FAVORED TO WIN

FAVORED TO WIN

MaryAnn Myers

LIGHTHOUSE
Literary Press, Inc.
Chesterland, Ohio

Lighthouse Literary Press, Inc.
P.O. Box 421
Chesterland, Ohio 44026

Copyright © 2000 by MaryAnn Myers
Cover design by Tamara L. Dever, TLC Graphics,
Folsom, CA.

First Edition
10   9   8   7   6   5   4   3   2   1

This is a work of fiction. Names, characters, places, and incidents either are the products of the author's imagination or are used fictitiously, and any resemblance to actual persons, living or dead, events, or locales is entirely coincidental.

Publisher's Cataloging-in-Publication
(Provided by Quality Books, Inc.)

Myers, Maryann.
    Favored to win / MaryAnn Myers. -- 1st ed.
    p. cm.
    LCCN: 00-190601
    ISBN: 0-9668780-2-7

    1. Horse racing--Fiction.   I. Title.

PS3563.Y477F3 2000   813.6
                  QBI00-392

FAVORED TO WIN is dedicated to John.
Thanks, hon. For everything.

Chapter One

"Hold it, where's your pass?"

Dawn turned, barely awake, and faced an armed guard. She hesitated. It was too early in the morning for this. It was too early in the morning for anything. "My name is Dawn Fioritto, and I write for *The Herald*. I'm here to do a story about the racetrack."

"That's nice." The guard glanced down to her legs then back up at all five feet ten inches of her. She had eyes the color of her olive-green shirt, and thick auburn hair braided neatly in a single braid down her back, waist length. Classy looking. "You still need a pass."

She had a press pass.

"That won't do."

"No?"

"No. You need to go to the secretary's office."

Dawn sighed, hoping to be spared the bother, and made several attempts to dissuade the man. "Timing," she pointed out, "is so very crucial." She even tried that old line about holding up the presses. But in the end, it all proved a waste of time. "The secretary's office...?"

The guard eased a pipe out of his pocket and pointed over her shoulder. "If you follow that path, it'll take you to it," he said. And sure enough she found it, but unfortunately right at scratch time. Everyone there was huddled around a middle-aged cowboy, who was shaking a jar and calling out numbers.

She walked up behind them and observed for a few minutes. "What are they doing?" she asked a man next to her.

"Drawing the *also-eligibles*," he said, leaning back then and looking her over.

"What for?"

The man probably would have ignored her at this point, since he was waiting anxiously to see if his horse drew in, but she was too pretty to ignore. "Today's racing lineup."

Dawn nodded as if that explained everything, and watched as this process gave way to another, "Picking up mounts." As horses' names were called out, so then were the names of "available jocks."

"They don't look like jockeys," Dawn said. Most were of average height or taller, and had what looked like hefty beer bellies.

"They're not. They're agents."

"I see."

"My boy'll ride him for you," one shouted, followed by another, "Billy's open that race. We'll ride him. We know the horse." Then another, "Give Jimmy a try, you get the weight." And another, "Hey, John, what about Visquel?"

Dawn lost interest as this went on and on, and looked around the room. Spotting a woman at a desk in the corner, she thanked the man for his time, and approached her. From there, she was directed down the hall, where she obtained her pass. An hour later, she was back at the stable gate, complaining to the guard.

"They made me wait forever, and then they interrogated me. I'm surprised they didn't fingerprint me!"

The guard laughed. "Well, they would have for a permanent pass. Yes, they would."

"Wonderful," Dawn said to herself, "rule number one." Waving over her shoulder, she headed down through the barn area to the racetrack amid a flurry of activity, and learned rather quickly to not only watch where she was going, but precisely where she was stepping along the way.

The horses going onto the track went through one gate, those coming off, another...a steady stream back and forth and an array of color, all decked out in leg bandages of green, yellow, red, and blue. Equally colorful, so to speak, were the comments and commands of some of the exercise riders.

For a while, she was content to just watch them come and go. Some put on quite a show, dancing, bucking, and kicking out. In time though, her mind wandered to something her Uncle Matt said yesterday. "Your signature is only a formality at this point. Don't give it another thought."

"Right." She'd hardly been able to think of anything else since. She drew a deep breath, then promptly sneezed, and figuring no one would want to read a story consisting entirely of polluted air, rainbow colors and profanity, she decided to ask some questions.

She approached a young man, who responded with an apparently ever-popular racetrack term, adding how he was new and didn't know much. She watched a few more groups of horses gallop by, then one or two by themselves, and after that, noticed an elderly man wearing a baseball cap, leaning on the rail and looking at her curiously.

She walked up to him. "Hi. Nice day."

"Not really," he said. He'd wanted rain.

Dawn studied his face as he looked out at the racetrack. "Why's that?"

"I got a horse that likes the mud."

Dawn poised her pen in her hand. "Really? Why would a horse like the mud?"

"Some horses just do." The old man looked at her. "Who are you anyway? You look like you might be lost."

"I'm a writer."

"Oh..." He cocked an eyebrow and nodded. "What are you writing about? Blackwell Stable? They're big news lately, leading stable by what...nine, ten wins."

"No. I'm doing a story about the racetrack in general, and about race people."

The old man lifted his hat and wiped his brow on his sleeve as he watched a horse gallop down on the rail. He mumbled something then, seemingly ignoring her now, and started to walk away, but stopped and looked back over his shoulder. "First thing," he said, "we're called horsemen. Not race people."

Dawn smiled, thanked him, and found herself watching him from a distance as he walked over to a horse coming off the racetrack. She squinted. When the jockey jumped down, both he and the old man appeared to be focusing on the horse's right front leg, quite a bit in fact. And the horse was nodding its head up and down, as if it totally agreed with what they were saying as it walked along.

Dawn spent the next few hours gathering comments from some of the other trainers and grooms, who she got really good at telling apart from the way they dressed and the condition of their boots, and noted their attitudes as well as their pointed observations. When the training activity slacked off around ten, she went into the track kitchen, drew herself a cup of coffee, paid, and sat down to go over her notes. As she looked around the room, not one friendly face gazed back. Instead, she was being eyed suspiciously, an obvious intruder.

A little while later, she sat in on a meeting called by the HBPA, the Horseman's Benevolent Protection Association, and observed what seemed to be an affair for venting grievances. The track condition was brought up repeatedly, along with a concern about a drop in purse monies, too many extras being written as favors...whatever that meant, and a need for tighter security. The meeting ended on a light note with a reminder about the annual picnic scheduled the following Monday. Rain or shine.

Dawn went back to the track kitchen then and took advantage of the daily breakfast special, served all day. A big platter of eggs, bacon, hash browns, and toast for $1.98 including coffee. By the time she was ready to head back to the paper, the stable area resembled a ghost town. Every few barns or so she would see a marauding cat or hear the sound of distant voices or a radio, but that was it. And she was almost to the stable gate when she saw a familiar face.

It was the elderly man she'd talked to earlier. She ventured toward him. "Hi, remember me?" When he smiled, she extended her hand and introduced herself. "My name is Dawn Fioritto."

He shook her hand warmly. "Ben Miller."

"Nice to meet you, Mr. Miller. Tell me, was I mistaken or did you look worried when you walked your horse back to the barn this morning?"

"You plan on putting my answer in your story?"

Dawn blushed. "No, I was just wondering. You seemed so concerned."

Ben shrugged. "Time'll tell."

"Is it bad?"

Bad...? The man wouldn't say. He didn't even want to think about it.

Dawn hesitated. "I'm sorry, Mr. Miller. I don't mean to pry. But if you don't mind, why *is* everyone so top secret around here?"

A smile slowly spread across Ben's face. He liked this girl. There was something about her. "Here." He handed her an empty water bucket and motioned for her to turn it upside down and have a seat. Over the next hour he told her all about the basics of claiming races, racing conditions, allowances for a horse's age and sex, lifetime conditions, and allowance races and stakes. A crash course of sorts. And she was thankful she had her tape recorder, as she hung on his every word. She was getting quite a story. Her editor would be pleased, maybe even pleased enough to use it as a Sunday magazine feature.

"Any questions?" Ben had an amused expression on his face as he watched her change the tape.

She looked up. "Yes. Claiming races. I still don't understand."

Ben sighed. "Well, let me see. I'll try and explain it better." He took off his hat and scratched his head. "Are you married?"

Dawn shook her head.

"Got a man?"

Dawn smiled.

"All right. Imagine if you had to put a price on him, to let people know how much he was worth."

When Dawn made a face, he laughed. "Oh, he ain't worth that much, huh?"

Dawn chuckled.

"Well then, let's just say he was a good one, and that he could be taken from you for the price you put on him. Would you go around telling everyone how good he was? Or would you maybe hold back a little, just in case...?"

Dawn nodded, beginning to understand.

"Exactly. Then imagine you get one that's so good, kinda like my wife Meg. Those, the good ones, you don't risk losing them for anything."

"I know." Dawn smiled at the analogy. "Those are the ones you run in the stake and allowances races. That way no one can take them from you. Right?"

Ben nodded. "You're doing good, but they can still be taken." He held his hand up when she started to object and proceeded to explain. "They can take a bad step. It could be a stone. An off track. They can stumble. The horse in front of them can stumble. They can get sick." He trailed off, and seemed to withdraw for a moment. "So many things can happen. Which is why the things you can control..." He looked over his shoulder at the horse in the first stall. It was the same horse Dawn had seen earlier up at the racetrack.

"That's Beau Born. The best I've had in years. Doc says we'll know more in the morning when we get the x-rays back."

"Oh no," Dawn said sadly. "Was he an allowance horse? One of the good ones?"

"What do you mean *was*?" Ben scoffed.

Dawn chuckled in spite of her red face. "Sorry."

Ben stood up slowly and walked over to the stall, with a look in his eyes then that for some reason reminded Dawn of her father when he used to tuck her into bed as a child.

She walked up next to them and reached to pet Beau's forehead. "He's so beautiful. I had no idea racehorses were this big."

"Not all of them are."

Dawn smiled. He'd said that proudly. "He doesn't look like he's in a lot of pain. Maybe it's not that bad."

Ben shook his head and walked back and sat down. "Good horses are funny about pain. They don't always show it. That's where class comes in."

Dawn ran her hand over Beau's silky-smooth neck. "How do you know if a horse has class?"

"How?" Ben couldn't help but smile. "Now that's a good one. But I don't think there's enough days in the year to explain it. And you little girl, I'm afraid, probably didn't bring enough tape."

Dawn laughed, and walked back to her seat. "Well, tell me something at least."

Ben paused. "I can tell you this. If a horse has it, they're something special." He swished a fly from his face. "Breeding is the biggest factor, mind you. But I've seen my share of common-bred horses with it too."

Dawn shifted her weight to get more comfortable.

"Why, they had a thirty-five-hundred-dollar claimer here a while back, with two of the biggest goddamned bowed tendons I've ever seen. And I've seen my share. But it weren't nothing compared to the size heart this horse had. He never quit. You gotta have respect for a horse like that. That's class."

"I'm confused," Dawn said, scanning her notes. "If a common-bred horse can have it..."

Ben grinned. "Hey, you're at the racetrack, remember? We're all gamblers here. It's what it's all about."

Dawn smiled, hesitating as she put her tape recorder away. "Do you mind if I come back in the morning to see you?"

Ben shrugged, his thoughtful gaze traveling instinctively to the horse in the first stall. "Sure, stop by. We'll be here, the good Lord willing."

The same stable guard from earlier greeted Dawn with a friendly nod from his bench, arms folded, and his pipe clenched firmly between his teeth. "Get your story?"

"Not quite." Dawn settled down next to him and went right to work. "But I did get some really good information. Do you mind if I ask you a few questions, Mr. uh...?"

"Charlie," he said, saying it with distinction, yet sounding humble. "I'm known only as Charlie." He'd been a guard here for more than thirty years now, he told her, and could talk forever. Dawn listened to tales of loose horses at night, attempted thefts, generations of families he'd watched grow up on the racetrack, and numerous drug scandals. Referring to the so-called trainers involved as, "Butchers who'd drug their own horses or anyone else's to cash a bet," he sighed in disgust. Then sadly, he recalled the details of a fire they'd had several years back that took the lives of an old groom and five horses, which led right into the speculative talk of new barns. "In the planning now, mind you, for more'n six or seven years."

When he paused to refill his pipe, Dawn checked her tape. "Do you know Ben Miller?"

"Ben? Oh yeah, I know Ben. Me'n him been good friends for years now. Damned good horseman too. Yeah, mc'n Ben go way back."

Dawn smiled. The two men looked about the same age, same school.

"Had himself a good one in '74. Dandy something. But he broke down in the prep and had to be destroyed. It was the same year his wife Meg got sick and passed away." He paused as he stared down the road between the barns. "I still find it hard to believe. She worked right with him, you know."

Dawn shook her head, staring in the same direction now, and probably should have asked what a prep was, but didn't.

"Got himself one this year, though, that's maybe even better," Charlie said, with an emphatic nod. "Yep, Beau Born. There's a big race for him day after tomorrow. He'll win it too. You wait and see."

Dawn lowered her eyes to the ground and thought about her conversation with Ben. How it didn't sound good for this Beau Born. And how it could possibly turn out just like the other one, this Dandy something...the same year his wife Meg died.

"Well," she said, tucking her recorder away. "I have a two-day pass, so I'll see you tomorrow."

Charlie nodded. "You said your name was Fioritto. Any relation to the west-side Fiorittos?"

Dawn hesitated responding, as always when asked about her family. "Why? Is there someone in particular you know?"

Charlie shook his head. He didn't know them, he'd just heard about them, read about them. Then again, who hadn't?

"I'll see you tomorrow."

Dawn woke the following morning fearing she'd overslept and was surprised to find it wasn't even five-thirty yet. She showered and dressed anyway, threw several tapes in her purse, and left. She waved to Charlie as she strode past the guard shack, and headed straight for Ben Miller's barn.

She rounded the corner feeling positive, convinced everything was going to be all right, a happy ending for a change. She even had a smile on her face. But her hopes vanished as she stared into the first stall. It was empty. Stripped completely of its bedding.

She glanced into the tack room and called out for Ben, turned, and looking down the walkway of the barn, called his name again. A young man came around the corner then, leading a wiry, bay horse. "Have you seen Ben Miller?" she asked.

He motioned for her to come to the inside; horses usually kick out, not in, when walking around a shedrow. She moved quickly so he could pass. "Well," she repeated, "have you?"

"Yeah, he was just here with Doc Jake."

"All right," Dawn muttered to herself, following the young man with her eyes until they turned the opposite corner out of sight. So where is he now? And what did the vet tell him? More importantly, where was Beau Born?

She refused to look into the first stall again, into the emptiness, her heart beating faster, and damned her editor for giving her this assignment. She didn't need this. Get somebody else, she should tell him. Leave now. Now. But all she could do was stand and stare into the tack room, a lifetime, an eternity, and had to back up and get out of the young man's way again as he came back around.

He said something to her, something she couldn't quite make out, not that she couldn't hear him. He'd practically shouted. She wasn't listening. What was it about the old man that made her care? Besides, how much was a person supposed to take? What if he had to put this horse down too? What if...?

She sighed, pushed the loose strands of hair from her forehead, and walked up to the racetrack. Six-thirty a.m., the sun peeked over the horizon, giving the dew on the infield the appearance of diamonds glistening on a blanket of lush emerald-green velvet.

She closed her eyes and breathed in the morning air, a mixture of dirt, grass, hay and straw, manure, liniment, and a distinct smell of coffee. A pleasant scent, a familiar scent, as opposed to yesterday. The routine of the horses going on and off the track seemed pleasantly familiar also, as if she'd witnessed their comings and goings a thousand times.

She leaned on the railing, elbows propped, and with her chin in her hands, just watched. After a while she detected differences in the sounds of the horses' hooves as they passed. Some pounded the surface like a jackhammer, while others touched as lightly as a pebble skipping across water. And she started playing a game, in which she would try to pick out similarities and then other obvious differences.

She smiled, admiring horse after horse, shaking her head at the antics of one, to then just gape in awe at another, and wondered how she could put this into writing. How could she describe the magic? The speed? The raw power and drive of a Thoroughbred. The same horse jogging on and playfully tossing his head, who would then turn and run as hard and fast as he could. How could she describe the special something Ben said set one horse apart from another? How could she describe the feeling? The sense of being swept along in the dreams of every horseman on the racetrack. The gamble. The hope...

"Good morning!"

Dawn jumped, startled. "Oh, Ben!" she said, catching her breath. "I was looking for you earlier. I stopped by your barn."

Ben smiled. "You'd better be careful. I saw that look in your eyes. I think this racetrack is getting to you."

"What?" Dawn frowned. "What do you mean?"

"You." Ben took hold of her hand gently, turned her wrist up, and pointed to the veins in her arm. "It's getting in there. It gets in your blood, you know."

Dawn shook her head and laughed. "No, it's not. I'm a writer and this is just a story. One that fascinates me, I'll admit. But a story nonetheless."

Ben smiled rather smugly, nodding, and turned to watch a horse being galloped on the inside rail. Dawn was taken by the intensity of his gaze, the caring, such a kind old man, and dreaded asking, "What happened to Beau Born? He wasn't at the barn when I stopped by. Did you? Is he...?"

Ben silenced her, touching her lightly on the arm and looking into her eyes as if he were searching for something. "He's fine. We're going to scratch him though, just to be safe." He paused, glancing to see how his horse pulled up. "We were probably at the wash rack when you came by."

Dawn looked away, overcome with a sudden rush of emotion. "I'm glad," she said, her voice cracking. "I was afraid..."

Ben stood quietly for a moment, observing her out of the corner of his eye, then motioned to a horse in the middle of the racetrack. He commented on it being sore, and Dawn turned to look at him, swallowing the lump in her throat.

"How can you tell?"

Ben smiled faintly. "Watch him."

Dawn studied the horse for a few seconds and did notice something unusual, though at a gallop it was impossible to tell if it was limping. "Tell me what to look for," she said.

Ben's smile faded, watching her. "It's in his eyes," he told her, and when she glanced at him, he looked at the horse and said it again. "His eyes gave him away."

Dawn nodded and focused back on the horse for a long, long time.

"You want a cup of coffee?" Ben asked.

"Sure." She picked up her purse and walked with him to the track kitchen, which also had a different feel to it than yesterday. Much different. She didn't know if it was just her or because she was there with Ben. But the reason why didn't really matter. What was important was that it felt right. Her being there felt right.

"So..." Ben eased into a chair across from her and took a sip of his coffee. "How's the story coming?"

"Good. I have an appointment with the track's general manager later this morning, then I'm going to talk to the track chaplain. I talked to the stable guard yesterday. He was really helpful. And I thought I should try to speak to a few of the jockeys. Then I guess I'm done."

"It sounds like you're doing a thorough job," Ben said. "I like that. You're getting a side of everyone."

Dawn blushed a little. "Thanks," she said, and sipped her coffee. For some reason, his opinion meant a great deal to her, and it felt good that he was pleased.

"Are you sure you've given it enough time?"

"I think so." Dawn paused, then smiled. "And even though what you say about my veins isn't true, I would like to come back when Beau races."

"I'll save you a place in the winner's circle."

Dawn laughed. "I'll be there."

Early Saturday morning, wide awake, Dawn looked at the clock. Six thirty-three. Only ten minutes later than the last time she'd looked. "Wonderful." She turned the radio on low, hoping it would lull her back to sleep. But it didn't.

She'd handed her article in yesterday and her editor liked it. Yes, it would be featured in the Sunday magazine section. So why think about the racetrack now? Beau Born wasn't running. She'd checked the paper yesterday for the entries. Still...

She got out of bed and got dressed. She wanted to go and that's all there was to it. Halfway there, however, she almost changed her mind and turned back. This is ridiculous, she thought. Utterly ridiculous. Yet she drove on, and arriving, started wondering again. What was she doing here?

Which is exactly what Charlie, the stable guard, wanted to know. "I thought you had your story."

"I do. I mean, I did."

"Got a pass?"

Dawn sighed. "No, I'll go get one."

Charlie nodded, and glanced at his watch. "It's gonna take a while. They're just now opening up."

Dawn stared in the direction of the secretary's office, remembering how long it took the first time, and reconsidered. "This is crazy," she said, thinking out loud. "I might as well just go home."

That's when Charlie got this big grin on his face. "Ben said you'd be back." He reached into his shirt pocket and handed her a visitor's pass. "Here. He left this for you."

Dawn shook her head and smiled, thanking him, and headed for the barn. Ben was standing outside, watching Beau Born on the walking machine, with his back to her as she approached. She hesitated for a moment, drew a deep breath, and walked up beside him.

"Ben, what am I doing here?"

He smiled as he turned and looked at her. "Why, you're here to write a story about race people. Isn't that what you said?"

Dawn stared. Her saying that seemed so long ago. Maybe she'd worked on the article too long, she told herself. Maybe she'd read it one too many times. Maybe she'd made it sound too good.

Or maybe, just maybe, she was running. Hiding...

"This was supposed to be just another story. Ben, I'm a writer."

"So," he said, "why don't you write a book?" And that was that. If she *was* hiding, this was the perfect place. He tipped his hat back, crossed his arms, and started planning ahead. "First thing, we'll have to get you a license. You know anything about horses?"

"Yes, riding horses. Nothing about racehorses though."

"No problem," Ben said. "That we can teach you."

"We...?"

"Me'n my partner, Tom." He tapped her on the shoulder. "Come on, I'll introduce you."

Chapter Two

Sometimes accidents just happen. In Dawn's case however, Ben would point out, they happened usually because she wasn't paying attention. At least in the beginning. "I'm okay. I'm okay," she'd always say. But he really wondered.

Fancy Pat finished an unimpressive, start-to-finish, trailing-the-field tenth out of ten. In her nine lifetime starts, she'd never once hit the board. In fact, she never even got close. Her talent seemed to lie in sensing the day she was to run, so she could stall-walk for hours, and leave most of what was needed for the race, back in the barn. They tried fooling her; giving her hay that morning, no bath, sending her to the track, you name it. But somehow she always knew. By the time she reached the paddock, what little energy she had left, washed-out completely in a frantic sweat. The gate crew dreaded loading her. And to keep her standing on all fours until the start proved even more of a challenge. She would either try to sit down or climb her way out, both seemingly at the same time on occasion. The latch would spring and out she'd come, for a lackluster run. Then it was back to the barn.

Dawn gathered up the Absorbine and leg wraps, and ducked under the webbing of the horse's stall before reaching for her. A big mistake. Fancy Pat was crankier than usual and lunged at her with ears pinned and mouth open. Taken by surprise, Dawn jumped back, and in doing so, bounced hard against the wall. The sound of the thud sent the mare into a mild fit, and in an instant, the situation had turned dangerous.

Dawn found herself staring at the mare's quivering, coiled, and well-muscled hind end. Doorway blocked.

"Oh Lord."

How she could've been so stupid as to enter the stall without tying her up first didn't seem important just then, though the thought crossed her mind. What mattered now, was that there was no way out.

Sensing the advantage, the mare, in a gesture of aggressiveness, started pawing the ground like a raging bull, scattering her bedding and exciting herself even more. When Dawn made a move, the mare cow-kicked and struck the wall, ripping a piece of hide off her hock. This seemed to only darken her mood. She began to swing her head back and forth like a pendulum, gnawing the wall with her teeth at the end of each pass, and was building momentum, when suddenly Tom appeared from out of nowhere.

"What the...?"

He'd snuck down the shedrow to check on Dawn, hoping she wouldn't see him, but now stood openly concerned in the stall doorway.

"Don't move."

Right... Dawn's expression said. What else?

Tom motioned for her to be quiet. The mare had stopped for a moment, but now started up again, gnashing her teeth on her feed tub with each swing. He'd have to time it just right, going with the offside of the swing. No one knew more than Tom how this bitch liked to bite.

He waited, waited, and waited...then lunging, reached for her, just as the mare lunged for him. He almost got hold of her halter too. In fact, he just missed. "Shit." He darted his eyes toward Dawn.

She needn't utter, "What now?" It was in her face.

Tom motioned again for her to be still, and glanced up and down the shedrow. Nothing. No shank. No rope. Nothing. He took off his belt in slow motion. It would have to do.

He nodded to Dawn, a nod that implied, "When I say when." She nodded back. And with that, he slowly raised the belt over his head, counted to himself, nodded again to Dawn, and let it rip.

Smack! He hit the mare high on the shoulder, which sent her flying to the back of the stall. "Quick!" Unsnapping the webbing then, he reached for Dawn, who for some reason just stood there. Next thing she knew, she was being yanked out of the stall and into the shedrow with such force, she landed in the ditch on the other side.

A ditch of fresh morning rain and old runoff urine from the muck bin.

Dawn sat trembling for a few seconds, trying to catch her breath, and looked up to thank Tom, but he was standing with his hands on his hips, bobbing his head in that way of his, and she declined.

"Well, I'm sure you'd of figured something out," he said. "But we thought we'd better check on you anyway."

Dawn waved her hand in front of her face, as if she were fanning herself and shook her head. She could picture the two of them, him and Ben, waiting up by the guard shack and flipping a coin to see who would go check on her. Though admittedly, she was actually glad they mother-henned her this time.

She managed a feeble, "Thanks."

Tom smiled with a sideward glance, like only he could, and threaded his belt back through his jeans as he motioned to the stall. "Don't bother doing the bitch up. Ben decided while we were waiting, to quit on her. He's calling Big Mouth tomorrow." Big Mouth was Tom's nickname for Fancy Pat's owner.

Dawn nodded, gazing down at her muddy jeans.

"Throw her a bran mash and call it a day." He walked down the shedrow, smiling now, and waited until he was almost at the end to look back. "Oh, and Dawn..."

She looked up with a reluctant sigh, and sure enough, that was all it took to start him laughing, quietly at first and somewhat restrained, then building to his customary roar. He couldn't even finish what he was about to say. "Never mind," he sputtered. And she could've sworn she heard him laughing all the way to the stable gate. Then Ben.

Terrific. "What's the point of a shedrow anyway? she'd asked Ben one day, one pouring-down rainy day. That conversation returned now as she pictured herself sitting in the ditch.

"Aside from their being the cheapest barn to build, more importantly," he said, "horses need fresh air and something else to look at besides a barn wall." Thus a shedrow. Stalls in a row, with a shed roof to allow for plenty of that fresh air. And whenever the subject of the plan for enclosed barns was brought up, he scoffed at the idea, as adamantly as he objected to the proposed year-round racing season.

"Why do they call the barn area the backside?" You had to drive past the barns to get to the grandstand, they were in front. So where did the term come from? It didn't make sense, not to her at least.

"It's because we're all horses' asses," Tom had said, coming down the shedrow that first morning to be introduced. "Ain't it so, old man?"

Ben laughed. "There's only one horse's ass around here, Tom, and that's you."

Dawn smiled. So this was Tom. The partner; as good-looking a cowboy as she'd ever seen: tanned, smiling eyes, toothpick dangling from his mouth, and nowhere near Ben's age. She guessed him to be somewhere around forty-five. She was off by a year.

"We're called the backside," Ben explained, "because we put on the show. We're the backside of the production. But keep in mind, we're the stars. Don't you ever forget that."

Dawn locked the tack room and walked down to see if Fancy Pat was eating, which she was, and left to go home. Thinking about it, she probably drove Ben crazy those first couple of weeks, always asking questions. Always wanting to know something. Always occupying her mind.

"Why do some horses stay sound and others go sore?"

Ben told her it had a lot to do with the trainer. Although in many instances, he said it was out of his or her hands. "The way a horse is put together is often the biggest factor. That, and the amount of trips around the track. Still," he said, "a good trainer can hold a horse longer than most, for that reason alone."

"Why? What's the most important thing?"

"What? About being a trainer?"

She nodded.

"Well..." He paused for a moment, as if he had to think about it. "You going to put this in your book?"

Dawn laughed. He loved asking her that. She could see it in his eyes. "Yes."

"Well then," he said. "What's important is to treat each horse as an individual, because there's no two horses alike. One'll take to training hard, where another'll fall apart. They're different. Each one. And if a trainer thinks he can do it any other way, he might as well just quit." Ben thought most trainers should've quit before they ever got started, his pet peeve being ex-jockeys turned horse trainer. He could go on for hours about that. "You understand?"

Dawn nodded.

Ben was from the old school, and ran his stable on a tight schedule. The horses were fed a scoop of oats at six a.m., and allowed a half hour to eat. The feed tubs were pulled then and hung outside the stall. This was done, he explained, to encourage them to eat up. Morning was no time for lollygaging. They were athletes, he said. When training was over, they could rest and eat at their leisure. But the morning belonged to their trainer, and the business of being a racehorse.

Routinely, the horses not scheduled for training on a particular day, were always hung on the walking machine first, and their stalls cleaned during this time. Ben liked to see a horse feeling good and "on-the-muscle," but always had them yanked off if they acted up too much. He'd seen too many horses injured, some severely enough to end their careers, from walking machine accidents. He preferred to hand-walk a horse, and in fact, still insisted on it the morning of a race. But even he had to admit, a walking machine was almost a necessity for a large stable. So consequently he used them, but begrudgingly, and with quick releases on both tops and bottoms of the shanks.

Once the walkers were done, training got underway. Beau, on scheduled days, always tracked first, and more often than not before sunrise, when the track was least congested. As a rule, horses weren't allowed to ship in and out during training hours. Nevertheless, right after Beau came off the track, Ben was paged to the stable gate to authorize an arrival.

Nothing made Ben madder than a glitch in his routine. Nothing. And to make matters worse, when he got back to the barn with this new horse, it was just in time for him to see Majorama's exercise boy getting a leg-up at the next barn.

Gone were the days when trainers had his or her own exercise rider. It was done mostly by freelancers now; exercise riders for the going rate, or jockeys for the mount in a race, and they all had routines of their own. If a horse was tacked and ready to go when they got there, they'd get on it. If it wasn't, occasionally they'd wait. Some would even tack their own if they were familiar enough with the horse. But usually, they just moved on. And if you were lucky, they'd make it back around in time before the track closed.

"Shit!"

Every horse in the barn decided to welcome the new arrival, as was customary, any horseman will tell you. Racehorses, standing around, sniff the air for anything to get them going. They buck and kick and squeal in their stalls then, charging their webbings and getting the horses on the walking machine going; leaping and kicking, rearing, and yanking the machine arms up and down with their antics…then running round and round…the pulley clanging and slipping, dirt clumps flying from the horses' hooves and landing on the metal roof of the barn, which only gets the horses in the barn acting up even more then.

Luckily all had settled down by the time Dawn got Beau back to the barn after his bath, or he'd have just made things worse. He had one of those whinnies that carried for miles, like the call of the wild, over and over, and answers would've come from everywhere.

The new horse was named Gibyag, and had shipped in from Sportsman's Park, where he'd run *a route* eleven times in less than three months, and finished all eleven times in the money. He was an eight-year-old gelding, standing a little over seventeen hands, and without a doubt was Dawn's favorite color, gray.

She and Tom gave him a bath, then scraped him off, hung him on the walking machine, and stood back to take a good look at him. Ben was still in a bad mood, but eventually came grumbling out of the tack room to join them, and was pleasantly surprised.

This was the first of Dave Bacardi's horses that had come to him not looking like it needed a long rest. He'd been training the man's horses for years, and liked him well enough, but always dreaded the ship-ins from his Chicago trainer. Not that Ben faulted the man on the amount of run he got out of a horse; he just didn't leave much for the next trainer to work with. More times than not, Ben served merely as a layover, before advising Dave to turn the horse out for a while. But not Gibyag.

Ben told Dawn to do him up with alcohol, only as a precaution after shipping. His legs looked and felt as good as a two-year-old's.

The first time Dawn tried to "do a horse up," the term used for bandaging its legs, she thought she'd never get it right and had been more nervous than usual that day. Watching Tom, it had looked so easy. It wasn't.

"Rub briskly," Tom told her. "No, more'n that." He showed her how. "Now here..." He told her to always wrap from front to back. "Why?"

"Because," he said, and smiled. "That's how it's done."

"Okay." Dawn started out all wrong. So concerned with holding the quilt wrap in place, she wound the bandage too thick at the bottom and ran out before she got to the top. Her second attempt was a little better, but Tom said it wasn't tight enough.

"It'll slip in a minute."

The third try looked good, but he made her do it again, pointing out how the tension had to be consistent, so it wouldn't put excessive pressure on the tendon. Pins always go on the outside, he told her, demonstrating how to fold the bandage back if it ended up otherwise. With Velcro, he said, it didn't matter.

"That's it?" Dawn admired her accomplishment.

"Yep, that's it," Tom said. "But remember the rubbing is just as important as the liniment. Rub it in till it's almost dry. It helps the circulation."

Dawn looked up at Gibyag as she finished pinning the bandage. She always used two pins on each leg. Tom said only one was necessary, but she liked how two looked lined up.

"There now," she said, talking softly to the horse. "All set." As she reached for the brush just outside the stall, she could hear Tom and Ben in the tack room discussing Gibyag's past performances. In his seventy-three lifetime starts, he'd finished one-two-three in sixty-two of them. He'd been claimed nine times, and was currently running for thirty-five-hundred dollars.

"Well, well," she said. "Aren't we the hard knocker."

The horse apparently liked the sound of her voice, because he stopped munching his hay to gently nuzzle the side of her face, then her hair, and with that, raised his head and sneezed all over her.

"Yuk!" There were slobbery green hay globs deposited everywhere. She batted here and there, leaning over and whisking them from the top of her head, and in this position, didn't notice someone had approached and stopped in front of the stall.

"Here," a man's voice said. "You missed some." A precise swipe or two, and he was gone.

Dawn started to stand, not recognizing the voice, or the legs, which were all she got a good look at, and caught her shoulder on the webbing. The man was two or three stalls down by the time she stood up and leaned out. She stared. He was obviously looking for someone or something. "Excuse me..." she said. Ben didn't like strangers in the shedrow.

He turned.

Muscular and tall from behind, now face to face, she found herself staring again.

"Is Ben Miller here?"

The man had piercing, deep blue eyes. "Yeah, uh..." She pointed to the feed room, then realizing her mistake, blushed and motioned in the opposite direction. "He's in the tack room."

When he passed by her, she turned and mumbled to herself as she buried her face in Gibyag's neck. "Oh my God."

She listened then. "So you're Doc Iredell," she heard Ben say. She leaned back and peeked out. He and Ben were shaking hands. Tom was chewing on a toothpick.

"Jake tells me you have two to worm and one to scope."

"That's right," Ben said. "But I don't believe he told me you were this *young*."

Dawn smiled. Doc Iredell, as Ben called him, said something then about going to get his equipment and coming right back. And she started brushing Gibyag. "Did you see him?" she whispered, mimicking an awestruck teenager. "The man could be a movie star. Or a lifeguard even."

She laughed to herself. Then there he was again.

"You talking to me?"

"No, I was..." She motioned to Gibyag and shrugged. Ben appeared then, and introduced them.

"Dawn, this is Jake's new assistant." He said the word "new" the way he'd said the word young. "Doc Iredell."

"Randy," he said, smiling. "Just Randy is fine."

"Nice to meet you," Dawn said.

His smile widened, and as he and Ben started down the shedrow, he glanced back at her over his shoulder.

By the time they were done treating the horses, Dawn had worked her way up to Beau, her favorite. She always saved him for last. From her kneeling position as she did up one of his hind legs, she watched Randy walk to his truck, then over to the barn across from theirs. He followed Bob Graptor's daughter into one of the tack rooms. When he came out a few minutes later, still talking and glancing at his watch as if making a date and deciding what time, Dawn stood up slowly, reached for a comb, and started doing Beau's mane.

Chapter Three

With the flip of a coin, Dawn won the task of cleaning Red's stall for another week, the third in a row. She examined the coin carefully, thinking Tom had somehow rigged the toss, and just to be safe, she threw it as far as she could so he couldn't use it again. "There!" She grabbed he muck basket, walked down to Red's stall, and hesitated before she ducked under the webbing. How one horse could shit this much, absolutely amazed her.

Red was Tom and Ben's pony, and probably the ugliest horse in the world. He had large appalling eyes, a hammerhead with blazed face and a roman nose, a sagging lower lip, and nothing but a cowlick where his forelock was supposed to be. He had legs like stove pipes, adorned with scars, wind-puffs, protruding monster-like ergots, and walked like he was straddling a bridge. His largest and most memorable scar, one of his many battle wounds from his years as a racetrack pony, was a good eleven inches long and at least half an inch wide, starting high up on his shoulder. When Dawn asked Tom how he got it, he began the story with a shudder.

"I thought it was fucking curtains for him that day. I'm not kidding. It scared the hell out of me. I was ponying this silly filly and we were just getting started. We were stabled on the other side that year, so ya had to enter up by the quarter pole." He took a breath; he loved a captive audience. "I'd just backed her up when they sprung the latch on some horses being schooled out of the gate, and right off one of 'em dumped its jock. A big colt, and as soon as it hit the main track, it turned the other way." He laughed. "Coming right at us. And let me tell you, this filly went bonkers! Honest to God. She was all over Red like a whore on Saturday night. Practically in my lap. Legs flying..."

Dawn made hurry-up get-to-the-point gestures when he stopped to relive it in his mind.

"Well, to make a long story short, the loose horse was coming right at us. I managed to get the filly out the gap. Ben was there; he took her. And me and Red took off after the loose horse. Goddamn, it was fun!"

Dawn sighed, rolling her eyes impatiently.

"Okay..." Tom raised his hat to smooth his hair, then tipped it forward, letting the brim rest low and cocky on his forehead. "Red spotted him coming around the turn, I mean bookin' it, and now this is where the story gets short."

Dawn nodded her approval.

"We got a jump on him and laid right on his shoulder. I leaned over as far as I could to try and grab the rein, but first time I missed it. Then the damned thing stopped dead right in its tracks. I mean on a dime. But so did Red. He was digging this. I remember thinking, this is about as good as it gets for a gelding I guess. He read that horse like a cowpony. I reached out, leaning way far over. This time I got the rein. And that was that."

Dawn stared at him. "What about the scar?"

"What about it?"

Dawn sighed. "You were supposed to be telling me about what caused it."

"Oh...well, it's the same story. Only I didn't notice it until I handed the colt over to its trainer, that Red had been cut. And I mean bad. Blood everywhere."

Dawn made a face.

"The stirrup must've got hung up in the gate when the horse broke out. It had a big jagged edge and Red's hide was stuck to it. That's what cut him." He tipped his hat back. "Took Doc Jake an hour to stitch it up. After that, he got a month off. He hated it though. He got downright mean. And he gained so much weight, he looked like he was gonna foal. Honest to God. Third week we had to cut his grain entirely, just give him hay." He paused, chewing on a toothpick. "Did I tell you how mean he got?"

Dawn nodded.

"First day back at the track, you ready for this, he bucked me off. Me! I kid you not! I was so sore I couldn't screw for a week. And let me tell you, if you want to talk about mean..."

Dawn laughed then, and thinking about it, laughed now. Somehow remembering that story made cleaning Red's stall a little easier. Ugly as he was, abundant shit and all, when it came to ponying, he knew his job, and did it with style.

Dave Bacardi, one of Ben's owners and frequent visitor to the barn, arrived carting a dozen of his bakery's freshest donuts. Dawn could smell them ten stalls away. She hurried and bed Red's stall down, raked the shedrow in her favorite crisscross pattern to the tack room, and reached for the box with sweet anticipation.

Too late. Tom had gotten to them already and was licking his fingers. "Three of them," he said. "And so creamy it made me horny."

Dawn could've thrown the box at him, and probably would have if Dave hadn't still been there. Custard was both their favorite, thus this ongoing competition with getting to them first. Tom was supposed to have been up at the track kitchen.

"You creep! You said..."

Tom grinned innocently.

Ben once asked Dave to bring the whole dozen in custard to avoid this, but Dave pretended to take offense. All his donuts were delicious, he said, not just one variety. Actually, he enjoyed these little games Dawn and Tom played, and looked forward to them.

Ben propped his elbow on his desk and gazed down at the condition book, affectionately known to some trainers as "the bible." The book, Ben told Dawn, on day one, that can make or break you. "Having the fittest and the best don't mean a thing if you don't enter 'em right."

Dawn thought it all seemed simple enough, glancing at the book he'd handed her. Find the condition that fit and enter. How hard can it be?

Ben peered over his bifocals at her. "It doesn't work that way. Here..." He pointed to the ideal condition for Son of Royalty. "It's perfect for him, but he can't win it. Wilson'll enter that horse of his, what's his name?" He looked at Tom, and when Tom rattled off a name, nodded. "Yeah, he'll win it, and Son'll run second. Next time out, he'll be a sure winner, even on the raise depending on the bunch, only he'll probably have been haltered in this race, so it'll be for somebody else, and..."

All right, so it's not that easy, Dawn thought. You always had to consider the possibility of having the horse claimed. Particularly, Ben said, this time of year. He said he'd rather take a third for five hundred more and not lose him, and run him back low and take the chance along with the win.

Dawn settled for a jelly-filled donut and sat down next to Tom, purposely stepping on his foot and dramatizing an ever-so-polite apology. Tom hated his boots scuffed. She reveled.

"Custard breath."

"Bitch."

Ben rolled his eyes, enough was enough. "What about this race?" He handed the book to Tom. Tom took a look and handed it back. Son of Royalty was due to be shod, and this race was four days away.

"If we wait, you chance his cutting himself all to hell." Tom spit on his boot and rubbed the toe with his fingers, then spit and spit and rubbed some more, toothpick still between his teeth. "You go and have him done now, he won't be able to walk." Son of Royalty had the worst feet they'd ever seen on a horse.

Ben hesitated. "We'll lose him. I can feel it in my bones."

"Nah! It's probably just your arthritis, old man. Don't worry about it."

Ben shook his head. What he'd also told Dawn early on, was sometimes you can get away with running a horse in someone's face, because it just may be that you want him taken. The gamble again.

"Run him," Tom said.

When Ben shrugged, which meant it was as good as settled, Tom reached behind Dawn to where he'd hidden a custard donut wrapped in tissue.

"Give it to me!" she said, seeing what he had and grabbing for it.

"No way!" Tom dashed out of the tack room. "I need the carbo's. I got a date with Sue Grape the Ape later."

Dawn could tell a song was coming on.

"I gotta do her right...do her no wrong." He was in rare form too, almost in tune. "Do her good, she knows that I could, yes, could, could, Susie would, would. And tonight, tonight, with a little bit of luck, I'm gonna be in for one hell of a..." His voice trailed off as he rounded the corner, almost sparing them the inevitable ending.

Dawn shook her head. Hopeless, she was used to him now, but could remember all too well her apprehensions when they first met. Right after his initial horses' asses comment and thus being introduced, he started. "Goddamn, old man, did you get her for me?"

Ben assured her there was no need for concern, that inside Tom there was a gentleman at heart. This he said as he smacked Tom hard on the arm. Tom scowled at him and then nodded, smiling. Still, for the next few days Dawn watched him, and day three, she did have some concerns.

"I'm sorry, Ben, his language is so offensive. And his songs."

Ben nodded. "I know."

"They're so, so...vulgar. I've never heard such lyrics."

"Of course not." Ben nodded again, trying not to laugh. "He makes them up."

"And the way he talks about women! Is that all true?"

"I'm afraid so."

Dawn shook her head. This wasn't going to work out. In addition, her Uncle Matt was pressuring her to quit. "I'm sorry, I just..."

"Listen," Ben said. "Come on, sit down."

Dawn obliged with a sigh.

"You're not the only one."

Dawn looked at him.

"When I told Meg I wanted to make him my assistant trainer, she all but had a conniption. She knew about his mouth, his womanizing, and his drinking."

Dawn's eyes widened. Drinking?

"Now mind you, Meg was with me a lot of years on the track, and she'd heard it all. But she drew a line with the four-letter words." He raised an eyebrow. "God forbid, whenever I let one slip."

Dawn smiled.

"Anyway." Ben took off his hat and scratched his head. "She told me if I could get him to clean up his mouth, stay sober, and keep his women out of the shedrow, it would be okay. But you know..." He chuckled as he put his hat back on. "I think she knew he'd never be able to do it. Not that she didn't like him, mind you. She did. But he was Tom. You know what I mean?"

Dawn nodded, and he paused, staring off for a moment. She hadn't known him long enough at this point to tell, but he was thinking about Meg now, the woman he'd loved, still loved, and who'd died painfully in his arms. "She'd had this cold for months, and couldn't shake it. And she was getting tired all the time." He wiped at his eyes, and picked up the condition book. "So anyway..." He cleared his throat and looked at her. "Tom agreed to it. No booze. No women in the shedrow. And no four-letter words."

When Dawn started to say something, Ben laughed. "No, it didn't last long. Not even half a day in fact. She got so tired of him swearing and then apologizing, saying it'll never happen again, over and over, she gave in. But I'll tell you what, he never showed up drunk, and he never brought a woman in the shedrow. Never. Not to this day."

Dawn hesitated. "Does he still drink?"

"No, not anymore." Ben's expression suggested his mind was wandering again. "I'll tell you, Dawn. Underneath all that bragging and swearing, is a good man. I don't think I could've gotten through Meg's death without him."

Barn Kitty meandered into the tack room, meowing, and Dawn picked him up and put him on her lap.

"She would've liked you, you know," Ben said, smiling sadly. "You'd have liked her too."

Dawn lowered her eyes to the cat and thought about Meg, a woman she'd never met, but whom she cared for. A woman whose constant presence in lingering memories, that reminded her of her mother. Her mother's wishes. And with the decision Dawn was facing, it was now or never, her father's.

Ben stared off and sighed. "No, Tom doesn't drink anymore. Used to be he was drunk every day by noon. But then he caused this pile-up on the freeway. Six people got hurt. One was just a kid." He looked at her. "The kid was hurt the worst and almost died."

Barn Kitty started purring.

"He was still fighting the booze when he came to work for Meg and me. He's a fine trainer, Dawn. I honestly don't know another horseman whose opinion I respect more. Or for that matter, one with such a mouth."

Gibyag's stay was short. He'd been the last to track, heading out just as it started to sprinkle, and returned in a downpour. Dawn and Tom hosed his legs, scraped him off and covered him with two blankets. Dawn attempted to hand-walk him then, while Tom rushed to finish his stall. The path down the middle of the shedrow was soon a slippery, sloshy mess. She almost got stepped on twice, through no fault of her own or Gibyag's. And with each pass, she became wearier.

When Tom waved her in, they quickly rubbed Gibyag down and put a dry blanket on him, and were headed for a much-needed cup of steaming hot coffee. Suddenly, from under the eaves appeared three figures in slickers, smiling like a sunny day.

Hunter-jumper people. It had to be.

"Excuse me..."

It was a man and two women. The man's accent was lovely.

Dawn smiled. "Yes?"

"We're with the Foxborough Hunt Stable and scouting for new talent, so to speak."

Dawn was amazed at how they always came in groups of three, regardless of which stable they were from. Equally amazing, was how they always seemed to look alike and almost always had an English spokesperson. A tall, lanky one.

"Are there horses for sale in this barn?"

"I don't believe so."

One of the women stepped forward. "That handsome gent you were just walking. The gray. Is he negotiable?"

Dawn couldn't help smiling again. Two English accents. "I don't think so," she said. And they all turned in the direction of Gibyag's stall, just in time to see Tom backing out of the one next to it, zipping up his jeans.

No problem. The trio didn't seem the least bit ruffled, as if urinating in a stall was proper horsemen's etiquette. Tom smiled as he walked by them, and the two women smiled back as the man spoke to Dawn. "I wonder if you would be so kind as to inquire with the gray's owner to see if..."

Ben emerged slowly from the tack room upon hearing this. "Make me an offer and I'll contact him, but I can almost guarantee you he won't sell. He's worth more as a racehorse."

The trio sloshed their way down the muddy path and peered in at Gibyag. "He looks pretty sound," the man surmised. "Mind if I feel his legs?"

"Not at all," Ben said, adding his own rendition of an English accent. "He's as sound as a bell of brass."

Dawn walked into the tack room and exchanged a knowing smile with Tom. Ben loved it when hunter-jumper people came around, although he'd never admit it. They always brought out a little of the old horsetrader in him.

While the eldest of the women held onto Gibyag's halter, the man went over him very carefully, skillfully. Meanwhile the drumming rain on the tin roof had stopped, and the youngest of the three made a decision. You could see it in her face. She wanted this horse. All she needed was a slight nod of approval from the man, and then she turned to Ben.

"How old is he, please?"

"Eight."

"What tag does he run for?" the man asked, coming out under the webbing and trying to appear less than anxious. Gray horses were dear as jumpers, not to mention one standing healthy at seventeen-two.

"Thirty-five hundred."

"I'll give you that for him."

Ben smiled, definitely enjoying this. "I'm sure you would. But he's sitting on a win. His share of the pot'll be close to twenty-seven hundred. I won't even bother my owner unless you match that, the claiming price, and then some."

The man stroked his chin, thinking for a moment. "I'll give you seventy-five hundred for him."

"I'll ask. Stop back later."

The young woman inquired about the horse's name.

"It's Gibyag," Ben said, smiling when the girl's eyes lit up at the sound of it.

"Oh, that's beautiful. He looks like a Gibyag."

Ben shrugged. He didn't know there was such a thing. This was when Dave arrived with a dozen donuts, an apparent annoyance to the threesome until Ben indicated that he was Gibyag's owner.

As Ben took Dave into the tack room to discuss the offer, Tom exited in a hurry. He had a thing about avoiding any and all owner-trainer negotiations. He tipped his hat to the two women in passing, melting the generation gap with his *Marlboro Man* smile. And vanished.

Dawn always took Tom's lead when becoming scarce was in order, and sat down on a bale of straw in the shedrow to wait. Ben emerged a few minutes later, a good time for her to hurry in and get the donuts.

"The price is twelve thousand...firm." He motioned over his shoulder at Dave. "The man really doesn't want to sell."

"Will you give us a moment?" the gentleman said.

Ben nodded, and when they huddled, winked at Dawn as she slipped past them to sit back down on the bale of straw. The conference didn't last long.

"We'll pick him up in the morning," the man said. "Is it all right if I give you a check for him now?"

Dave said a check was fine. Ben looked it over then and handed it to him, and the deal was made. Ben said he'd have the papers ready for them tomorrow, and they shook hands.

As the three walked away, Dawn overheard the older woman telling the man about what a steal Gibyag was, and how she probably would have given a few thousand more for him if they'd asked for it, that he was probably worth it, and...

Dawn wolfed down the rest of her donut, called Ben out, and motioned for him to walk with her down the shedrow. "I need to show you something in the fifth stall," she said, for Dave's benefit.

Ben couldn't imagine what, as he followed her. The fifth stall was empty. Since it was so late in the year, they'd been using it just for icing horses.

"What?"

"Nothing," Dawn whispered. "I just didn't want Dave to think..."

When she told him what the woman had said, Ben smiled. "Listen. He could've been claimed for thirty-five hundred, and there's no guarantee he would've won. We just got twelve thousand with no risks. Every time you lead a horse his age over there, you take a chance. A bigger chance. Who knows how many more trips he had."

"But...?"

"Look at it this way. Surviving all the trainers he has, he deserves to retire sound. Besides, between you and me, he should be a hunter. He's got the personality for it."

Dawn didn't disagree. She just didn't understand. "But he's a good racehorse. And like you said, he's still sound."

"Right." Ben nodded. "And you want to know why? Because he never ran hard enough to hurt himself. He's a Thoroughbred, Dawn, but that don't mean he wants to be a racehorse. If you could ask him, he'd probably say so. And let's not forget the most important thing here. The smile on that little girl's face."

Dawn marveled. He was such a softy.

"Why, he'll be pampered and never want for anything. He'll have it made, and I say God bless him."

Dawn smiled, and as he walked back to the tack room, thought about what he'd told her a long time ago about class.

"And another thing," Ben said, stopping and looking back at her. "You say they would've given a few thousand more. Then the way I figure it, we split the difference. Because Dave had already agreed to take a few thousand less."

Gibyag shipped the following morning, less than a month from the day he'd arrived, and with just two weeks left in Dawn's first racing season. She was looking forward to the time off, but admittedly, was going to miss the track. Most of the trainers at Nottingham shipped elsewhere to race after the meet, but not Ben. Occasionally he shipped a horse to another trainer for the winter, but more often than not, they were given the time off and turned out. Tom planned on migrating to Florida, as he did every year, and Dawn was going to work on her book. Her novel.

She sighed, remembering the day Ben suggested she write it, that morning, as if it were yesterday. "How's a hundred-fifty a week to start. That's pretty standard. Plus you'll get stakes."

"Stakes?"

Ben nodded. "Kinda like a tip when a horse you groom wins."

Dawn hesitated.

"What? Not enough money?"

Dawn shook her head. No, it wasn't the money. Actually, it was everything but the money.

"You'll get afternoons off when there's nothing in. You and Tom can rotate feeding, plus Mondays and Tuesdays when there's no racing. It'll be a lot of work. Hard work. And I have to be able to count on you. So if you don't think..."

Perhaps hard work was exactly what she needed. Because maybe, just maybe, if she worked as hard as she possibly could, she'd be able to distance herself from her past and give some meaning to the future. How insane, she thought. What was working at a racetrack going to do? How would it help? How would anything help?

"What's the problem?" Ben said.

"Nothing. I guess I uh, just wish I knew more about what I was doing."

"Don't worry, you'll learn," Ben said. "And you're going to love it."

He'd sounded so positive, never a doubt. And with the season almost over now, she had to admit, she did love it. All of it.

Ben told her that every year, when it got close to the end of the season, he always thought of retiring. "Sometimes I sit here and wonder if I want to come back. Especially when the years haven't been as good as this one."

He looked from her to Tom, then shrugged and stared off, and they both knew he was thinking about Meg now, the summer she died. Dawn reached over and squeezed his hand, and he glanced at her for a second, then nodded, and took off his glasses and wiped his eyes.

"Yep, it's been a good year," he said, and he wasn't just referring to the six stakes Beau won, or how well most of the other horses had done. "There's gonna come a day when I will retire though. And I'm gonna sit on my front porch, maybe even get me a rocking chair, and do nothing but watch Beau's offspring grow. Lord knows the Ohio breeding program could use a good stud." He sighed, then smiled and put his glasses back on. "But Beau's not done with this racing business yet, and neither am I."

"Well, you can count me in for next year," Dawn said.

Ben grinned. "I never doubted it for a second."

Tom didn't like it when the old man got sentimental, because it made him feel sentimental then, and that wasn't in keeping with his image. He was glad it had passed. He propped his feet on the tack trunk, tipped his hat back, and pulled a toothpick out of his shirt pocket. "Well, I'll be back. That is, unless some rich broad holds me down and won't let me go. Hell, maybe she'll have a daughter, or a sister, or maybe a Momma that's richer." He raised his eyes, liking the sound of that, and went right into his own version of "Momma's gonna buy me a new pair of shoes."

Dawn had been an eager apprentice, and had learned about as much as an aspiring horseman could. She'd bathed, brushed, done up, and picked and shoveled her fair share. She'd been kicked, broken a finger, and sprained an ankle in the process. She'd weathered rain, heat, hail, and snow...sunshine and a flood. And all the while, had become more attached to Ben and Tom, and deeper and deeper in love with Beau Born.

She'd had the pleasure of standing in the winner's circle on many occasions, but learned to accept the reality of returning to the barn a loser on even more. She found out firsthand what it was like to have a horse she was fond of claimed from them, had seen numerous horses come and go, and even managed to get talked into betting a week's pay on a horse that couldn't lose, but did. She'd been teased, set-up, laughed at, laughed with, and cared about, and somewhere in the midst of all this she'd started to put her life back together. Of course she'd be here next year. The racetrack was a part of her now.

They were down to one race.

The Overton.

And Beau was favored to win.

Chapter Four

Ben always breezed Beau a half mile two days before a race to get him tight, to bring his conditioning to a peak, and as usual, Tom and Red had to help Miguel pull him up.

"Jesus!" Miguel jumped off at the gap and walked along with Ben. "I have a strangle hold on heem! Look!" Deeply etched grooves from the reins were still visible in his palms. "I say no one will beat heem."

Ben wished the man would talk slower. His accent made him hard enough to understand. "Just don't come to the paddock..."

"No problem, Mr. Miller. I am straight."

Ben glanced at him, wondering. Half the time he could swear the man was higher than a kite.

"Thank you for naming me on heem! I tell my agent no more you take me off the Miller horse."

Ben nodded sarcastically. "I don't suppose looking up Beau's ass in the Ballymore had anything to do with convincing him, now did it?"

Miguel didn't answer, knowing anything he'd say would only aggravate Ben more. Besides, it was true. He waved instead, and ducked into one of the barns.

"Agents," Ben told Dawn, "most of them anyway, are nothing but handicappers with a part-time job." Another of his pet peeves.

"Do they ever pick the right horse?"

"Sometimes," Ben said. "But it ain't often."

A person didn't have to be around Ben long to know who and what he liked and didn't like. He was brutally honest and always said what was on his mind. Always.

Dawn gave Beau a quick bath, since the temperature was dropping, and after scraping him off, covered him with two blankets and offered him a drink of water. He played with it, smacking his lips and splashing her, his lack of thirst another indication of his fitness.

From under the eaves of the barn, Ben watched as Dawn hung Beau on the walking machine, and was deep in thought, contemplating the days ahead, when she appeared at his side.

"I still don't understand why you named Miguel back on him. Tom says he's the biggest doper on the track, and will stiff a horse in a minute if..."

"You don't always have choices, Dawn."

This was the same answer he'd given her before. "Why? Why not?"

Ben glanced at her, then sighed and explained, reluctantly, because the fact of the matter bothered him as well. "Miguel fits Beau better than any rider here. He's a tough horse to ride and Miguel gets the job done. It's as simple as that."

"But he wasn't on him in the Ballymore, and..."

"That race was a little easier than this one, and don't forget I named him on the horse. I wanted him then, and I want him now. This late in the year and what with the track the way it is, I've got to take my best shot."

"What if he holds him?"

Ben smiled. "Claimers are where you have to watch him. He's too smart to stiff a horse with this much money involved."

Dawn nodded hopefully, thinking, we'll see, and just then a large bay horse came running down between the barns. No tack, no halter, no direction. And drawing shouts from points near and far.

"Loose horse!"

"Loose horse!"

"Shit!"

"Loose horse!"

Always, as with any loose horse, you either try to catch it or get out of its way. The safest route is just to get out of its way, but it could very well be your horse next time, so...

"Turn the machine off!" Ben yelled. Dawn was already headed for the switch. All the horses started going crazy in their stalls. Beau started rearing, then leaping in the air and kicking out. Ben couldn't get near him. And damned if the loose horse didn't trot right up between the two of them.

"Turn it back on!" Ben yelled. "Turn it on!"

Dawn hit the switch again.

Majorama snapped the top of her webbing, leaning all her weight against it, kicking and bucking. Dawn ran to shut the bottom door of her stall. When she turned, her heart sank.

Beau was pulling back on the walking machine arm, striking out at the loose horse, and the loose horse was striking back. Ben was helpless. He couldn't even begin to get close to them. With each strike, one would then leap. The machine would yank Beau forward. He'd fight it, yanking back, and would strike again. Then down through the barn area came Tom on Red, leading Third Time A Lady.

One look, and he yelled for Dawn to come get her. He jumped off Red and slapped him on the rear. Red trotted down the shedrow and into his stall, and Dawn led Lady quickly in the opposite direction.

"Whoa..." Tom said, arms spread as he approached the machine. By now, Bob Graptor had come out of his barn and was attempting to do the same from the other side.

"Whoa...easy now. Whoa..."

Something spooked the loose horse. It jumped low to the ground. Beau squealed! And the two of them struck at each other again.

"Oh shit!" Tom said under his breath. It would've been too much to hope that it could've been a filly or a mare. It was a goddamned stud horse. Battle lines drawn. "That's just great!" he said in a soothing voice as he advanced. "Let's talk about who's got the biggest balls."

Beau stomped the ground.

The loose horse stomped back.

"Easy now..." Tom came around the inside of Beau, figuring it to be the only option at the moment, with both horses squared off, necks bowed and squealing. Timing his move precisely, he grabbed Beau's halter, yanked back on it, and with the other hand, reached up and grabbed hold of the loose horse's ear.

No horse alive likes its ears handled, let alone one head-shy, as a lot of stud colts are from being continuously corrected since the day they were born. It started backing up in high gear. Toward the barn. Through the ditch. And into the shedrow...with Tom still holding onto its ear.

"Go ahead, cocksucker!" Tom kept saying. "Go ahead!"

The horse backed himself right into a wall.

Graptor crept up and put a halter and shank on the horse. Ben got Beau off the machine. The loose horse's groom arrived, grateful and red-faced, to take the horse away. It would appear neither horse had landed a blow. So all was well. No harm done.

Except for Red, who instead of staying in his stall, took advantage of all the excitement and found his way to the feed room. He ended up slightly colicked later, laying flat out on his side and moaning, but managed to be up by dinner time.

The following morning, every horse in the barn walked, so chores were finished well ahead of schedule. Ben left to go home, and Tom was going to McDonald's to pick up lunch for Dawn and him. Typically, he teased her about how much she wanted to eat.

"Two cheeseburgers, large fry, hash browns if it's not too late, a chocolate milkshake, and a large Coke. What? No apple pie?"

"Well, now that you mention it, yes. Only make sure it's done this time. The last one was frozen in the middle."

Tom bowed at the waist, then saluted. "Yes ma'am! Will there be anything else?"

"No, that'll be all." She dismissed him with a trivial wave and laughed. "Now run along." When he'd gone, she stretched her legs out and looked in at Beau, who was up to his chest in an ice tub. It was all right to joke about giving orders, especially since she'd made the last two or three lunch runs herself. But in reality, it always made her uncomfortable.

She was no hypocrite. Hardly. She was who she was, and there was no denying that. Still... As her mind wandered, she thought about her mother and father. Beau sloshed in his ice tub then, and quickly brought her back to the matter at hand. It was routine to ice

Beau the day before a race, and although ice boots would be much easier, the ice tub was Ben's way.

"It's uniform," he'd said. "With boots, where the ice starts to melt, there's gaps."

So here she was, sitting on a water bucket padded with quilted leg wraps, keeping vigil over him. Oh, Mother, if you could only see me now. She smiled to herself, imagining the conversation they might have.

"Dawn, what are you doing?"

"I'm watching this horse, Mom."

She could see her mother's face. Her puzzled expression. "What for?"

Dawn chuckled, while in her mind, she explained. "He's in a race tomorrow and icing his legs is good for him."

She pictured her mother looking in at Beau, from a distance of course, and frowning. His front legs were completely immersed in icy water. "How on earth did you get him in there?"

"Not all that easily, Mom. The horse has to be coaxed up close, then one leg lifted and bent. Then you coax them a little more so they lean forward, and in goes that leg. The quicker the better, because it's pretty much instinct for them to lift the other one then. Tom always bends the top of the tub back at that point. See, here look, it's somewhat flexible. Then you bend the other leg, get it in, and get them to stand squarely. And here I sit. They have to be in ice for at least an hour and a half. Anything after that, Ben says, is a waste of time. And you take them out just about the same way, first one leg and then the other."

"Really?"

Dawn sighed. It was a nice fantasy, talking to her mother. But even stretching her imagination, if her mother were alive, she couldn't picture her anywhere near this racetrack, let alone the backside. Not that her mother looked down on places or things. It was just that her posture was so...that, well, she only saw things straight ahead or up.

Beau sloshed some more, lifting one leg and leaning back on his haunches a little, and Dawn talked to him. "Come on, it won't be long now." She clicked softly and he pricked his ears. "Come on now." When she tugged lightly on the shank, he put his leg back

down, looked at her for a moment, then pulled a mouthful of hay out
of the hay-net hung just outside his door.

It had been months since Dawn had allowed herself to think about
her parents, really think about them. And even though she refused to
let it consume her anymore, as she thought about them now, it was
the same old anguish. She damned her father's private plane. His
pilot's license. The accident. And as always...her part in what
happened that day.

Tom started down the shedrow singing, with Barn Kitty tagging
along behind and meowing enthusiastically. They'd often marveled
about this particular cat's uncanny ability to smell food from five
barns away. Tom had a song about him, something obscene about the
"sniffing little puss puss." He sang an encore for Dawn, improvising
here and there. And at the sound of his voice, she looked up at him
and smiled. She'd been miles away and hadn't heard a word he'd said.

Dawn was looking forward to a long hot shower, a meal of sweet and
sour pork, and a little quiet time to write, and hadn't been home a
minute when her cousin Linda informed her of other plans. She and
Dawn had been roommates for three years now, after practically
growing up together on their families' adjoining estates. The two of
them couldn't have been closer if they were sisters.

"A couple of hours, Dawn. What's the big deal?"

"None. I just don't want to go."

"Why not? Harland says he's very nice. And it's only for dinner.
Come on, it'll be fun."

"No thanks. I don't like fun."

"Dawn..."

She'd started down the hall.

"You can't just write about life, you know. You have to live it
too."

Dawn stopped and looked back. "Phil Donahue. Right?"

Linda laughed. "Dawn, come on. Please...for me."

Dawn glanced down at the floor and shook her head. "I'm sorry, I
just don't want to go. I don't want to go anywhere. I'm home, and I
want to stay home."

"Why? What for? You haven't been out in months, ever since you
dumped Dave."

"Right. Did you hear what you just said? Ever since I dumped Dave. Which means it was my choice. I want to be alone."

"No, you don't," Linda said. "You just didn't want Dave around anymore."

Dawn laughed.

"Please. I promise, we'll be home by eleven."

Dawn stared. "That's too late. Beau's in tomorrow, and you know how my stomach gets."

"Fine. How's ten?"

Dawn was as bad as Fancy Pat when it came to getting nervous about a big race. The only difference was Dawn began fretting the night before. She drew a breath and sighed heavily. "What relation is he to Harland?"

"They're cousins. First cousins. Isn't that great?"

Dawn rolled her eyes. "Wonderful."

Linda meant well. She just wanted to get Dawn out of the apartment, fearing she was withdrawing again. But so much for good intentions. Dawn excused herself to go to the ladies room for the third time since arriving at the restaurant, and on the way back to the table, started thinking about how she was going to get even with Linda for this.

She could be home right now, where she wanted to be, where she'd planned to be, and should be. She'd certainly be more comfortable.

Her stomach growled as she sat back down, the kind of growl that hurts, and she gave Linda the I-want-to-go-home look. I want to go home.

Linda was glad she'd arranged for Harland and his cousin to pick them up. Dawn had been flashing her this look for some time now, and it wasn't even eight o'clock yet. She glanced from Harland to his cousin, desperately trying to think of something interesting to say. "Dawn works at the racetrack."

"Oh?" Harland's cousin said.

When he turned and looked at Dawn, she just stared. In another minute or so, she was going to be once again lining the toilet seat with tissue. It's hard to make conversation with this pending.

"Tell me about it."

"Well..." She sighed, her stomach growling some more. "I'm a groom."

"A what?"

"A groom. I take care of the horses."

"Oh, what fun! Really? Why?"

Dawn flashed another one of those looks at Linda. Now! I want to go home *now*. Feeling bad was bad enough, but this man was a bore. A geek. Pompous and arrogant. Dawn looked at Harland. There was a slight family resemblance.

"I don't know. Because I enjoy it."

"I'll bet you do. Are you a jockey?"

Geek. Geek. Geek. "No."

"I see."

Dawn stared, then excused herself again. When she returned, it was obvious Linda had done some prompting to help the man along. "I hear your favorite horse is running tomorrow."

"Yes." Dawn forced a smile. "Eighth race."

"Is it true they still shoot horses when they break a leg?"

He'd come up with this on his own, and needless to say, Dawn's expression in response had Linda fidgeting uncomfortably in her chair. Dawn wasn't going to answer him. She could tell by the way she sat back. But then suddenly Dawn smiled an odd smile. "Yes, and isn't that sad."

"Terribly," Harland's cousin said, nodding then when Dawn nodded.

"That's why I always make a sacrifice."

Linda's face flushed.

"A sacrifice...?" Harland asked. "What do you mean?"

Dawn turned innocently to Linda. "You didn't tell them?"

Now it was Linda giving the looks. Don't you dare. I mean it, don't you dare.

Wrong look. "A burnt offering. Chicken bones. Calves' blood. And chicory. Have you ever smelled chicory burning? Fresh chicory that is." Dawn lowered her voice. "It smells like hell. Literally. It does. If you know what I mean." She stood. "Now if you'll excuse me, I need to see the chef again. He's preparing me a very special doggy bag."

Harland and his cousin stared up at her with mouths agape, watching her every move. And suffice to say, the evening pretty much came to end with that.

"She's kidding. Right?"

Linda sighed. "Harland, I'm sorry. But I seem to be getting a headache. Can we go?"

At the apartment, Linda lingered in the hall saying goodnight to Harland, then turned, and closed the door. An evening's worth of pent-up frustration simmered in her eyes. "Do you have any idea what Harland must be thinking right now? What his cousin must be thinking?"

"Who?"

"All right. So maybe I shouldn't have told Harland you haven't been dating. Maybe I shouldn't have set this up. All I was trying to do was get you out so you could have a nice time. But nooooooo!!! You have to go and act like some kind of, what was that? A devil worshiper act?" Linda threw her hands up. "My God, I can't believe you did that! Of all things! Harland's probably thinking, no wonder you don't go out. And me! What about me, living here with you? What do you think he's thinking about me? I hope you're happy! Are you happy?"

"I don't know." Dawn shrugged. "The evening did have its moments."

Linda stared in disbelief, just stared, remembering, and with that, the two of them burst out laughing.

"Chicken bones?"

"And chicory. Let's not forget the chicory."

"I know. It smells like hell."

Hand-walking Beau the morning of a race was next to impossible. Tom was the only one who'd even attempt it. While he struggled to keep Beau on the ground, Dawn stripped his stall of all its bedding. This was done as part of the *drawing* process, to make sure a horse runs on a relatively empty stomach. They were given half their usual ration of hay at feeding time the evening before, and none the next morning, just a scoop of oats. The straw was always removed as well, because most horses will eat it in the absence of their hay.

Dawn had been back and forth to the ladies room more times than she cared to count since arriving this morning. And to make matters worse, Tom always made a point of letting her know he knew where she'd been. He thought it was funny.

It made for a long morning of doing stalls, and she was finally down to her last muck-basket full. As she heaved it up over the side of the manure bin, she lost her grip. No problem if the bin were filled, but it wasn't. Consequently, she had to climb up onto the side and lean over as far as she could to grab the handle. The basket had landed right-side up and was still full, so she had to jog it back and forth, her empty and nauseous stomach rubbing into the side of the bin the entire time. And for a moment, she felt like she was going to be sick.

"Oh Lord..."

"Dawn, you need some help?" Tom called from the shedrow.

She shook her head with determination and lifted with all the strength she had left, grabbed hold of the other handle, and with her stomach really on the verge now, tipped the muck basket and emptied it. What an accomplishment.

"Jesus, Dawn..." Tom said, walking up behind her and giving her a scrutinizing look. "You'd think you'd be fitter by now."

Dawn rolled her eyes. Why he got such a big kick out of teasing her, was beyond reason. But then, like always, he did something so endearing, she could only smile. Using the upper part of his sleeve, he wiped the perspiration off her brow. And somewhat gently yet.

"Go take a break. To look at you, people'd think you did all the fucking stalls. Jesus Christ."

Dawn shook her head. She'd done four that morning, Ben two, and Tom five. And on top of that, he'd ponied three horses for them, the three shipping on, in addition to two for a trainer on the backside, and had galloped a two-year-old for Graptor as a favor, when no one else on the track would get on it. He was the one that should be tired. He shifted his toothpick. "God, you're sexy when you're sweating."

Dawn laughed.

When Ben returned from the secretary's office, calm as can be, Dawn couldn't help but wonder why she was the only one who reacted to Beau's races this way. After all, there was so much at stake. Ben's future, his retirement, Beau's retirement. The pressure. Each race became a lifetime statistic, which would have a bearing on his standing at stud, each and every one monumentally important in terms of percentage. Not to mention how he could also get hurt.

That thought had her stomach cramping again, and off she went on yet another trip to the ladies room. As she rounded the corner she ran smack dab into Randy Iredell, who was coming from the opposite direction.

"Oh Jesus..." She hugged her sides. "What?"

"What?" The way she'd asked, annoyed him.

She drew an agonizing breath. "I'm sorry. What do you need?"

"Nothing," he said, and paused. "You need me. Jake says you have a horse to be tranquilized for shipping."

Dawn stepped back, motioning to Tom, who was halfway down the shedrow, and walked away. He could ask him. When she returned, she sat down on the stoop by the tack room and, with her elbows on her knees, buried her face in her hands. This was only the second time Randy Iredell had been to their barn, since Doc Jake normally handled all their calls. She could hear him and Tom talking down by Majorama's stall. When she heard another voice, she looked up.

It was Doc Jake. He'd just handed something to Randy, and was walking toward her. "Is Ben around?"

"No, I think he's up at the kitchen."

Doc Jake stopped in front of her, gave her a quick once-over, and shook his head. "The big horse's in, huh?"

Dawn nodded.

"You gonna make it?"

"I don't think so," she said wearily.

Doc Jake chuckled, patted her head affectionately, and walked on. Tom and Randy were still down by Majorama's stall. She stared at them. It was obvious from their actions, and the looks they were giving her, that they were talking about her. Randy leaned in closer, listening, and then the two of them laughed.

Too miserable to play along and ask, "What's so funny?" she buried her face in her hands again. They were walking toward her now, their hushed voices growing closer and closer. Then they stopped.

She looked up at them.

They both smiled. Grinned actually.

"How are you?" Tom said.

Dawn rolled her eyes. "Fine, Tom. And how are you?" She stood up, thinking they wanted past her into the tack room. But despite her sarcastic reply and apparent disgruntlement, both of them continued to stand there and smile amiably.

Randy was taking in how tall she was, this being the first time he'd spent longer than a second or two standing next to her. She was taller than he'd realized. He liked tall women, and this one was very tall; five ten or eleven at least. And pretty, though somewhat plain. He ran his eyes down to her feet, then back up, quickly, but expertly. Tall enough to maybe stand for sex. His smile widened.

Dawn couldn't help but notice she was being sized up, although she had no idea to what extent, and even managed to do a little sizing up herself. Once again, she was taken by how muscular the man was. Then she thought, how ridiculous, as if veterinarians didn't need to be strong, particularly ones who practiced on large animals. He'd have to be. And those blue eyes, and that mustache.

Tom broke the momentary silence. "I was just telling Randy here about this ritual you have of drawing yourself for Beau's races."

Dawn stared at him in disbelief, then glared. Was there nothing sacred with him? "Tom..."

He moved out of striking distance, laughing, as Randy turned, trying not to laugh.

Dawn could've strangled him right then and there. Or worse. But when she opened her mouth, never at a loss for just the right thing to say having inherited her Aunt Maeve's acid tongue, her stomach cramped again.

Tom and Randy stepped back out of her way, first one then the other. They both pointed ceremoniously to the ladies room. And shaking her head, she left them.

When she returned, she was thankful they'd gone. Tom especially. Him and his childish sense of humor. All she wanted to do was go into the tack room and lie down on the cot for a while. She startled Ben when she walked in, and he jumped, dropping a number of pills on the floor.

"I'm sorry." She watched them spiral round and round, then bent down to pick them up. "Do you have a headache?"

Ben didn't answer, trying hard to get down low enough to pick them up himself. Dawn examined one. They weren't aspirin.

"Are these blood pressure pills?"

Ben shrugged.

"They look like the kind my mother used to take." She dusted them off, handed them to him, and leaned down to get the last one. "I didn't know you had high blood pressure."

"It's nothing," he said, avoided eye contact, and walked out. "I'll be back in a little while."

Dawn lay down on the cot and stared up at the ceiling. There were cloudy cobwebs in each corner, the largest one in the area closest to the bridles and saddle rack. Her stomach ached and growled. Perhaps it would feel better if she turned onto her side. First her left. It didn't help. Then her right. But always facing the door. Always. She did this instinctively, her head at the top and then the bottom.

Her stomach rumbled again and she sighed. Blood pressure pills? Even though Ben said it was nothing, she wondered. Worried. Age for the most part had been kind to Ben, his gray hair more silver than white, and still thick. And he appeared healthy and strong, though slightly bent at the waist. His hands were large and callused, his shoulders thick and wide.

She smiled to herself. He certainly was healthier than she was at the moment. Besides, a lot of people take blood pressure pills. It's nothing, just like he said.

Ben was doing some thinking too as he walked up to the racetrack, thinking about Meg, and thinking about Dawn. Meg couldn't have children, and always felt she'd let him down because of it. Even now, years after her death, he ached at the idea of her ever letting him down. She would've given him a daughter just like Dawn if she could've. Just like her. And sons too.

Tom handed Beau over to Dawn when they reached the paddock entrance, and joined the other ponies assembled out on the track by the winner's circle, to wait.

Dawn called out Beau's name to the paddock judge as she led him past, a role-call formality which hardly seemed necessary in Beau's case, since almost everyone recognized him on sight. Not only was his massive size a trademark, a tower of brand-new-penny shine and classic veins standing out under thin skin...he had an air about him, a presence, one that seemed to say, "Well, here I am. Now try and outrun me."

Dawn circled the paddock area twice before Ben motioned her in. Relax," he said, teasing her for this do-or-die expression she always sported right about now. "We're going to win in hand. Give the maintenance crew a rest."

Dawn laughed self-consciously, then glanced at the level of spectators above, who were hanging over the railing looking for tips on which horse to bet. Maybe the one that kept tossing its head. Or perhaps the one that acted the rankest. The one kicking or rearing. Or the one standing the quietest. Any little sign. Anything. Dawn even heard a spectator once telling the person next to him that if you watch how high a horse holds its tail, you'll know.

At the time Dawn just shook her head, but even now, as ridiculous as it seemed to watch for such signals, it made about as much sense to her as reading a racing form. Especially since Ben told her it wasn't so much what a form showed that was important, but what it didn't show. It's complicated, he explained, and summed it up by saying, "You have to be able to read between the lines."

A large bay horse being saddled in the stall next to them started acting up, easily dragging its poor groom around. Pettibons King, a ship-in from Chicago, was being saddled at a walk and would rear and throw his weight up against the valet at the slightest hesitation. Here and there were stern commands. The number five horse, a small but flashy chestnut, danced around the paddock obediently, and if horses could smile, with a smile on his face.

Dawn's stomach grumbled.

Beau stood still to be tacked, frozen in a statue-like stance, his muscles quivering as the saddle cloth was laid across his back. The saddle pad and saddle were next, and the girth passed underneath. Beau's eyes widened, his quivering escalating into trembling as he stared straight ahead, his gaze fixed. The overgirth was put in place and Ben reached down to thread it through the buckle, pulling it hard and tight and then passing the leather back for the valet to tuck in securely.

The paddock judge approached, smiling first at Ben, and cringing as he took hold of Beau's upper lip to check his tattoo. Beau kicked out. It was something you could always count on. The sound as he connected with the wall resonated like a cannon blast.

Miguel, in scarlet and gray silks, was the last rider out of the jocks' room, which was another thing you could always count on. He walked over slowly, adjusting the Velcro on his sleeves as he looked around the paddock, and nodded to Dawn and then Ben as he came nearer.

Ben drew him close. "Let him break on his own. Don't hustle him."

Miguel nodded as he wound the reins, and pulled back on them to tighten the all-important rider's knot.

"There's some early speed in the race, but don't let the pace fool you. Stay close."

The paddock judge called, "Riders up!" And the jockeys were legged-up in order of their starting positions, and led out onto the track.

As soon as Dawn handed Beau and Miguel over to Tom, she headed for the ladies room. At the two-minute-to-post warning, she walked down to the rail and jumped up onto the fence support, her favorite spot to watch a race. Ben came down right after that to join her.

Since the race was a flat mile, the starting gate was directly in front of them. The tote board changed as the horses approached the gate, making Pettibons King even money and Beau three to one. Ben explained once to Dawn how for big races, even the most faithful will bet the ship-in. Popular opinion being, that if they were willing to travel, they must think they can win it.

Ben liked the odds.

The last horse to be loaded balked, backing up and ducking numerous attempts by the gate crew to get him in, while the others became restless. "No boss! No boss!" different jockeys yelled. "Not yet boss!" Pettibons King reared, his rider jumping up onto the side of the gate before mounting again. Two of the gate crew got behind the last horse, clasping their hands together to push and shove. At one point, they practically lifted the horse off his hind legs, before finally getting him loaded.

"No boss! No boss!"

"No boss!"

"No! No!"

Then silence, time seemingly suspended as the latch sprung. The bell rang. "And they're off!"

Beau broke well and laid third through the first turn, dropping down on the rail when it opened up, two or three lengths off the lead. Pettibons King was out in front, covering the first half mile in forty-five seconds flat. Still laying third down the backside, as they entered the far turn, Beau loomed up on the horse running second, and at the head of the stretch, took over the lead.

Dawn's eyes were riveted on him, hearing only his name, as the others blended together, just his. Just him. With a sixteenth of a mile to go, Beau was in front by five lengths. Pettibons King was being challenged now by a pack of horses for second.

Approaching the wire, Beau continued to reach out, lengthening his lead with each stride...Miguel hand-riding him with the reins pushed high on his neck and his whip uncocked.

"And it's Beau Born in ccoommpplleettee ccoommmannnnddd!!!" the announcer called. "Ladies and gentlemen, Beau Born is the unofficial winner of the twelfth running of the Overton Stake. There is a photo for place and show."

Ben clutched the fence, lowering his head, and mouthed a silent prayer. When he raised his eyes, he watched Beau being pulled up. After they turned, jogged, and broke into a fluid canter, then and only then, did he turn to Dawn and smile.

The winner's circle was filled with jubilant people; several of Ben's friends, the owners of the Overton Racing Stable, their family and friends. And the track's general manager was on hand to make the trophy presentation.

Tom dismounted Red and led Beau in as Miguel looked up toward the stewards' box above the grandstand and waved his whip in a traditional jockey's salute. The photographer snapped the picture as everyone huddled together, grinning and laughing. Beau stood proud. And the official sign was posted. Pettibons King held on for second. Jimmy Crickett, the little horse with the smile, finished third.

Chapter Five

How or why Gloria Mitchell happened onto the Miller barn one day, was a mystery. She was pretty, spunky, recently retired, and widowed. To Ben however, she was just an annoyance.

"I don't like the way she looks at me."

Tom laughed. "What do you expect out of an old nurse? She's been looking at men "on their way out" her whole life. Hell, you're prime in her eyes."

Dawn chuckled, smacked Tom on the arm, and turned smiling at Ben. "Well, I think she's nice. Besides, all she wants you to do is find her a horse."

Tom nodded in agreement, somewhat. "Right, and how can a woman that smells like a lilac bush be all that bad?"

"She smells like a goddamned funeral parlor," Ben said. "That's what she smells like."

Tom laughed, while closely examining a hangnail on his left thumb that had been bothering him all morning. "She's got the hots for you, old man. It's as simple as that. Go for it!"

"I'll give you, 'go for it.' If you're so gung ho, why don't you..."

"I can't, I tried. She won't have anything to do with me. She wants you. No one else'll do."

Ben didn't find any of this funny and left the tack room. They were barely into the third week of the new racing season, and already he was grumpy. Most of the horses had shipped in about seven weeks earlier and were doing well, but the Wagners had switched stables over the winter, and it bothered him. He'd been their trainer for years now and had won a lot of races for them. Why would they change? For lack of any other reason, he chalked it up to his suggesting they retire Majorama. With bone chips in her knee too numerous to count, and the joint having been drained of excess fluid too many times, ending her racing career to become a broodmare was sound advice.

Tom had tried consoling him in his own way. "Screw 'em, who needs 'em. So they got a bug up their ass. Who cares?"

Still, it played on his mind, and every time he'd watched Majorama head for the track in the morning, it upset him more. So much so, one would've thought when he heard she'd "broke down" and had to be destroyed, he'd have felt some satisfaction. But not Ben. He called it a waste, a crying shame, and probably would have punched old-man Wagner if he'd been within reach.

Gloria Mitchell's timing was off. Majorama was about to become a by-product, and she was trying to flirt with an angry man. "Well, Mr. Miller. Are we going to claim a horse today?"

Ben shook his head in disbelief. Did she think on any given day there were horses worthy of claiming? "Now, Mrs. Mitchell, that's not how it's done. Surely you understand that a little clocking is in order. I don't want to halter a dink for you, nor do I want to train one."

Clocking? Halter a dink? Gloria pursed her lips. "Excuse me...?"

"Claim a sore horse," Ben partially explained. Haltering is a common racetrack term for claiming. Clocking in this context refers to checking a horse out, watching it train in the morning, asking around about it, following it to the race, that sort of thing. "Claiming a horse is risky business."

"Oh, but of course it is, Ben...may I call you Ben? And please," she said, "you call me Gloria. It's just that I'm so excited. I want a horse so badly. A black one. I like black horses. What about you? Remember *Fury*? I loved that show. Let's look in the racing form to see if there are any black horses running today."

Ben gazed down at the tack room floor, sighing. Why me, he wondered? A black horse. As if color had anything to do with making a sound choice.

"Ben?"

He looked at her, showing signs of giving in, giving up.

"Today...?"

Ben nodded. Maybe if it weren't for the Wagners leaving him with empty stalls. No trainer likes giving up his or her stalls. "Okay, we'll do it. You pick one out and we'll talk about it. Now let me get back to work."

Gloria could hardly contain her excitement as she headed for the track kitchen, racing form in hand and singing over her shoulder, "I'll be back."

Ben looked at Dawn and shook his head. "I'll tell you what. When I die, I don't want any flowers." The aroma of lilac hung heavy in the air. "You hear me? None!" He buried his face in the racing form, mumbling to himself about corpses, funeral parlors, black horses, and then Woolworths for some reason, perhaps the fragrance. Dawn had to leave the tack room to keep from laughing.

Midday, Gloria returned to the barn, dressed in lavender from head to toe, and waving triumphantly. "I've picked one out! I've picked one out!"

So had Ben and Tom. They'd spent the last two hours going over the form themselves, and had ruled out all but one. A solid hard-knocker running for $6250. He'd been sprinting and looked like he just needed a little more ground.

"I knew I'd find one!" Gloria beamed. "My horoscope for today said I'd find exactly what I was looking for. And the best part is..." She perched herself on the chair across from Ben and Tom, next to Dawn. "He's black!"

When Ben started to object, Tom tapped him on the arm and pointed to their choice in the form. He too was black.

Gloria crossed her legs at the ankles and put her purse on her lap. "His name is Too Cajun. Isn't that a pretty name?"

Ben and Tom both glanced at the form. "Just lovely," Tom said, somehow managing to sound quite serious. "How did you pick him out?"

"Simple," Gloria replied. "He's the only black horse running today."

Ben instructed Dawn to stay on the backside until post time of the third race. "Hide the halter and shank in your jacket. If for some reason we don't take him, don't let on. No use advertising we're looking."

Dawn had some time to kill, so she decided to pull some manes, even though her fingers were still sore from the three she'd done earlier in the week. Cutting a mane to a shorter length with scissors would certainly be easier, but that's not how it's done. A comb is used to tease the hair back, leaving just a few strands, the longest ones, which are then pulled out. Start at the top and work your way down, she'd been told. That way, when you're done, you not only have a shorter mane, but one that's thinned out and laying nicely as well. Horses don't have nerve endings in their mane and tail, so they basically feel nothing but the pull, though it does take a toll on a person's hands. The hair when yanked can slice your fingers like a paper cut. Tom always taped his with Vet Wrap whenever he did any, that is whenever Dawn allowed him to do any. But he wasn't as fussy as she was, and the manes didn't look as good either.

"When you tape your fingers like that, you pull out more at a time than you should. I'll do it my way, thank you very much. And please, do not go near Beau."

Dawn finished a few minutes before she was to go over to the grandstand, and decided to walk up to the kitchen for a can of Coke. When she found the machine out of order again, that was that. They had fountain cola inside, but to her, it just didn't taste the same.

She walked around to the back of the kitchen and sat down on one of the benches facing the first turn of the racetrack. There was a well-worn path at her feet. Though not exactly the ideal place to view a race, this was where one could hear exactly how it all went. The jockeys' explicitness as they pulled up usually left no doubt. But she wasn't going to be here that long. The plan was for her to head over at post time. Not before and not after.

Dawn thought about how the jockeys' comments would change by the time they got turned around and delivered the horse back to its trainer. Excuses. Next times. It's what most trainers wanted. And it's what most jocks gave.

"We got boxed in."

"We got bumped coming out of the gate."

"She'll be all right. She just got a little tired."

"He just come up short."

"We don't get cut off, we win."

"We'll get 'em next time."

"Name me back."

"Yes, name me back."

On and on.

Not Ben though. He had a reputation for not talking at all to a jockey right after a race. He'd just witnessed what had happened, and sure as hell, he'd say, didn't need anyone telling him how it went. Nor did he want any excuses for "running up the shit-house," as he put it. Occasionally though, he'd been known to ask a jock to come watch the videotape of the race with him the next day, if something bothered him.

As Dawn started toward the grandstand, Tom took his place beyond the office door next to the paddock. When the horses for the next race were led in, Ben tried clocking Too Cajun, but it was nearly impossible with Gloria in his ear. He was never so happy to see Dawn.

"Here..." He motioned her over and slipped her a five-dollar bill. "Go get some coffee. Get a hot dog. Anything!" he whispered. "Just take her with you."

Dawn nodded, smiling. With them gone, Ben was able to get a quiet look. Turned slightly, he appeared to be giving each horse equal attention. There were eight in the race. When he looked over at Tom then, both giving the other a hint of a nod, Tom went in to "drop" the claim. They were going for him.

"Just coffee, dear." Gloria was too excited to eat. "I just can't. But thank you. You're so sweet."

Dawn guided her down to the fence to watch the race. Ben and Tom joined them just before the start.

"Did we get him?" Gloria asked, eyes all lit up.

"We won't know till the race's over," Ben said. "There were five other claims dropped."

Gloria gasped! "For him? For Too Cajun?"

"Shhhhh..." Ben frowned. This woman. "I don't know. He's the only horse worth taking, so could be."

"How will they decide?" Gloria asked, in a hushed voice and with her hand to her mouth.

"We'll shake for him," Ben said, nudging her to put her hand down and turn around. "Watch the race. They're at the gate."

Gloria sighed. It was a six-furlong race. The gate was clear across the racetrack, and she couldn't see a thing. She hummed anxiously. Ben glanced at her. She'd closed her eyes. Was she praying, he wondered? Must be. He shook his head.

Too Cajun broke slowly, trailed the field for most of the trip, then closed some ground down the stretch, to finish third. He'd been beaten by at least ten lengths, but it didn't seem to bother Ben or Tom. They were both thinking the same thing; he'd just flattened out. Surprisingly, Gloria's opinion echoed theirs, though expressed differently. And tenderly. "Oh, he just got tired, that's all. He had to run too hard to catch up."

Too Cajun wasn't the only horse singled out by the paddock judge when they got back to the grandstand. A gray horse was tagged as well, one that bobbled with each step as he was led past them to the indoor paddock.

Dawn and Gloria stood with their backs against the wall opposite the paddock, looking somewhat discreet, though at this stage it hardly mattered. Ben and Tom were in the claim booth; the room where decisions were made.

Gloria was hypnotized, her eyes glued to the black horse she hoped was hers. Dawn watched the gray. Its groom was patting and rubbing its shoulder, refusing to look at him. Dawn knew what the young man was feeling, having lost their share the same way. You're not supposed to get attached to them. But you do. And right about now, it hurt to even look at them. This was good-bye.

A few minutes later Tom and Ben emerged. Tom motioned for Dawn to bring over the halter and shank. "Well, we got him," he said.

Gloria squealed with delight. "I knew my horoscope was right! I just knew it!"

Dawn stood back while Tom talked to the groom, pumping him for information about the new horse, like only he could. Amidst his bragging about his latest conquests, full of obscenities and hand gestures, he was carefully making note of the dropped noseband, snaffle bit, tongue tie, and all the groom had to offer.

"Was there more'n one claim in for him?" the young man asked, as they started to walk away.

"No, they're all in shaking for the gray." Tom turned and watched as the gray horse took a step and almost went down on its knees. "They'll be lucky if they fucking get him back to the barn."

The next morning, Doc Jake examined Too Cajun, as was routine for any new horse in the barn. Tom and Dawn had been sitting on the tack room stoop for some time, laughing and amusing themselves as he went back and forth to his van for vial after vial of various medications. The horse had thrush in all fours, "hoof rot" as Tom called it, ringworm and girth gall, which he dubbed "fungus amungus." And its mane and forelock were ridden with lice. Tom didn't have a nickname for this, it was just plain lice.

"Lice...? I'm not going near him," Dawn sputtered.

"Me neither! I got more hair than you. I got it everywhere!"

Ben leaned out the stall. "That's enough! All right?"

Tom and Dawn nodded, staring ever so obediently, and even managed to stay quiet for a moment or two before starting up again. "Let's flip for him. Heads, he's yours. Tails, mine."

"Yeah, right," Dawn said, knowing there was no way she'd win. "I'm not flipping anything with you. You cheat!"

Ben ignored them as Doc Jake drew blood for an analysis. "We might as well worm him. I'm sure he's full of them." He kicked a fresh pile of manure with his boot. "Look at this shit. Hard as a rock. It's a goddamned wonder he's not impacted."

Ben nodded. His sentiments exactly.

"Who'd you get him from? No, never mind, don't tell me. I don't even want to know."

When the two men were done worming the horse, they started down the shedrow toward Tom and Dawn, who were pushing at each other, still joking and laughing.

"Hey, Doc," Tom said, pointing while trying to compose himself. "How's come that horse jerks his head like that?"

Doc Jake turned and looked back at Too Cajun. "Like what?" he asked. And just then he did it again; a little jerk down and up, more like a twitch actually. Only this time, he fluttered his ears as well.

"Shit!" Doc Jake walked back, got out his pen light, and took a look. "He's got ear mites too."

This was enough to start Tom and Dawn up again, until Ben glared at them. They both stood then, saluted, and scattered in search of something to do.

Ben sighed, already thinking of the inevitable conversation he'd soon be having with Gloria. Doc Jake put salve in Cajun's ears and stood back. "Well, all things considered, he's about as sound as they come. A bit neglected, but..."

Ben smiled, of the same opinion. The horse was small, but put together nicely. He'd run down a little, but aside from that, his legs were in good shape. "They'd better get around to doing some serious maintenance on this track or there won't be anything left to run on it."

If a horse had "run down," peeling layers of hide and tissue off the backs of their fetlocks, it was usually because they couldn't get hold of the racetrack; spinning their wheels so to speak, and having to dig in deeper. Too much sand in the track made the problem worse.

"Maintenance? Sheeeettt!" Doc Jake said. "They'd build a new clubhouse first."

Ben chuckled. "Nah, I hear tell they're thinking of a new executive lounge up by the offices." They both laughed, shaking their heads, then fell quiet. They were old friends and had been through a lot together. They'd seen it all.

Doc Jake stared off. "I went to the cemetery yesterday. It would've been me and Audrey's forty-fifth wedding anniversary."

Ben nodded. He knew. Not the exact date, Meg was the one who remembered the days. But he knew it was around this time of year.

"How is it she's been gone three years now, and I still wake up in the morning expecting her to be in bed next to me?"

Ben put his hand on Jake's shoulder.

"I'll tell you, Ben. I dream about her all the time lately. She's sitting up on this hill." He paused, remembering every detail. "Her hair's in curls, just like when I met her. And she's holding her hands out to me." He showed Ben the exact way. "It's the damnedest thing. What's even crazier, I'm making my way up that hill, and I can't be more'n twenty years old."

Ben listened, nodding.

"I always wake up though before I get to the top."

. Ben could feel Jake's pain...his own pain. My God, Jake, he thought, studying his friend's eyes, you look old. You *are* old. We're old. You look so tired. And I know I'm tired. What's going to come of us? We weren't supposed to outlive our wives. Women are supposed to live longer.

Jake shook his head and repeated himself, sadly. "I always wake up before I get to the top."

They walked over to Jake's van and he put his equipment away, closed the back doors, and got in behind the wheel. "Put that salve in his ears twice a day. I'll have Randy drop off some more of it."

Ben nodded and stepped back.

Jake hesitated. "Did you see that new truck of his? Jesus, it's got more compartments in it than Carter has pills. Three even refrigerated. Shit, he could make lunch."

Ben laughed. Jake waved and pulled out, and at the sound of a voice behind him, Ben cringed.

"Yoo hoo..."

The scent confirmed it. He turned reluctantly.

"How did we do? What's he like? He looked so pretty in the paddock."

Ben started down the shedrow with her, thinking of how best to break the news. "Well, aside from a few minor kinks, he seems just fine."

"Oh goody!" Gloria said, clapping her hands in delight, and promptly sending three horses flying to the backs of their stalls. "Oops."

Ben rolled his eyes and stepped back to look in at one of the horses, before walking on.

"So when will he run again? I can hardly wait."

Ben drew a deep breath, stalling. She wasn't going to like this. "I figure about a month. Three weeks at the earliest."

"What?! Why?! What's wrong with him?! Is he sick?"

"Sick...?" Ben said, scratching nervously at his ear. "No, not exactly. He has a parasite problem, among other things, though it's not serious."

"Thank heavens. You scared me. What do you mean parasites? Like worms?"

"Uh...yes. Worms. He has worms," Ben said, as if that were all of it. "Worms."

"So get rid of them."

"I will. I mean, I did," Ben stammered, realizing how foolish he sounded and wondering why he just didn't tell her the truth, all of it. Having reached Cajun's stall though, he just gazed in at him and nodded somberly.

"Poor baby," Gloria said. "You got worms." She looked at Ben, still standing there with an expression on his face like a mortician's. "A month for worms? Good grief! What kind of worms does he have?"

"Oh..." Ben sighed heavily, looking even more sorrowful. "Rare ones." A picture of Dawn and Tom laughing earlier came to mind, and for a second he almost laughed himself. He cleared his throat and furrowed his brow. "But I promise you, he'll be just fine. He seems quite sound."

Gloria looked as if she were going to cry, the last thing Ben expected her to do. He put his hand on her shoulder. "Come on now, he'll be all right. Besides, we wouldn't want to rush him, now would we?"

Gloria's face lit up with the sound of the word "we" Ben had said purposely. "Heavens no, of course not." She bounced back at once, thinking. "Well, I do have to pick out my colors," she said, referring to the color and pattern of her jockey silks. "What do you think of purple? Violet actually? Should I get silk or nylon? Oh my, I hope I can get it all done in a month." She smiled at Too Cajun, then at Ben, and turned in a swirl.

"Sorry I can't stay and chat," she sang over her shoulder.

"Oh, that's okay."

"I'll see you tomorrow."

"Lucky me," Ben said to himself.

Jake woke in a sweat, thinking he'd heard someone calling his name, and after lying still for a moment, realized it was a dream. That same dream where Audrey was calling him to the top of the hill. So beautiful, and so young...she made him feel young again. He closed his eyes, wanting the dream to come back, wanting her to come back. She was so close, much closer this time, and she was holding her hands out to him, smiling as she whispered his name. She whispered it again, then again, and he felt the softness of her skin, her familiar touch. The scent of her hair. And he embraced her.

When Ben pulled his truck in through the stable gate shortly after five-thirty, Charlie was watching for him as he had for years, always there to greet him with a smile. As Ben approached, he rose slowly from his chair.

"Morning, Ben."

Ben smiled, raising his hand to touch the brim of his hat as he always did in greeting him. He stopped midway. There was something in Charlie's eyes.

"What's happened? What is it?"

Charlie swallowed hard. "It's Jake, Ben. He's dead." Charlie's voice cracked, he looked away, and Ben lowered his eyes to the ground.

"How?"

"His daughter found him," Charlie said, his chin trembling noticeably. "His answering service had been trying to get him for hours and..."

Ben looked up with tears in his eyes, and for a moment the two men just stared at one another. "Where did she find him?"

"He was in bed. He died in his sleep."

Ben nodded to himself, then nodded again and gripped Charlie's arm. He gripped it tightly. Of the original group of friends, they were the only two left now. Just the two of them. Everyone else was gone. As Ben walked on, Charlie sat back down and stared stoically at the incoming traffic.

Chapter Six

In less than two weeks, Too Cajun was a different horse. All the bugs were gone, his girth gall was practically healed, and they'd managed to put some much-needed weight on him. Ben was training him long and slow. He'd taken well to this regimen. So all in all, except for the twitch, which was obviously here to stay, he was just about one hundred percent.

Gloria, as Ben had feared, showed up every day at the barn now, like clockwork, though at least she waited until training hours were over. He was thankful for that. Still, she asked too damned many questions. Why this and why that?

"I want to be an active owner. I want to know everything there is to know."

How about the way to the clubhouse, Ben thought. He'd never trained for a woman before. He'd racked his brain trying to think of one. A husband and wife maybe. A father and daughter once. But never a woman herself. Never. So why start now?

He sighed.

Gloria wanted to run. "I know you said three weeks to a month, but it is my birthday. And a very special one at that. Come on, I can't wait. It'll be so much fun. All my lady friends'll come. Maybe my granddaughter too. Oh, Ben, please..."

"We'll see," he said. "I'll check the condition book."

Gloria fished one out of her purse. "Here, use mine."

Ben stared. Use mine? Oh God. An owner with a condition book.

Gloria held it out until he took it; opened and folded neatly to Friday's date, six races circled, and reeking of lilac. "What about this one here?" she asked. It had a perfectly-drawn star next to it.

The condition didn't fit. In fact, for that day, there was nothing even close. "You know, you really don't have to bother yourself with..."

"Oh, it's no bother," Gloria said. "I enjoy it. You know me."

Ben just looked at her.

"Well...?"

"Like I said, we'll see." There was always a possibility of having an extra race written that might fill. Ben handed back her condition book, nodded, and turned to walk away.

"But when will I know?"

"Tomorrow."

"Tomorrow? I have to wait till then?"

Ben kept walking, feeling short of breath, and headed toward the men's room to discourage her in the event she decided to follow him. He and Tom had talked earlier about maybe running Cajun this weekend. One day sooner wouldn't make all that much difference. They weren't going for a win. It would be the first time he'd ever run long in his life. He'd need at least one.

Gloria got tired of waiting for Ben to return and left, but not before confiding in Dawn that she was planning on inviting him to dinner at her house for her birthday.

Dawn tried discouraging her in a subtle way, but with no success. Gloria even had the menu planned already. When Ben finally did return, Dawn debated whether or not to tell him, to warn him, but decided not to for the moment. Ben had a way of letting you know when he wanted to talk, and now wasn't the time. She was sure his moodiness lately had a lot to do with Jake's death, and wished she could talk to him about that too. But Ben kept things to himself. And being much the same, Dawn never pushed.

Tuesdays at Nottingham, as well as Mondays, were dark days, no racing, and though training was usually the heaviest on these mornings, today's· was light. Beau hadn't tracked, and normally would have been hung on the walking machine first. But he'd obviously spent the majority of the night urinating in the center of his stall so he could roll in it, and needed a bath. The weather was unseasonably cool, so he and his bath had been put off until last.

In spite of his refusing to stand still, keeping his head much too high for rinsing, and swishing Dawn in the face more than once with his wet, sudsy tail, she managed to get him done, alone; a feat that both baffled and amused Ben and Tom, who'd stopped offering to help after she kept insisting they just got in the way.

Randy Iredell stood in the shedrow across from the wash rack, watching her and smiling to himself. He'd seen Dawn several times since the season started, but always at a distance or when he passed a stall where she'd be down on her knees doing a horse up. He'd say hi, she'd say hi, and that would be it. He'd just walk on then. She wasn't easy to talk to. He'd asked around about her, but no one really knew her. Some thought she was related to Ben, others didn't think so. No one knew for sure.

Dawn got back to the barn and reached for the sweat scraper. When it wasn't on the hook where it was supposed to be, she called out for Tom. He'd used it last.

"Looking for this?"

Dawn turned, not recognizing the voice, and nodded then as she reached for it. "Thanks."

Instead of handing it to her, Randy started scraping Beau off. "So how are you?"

Dawn shrugged. "Fine."

Randy nodded as he scraped down over Beau's shoulder. When he glanced at Dawn she pushed some wet strands of hair off her face, and for a second or two, he found himself staring at her.

Dawn could only imagine how she looked, the way she always looked after a bath with Beau. She wiped her face with the back of her sleeve.

Randy tried to think of something to say, something clever, but couldn't. He was exhausted, his mind a blank. He concentrated on scraping off Beau instead.

Dawn watched him as he walked around to Beau's other side. "You look tired," she said, as if she knew how he looked when rested.

Randy smiled faintly. "I can't seem to catch up." He paused, staring off as he ran his hand under Beau's belly to make sure he'd gotten most of the water. "I looked at a horse this morning..."

Dawn waited a moment before asking, "And?"

"I didn't know what the hell was wrong with it." He sighed and stepped back. "I miss that old man. I don't know, I guess I thought he'd be around forever."

Dawn gazed sympathetically at him, relating his loss to that of Ben's. "Well, did you figure it out?"

Randy hesitated, as if he had to think about it. "Yeah, finally."

Dawn smiled, giving the impression she knew he would all along. Randy appreciated the gesture of confidence. "My service says Ben has a horse he wants looked at. Do you know which one it is?"

"No, but Ben's in the tack room."

Randy had an assistant working with him now, a young woman who anticipated his needs and saved him a lot of steps walking back and forth to his truck for different items.

With Beau hung on the walker to dry and with Tom having caught his stall, Dawn poured herself a cup of coffee and sat down on the stoop to take a break. The young woman smiled at her in passing during one of her trips to the truck.

"I don't know what I would do without her," she heard Randy telling Ben. "Especially on farm calls."

Dawn sipped her coffee, watching Beau.

"It helps even more her living with me," Randy added.

Dawn frowned, glancing at the truck to where the woman stood searching for something in one of the compartments. She was very pretty.

"She's my kid sister."

Dawn looked at Beau and smiled. How nice.

One more trip back and forth, and Randy's sister and he were walking down the shedrow to leave. "Let's go get something to eat," he said, draping his arm around her shoulder.

Dawn sipped her coffee and looked up then when he stopped in front of her and his sister walked on.

"Do you want to go get some lunch?"

Dawn shook her head. "No, thanks, but..." She glanced down at her clothes, still wet from Beau's bath, particularly the bottoms of her jeans.

Randy smiled. "You look fine. Besides, we're just going to Wendy's."

"Go ahead and go," Ben said. "I'll put Beau away and lock up."

Dawn's reluctance was obvious. But Ben had gotten such a big kick out of putting her on the spot, he was actually smiling for a change, so she agreed. "You'll have to give me a few minutes to wash up."

"No problem," Randy said. "I've got to check with my service anyway. I'll meet you back here."

When Dawn came out of the ladies room, she was surprised to find the truck parked right in front. Randy got out and motioned for her to come around and get in on his side. As he slid in behind the wheel, he introduced her to his sister Cindy.

They both smiled and said hi.

Cindy was friendly and easy to talk to, for which Dawn was grateful. She felt odd sitting so close to Randy, a man she hardly knew. They talked about the weather first and then about the term paper Cindy was working on.

"Human sexuality...of all things." Cindy chuckled. "Try putting that into words."

"No thanks," Dawn said, thinking if she did, it wouldn't make any sense and nobody would buy it. "I'll pass."

At Wendy's, seated, eating, and having been unable to get a word in edgewise, Randy tried striking up a conversation with Dawn himself. "Are you in school also?"

"No," she said, "I'm out." She'd hardly been ignoring him though, and seriously doubted if any woman could.

Randy glanced at her tray. "How can a person eat as much as you and be so thin? There's nothing to you," he said, saying this purposely so he could run his eyes down over her. "Where do you put it?"

Dawn just shook her head and smiled. No comment, nothing. And Randy had to think of something else to say. "How long have you been at the track?"

"This is my second year."

"What did you do before that?" he asked, hoping to figure out her age.

"School, work...the usual."

"How long?"

"A couple of years."

"How old are you?"

Cindy smacked him on the arm. "Randy! Jesus! Give her a break. You sound like a game show host."

Randy blushed, but laughed as well. "I was just curious."

"Yeah, right!"

When Dawn and Cindy turned back to one another, excluding him again, he found himself glancing idly around the restaurant. Two teenage girls were sitting across the way staring at him. They giggled self-consciously when he looked at them. He smiled, giving them a pretty thorough once-over, until he noticed Dawn watching him out of the corner of her eye. He looked away then, feeling like a kid caught with his hand in the cookie jar.

He stared out the window for a moment. It was almost time to go. "You're going to have to help me with farm calls this afternoon," he said to Cindy.

Cindy shook her head. "Not if I'm going to get my paper done. Why don't you see if Janet'll help you."

Randy frowned. "Sorry, but I can't. She's mad at me, so I know better than to even ask. Besides, she's not much help. She's dumber than a sack of rocks." No sooner said, he wished he could take that last part back. And Dawn's expression only accented the fact.

Cindy rolled her eyes and sighed. "Dawn, do you think you could help him? I wouldn't ask, especially after..." She cast Randy a critical look. "It's just that if I don't get this done..."

"Perhaps I can do your term paper for you," Dawn said.

Cindy laughed. "Please. Come on."

Dawn hesitated. "I don't know. I mean, who's to say if I'll be smart enough. Is there a test or something I can take first to rule myself out?"

Randy was thoroughly red in the face now, and waited for them to stop laughing to look apologetically at Dawn. "I'm sorry. I really could use some help."

Dawn gazed back at him, wondering how often his good looks got him out of situations like this. He was hard to resist. Not to mention Cindy's pleading, pleading, pleading eyes. "All right, I'll help you. But it's my turn to run stalls and feed, so..."

"What time?"

"Three, three thirty."

Randy glanced at his watch. "Perfect. We'll get the calls at the track and your chores out of the way first." With that settled, they got up to leave. On the way out, Randy winked at the two teenage girls.

Fifteen minutes into the routine and Dawn had already handed him the wrong thing twice. Both times, after describing what he needed, he watched her walk to the truck, pleased with himself, and glad he'd solicited Cindy's help in pulling this off.

Before they moved on to another barn, Dawn insisted on a crash course. "What's this? What's that? What do you use most?" She made mental notes as Randy pointed out the different instruments and supplies. Then they moved on.

"Whatever you do at this barn," Randy said, as they started down another shedrow, "don't ask any questions. And if for some reason they ask you something, don't answer."

Dawn looked at him. "Perhaps this is where dumber-than-a-sack-of-rocks Janet would've come in handy."

Randy laughed. "God, I wish I hadn't said that."

Her feelings exactly. "So uh, why am I not supposed to talk here?"

"Because." Randy lowered his voice. "Some of these old trainers are funny. Jake had been around so long, for some he was the only vet they ever had. They trusted him."

"And they don't trust you?"

Randy shrugged. "I don't think they distrust me. It's just..."

"What do they think you're going to do? Steer them wrong?"

"No." He smiled at her, taking in her pretty green eyes as she looked up at him. "I guess there was a vet here a couple of years back that used to tout horses for claiming to his friends. He even went so far as to have a few claimed for himself."

"Oh wonderful," Dawn said. "We just claimed a horse. How's that going to look?"

Randy hesitated a second, thinking this might not be such a good idea after all, then shrugged. "I don't think we have to worry about it with Ben. His reputation's..." He trailed off as the trainer walked toward them. "Just don't talk."

Dawn didn't say a word, not that she ever said that much anyway, and halfway through the third call, she realized she was enjoying herself. Randy was easy-going, smiled a lot, seemed well-liked by most everyone, and was fun to be with. Over the next few hours, they wormed several horses, administered vitamin, mineral, and electrolyte injections, examined at least five lame horses, gave an enema to a colicky one, and even looked at a growth on a goat's stomach.

When it was a little after three, Dawn told Randy she was going to walk down to the barn to start chores.

"No, wait," he said. "One more call and we'll drive down. I want to keep up my end of the bargain."

Dawn smiled. "Are you sure you can handle it?"

"Don't worry about me." Randy laughed. "Just tell me the game plan."

At the barn, they both pulled feed tubs and brought them into the feed room. Then with Randy starting at the one end and Dawn the other, they "ran the stalls," picking out the manure and wet spots and fluffing the straw.

Dawn was mixing feed when Randy appeared in the doorway. "It doesn't surprise me that you finished ahead of me, sticking me with that big-shit of a pony's stall."

Dawn chuckled. "You were the one that chose that end." She glanced up at him. "Besides, I didn't complain when that goat peed on my boot, did I?"

Randy smiled. She'd taken her jacket off, and it was the first time he'd seen her without one. Unfortunately though, she was wearing a blouse and a heavy sweater, which still made it impossible to tell how large her breasts were; something he was dying to find out. As she started measuring various things into the feed tubs, he leaned against the doorway and studied her. He loved long hair, long and thick, and though he'd never been wild about the color red, he thought hers was just beautiful. Then the more he looked at it, he decided it really wasn't red at all. It was auburn. And although braided was the only way he'd ever seen it, he was sure loose, it had to go all the way down to her waist.

When Dawn looked up and caught him staring at her, he tried to appear casual about it by walking over and sifting his fingers through the different feed tubs. To some she'd added flaxseed, bran and cracked corn to all. A few got barley. Sweet feed had been added to each one. And she topped that off with salt, Brewer's yeast, and a squirt of liquid vitamins. When she started scooping oats out of a steaming barrel behind her, he commented on it.

"Not many trainers cook their oats anymore."

"Ben believes horses in training should have a hot mash every day, not just when they run." Routinely, he started them cooking every morning about ten. A scoop and a half of oats per horse, water added to a certain level depending on how many horses, and an electric heating coil immersed in the center. He'd cut a hole in the barrel lid, large enough for the cord, and once the lid was put on, no one had better lift it until feeding time. "It's like cooking rice," he'd told Dawn when he'd first showed her how. "You want the oats to absorb the water, to puff up and swell. It's good for a horse's digestion."

Randy stepped back and leaned against the other side of the doorway, crossing his arms. "You think a lot of him, don't you?"

"Who, Ben?"

Randy nodded.

"Yes." She smiled. "He's kind of been like a..."

"A father? Like a father to you?"

"Not quite," Dawn said softly. "But almost."

"Is he anything like him? Your dad I mean."

Dawn stared a moment, thinking about her father, always tanned, meticulously groomed, hands weighted with gold. "No, he's nothing like him."

"What did you say?" Randy leaned so he could see her eyes. "I didn't hear you."

Dawn hesitated. "I said, he's nothing like my father. My father isn't even alive. He died in a plane crash."

"I'm sorry. And your mother?"

Dawn dished out another scoop of oats. "She's dead too. She was with him. They both died early last year," she said. And to avoid any more questions, she handed him the stir-stick and pointed to the two feed tubs closest to him. "That one goes to Beau, and that one there, the horse right next to him."

Chapter Seven

In the truck and driving down the road, Randy handed Dawn a clipboard. "Where's the first call?"

Dawn read through several scribbled notations at the top of the page. "Well, according to this..." She turned the board sideways. "Riverwood Farm, Buckeye and uh...Kinsman, for a butt exam." She looked at him. "A butt exam?"

Randy chuckled. "Oh yeah, now I remember. It's a mare to be checked for breeding."

Dawn shook her head. "Lovely terminology."

"It's my own method of shorthand. You should've seen some of my notes in school."

Dawn laughed. She could only imagine.

They rode for some time after that, hardly talking, unless it was to comment about a certain song on the radio or the news, and the lack of conversation was driving Randy crazy. He'd never been at a loss for something to say to a woman before, and was starting to take it quite personally, until he rationalized the situation and came to the conclusion that it was all Dawn's fault.

"Are you always this quiet?"

Yes and no. She shrugged. "I'm hungry."

Randy glanced at her, then glanced at her again, wishing he could just look and look and look at her, studying each one of her features until he knew them by heart. "What are you hungry for?"

Dawn sighed softly, staring out the window and thinking. "I don't know. Pizza?"

Randy smiled. "Before or after the first call?"

"I don't care. Before...no, after."

"Do you have a tough time making decisions?"

Dawn laughed. "No, not really. Just sometimes."

Randy shook his head, smiling. "Well, we're almost to Riverwood, so let's make it after."

Riverwood was a relatively new farm, very elaborate in its Tudor design: house, garage, and barns alike, with acres and acres of plank-fenced paddocks, and a brick-paved road to take you from one building to the next.

"Some place, huh?" Randy said.

Dawn nodded.

Randy parked by the main barn, got out, and started gathering the instruments and supplies he'd need. He handed Dawn a stainless-steel bucket, filled the bottom with cotton, squirted some iodine scrub solution on it, and placed a large speculum on top of that. The sheer size of it made Dawn cringe.

"This is a far cry from the farm I grew up on," Randy said, as the two of them walked to the barn.

Dawn glanced up at him, smiling. "And what kind of farm was that?"

"Oh, your typical Midwestern I guess. You know, house, barns, silo, wire fence..."

"A dairy farm?"

"No, pigs."

Dawn opened the door for him, but then he braced it with his foot and waited for her to go ahead. "Whiteshires," he said. "My dad still raises them. Though not as many. Best damned pigs in the state too."

Dawn smiled.

"What about you? You grow up on a farm?"

"Me...?" Dawn thought a moment and nodded. "I guess you could call it that," she said, though she'd never heard it referred to as anything other than an estate.

Joan Richmond came around the corner to greet them. "Hi, Randy! I thought you were coming by yesterday." She stuck out her bottom lip and batted her lashes. "I waited for you."

Randy smiled. "Sorry, but like I told you on the phone, it was doubtful I'd make it."

Joan wrapped her arm around Randy's, purposely nudging Dawn as she wedged between them. "I know, but I was still hoping."

As Dawn walked along next to them, she glanced at the woman, and when they stopped in front of one of the stalls, took an even closer look. Joan Richmond reminded her of a call-girl approaching forty and not aging all that well.

Randy freed his arm. "Dawn, this is Joan Richmond. She and her husband Glenn own Riverwood Farm. Joan, this is Dawn Fioritto."

How formal, Dawn thought. Mother would've been proud. She'd been a stickler for proper etiquette, one of her bibles being the Amy Vanderbilt version. And though Dawn couldn't care less who was presented to who or whom, she knew it was always safe to respond with a polite hello, which she did, and which Mrs. Richmond promptly ignored, having focused all her attention on Randy. The woman was practically purring.

"I think she's started horsin', Randy," she said, meaning she thought the mare was coming in heat. "I guess I should've told you. Is that going to be a problem?"

Randy shook his head, looking in at the mare. "It shouldn't be, but we'll twitch her anyway just in case. I don't want her kicking me on my ass if I don't measure up."

Joan laughed, throwing her head back, and Dawn glanced away, rolling her eyes. It wasn't *that* funny.

One of the stable-hands twisted the chain twitch around the mare's nose, tightened, and clamped down on it to occupy her mind while Randy wrapped her tail. After he scrubbed her, he put on a disposable glove that went all the way up to his shoulder, lubricated it with K-Y Jelly, and eased it into the mare's rectum to palpate her.

Dawn stared in the opposite direction, reminded of the first time she had a gynecological exam. She'd just turned sixteen, a virgin, and was scared to death. So what if Dr. Adler had delivered her and seen her naked before. That was before puberty and breasts.

"He doesn't look at you really," her mother tried convincing her. "In fact, he hardly looks at you at all."

"So how's school?" Dr. Adler asked.

School...? How's school? I'm shaking, bare to the bone, you're looking at everything I've got, front and back, I think I'm going to have diarrhea, if I do I'll die...and you want to know, "How's school?"

"Well?" Dr. Adler said, as he put his plastic gloves on.

"Fine," Dawn managed, tightening her pelvic muscles as hard as she could. "Just...f-f-fine."

"Relax, Dawn. This will all be over in a minute. Just relax."

At the sound of a plastic glove being removed Dawn turned to see Randy soothing the mare. "There now, Momma, that wasn't so bad, was it? Dawn, run some warm water on the speculum."

When she returned, Randy thanked her and smiled. "You okay?" he asked.

"Fine," she said, but looked away again, remembering how she'd stared over the sheet across her spread legs and watched as Dr. Adler ran warm water on the speculum. "This won't take long," he said. "You're almost done, and you're doing just fine."

"Relax, darlin'," she heard Randy saying softly. "You're almost done. Just relax and it'll all be over in a minute." He completed his examination and removed the speculum, stepped aside, and instructed the stable-hand to take the twitch off. The mare shook her head several times, scrunched her nose, then rubbed it on her feed tub, and rubbed it again.

"She's clean," Randy told Joan as he gathered his things and walked out of the stall. "About to go out of heat though, not just coming in. Mark this date and ship her in about two weeks." He walked over to the hose and washed off the speculum. "How far does she have to go?"

Joan had followed him. "About a two-hour ride."

Randy nodded.

Joan stepped closer. "Would you like some coffee?"

Randy looked into her eyes briefly, then glanced at Dawn. "Thanks, but not today. Dawn's starving and I promised to feed her before she faints."

"Oh, that's too bad." Joan traced his shoulder with her fingertip. "Maybe next time."

Back in the truck again and pulling out of the driveway, Randy looked at Dawn and marveled. He'd never known anyone this quiet. "I forgot to tell you," he said. "You're allowed to talk on farm calls. In fact, it actually helps me out. That way I don't have to."

Dawn stared out her window. "Sorry. Permission granted or not, I didn't have anything to say."

Randy smiled. Quiet, yes. Shy...no. He hesitated. "What are you thinking about?" he asked.

"Nothing," she said. She was thinking about how if she hadn't been along on the call, and Joan Richmond had her way, Randy and the woman probably wouldn't be doing any talking right about now either. And she was thinking about the mare, her hind end smeared with lubricating jelly, violated.

"It was okay," she remembered telling her mother after her exam, relieved beyond belief that it was over. "You were right, he didn't really look at me. And it didn't hurt. He says I have good pelvic somethings. I'm hungry. Can we go to McDonald's?"

Her mother nodded, smiling, but then grew serious. "Do you have any questions? Anything you want to know?"

"No," Dawn said. "Nothing."

They were both relieved then. They'd gotten through it.

Dawn wondered if the mare had any questions.

Randy stopped at the first pizza place they saw. Once inside, Dawn headed for the ladies room, Randy, the men's. When he came out, Dawn was talking on the pay phone over by the bar. It bothered him for some reason. And the longer she talked, the more aggravated he became. He couldn't believe he'd practically spent the whole day with her and hadn't once thought of a way to ask if she was involved with someone. What if she was? What if that's who she was talking to now? What if she was married? He'd been so preoccupied with the rest of her body, he'd never once looked at her hands to see if she was wearing an engagement ring, or worse, a wedding band.

When Dawn laughed and hung up, Randy shook his head and stared in the opposite direction.

"Has the waitress been by?" she asked, sitting down across from him. "I'm dying of thirst."

Randy kept his eyes focused elsewhere, still wondering who she'd phoned. "No. Besides, how would I know what you'd want anyway?"

Dawn looked at him curiously. "I don't know. I think water might've been a safe bet. Though I normally prefer white wine with pizza."

Randy turned and looked at her right as the waitress approached the table. "Drinks?"

Dawn nodded. "I'll have a glass of white wine, Chardonnay if you have it, please." She glanced at Randy. "That's if you don't mind?"

Randy quickly lowered his eyes to her left hand, then just to be safe, her right. Empty. No rings. "Anything you like. I'll have the same."

It was odd that he'd ordered wine, since he really didn't care for it. Though he had to admit, it didn't taste half bad with pizza. "Do you want some dessert?" he asked, when they'd finished eating.

"No thanks." Dawn gazed nonchalantly around the restaurant. "I'm full."

It's no wonder, Randy thought. She'd eaten half a pizza, half a twelve cut. "Well, I think I'll have something. I'm still hungry."

Dawn glanced at her watch. "I think we'd better get going, not that I'm trying to tell you what to do. But if we're going to get done at a decent hour..."

Randy had to smile. She was already putting on her jacket, as if it were settled. He stood up without a word and walked over to the counter to get the check and pay the bill. Dawn waited for him at the end of the bar. As he walked back to the booth to leave a tip, he noticed two men trying to strike up a conversation with her. If she hadn't been giving them the cutest damned cold shoulder he'd ever seen, it would have annoyed him. But as it was, he was smiling as he reached for her arm and opened the door.

The next farm call was only a fifteen minute ride, but again, it was a relatively quiet ride. The barn was dark when they arrived, so Randy walked up to the farm house and knocked on the door.

A man opened it and leaned out the screen. "Yeah?"

"I'm Dr. Iredell. I'm here to worm your horses."

"Really? Well, you should've been here hours ago."

"Sorry, I've had a busy day," Randy said, trying to sound as pleasant as possible. People like this irritated him. "But I'm here now, so..."

"You're too late."

Randy's face reddened. "No lights in the barn?"

"No, I got lights. But I got me another vet, too. One that comes on time." He slammed the door shut.

Sitting close enough to hear, Dawn lowered her eyes with this, as if she were looking at the clipboard.

Randy stared at the door for a few seconds, thinking about knocking again and having the last word, but changed his mind. He walked back to the truck, got in behind the wheel, and pulled the door shut. "I don't make exact appointments for farm calls," he said, through clenched teeth. "The son of a bitch."

Dawn glanced at him and nodded, then drew a line through the man's name. "One down and three to go."

The next two calls were within a mile of each other, both went routinely and quickly, and they were off to their last. As they pulled down the driveway, a bubbly teenage girl with a big smile and a mouthful of shiny braces rushed out to greet them. She talked all the way to the barn, with questions galore, and grew quiet only when Randy was about to draw blood from her horse. She held her breath and covered her horse's eyes.

"All done," Randy said.

The young girl exhaled. "We're going to our first show next week, so I have to have the Coggins report back by then or we can't go. Will I have it by then?"

Randy was holding the wrapper from the test vial in his teeth and couldn't answer right away.

"Will I?"

Randy marked the vial and put it in the wrapper. "Boy, I don't know. That's pushing it. It's been taking about ten days."

"Ten days?! Oh no! We won't be able to go then!" In an instant, the girl bordered on tears. "Why do we need one anyway? It's not fair."

Randy explained briefly about equine encephalomyelitis and how rapidly it had spread across several states south of them, then paused, glancing at Dawn before he continued. "And while your horse may be fine, don't you want to be sure about the others?" He patted the horse's neck. "I'd hate to think you'd want him exposed to other..."

"But," the girl interrupted, "I just have to have it before the show!"

Randy put the vial in his shirt pocket and walked out of the stall. "Well, perhaps you should've called me sooner then. That way I could've made sure you had it in time."

"But I didn't have all the money till this morning. I baby-sit." She dug into her jeans' pocket and came up with a fistful of one-dollar bills and a bunch of change. "Here." She reached for Randy's hand, deposited the money, and folded his fingers around it, so none would fall out. "I earned it all myself."

Randy stared at his hand a moment, then raised his eyes, shaking his head and smiling. "All right, if we don't get the results by Friday, I'll call the lab for it and write you up something to get you into the show."

"Honest?"

Randy nodded. "Honest."

The girl beamed. "Is Magic going to be all right after the blood you just took?"

Randy glanced back at the plump pony, bed knee-deep in straw and munching his hay. "He'll be just fine." He turned to Dawn. "He really is pretty, isn't he?"

Dawn smiled, their eyes connecting for just a second before she gazed in at the pony, agreeing. "I'll bet he makes you very proud."

"Can I drive you home?" Randy asked, as they pulled out onto the highway. He wanted to see who was waiting for her.

"My car's at the track," Dawn said.

Randy nodded. "I really appreciate you helping me today."

Dawn shrugged, yawning, and edged down a little in the seat, resting her head on her arm against the window. Today had been fun, but now she was tired, and when she was tired...

After a few minutes of relative silence, Randy turned the radio on, not high, but apparently loud enough to startle Dawn, and she jumped.

He turned it down. "I'm sorry. Were you sleeping?" How was he supposed to know, as quiet as she was?

"You're driving," Dawn snapped. "Not me."

Randy arched his eyebrows and made a face. "Well, excuse me. Go back to sleep. I'll wake you when we get to the track."

It was after ten. No wonder she was tired. She burrowed down again and within minutes was snoring softly. At every light, Randy found himself just gazing at her.

He waved to the night guard as he drove through the gate at the track, and pulled into the horsemen's parking lot. There were only eight or nine cars there, four parked in the front row. Figuring one of these had to be hers, he slowed to a stop and put the truck into park.

He hated to wake her, he really did, and would've been content to just watch her sleep. She was so beautiful. And her hair... He wanted to touch it, to lace his fingers through it, to touch her face...

"Wake up," he whispered. "Wake up and look at me."

Dawn never even stirred.

He ran his eyes down the length of her body, wondering again about who she'd phoned earlier, knowing if she belonged to him, there'd be no way he'd let her out at night by herself, let alone with another man.

He shook his head, berating himself. He hardly knew her. What was he thinking? He touched her arm lightly. "Dawn..."

Nothing, not even a flinch. He smiled at how soundly she slept. Then suddenly something out the window past her in the distance caught his eye.

"Holy shit! Look at that car!"

Dawn jumped, wide-eyed and clutching her chest.

"Look at it!" He pointed past the guard shack. "The Jaguar! Look! Right there!"

Dawn stared, trying to swallow and catch her breath at the same time.

"Come on, let's go look at it." He got out and came around to open her door. "Come on," he said, tugging at her arm.

Dawn picked her purse up off the floor, rubbing her eyes as she followed him. He circled the Jaguar twice, shaking his head and whistling under his breath. "This is a classic, Dawn."

The guard peered out, put his newspaper down, and came out to join them. "Pretty, ain't it, Doc?"

Randy nodded. "It's beautiful. Whose is it?"

Dawn was just about to tell him, but the guard spoke first. "Charlie says it belongs to some broad. I've only seen it here this late once or twice, but apparently this is where it's parked all the time." He motioned to the overhead light. "The broad must be afraid of the dark or something."

Dawn turned to the man. "Is "broad" your term or Charlie's?"

When the guard shrugged, cocking an indifferent eyebrow, Dawn stared him down, her green eyes steel like a cat's in the night. And with that, he turned and walked back to the guard shack. Randy was circling the Jaguar again.

"I'd give my right ball for a car like this."

Dawn gave it some thought as he ran his hand across the hood. "It's lacquer. Jesus! Hand rubbed I bet."

Dawn nodded.

"I don't believe this, a Jaguar XKE Roadster. It's got to be a '67 or a '68. '68 I bet."

Dawn nodded again. "Randy, it's been a blast, but I've got to go home. I'm tired." She wanted him to move out of the way. But he just stood there, staring, and for a second her mind wandered. She could see her father's face. His finding her this car was the way he did things. He'd searched and searched himself. It had to be perfect. Right color, red with black interior. Right year. And all the options. She could see the gold ribbon wrapped around it. "Randy..." She nudged him. "I really am tired."

He stepped back and turned slightly. "We never discussed what I was going to pay you."

Dawn yawned. "Well, you did feed me twice."

Randy smiled. "I have to pay you something."

Dawn waved a weary hand. "Fine, but let's talk about it tomorrow." She took her keys out of her purse and unlocked the door. "I'll see you tomorrow."

"Wait a minute." Randy's eyes widened. "This is your car?"

Dawn nodded and got in behind the wheel, leaving Randy just standing there, with his mouth agape in disbelief as she started it and drove away.

Chapter Eight

"The birthday girl is here!"

Ben cringed.

"And I've come for my birthday present!" Gloria rounded the corner of the shedrow with three of her lady friends trailing behind, tiptoeing and watching their step. "This is Jeanne, this is Nancy, and this is Elizabeth."

Ben nodded politely, still unable to believe he'd agreed to have dinner with this woman.

"Now don't get any ideas, girls, I saw him first." Gloria declared, all aglow. "And isn't he everything I said he was?"

Gloria's lady friends giggled.

"He's such a peach. He even had a special race made just so my little Cajun could run on his Momma's birthday."

Ben sighed. Getting an extra race written wasn't all that difficult. He'd told her that three times already.

"Let's go see Cajun," Gloria said. "Come, let me show you." The four women filed out of the tack room in a flurry and a myriad of flowery fragrances.

Ben took out his handkerchief, sneezed, and blew his nose.

The women oohed and aahed in front of the stall.

"Are you going to win, Cajun honey?"

"Should we bet on you?"

"Are you going to talk to us?"

Cajun twitched.

"He said yes!" they chorused. "He said yes!"

Cajun twitched again.

"Yes! Yes! He's trying to tell us something!"

They coaxed him for more information. He twitched and twitched and twitched as they giggled and laughed. Then they scurried down the shedrow and headed for the clubhouse.

"I'm going to have a Rueben sandwich for lunch. What about you?"

"Who me? No, I just started a new diet. I'm having a salad."

"What?" Gloria had her heart set on a Reuben and a salad. After all, it was her birthday. "Start your diet tomorrow."

Cajun was so even-tempered he didn't need a pony in the post parade. Tom and Dawn walked him over to the paddock. Ben had reluctantly agreed to sit with Gloria and her lady friends in the clubhouse and had left several minutes earlier to join them. He was dreading it, but feared they'd come waltzing into the paddock otherwise and figured this was the lesser of two evils.

Johnny Burke, the young apprentice jockey named to ride Cajun, came out of the jocks' room first, grinning, in spite of wearing lilac and pink polka dots.

Tom put his arm around him and leaned down to talk. "I don't care if you're looking up the asses of the whole fucking field at the quarter pole, you sit on him until then."

Johnny nodded.

"Ask him for some run, but don't abuse him. If he wants to go, then ride him out. Got that?"

Johnny nodded again, smiling at Dawn as she led Cajun in past them. "He might come up short," Tom added. "But chances are he's gonna close full of run."

The race was a flat mile. Cajun broke slowly, trailed the field all the way to the head of the stretch, and was at least ten lengths out of it when Johnny asked him for some run. He started picking up horses on the outside then, practically in the middle of the racetrack, and got up just in time to nose a horse out for second, beaten only half a length for all of it.

Gloria and her lady friends were ecstatic, jumping up and down and screaming. One of them even cried, sobbed no less. Gloria hugged Ben and kissed him on the cheek. This, while she was still jumping up and down. And that was enough for him. He mumbled something and made a quick exit.

Horses finishing first and second always went to the test barn, commonly called the spit barn, since in the old days they used to test a horse's saliva for the presence of drugs. They test their urine now, or blood if the horse won't oblige. Either way, it's still called the *spit barn.*

Cajun bounced alongside Dawn, tossing his head and pushing up against her. Like he knew he'd done good. Tom headed for their barn to get his halter and shank. By the time Dawn reached the spit barn, having to take the customary designated route under the watchful eye of a state official, Tom was waiting for her. They watered Cajun, allowing him to drink about a quarter of a bucket, bathed him, scraped him off and put a light blanket on him. He was allowed another drink then. And while Dawn finished cooling him out, Tom took his bridle and went back to the barn to clean his stall.

Cajun couldn't have been more cooperative. In a little less than half an hour, Dawn was leading him back to their barn. She glanced up and down the road for Randy's truck, the third time she'd looked for it that day, and this time spotted it, then him. He was three barns away, talking to some woman. They were laughing.

Tom was watching for her, leaning against the outside of the barn, arms crossed and chewing on a toothpick. "I had to practically kick the old man out of here."

Dawn chuckled.

Tom motioned for her to hold up, and ran his hands down Cajun's legs. He too had a date. But unlike Ben, Tom was looking forward to his, and in a bit of a hurry. "Do him up in alcohol, but smear some Furacin on these cuts first." He stepped aside. "You gonna be all right by yourself?"

Dawn rolled her eyes. "Yes. I'll be fine."

Tom hesitated. "Everything else's done. I mixed his bran mash."

Dawn nodded, glancing back over her shoulder as she led Cajun down the shedrow. "Have fun."

"Always," Tom said, and went right into his own rendition of, "They'll be a hot time in the old town tonight," loud as could be and woefully out of tune.

Dawn gave Cajun a few turns around the shedrow, then put him in his stall and watched him. "What are you looking for?" she'd asked Ben the first time she saw him do this.

"Lots of things," he told her. For one, "whether or not they're hungry." Ben liked to see a horse go into its stall and first thing, grab a mouthful of hay. "Then you watch to see if a horse rolls. A lot of them will lay down in the spit barn and roll, itching after a bath, but a good many will roll again when they get to their own stalls. Habit. You have to watch carefully." He explained how a horse in distress will roll as well as a horse feeling good. "But there's a difference. You'll get so you can tell." You also looked for the obvious, whether or not they were bleeding anywhere. Whether or not they were favoring a leg. "Sometimes they won't show it till they get down and go to get back up."

Cajun rolled, then got up, shook, turned around, and rolled again. He broke out in a sweat then. Most all of them will break out a little. It's when they start sweating too much you have to be concerned, Ben had said. It might be they just haven't wound down yet. But it might also be because they're hurting or not properly cooled out. "Remember, every horse is different."

Cajun had only broken out a little. Dawn waited until he started eating his hay, then walked down and gathered his leg wraps, waited a little while longer before giving him his bran mash, and was humming to herself as she entered his stall and began brushing him off.

Randy came around the corner of the barn a few minutes later, looked into the tack room, then glanced down the shedrow, and followed the sound of her voice.

Dawn had just gotten down on her knees to do Cajun up and was reaching outside the stall for his wraps. Randy handed them to her.

She looked at him and smiled as he bent under the webbing and sat down in the straw just inside the doorway.

"He run good, huh?"

She nodded. "Did you see the race?"

"I caught the last half. He finished strong." He felt Cajun's knees and ankles. "Looks like he came back okay." He pointed to two cuts on the inside of Cajun's right leg. "Put something on those before you do him up."

Dawn smiled, shaking her head, and motioned to the jar of Furacin in the bucket next to him. He opened it, smeared some on the cuts, wiped his finger on the straw, then closed the jar and put it back. "So where did you get the Jaguar?"

Dawn splashed some alcohol on Cajun's left leg, and glanced at him. "It was a gift from my father."

Randy gazed into her eyes. "It's really beautiful. I stopped by it this morning in the daylight to look at it." He paused. "Why didn't you tell me it was yours?"

Dawn could've answered, "Because the guard beat me to it," but chose to remain silent.

Randy glanced down the shedrow and back. "I owe you for yesterday."

Again Dawn remained silent.

"So, if I buy you dinner, will you take me for a ride in it?"

Dawn smiled. "Sure..."

Randy watched as she rubbed Cajun's legs. Down and over. Then down again, gently yet brisk. Just the right amount of pressure...again and again. Such beautiful hands too. Such long, slender fingers. He leaned his head back against the wall, absorbed in the rhythm.

While Dawn locked up, Randy waited in the truck. She checked her watch as she climbed in. "I have to make a phone call before we leave," she said, and didn't notice his sudden mood swing as they rode to the pay phone outside the guard shack.

Dawn dialed, then turned her back so Randy couldn't hear. "It's me."

"Where are you?" Linda asked.

"At the track. Randy asked me to dinner. We're going now. That's why I'm calling."

"Aunt Maeve's here."

"What?!" Dawn whispered. "When did she get there?"

"She flew in just a few hours ago. She wants to take us to Antonio's. We're waiting for you."

Dawn shifted her weight and glanced at Randy, then shook her head and sighed. "How long is she planning on staying?"

"Just tonight. She's leaving for Texas in the morning for some benefit. It's in her behalf."

What timing. "All right." Dawn stared down at the ground, resigned to the fact. "I'll be home in half an hour."

Her face was flushed as she hung up and walked around to Randy's side of the truck. He rolled his window down the rest of the way, looking like he already knew what she was about to say.

"I'm sorry, but we're going to have to do this some other time."

"Problem?"

"No...just family. I'm really sorry." She hesitated, then turned, and without offering any further explanation, walked to her car.

Randy watched her, fuming, and thought about calling after her and demanding to know who she'd just phoned. It seemed the most important thing in the world at the moment, knowing. Whatever the answer. But instead, he swore under his breath, smacked the steering wheel, and drove out the stable gate. The hell with her. He never had to chase after a woman before. Why bother now?

Ben refused to discuss any details of his dinner date, and halfway through the morning, threatened Tom's life if he even so much as thought about bringing it up again. "Enough, all right?!"

"Oh, who gives a shit," Tom said. "I don't want to know anyway." He smiled, deciding to drop it for a while, and reached for the sale catalog Ben had in his hand. "Find one yet?"

Ben scowled at him. "Hip #12."

Tom flipped through the pages, nodded, and laid the catalog down and picked up Ben's condition book.

"Give me that!" Ben said, snatching it back. Dawn came into the tack room. One look at Tom and that innocent, guilty-as-sin grin of his, and she knew they were still at it. She poured herself a cup of coffee and sat down with the sale catalog.

The Vandervoort Estate was having an auction to liquidate their entire breeding and racing stock. Ben was in the market for another broodmare, so he and Tom were planning on going.

Dawn skimmed through the pages halfheartedly, still somewhat melancholy because of the missed dinner date with Randy, and languished over the horse on page twenty-two. "When you guys go, I'd like you to bring back this filly for me."

Ben and Tom glanced at her, then turned back to the condition book.

"She's a three-year old and her name is All Together."

Ben and Tom both looked at her with similar expressions. "Sure thing," Tom said.

Dawn walked over and spread the catalog in front of them. "Isn't she pretty?"

Ben nodded, briefly studying the page. "Yes. Pretty and out of our league."

"Why?"

"The breeding. She'll no doubt be the highest bid horse in the sale." He handed the catalog back to her. "Out of our league."

"Hmph. I have good taste then."

Tom chewed and chewed on a toothpick. "We're talking major big bucks here, Dawn."

Dawn sighed as she stared down at the picture. The filly was gray. "I love gray horses."

Ben rolled his eyes. She was thinking of Gibyag. She'd pouted for a week after he'd sold him. "Color has nothing to do..." What was it with women? He shook his head and sat back. "Oh forget it."

Dawn and Tom looked at him.

"Did you know," he said, "that silly woman puts Ketchup on her steak."

Tom laughed. "Hot damn, old man! I knew you'd tell us something sooner or later."

Ben took off his glasses and rubbed his eyes. "And talk! That woman never shuts up. I was driving out the driveway and she was still talking."

Dawn chuckled.

"What else?" Tom said, handing Ben's glasses to Dawn when she motioned for them. "What else did you do?"

"Nothing."

Dawn cleaned Ben's glasses with the bottom of her shirt and handed them back to Tom.

"I ate. I let her talk my ear off. Then I left. That's it." Ben reached for his glasses, looked through them, and put them back on. "Nothing more."

Dawn smiled at him, then noticed something; a slight quiver in his chin. He got choked up so easily lately. She shook her head at

Tom to alert him, and changed the subject. "Well, I still want this filly, so..."

"You're crazy," Tom told her. "Weren't you listening?"

"Listening...? Yes." What had started out as a whim and now a diversion, on second thought, began to appeal more and more to her. "But there's no minimum bid, so I don't see why..."

"There's no minimum bid because it's understood."

"You don't know that for sure."

When Ben got tired of hearing the two of them, he tried a different tactic. "Why don't you ride down with us." He figured once the bidding started and she saw how much the filly was going for, he wouldn't have to say another word. "Coshocton isn't that far from here. We can get down there and back before feeding time, no problem."

"All right," Dawn said. "Maybe I will." She knew from Ben's tone, he was being more patronizing than anything else. Humoring her in a sense. But that didn't matter. She'd just made a major decision. "Yes, I think I will."

They started training especially early the day of the sale, finished with time to spare, and Tom and Ben went to the men's room to wash up. Tom had been razzing Dawn all morning about the filly she was going to buy, but Ben had been exceptionally quiet. He'd had to scratch Beau from a race because of a poor work the day before and his good mood, albeit brief, had gone steadily downhill. Beau wasn't right and they all knew it, only no one wanted to admit it. Especially Ben. First he blamed it on his just not being fit. Then he blamed the lousy track conditions. And now it was the blacksmith's turn.

Dawn had stopped at the deli on the way home yesterday to pick up sandwiches and a twelve pack of Coke, which she put in the cooler in Tom's truck. And she had her checkbook tucked safely in her purse. She was ready. She'd been ready. So ready in fact she was nervous and raking the shedrow for the second time just for something to do, when Randy came walking around the corner of the barn.

He was annoyed with himself for being there. "So, how you been?"

"Fine."

He glanced down the shedrow. "How's the family?"

"Fine..."

"What? No crisis?"

Dawn shook her head. "There was no crisis. My aunt was in town for the night."

Randy stared. How a person could look you square in the eye, lie, and look like they weren't, amazed him. Infuriated him. "What are you doing today?"

Dawn couldn't believe his sarcastic attitude, and responded with a little of her own. "If it's help you need, you haven't paid me for the last time yet."

Randy shook his head and told himself he should walk away, but hesitated. "I thought we might do something. I doubled up the last couple of days so I could have the afternoon off."

Oh really? Dawn turned. Even that remark could have been taken sarcastically, not to mention presumptuous, had he not looked so sincere. "Thanks, but I'm going to..."

He threw his hand up. "Wait! Don't tell me. You have to make a phone call first." This time he was walking away for sure. He started down the shedrow. That's when Tom and Ben drove up next to the barn.

"Your chariot awaits, little lady," Tom said, getting out, extending his arm and bowing at the waist.

Ben smiled at Randy. "Did she tell you where we're going?"

Randy shook his head, wishing he could care less. It had taken him three days to get over her last refusal. He hadn't expected another one. "No, we didn't get that far."

Ben leaned across the seat. "We're going to the estate sale in Coshocton."

Randy nodded, gazing back at Dawn in spite of himself. "Quite a few people are going down. I hear they've got some nice broodmares."

Dawn took a tentative step toward him. "Did you say you had the afternoon off?"

"Yes...why?"

"Why don't you come with us?"

Randy glanced at Tom's truck.

"We can follow them in my car," Dawn said, trying not to sound too anxious.

Randy looked at her. "Can I drive it?"

Dawn smiled. "No."

Randy paused, as if he had to think about it now. "All right. I'll park my truck up by the guard shack."

Ben tossed him the sale catalog. "We're going to bid on Hip #12." He winked at Dawn. "And the little lady here wants Hip #27. They're both marked."

Chapter Nine

Tom cruised along on the freeway at just above sixty-five miles per hour, with Dawn right behind him. "You know, Ben," he said, glancing in his rear-view mirror. "I think Dawn has the hots for Randy."

Ben stared at the road.

"You hear me, old man. I'm talking to you. I said I think Dawn has the hots for Randy."

"So..."

"So, what do you think of him?"

Ben shrugged. "He's all right I guess. Jake thought an awful lot of him as a vet."

Tom frowned, glancing at him. "Dawn's not a goddamned horse, you know."

"What's your point?"

"Nothing. I like him, and was just wondering what you thought of him."

Ben sighed, looking out his window at the trees whizzing by. "Like I said, he's all right."

Tom nodded and, thinking, switched his toothpick from one side of his mouth to the other. "Does she ever talk about a boyfriend?"

"No, why?"

"Why...?" Tom glanced at her in his rear-view mirror again. "Because that back there at the barn looked like a little bit more to me than, 'Hey, you wanna ride along?' That's why, if you know what I mean."

Ben drew a deep breath and exhaled heavily, not wanting him to get started on this. "Why don't you just stay out of it."

"What? I ain't in it. I'm just talking." Tom looked at him, shaking his head, and they rode on for a few minutes in silence. "But come to think of it, I do remember her saying something a while back about some guy. They'd been to a play or something. Remember...?"

Ben nodded, feeling a little like a father whose daughter had just come of dating age. He'd never really had to think of Dawn as a woman before. "And yes, I like Randy."

Tom grinned. "See, now that wasn't so hard, was it?"

Ben just looked at him.

"Well then, I guess it's good we both like him, because it's obvious as hell Dawn does too."

Ben nodded. He didn't need Tom to tell him this; he'd had a feeling himself. But if he had a say, he'd rather she not date anyone at the track, because he hated the gossip. And no matter what, there was always plenty of it. He sighed, knowing he really didn't want to ask, but asked anyway, "What do you know about this vet?"

Tom cocked an eyebrow. "Whoa...the old man wants to talk now."

Ben shook his head and stared out his window.

Tom glanced at him. "Okay," he said. "I can see you're serious. What do you want to know?"

Ben hesitated. "Does he sleep around?"

"Some."

Ben looked at him. "What do you mean, some? How much is that?"

Tom tipped his head. "All right...a lot."

"A lot?"

"Not as much as me."

Ben rolled his eyes. He should've known better than to ask.

"He was fucking Bud's daughter Ginney for a while. Still is, I think."

"What? That slut?"

Tom laughed. "Hey, that slut is one hell of a fuck. And she ain't that bad looking either."

Ben sighed disgustedly.

"And I think he's sleeping with Kathy Randall too. You know, that woman stinks. I mean, really stinks. Right out of the shower." He made a face. "And then there's that new groom of Turner's..."

Ben raised his hands. "Let's make this simple. Is there any woman on the track you and this vet haven't slept with?"

Tom nodded. "Yeah...one. Dawn."

Ben smacked the dashboard. "Goddamn you, Tom! Just shut up and drive! All right?"

They rode in silence for at least ten miles, until finally Tom had to say something. "Hey, Ben, I'm sorry. I didn't mean anything. You know me."

Ben looked at him.

"I never think of Dawn that way, honest."

Ben leaned his head back and sighed. "I know."

Again they rode in silence. It was Ben who spoke next. "It's just that I'd hate to see her get hurt."

"Me too." Tom nodded, flicking his toothpick out the window and reaching into his pocket for another. "But you can't live her life for her. She has to make her own decisions. Right or wrong."

Ben looked at Tom and smiled, still amazed after all these years whenever he showed his serious side. "I'm sorry I jumped on you like that."

Tom shrugged it off. "It's okay, don't worry about it." He glanced out his side window, chewing on his toothpick and grinning as he looked back at Ben. "Besides. Between you and me...I don't think Dawn fucks anyway."

Ben shook his head and laughed. Leave it to Tom. He'd never change.

Dawn and Randy followed close behind, talking about everything, and at the same time, basically nothing. Randy figured they'd covered just about every trivial subject under the sun, and tried once more to get her to open up about herself.

"Which birthday did you get the car for?"

Dawn smiled. "The one I had three years back."

Randy nodded, baffled, yet all the more intrigued by how evasive she could be. "Ever had any trouble with it?"

"Not much."

Randy chuckled. "Did you ever work for the CIA?"

Dawn smiled. "I quit last year."

Randy held up his hands, as if he were giving in. He figured no matter what the question, her reply would be just as vague. But then the quietness got to him, and he started telling her about his family, hoping a different tactic would draw her out. He bragged about his mom's cooking, and told her about his wish to have his sister go into practice with him. Then he talked about his love of camping, "Ever since I was a little kid," and told her about his dream to raise Charlois cattle. He talked, she listened, commenting here and there. And all the while he studied her features, her arms, her legs, and what he could see of her skin. She wore driving gloves, which he thought quite fitting. But much to his disappointment, she was wearing another bulky sweater. One which gave only a hint of the curve of her breasts, and still kept a secret of their size.

As Dawn listened, bits and pieces of the conversation she'd had with Linda the night she got home after helping Randy with his farm calls, crept in. "He wants to pay me for helping him. I think I ought to let him."

"Oh great! Start out a relationship by getting paid for your time. What a novel idea!"

Dawn had laughed, but still felt it wise. "I don't want it to be an issue. I don't want me to be an issue. Besides..."

Linda smiled. "For what it's worth, I don't think he sounds like the kind of guy who would..."

"I know. That's what I mean. I think it would affect him the other way around. Besides, as I was about to say, it's not like it was a date or anything. Let's not get carried away." But then again, he did ask her out the next day.

Halfway to the sale, Tom pulled into a rest area so Ben could use the men's room. During the stop, Dawn got some sandwiches and Cokes out of the cooler and Randy stretched his legs. Back in the car, on the road again, and with both of them eating sandwiches, Randy leafed through the sale catalog a second time. "This filly, this All Together. She isn't going to go cheap." When Dawn nodded, he looked at her with his mouth full. "And yet, you're going to buy her?"

Dawn's mind raced. "Actually, Ben's going to buy her. I'll just think of her as mine."

Randy gazed at her a moment. "Well, like I said, she won't go cheap."

"So I've been told."

The Vandervoort estate was vast and rambling; the main drive and one paddock filled with cars, trucks, trailers and horse vans. Dawn parked at an angle between Tom's truck and a semi. They couldn't have timed it better. As soon as they reached the indoor arena, which had been set up as the auction area, registered and found their seats, the sale began.

The broodmares were first, the initial eleven selling for prices ranging from nine hundred and fifty dollars to seventy-two hundred. Then Hip #12 was led into the ring. She was a bay mare with a back swayed from the numerous foals she'd carried, and her left knee was large and disfigured from a racing injury. The bidding opened at fifteen hundred.

Tom and Ben discussed the mare's conformation between themselves. She wasn't anything to brag about, but if you looked hard, there was that certain slope to her shoulder, and breadth of her chest, the angle of her hip...

Ben held up his number.

"I have $1500," the auctioneer said. "Do I hear $1550?" He pointed over Ben's shoulder. "I got $1550. Do I hear $1600?" Ben raised his number again. "I got $1600. Do I hear $1650? I got $1650. Do I hear $1700?" Ben held up his number. "I got $1700. $1800? I got $1800. $1900? I got $1900. I got $2000." The bidding climbed. "$2050. $2100. $2200. I got $2300. I got $2300. Do I hear $2400? Do I hear $2400?" The auctioneer scanned the crowd. "$2300. $2300. Sold at $2300!" Ben raised his number for the clerk to record.

Dawn watched a few more horses change hands, but then got so anxious she had to take a walk. "I'm thirsty," she said. "I'll be right back." When she returned, they were auctioning off Hip #26, a heavy three-year old chestnut colt who'd raced as a two-year old, but hadn't started this year. He went for $7250. Dawn held her breath when the auctioneer called for the next one.

Hip #27 leapt into the ring, dragging her handler with her. She was large. Too large for a filly, Ben thought. Just big enough, Dawn thought. Tom wouldn't allow himself a thought, he wanted no part of it. They'd gotten what they came for, and he was ready to leave. Randy on the other hand, in no hurry whatsoever, was simply nodding his head in silent approval.

The filly reared and struck out sharply with her left front leg, just missing her handler. She stood still then, raised her head high, and bellowed a long, loud whinny...that vibrated every ounce of her body.

Dawn leaned across Tom's lap to say something to Ben, something muffled but sounding like, "I love her, let's buy her." Ben nodded, smiling. And with that, Tom sat back, crossing his arms and shaking his head.

He looked from one to the other. "You two are crazy. You know that, don't you? She has to have a hole in her as big as a goddamned cannonball. There's got to be a reason she hasn't started."

Ben frowned at him, but admittedly was thinking the same thing, and turned back just as the filly struck out again, connecting with the wall this time. The sound echoed through the rafters. She threw her head up and whinnied again. And then again.

"She's a witch!" Tom whispered. "A goddamned witch!"

The filly stood proudly, her coat a silver blanket, with dapples covering her sides and rump. She stared out into the crowd, her head high and eyes wide. Then she tossed her head, jerking her handler up off his feet, just as she struck out again. This time she caught the man high on his thigh. Another handler rushed out to assist him, and the filly swung around, staring out at the other side of the crowd, head high and nostrils flaring.

"She's probably a fucking nut," Tom said. "No fucking wonder."

Ben wasn't listening. He was too busy marveling to himself. "What a grand bitch."

Dawn nodded, and leaned across Tom's lap again. "I want her."

Tom chewed through his toothpick. "I tell you, there's a hole in her." He pointed to the sale catalog. "It says here she ain't even broke. See this...no training."

The three of them turned to Randy, who, enjoying himself, was just staring at the filly in awe. He glanced at them after a few seconds when he noticed them looking at him. They obviously wanted a professional opinion. He shrugged. "I like her."

Tom leaned across Dawn's lap to look up into his face, rocking, and kind of bobbing his head. "That's it?! 'I like her.' What the shit? Thank God we ain't paying you!"

Randy laughed, winking at Dawn before they all turned back to look at the filly. The auctioneer opened the bidding.

"$20,000. Who'll give $20,000?"

Tom leaned back and sighed when, as Dawn and Ben looked at one another, Ben raised his number. "Oh Jesus Christ."

"I got $20,000. Do I hear $25,000? I got $25,000. Do I hear $30,000? I have $30,000." The filly reared, hitting the wall with both front legs when she landed. "I got $35,000. I got $40,000. I got $50,000. $55,000. I have $60,000 right here." The auctioneer pointed. "Do I hear $65,000? I got $65,000."

A loud voice came from the back. "$80,000!"

The auctioneer nodded. "I got $80,000. Do I hear $85,000?"

Dawn turned to try to see who had jumped the bid, then leaned across Tom's lap, looking into Ben's eyes, pleading.

Ben, at that point, couldn't believe he'd gotten caught up in this. He looked at Dawn and shook his head. "I'm sorry, but that's it for me."

"Ben...?"

The auctioneer pointed to the back. "I got $85,000. I got $90,000." The filly reared again. "I got $95,000. I have $100,000."

Dawn was still pleading with her eyes. "Ben, please..."

"I have $100,000. $100,000 once."

"I can cover it," Dawn whispered. She darted her eyes to the number held in Ben's trembling hand. "Please. Bid."

"$100,000 twice."

Ben raised his hand.

"I got $105,000. I got $110,000. Do I hear $115,000? I have $115,000. I got $120,000. Do I hear $125,000? I have $125,000 right here. Do I hear $130,000?"

Dawn pivoted with every bid, searching where it came from, and reached across Tom to squeeze Ben's arm.

"Do I hear $130,000? I have $130,000. Do I hear $135,000? Do I hear $135,000?" The auctioneer scanned the crowed as the filly struck out again. "I got $130,000. Do I hear $135,000?"

Dawn glanced over her shoulder and held her breath as she turned back. "$130,000 once." It seemed an eternity. "$130,000 twice." She prayed. "Sold!"

Ben held up his number for the clerk; the sound of the gavel drawing jubilant applause from everyone. But no one there was as excited as Dawn. She jumped up and hugged Ben, then Tom, and then Randy. Tom was mumbling and shaking his head. This, as Ben's mind scrambled to think of how he was going to come up with the money. What was he going to have to sell? The filly was led out of the ring. Dawn beamed. And Randy was pleased as well. Pleased with the hug, and pleased with Dawn's breasts. Nice firm ones.

They watched one more horse get auctioned off, then left and found their way to the filly's barn. Her stall was at the far end of the main aisle. As they approached it, she raised her head and pinned her ears.

"Oh, isn't she pretty?" Dawn said.

"Pretty...?" Tom shook his head, eyebrow furrowed, hands in his pockets, and trying to appear disinterested. "She's built like a goddamned colt. How can she be pretty? And she's still growing for Christ sake."

"It doesn't matter," Dawn said. "She's still pretty. Look at her face."

Tom took his hands out of his pockets, crossed his arms, and ventured a glance right as she pricked her ears. "All right, so she's got a pretty face."

Dawn smiled at him. Mr. Tough Guy.

"But I tell you, she's got to have a hole in her. Look at the ass on her, and her shoulders. Why no training? Huh?"

"Damn it, Tom!" Ben said. "Shut up a minute. I can't even think straight."

Tom looked at him and shrugged. "Fine, old man. But I'm telling you, there's a hole in her."

Ben sighed, glaring at him, and gazed back at the filly. For all he knew, Tom could be right, because this horse did look perfect. Too perfect. And when Randy turned, saying, "I'm going to go find her groom," even Dawn started to wonder.

She grabbed his arm. "Why? Do you think there's something wrong with her?"

"No, I just want to get a closer look. But after the way she behaved in the ring, I want someone in there with me that knows her."

Ben nodded, agreeing with that logic. Dawn stepped back out of the way, and no sooner had Randy made the corner, Tom put his hands on his hips and started bobbing his head.

"Okay. So how do you intend to pay for this bitch?"

Ben stared off, still unable to believe he'd bid a hundred thirty thousand for her. But then again, horses like this didn't come along every day. He sighed, tipping his hat to rub the ache in the back of his head. "I can cover about fifty-nine or sixty thousand. The rest I'm going to have to scramble for."

"Oh great!" Tom stated, bobbing some more. "This is just great!"

Dawn edged close, her voice low. "Ben, I told you I'd cover the rest."

Tom narrowed his eyes at her. "Yeah, and that's just fine. But while you're out trying to sell the Jaguar or something, they're gonna be throwing the old man in jail here for fraud!"

Dawn shook her head and dug into her jeans' pocket for the check she'd stashed earlier. "I don't want this to go any further than us." She reached for Ben's pen and motioned for Tom to turn around so she could use his back to sign it, then handed the check to Ben. "You fill in the amount. Whatever you need."

Ben stared down at it, and had to clear his throat to speak. He'd expected her to come up with something. She said she would. And whatever the amount, he'd have made her a full partner. He didn't expect this though. "Are you sure you...?"

"Yes," Dawn said, encouraging him to put it away. "Positive. Now please..."

"Goddamn, old man!" Tom said, peering over Ben's shoulder. "Maybe you're not gonna go to the slammer after all."

Ben folded the check and put it in his shirt pocket, all the while looking into Dawn's eyes. "Remember," she said, whispering to both of them. "I don't want anyone to know about this. Especially Randy. I'll just tell him I pitched in a little. Okay?"

Ben nodded, but Tom wasn't even listening. Because for the first time since he'd heard this filly's name mentioned back at the track, he was beginning to like the whole idea.

"Damn! She's a grand-looking mother!"

Randy returned a few minutes later. "Well, I found him. He'll be right here."

"Did he say anything about her?" Ben asked.

"Just that she wasn't as mean as she seemed in the ring."

Dawn heaved a sigh of relief. "Thank God."

When the groom arrived, Randy went over the filly completely. Not once, but twice. Then Ben went over her, and after that, Tom. She baffled them. Not that they wanted to find anything wrong. They walked out of the stall and stared back in at her.

"What do you think?"

"I don't know," Randy said. He turned to the groom. "Do you know why she hasn't been broke?"

The young man lowered his eyes. "Not really."

"What?" Tom looked at him. "What do you mean, not really? What the hell kind of answer's that?"

When the groom shrugged in response, Tom grabbed him by the arm. "Wait a minute. You know something, don't you? I can see it in your eyes. What the hell's going on here?"

"Nothing."

"Nothing...?" Tom got in his face. "Well, I think there is. No one has a filly bred like this bitch and just decides not to run her for no reason." He glanced at Randy and Ben, a thought just occurring to him. "I'll tell you, if someone's fucked with her papers and she ain't who she's supposed to be..." He gripped the groom's arm tighter.

"I don't know anything. I don't!"

"Yeah, right." Tom wasn't the only one not buying this. Randy didn't believe him either. "Well, we'll see." He walked down to the other end of the aisle, where he looked one way then the other, as if he were checking to make sure they wouldn't be heard. When he turned around and headed back toward the groom, the young man started talking fast.

"There's nothing wrong with her, I swear. Honest! It's just that old-man Vandervoort was senile. She was his favorite horse."

Tom let go of his arm.

"See, he never let anyone touch her. Slim, her groom, was the only one that ever went near her. She wasn't even halter broke up till a month ago. She just ran free. She even had her own barn." He pointed over Ben and Dawn's shoulders. "Over there, behind the big house. She was never handled. She went in and out of the barn whenever she wanted. Slim used to sit out in the pasture with her and she'd graze right around him. She ain't mean." He looked in at the filly. "She ain't mean at all."

Tom stared skeptically when the young man fell quiet. "That's it? You want us to believe that's it? That's nothing."

"Well..." the groom said sheepishly. "I guess there is more."

"You guess?" Tom bobbed his head. "What?"

The young man fidgeted. "Slim got drunk one night. Well, actually, he got drunk a lot."

Randy motioned for him to get to the point.

"Slim told the rest of us grooms, this one night I mean, when he was really drunk more'n usual. He told us that old Vandervoort thought the filly was his daughter. His dead daughter, come back."

Dawn shook her head slowly, she and Ben glancing at one another as the groom continued. "See, his daughter got knocked up by one of the stable-hands that used to work here. She died I guess when the baby was born. The baby died too."

Tom shifted his weight, chewing hard on his toothpick and getting into the story now. "Why'd the old man think this horse was his dead daughter?"

Dawn gazed in at the filly.

"I don't know." The groom motioned them over to the corner and lowered his voice. "I don't even think Slim knew. I told you, the old man was senile. But this night, the one I was telling you about, when Slim was real drunk. Well, all of us were drinking." His face reddened a little. "Anyway, I know it was wrong and all now, but what we did was..." He hesitated, a hesitation that drew Ben, Dawn, Randy, and Tom in closer. "We uh, we turned the stud pony, Rassuz, the one we use to tease the mares. We turned him into the pasture with the filly, and the next morning when the old man was having his coffee... See, we tried catching him and all, but he run off, and we couldn't see him in the night. The filly wasn't wanting anything to do with him anyway. But then I guess..." He cleared his throat. "Well, the next morning like I said, there they were, the filly squatting and Rassuz climbing all over her. The old man went berserk! We heard it right from the maid. He ain't dead, you know. That's just a lie. He's in the nut house. That's why the sale. They took him away."

Everyone stared, huddled together there for a moment...the young man nodding with authority, Ben, Tom, Dawn, and Randy all shaking their heads. Then it was Randy who grabbed the groom by the arm, and so suddenly, it startled everyone.

"When did this happen?"

The young man swallowed hard and stammered, considerably more frightened now than when Tom had a hold of him. His head barely reached Randy's shoulder. "About a m-m-month ago."

"I need to know exactly when." Randy pulled him closer then gave him a little shove for emphasis. "So you go find out when this happened. And don't make me come looking for you. You understand?"

The young man nodded, hightailing it, and Randy turned to Ben. "I'm going to go find the vet assigned to the sale," he said, already rolling up his sleeves. "He can check her or I will."

Dawn was right behind him, sick to her stomach and on her way to visit the nearest ladies room. "See if you can find me a twitch," he called to her over his shoulder.

She nodded, going one way, Randy another, and Ben leaned back against the wall, shaking his head.

Tom sat down heavily on a bale of hay. "It's ironic as hell, don't you think? One never knows." He drew a breath and sighed as he looked at Ben. "Here we are...and the old coot's daughter might be knocked up again."

Within minutes, Randy had found a Dr. Greene, the veterinarian covering the sale, and explained the situation to him. He gave Randy what supplies he needed, offered to check on a possible ruling, and said he'd come to the barn as soon as he acquired the information.

Randy ran into the groom on the way back to the barn and dragged him along with him. Dawn was staring into the filly's stall, thinking how terribly sad the whole story was, when Randy walked up behind her.

"Our little friend here says this all happened forty-five days ago."

The young man nodded at Ben and Tom. "I checked with the maid. She remembered when they took him away." No sooner said, he turned to leave.

Randy stopped him. "You're not done. You get to hold her." He took the twitch from Dawn and handed it to him. The young man didn't argue.

Randy stacked several bales of hay just outside the stall door and had the groom back the filly up flush to them. If she was going to start kicking, it would serve as protection. When he got her into position, out came the plastic glove and lubricating jelly.

During the examination, his expression varied. He'd grimace, then frown and look off, then grimace again; this whenever the filly would hump her back and strain, a natural reflex when trying to expel something. Then he'd move, changing the angle of his arm somewhat, frown, look off, and grimace some more.

"Get her to relax," he told the groom. "Come on, talk to her." She was squeezing the life out of his arm. "No, don't do that." The groom was about to tighten down on the twitch. "Just talk to her."

When she relaxed, he was able to palpate her. Dr. Greene soon appeared at his side. The two of them talked follicles then, heat cycles, and a few things Dawn had never heard of before. Randy joked with Dr. Greene at one point about trading places with him. Greene chuckled, saying no thanks, to look at the filly's eyes. "I'll pass," he said. Though no longer straining, she'd taken to picking up one of her hind legs in an increasingly threatening way, first her left then her right.

"Almost done, Momma," Randy said. "Hold on. Hold on..." The groom was cooing softly a mile a minute to her. "There now. There now." Finally Randy eased his arm out and stepped back, turning the glove inside out as he peeled it off and dropped it to the ground.

He looked at Ben. "Well, I'm almost sure she's not in foal, but..." He glanced at Dawn and hesitated. "I just wish there wasn't so much at stake here. A hundred and thirty thousand dollars for a three-year old filly in foal to a stud pony..." He shook his head, as the tremendous weight of that statement hung in the air. He turned to Dr. Greene. "What did you find out?"

"You can void the sale. You should've been told of the possibility."

Ben and Tom nodded, no doubt about it. "So now what?" Tom asked.

Ben shook his head.

"I wish I could be totally positive for you, Ben," Randy said. "But it's too soon."

Dr. Greene concurred. "Maybe another week or so. But unfortunately, if you're going to void the sale, you have to do it now before any money changes hands."

Ben looked at Dawn, wanting to ask her how she felt about it, but couldn't. Not if he was going to respect her wish that Randy not know how involved she was. He held his hands out. It was the only thing he could think to do. A rather helpless gesture he hoped she'd understand. Dawn nodded.

All right, he said to himself, and turned to Randy. "I'm a racetracker. Give me some odds."

Randy smiled. "On her not being in foal?" He didn't want there to be any misunderstanding.

"Yes."

Randy glanced in at the filly; standing in the back of her stall, head down, ears pinned and pouting. "How's two hundred to one?"

Ben smiled. "Good enough for me." He tapped Tom on the arm. "You go make arrangements to have them shipped and I'll go settle up."

Tom and Ben drove straight through on the way back. Dawn and Randy on the other hand, stopped about halfway for something to eat. "I'm starving," Dawn said, and as soon as she started to order, Randy found himself wondering if he'd have enough money to pay. He did a quick mental count of how much he had in his wallet.

"I'll have the prime rib, rare please," she said, "baked potato with extra sour cream. No butter on the potato please. And blue cheese on the salad, no radishes."

The waiter smiled. "What would you like to drink?"

"A glass of light beer, preferably draft if it's very cold. Otherwise, bring it in a bottle, no can please. I'll pour it myself," she added, smiling as she handed him the menu.

Her insistence on having things precisely the way she wanted them had been passed on to her by her mother, who'd been careful to point out that in order to have it that way, one must be very precise with their requests.

"Your order, sir?" the waiter asked, addressing Randy but barely taking his eyes off Dawn.

Randy handed him his menu. "I'll have the same, but with Italian dressing on the salad."

The meal was served to perfection, delicious, they each had another beer, and much to Randy's relief, he had enough to pay the check. Dawn insisted on leaving the tip though, and he couldn't help notice as she opened her wallet, that it was crammed full with credit cards. At least twenty of them, maybe more. He wondered how a groom at the track, who probably got somewhere between a hundred and a half to two hundred dollars a week, could have so many. Plus a wad of cash. And he was still thinking about it as they walked to the car.

Dawn yawned, covering her mouth with her hand.

Randy smiled. "Do you want me to drive?"

"If you don't mind." She linked her arm in his. "We started really early this morning. I'm exhausted."

Mind? He didn't mind. He wasn't even tired. How could he be? His mind was a whirl of unanswered questions. He'd just spent another entire afternoon and evening with her, and still didn't know anything about her...aside from the fact that she had a roommate, whom she didn't phone today, that she cared a great deal for Ben and seemingly Tom, and that she loved horses.

They weren't on the road five miles when Dawn stretched her legs to the side and burrowed down on Randy's shoulder. She murmured something about the setting sun and not being able to keep her eyes open. Within minutes, the rhythmic sound of her breathing told him she was asleep. He adjusted the volume on the radio lower, and glanced at her and smiled. She was so pretty.

And the car. Driving it was every bit of what he thought it would be. On a stretch of road without another car in sight, he took it up well past ninety before easing up on the gas, then did it again, just for fun. He loved driving it. But more importantly, and with every passing moment, quiet, vague, playing hard to get or not, he loved being with Dawn.

It wasn't until he parked next to his truck at the racetrack and turned the engine off, that Dawn woke. She sat back, tucking some loose stands of hair off her face and into her braid.

"Hey, sleepy head..." Randy touched her cheek gently, so soft, and leaned close and kissed her... Then kissed her again...

The stable guard tapped on the hood, startling both of them. When Randy turned and rolled down the window, the guard peered in.

"Thought that was you, Doc. We've got an emergency in the first barn. A horse caught his neck on the sheet metal on his door and damn near slit his throat open. You better hurry. I haven't been able to get a hold of anyone else."

Randy tilted his head back and sighed. "I'll be right there."

Dawn made a squeamish face. "Are you going to need help?"

"No. If it's as bad as it sounds, there'll be blood everywhere. You don't need to be there."

After he got out, Dawn moved over behind the wheel, adjusting the seat and getting comfortable before putting on her gloves. When she looked up at him, he was smiling at her.

"What?" she said.

"Nothing," he replied, his smile lingering. "Just you." The way she was, the way she did things, everything. He leaned down and kissed her. "I'll see you tomorrow."

Chapter Ten

It was after eleven the following morning before Randy got a break and made his way to the Miller barn. He checked the tack room first, which was empty, and called out for Dawn.

Tom poked his head out the third stall. "She's gone."

"Where'd she go?" Randy asked, walking toward him.

"I don't know. She mentioned something about lunch with her cousin."

Randy glanced at his watch. "Will she be back today?"

"Not until feeding time." Tom eyed him curiously. "Why? What's up?"

"Nothing." Randy reached into his shirt pocket and sorted through his umpteen messages. "I just wanted to talk to her."

"Guess it'll have to wait."

"I guess it will." Randy started to walk away, but stopped. "Tell me, what do you know about her?"

Tom smiled. "Not much."

"Come on, anything's more than I know."

Tom laughed. "My God, man, you spent four whole hours alone with her yesterday in that cracker-box car of hers, and you don't know anything about her?"

"As a matter of fact, no. On the way there, we talked about where we were going. And on the way back, she slept."

"At least she wasn't eating."

Randy laughed. "No, she did that first." He glanced away, shaking his head. "Does she live close by?"

"About twenty minutes from here."

"Where at?"

"I don't know. I've never been there."

Tom was starting to aggravate him. "Then how do you know it's twenty minutes from here?"

"Because she said it was." Tom grinned. "That's if she doesn't catch any lights."

Randy folded his arms across his chest. "You're having a real time with me, aren't ya?"

Tom shrugged, his grin widening.

"Screw you," Randy said, walking away.

Tom leaned out the stall. He'd had his fun. "Her address is on the bulletin board in the tack room. She wrote it there a long time ago for Ben's accountant."

Randy wrote down the number on his hand, thanked Tom, and left.

Ben had gone home early to wait for the arrival of All Together and the broodmare, and was sitting in the kitchen, Meg's kitchen, drinking a cup of coffee. When his head started pounding with the second cup, he remembered he hadn't taken his blood pressure pill. He went into the bathroom to get one and downed it along with two aspirins for his headache. They were his last. He'd have to get some more. This was the third headache he'd had this week. As he was walking back to the kitchen, he looked out the window and noticed the van had arrived.

George, his farmhand, led the broodmare down the ramp first. Ben greeted the driver and shook his hand. "How was the trip?"

"Well, aside from that one there raising hell the whole way," he said, referring to All Together who was whinnying, tossing her head, and pawing. "Everything was fine."

When George returned, he and the driver walked up the ramp and clamped a lead shank on her, removed the bar keeping her in place, unhooked her, and led her out.

Ben marveled. Without a doubt, she was one of the finest-looking Thoroughbreds he'd ever seen. And this, right off the farm. He could just imagine what she'd look like tucked-up and in racing condition.

On the ground, she whinnied and whinnied with her head high, darting her eyes in all directions as she danced circles around George.

"Here, I'll take her." Ben led her into the barn with a smile on his face. A smile that took on added meaning, when she stopped in front of a two-year-old colt's stall, and promptly raised her tail and showed signs of being in heat.

He tugged at her, laughing. "Put it on ice, sweetheart," he said. "You're going to be a racehorse first."

Randy was a good forty miles from the track at feeding time and having one of those days when nothing goes as planned. He didn't get home until well past seven. He was tired enough to just have a beer and fall into bed, but he had something more important on his mind. He showered, dressed, splashed on some cologne, and started out.

Dawn had also had a full day, and stood tired and hungry as she rummaged through the refrigerator. "When did you buy this yogurt?" she asked Linda.

"I don't know, a couple of days ago. What's the date?"

Dawn sighed. "The date means nothing once it's open." She checked the date anyway. Three days from now. "Did you open it yesterday or the day before?"

Linda shrugged. "I can't remember. Isn't there any more?"

Dawn shook her head, staring into the container. Apricot crunch. It looked good, still... She smelled it. It smelled like yogurt. "Jesus, why do you do this? How am I supposed to know?"

Linda had opened it just for a taste. She was on a diet. She was always on a diet. And she'd had a craving. "I wish you could appreciate my discipline," she said, pointing out how she'd only had two or three tiny spoonfuls. "Instead of..."

Dawn sniffed the container again, then shook her head and dropped it in the wastebasket. Why take a chance? "I'm going to take a shower." She started down the hall.

"Wait, I forgot to tell you, Ben called. He said to tell you the filly arrived and that she's horsing."

Dawn smiled.

"What's that mean?"

"It means she's not in foal."
"Oh. I see. That's good, right?"
"Right."

Randy parked in front of Dawn's apartment building, turned the ignition off, and just looked around for a moment. "Jesus Christ," he muttered. They didn't have neighborhoods like this back where he came from. In fact, the only other time he'd been anywhere similar was on an emergency call that turned out to be a pampered poodle with its own bedroom and color television. The growling, yapping, snapping little thing was having a bad day. It needed its anal glands expressed. Fun job.

He stepped down out of the truck and looked around again. What was Dawn doing here? Part of him hoped he'd gotten the wrong address. But there was her Jaguar. He shook his head in amazement and walked up the steps.

It didn't surprise him to encounter a lobby attendant as soon as he opened the thick steel door and ventured inside. But it did unnerve him a little to see that the man was armed.

"May I assist you?"
"Yes. I'm here to see Dawn Fioritto."
"Your name, please?"
"Randy Iredell."
"I'll ring her. Please be seated."

Randy was too antsy to sit down, and walked around the lobby instead, staring idly at the pictures on the walls. From somewhere, he thought he smelled Chinese food cooking.

Linda answered the intercom. "Yes, Richard?"

Randy turned. The voice didn't sound like Dawn's.

"There's a gentleman here to see Dawn. Are you expecting someone?"

"No. Who is it?"

"A Randy Iredell."

A momentary silence made Randy's armpits start to perspire.

"Send him up."

The attendant pointed to the elevator. "It's Suite 503. Turn left when you get off."

Linda clicked off the intercom, ran down the hall, and threw open Dawn's bedroom door. "Your vet's here!" she yelled. "Hurry and get dressed!"

The doorbell rang then, and she rushed back, pausing to take a deep breath before she opened the door.

Randy smiled. "You're right," he said, referring to her comment on the intercom. "I'm not expected. Is Dawn home?"

Linda nodded, silently agreeing with Dawn about how incredibly good-looking he was. Gorgeous was the word, and even bigger than she'd described him. "How tall are you?"

Randy chuckled. "Six four."

Linda smiled, gazing up at him all dreamy eyed.

"Is uh...is Dawn home?"

Linda blushed. "Oh yes, I'm sorry. She is, yes, come in." She stepped aside and motioned to the couch. "Have a seat. I'll go get her." She walked down the hall to Dawn's room and after closing the door behind her, promptly started jumping up and down.

Dawn came out of the bathroom, saw her, and gave her a funny look. "What are you doing?"

"Didn't you hear me?"

Dawn was still in her robe, her hair wrapped in a towel like a turban.

"He's here!"

"Who?"

Linda fell back on the bed, swooning at the ceiling. "Randy! Your vet!"

"What?!" Dawn jumped onto the bed next to her. "What do you mean he's here? Where here?!"

"Here," Linda said. "In the living room. And my God, is he ever..."

Dawn couldn't believe this. "How did he find out where I lived?"

"I don't know. But did you know he's six-foot-four?"

Dawn looked at her. "What? Did you ask him?"

"Yes. Now hurry and get dressed."

Dawn stared blankly, her gaze descending to the floor as if she were in a trance, and Linda stood up and pulled her to her feet. "Get dressed!"

Dawn nodded and nudged her toward the door. "Go talk to him. I'll be right out."

"Got it." Linda turned her head and pointed her hands like an Egyptian goddess to make her exit. "I will entertain him," she announced, her silliness transforming itself into dignified behavior before her return to the living room. "She'll be right out, Randy. You caught her a little off guard. Please, sit down."

Off guard? Randy stood still. First the apartment, more like a penthouse, now this. Off guard...? What the hell did off guard mean? Jesus, if she's in there with a man, I'm going to look like a fool. Not to mention how he'd feel.

"Would you like something to drink?"

Randy glanced around the apartment again, thinking she probably meant Perrier or something similar.

"A cold beer maybe?" Linda suggested.

Randy nodded. "That'd be nice." When Linda left, he shook his head over what he'd just said. 'That'd be nice?' He sounded like a country bumpkin.

Linda returned with a bottle of beer and a glass, handed them to him, and motioned down the hall. "I'll go see what's keeping Dawn."

Randy nodded, smiling as he watched her walk away.

Inside Dawn's room, Linda's calm-and-cool went ballistic again. "Aren't you ready yet!?"

"Almost," Dawn said, a rubber band dangling from her teeth as she finished braiding her hair; not an easy task, it being so long and thick.

Linda motioned for her to hurry up.

Finally. "There." Dawn held her arms out and twirled around. "How do I look?"

"Beautiful, like always," Linda said. "Now come on."

Randy meanwhile, was finding comfort in the absence of any signs of a man living here, at least in the living room. Still, he couldn't help but wonder what caught off guard meant. When Dawn entered the room, he was standing by the terrace doors, looking out.

"Hi, Randy."

He turned, and clumsily dropped his keys, realizing only then that he'd still had them in his hand. "Hi," he said, as he bent down and picked them up.

"You've met Linda?"

"Sorta..." He smiled, and instinctively should've turned his attention to Linda at this point. But he couldn't take his eyes off Dawn. He'd never seen her in anything other than jeans and a bulky sweater. She was wearing a white button-down blouse made of some kind of silky material and light-colored slacks that, while loose fitting, hugged her hips. Perfectly.

Dawn introduced them. "Randy, this is Linda. My cousin and roommate."

Randy's eyes sparkled.

"Linda, this is Randy Iredell. Dr. Iredell actually."

When Linda extended her hand, Randy grasped it gently. "Do you have the same last name?" he asked, for lack of anything better to say.

"Yes, we do..." Linda said, and frowned at Dawn as if to scold her for her lack of proper etiquette; the two of them laughing then. "Now if you'll excuse me." She mumbled something about having to get ready for a date.

The room fell quiet when she left, too quiet, as Dawn and Randy just looked at one another, and it was Dawn who turned away first. She sat down on the couch and tucked her legs underneath her. "I was surprised when Linda told me you were here. How did you find out where I lived?"

Randy sat down next to her. "Your address was on the board in the tack room," he said, thinking if she wanted to talk about surprises, how about this penthouse. "So I decided to take a chance and see if you were home."

Dawn searched his eyes when he started to say something else but apparently changed his mind. "And...?"

Randy glanced away. "And well, here I am."

Dawn smiled sadly. She knew it would be this way with him. He was uncomfortable. Very uncomfortable.

He stood up and walked over to the terrace windows again. "Why didn't you tell me you lived here?"

Dawn looked at him. "Here? What do you mean? In this area? This apartment? What?"

Randy stared down at the cars parked along the street, Mercedes, Cadillacs, Saabs, and all the rest, the Jaguar looking right at home.

He sighed. His reason for coming over here tonight was to ask if she was involved with someone.

"Randy...?"

He shook his head and looked at her. "Never mind."

"Never mind?" Dawn smiled, hesitating. "I don't think I've ever seen you at a loss for words before."

Randy ran his eyes over her, so pretty and so poised sitting there. So sophisticated. Jesus, she belonged here. He shrugged. "Well, that's because I've been trying to get your attention for so long, now that I have it, I'm speechless. I don't know what to say."

Dawn chuckled. "Right."

"I'm serious." He walked back and sat down, crossed his arms and gazed at her. "See. I've got nothing to say."

Dawn laughed, the tension between them easing. "Have you had dinner yet?"

"No, I thought maybe we could go out for something."

Dawn shook her head. "I'm too tired. I was just going to order up Chinese. There's a restaurant in the basement. Do you like Chinese food?"

"Yes."

Dawn reached across him for the phone, her arm brushing his thigh. "Should I just order the special? Everything they have is delicious."

Randy smiled, consuming her with his eyes as she leaned back and dialed. "My treat," she said purposely, just to be sure. "I'll put it on my tab. You've been feeding me all week."

Randy's face flushed instantly. "No, that's okay. I'll pay if you don't mind."

"Suit yourself," Dawn said. "The special okay?"

Randy looked at her, then glanced away. "Yeah, fine."

Dawn placed the order and hung up, told him it came to fifteen dollars, and held out her hand.

Randy was brooding again, totally preoccupied as he reached for his wallet and gave her the money. "Who'd you call the other day?" he asked.

"When?" Dawn folded the money and put it in her pocket.

"When we were at the pizza place."

"I called home. Why?"

"What about at the racetrack, when we were going to go for dinner?"

"Linda again, why? What's with the...?"

Randy smiled faintly. "I figured it was someone you lived with, only I was afraid it was a man."

Dawn frowned at the implication. Did he actually think she'd have agreed to go out with him in the first place, if she was already involved with someone? "Randy? What kind of...?"

"I'm sorry," he said, interrupting. "But you never offer anything. How was I supposed to know otherwise? Not one stinking soul at the track knows anything about you, not even Tom."

Dawn just looked at him for a second. "That's because there's nothing to know." She reached for his hand. "Come on, let's go get the food."

There was another passenger in the elevator on the way down and two on the way back up, so they virtually went and returned without talking to one another. "Do you want a plate?" Dawn asked, heading into the kitchen for drinks.

Randy glanced at the containers. "Not unless you do."

"Nope, not me. Beer?"

"Yes, thanks."

Dawn came back with beers and silverware, sat down next to him, and opened all the containers. The special for the day was sweet and sour pork. "It's the best. You're going to love it."

Randy smiled and just watched her for a moment, at home in a penthouse eating out of take-out food containers. "How long have you lived here?"

"A couple of years."

Randy paused. She was back into that customary vague mode of hers again. "Just like the car, huh?"

Dawn stared a moment. "Actually, I got the car first."

Randy nodded, intentionally keeping quiet to see if she'd add anything, to see if she'd elaborate. But she didn't, which came as no surprise. And as usual, he had to do most of the talking, but that was okay. He was getting used to it.

Linda emerged from her bedroom in a rush, right about the time they finished eating. "I gotta run. How do I look? Are you sure? It was nice meeting you, Randy." And in a flash she was gone. The two of them were alone.

Dawn stacked the food containers and took them into the kitchen to throw away. "Do you like *Webster*?"

Randy frowned, wondering if she was referring to some kind of art.

"On TV. You know, the little Papadopoulos kid." She turned on the television when she came back in, and sat down. Randy put his arm around her and she nestled up close to him.

Webster was having a bed-wetting problem.

During the first commercial, Randy moved slightly to get more comfortable. Dawn put her feet up then, stretched out, and grabbed a throw pillow to rest her head on his lap.

Randy took this opportunity to stroke her hair gently. It was so pretty. And to touch her face with the back of his hand. She had such soft skin. Creamy smooth, he thought. And such high cheekbones and slender neck. His breathing began to quicken as he ran his hand down over her shoulder to her waist, and traced her thigh with his fingertips. Slowly, tenderly, again and then again. And it was then, that he heard her snoring softly. She'd fallen asleep.

He leaned his head back and sighed in exasperation. He couldn't believe it. *Sleeping*. But then again, it wasn't as if he wasn't tired himself. Shortly after Webster hid his sheets in the closet, Randy was asleep as well.

Linda woke them when she came home a little after twelve. "How long have you two been sleeping?"

Dawn yawned, rubbing her eyes. "I don't know." She looked at Randy and yawned again. "Do you want some coffee?"

He nodded, smiling, and while Dawn was in the kitchen, made a trip to the bathroom.

"First door down the hall," Linda told him.

When he returned, Dawn was nowhere to be seen. He figured she'd be right back, and sat down on the couch opposite Linda in a chair. "So how was your evening?" he asked.

"Nice," she said. "How about you?"

Randy shrugged. The way she was staring at him made him wonder. Was this a common occurrence, coming home to find Dawn asleep with a man? What an irritating thought. He glanced at her again. She was still staring.

"What's your sign?" she asked.

"What?"

"Your sign."

Randy had to think. He didn't always make a whole lot of sense when first waking up. "Gemini. Why?"

"Just wondering."

Wondering what, he thought. Was she coming on to him? Could be, the way she was looking at him. After all, it wouldn't be the first time a friend of someone he was seeing, did this. In fact, she reminded him of that one girl...no, he looked at her again. She reminded him of Mary Lou. His mind wandered. He and Mary Lou were fifteen and it was the first time for both of them. Oh God, what a euphoric mess. He'd never forget it. "My mom's gonna kill me," Mary Lou had said afterward. "Look at my dress. That stuff's all over it."

"Randy...?"

He turned and looked at Dawn.

"Cream and sugar?"

"Yes." He nodded. "Please."

"So," Linda said, when Dawn left again. "What are Gemini characteristics?"

Randy hesitated, what did he know. "That we're uh, born in May or June."

Linda laughed and watching him, noticed how he looked into the kitchen then at Dawn. The intensity in his eyes. And suddenly, a wave of sadness washed over her. For Dawn, and what she'd been through. And for Randy, if he weren't a patient man.

"Do you need some help?" he called to Dawn.

"No, I got it." She came in with a tray, put it down and handed him his cup first and then Linda, before curling up next to him with one for herself.

In a short period of time he'd come to realize her cousin Linda talked a lot, nonstop to be exact, and about anything and everything. When he'd finished his coffee, and while she and Dawn went for another and something to snack on, he stood up and walked over to the terrace doors where he found himself staring out into the night, frustrated as hell.

He sighed, then something caught his eye, or rather the lack of something caught his eye, and he turned. "Oh Christ! Dawn, the Jaguar's gone."

She came back in just then. "No, it's not. The valet parked it. They park it every night before ten."

"Oh." Randy let out a sigh of relief, and walked back and sat down next to her. "They park the cars for everyone in the building?"

Linda returned with a bag of stale cookies she'd found stashed in the back of the cupboard where she'd hidden them in a weak moment. "No, just for the residents that pay for the service. It really comes in handy, especially with the parking ban."

Randy took a sip of coffee. "What parking ban?"

Dawn and Linda turned to one another.

"Oh shit!"

Chapter Eleven

The police dispatcher was polite, but firm. Randy would have to come down to the station in the morning to pay his fine. Then, and only then, would he get his truck back. He tried to argue that his position as a veterinarian and the possibility of a medical emergency should merit some consideration. But evidently not. Slamming the phone down in frustration, he threw his hands up and walked across the room.

Dawn was reluctant to approach him. "Randy, I'm sorry. I just never gave it a thought. This has never happened before."

Randy shook his head. He should have found some comfort in that remark. Instead, he took it to mean that her regular callers were from the neighborhood and familiar with the towing policy.

"Take my car home," she suggested, "and come back and get me in the morning."

Randy glanced at his watch. It was after one and his apartment was a good forty-five minutes away. "A lot of sense that makes. I'll end up with about two hours sleep."

"I said I was sorry."

Randy looked at her a second, realizing she thought he was blaming her, and smiled apologetically. "No, I'm sorry. It's not your fault." Of course it wasn't. It was just him and how he was about being independent, standing on his own two feet, not relying on anyone. It was how he'd been raised. And here he was, at someone else's disposal.

Dawn slipped her hand in his. "Why don't you just stay here," she said, with a tactful glance at the couch to clarify what here meant. "This way you can get some sleep."

"Oh, come on." Linda laughed. "You guys don't need to sleep, you've been sleeping for hours. Let's play Trivial Pursuit."

Trivial Pursuit? Oh great, Randy told himself, just what I had in mind. Dawn seemed willing though, eager actually, so how could he say no.

"I'm a bit nocturnal," Linda said, getting the game and spreading it out. "I'm up all hours of the night."

What a pair, Randy thought. Couldn't she see he wanted to be alone with Dawn? Particularly now, with Dawn seemingly wide awake.

Linda didn't feel she was intruding in the least. It never even crossed her mind, and for several reasons. One, she and Dawn had made a pact when they became roommates that there'd be no overnight male guests to surprise one another in the morning. Background checks and all. Two, they were both on their periods.

"Did you ever play this game before?" she asked Randy.

He shook his head.

"It's great. Dawn and I are hooked." She tossed him the die. "You go first. You'll learn as you go."

At twenty minutes to four, Randy answered the final question of the second game, and won again.

"Well, that's it for me," Linda said, as if they'd been keeping her up. "I'm going to bed."

Dawn glanced at Randy as she put the game away and smiled. "I'm going to go take a shower and get ready to leave. Do you want me to make another pot of coffee?"

Randy widened his eyes in exaggeration. "No, I won't be able to sleep for a week as it is," he said. Or so he thought. She wasn't gone two minutes when he dozed off.

Dawn nudged him. "Randy, it's time to go."

He blinked hard and looked around, then stood up groggily and went into the bathroom to splash some water on his face.

Dawn was a morning person. "Not that I've always been," she told him, when they were on their way. "My first few weeks at the track I was a zombie."

Randy felt like one now.

Dawn put on her turn signal as she neared her favorite donut shop. "You want some coffee?"

Randy shrugged in the midst of a yawn, as if he didn't care one way or the other.

"I'm a creature of habit," Dawn said, pulling in and parking. "I've got to have my cup of coffee and blueberry muffin to go."

Inside, under the bright lights, Randy started to come back to life. He drove from there, allowing Dawn the extreme pleasure of eating her breakfast unimpeded by driving. She thanked him over and over, and each time he just shook his head and laughed.

When he backed the Jaguar into its regular parking space, Charlie rose from his bench at the guard shack, barely able to conceal his expression of disapproval. He said good morning to Dawn and handed several messages to Randy.

Randy glanced through them and gave Dawn her keys.

"What about your truck?" she asked.

"I'll get somebody to run me over."

"Okay." Dawn smiled. "I'll see you later."

Charlie observed Randy with that same disapproving expression on his face as he watched Dawn walk away. "Cindy just called too. She said to remind you to pick her up at eleven."

Randy thanked him, tucked his messages into his shirt pocket, and walked down to Chapman's barn. He didn't like Chapman, and doubted if anyone did. But he'd inherited him from Jake, who'd been the only vet on the track that would have anything to do with him, and he could understand why. The man was obnoxious. Without so much as good morning or hello, Chapman grunted and pointed to the first stall.

Randy looked in at the horse as Chapman again, without uttering a word, dropped the webbing, grabbed hold of the horse's halter and just stood there. Randy shook his head and walked in past him.

Examining the horse, Randy found the ankles warm yet similar in degree of heat. The pastern, however, the area between the ankle and the hoof, was considerably warmer on the right leg than the left. There was also a significant amount of heat in the coronet band encircling the top of the hoof.

Randy straightened up. "Do you have a hoof tester?"

Chapman spit. "If you gotta put him down, you gonna want me to give you a syringe too?"

Randy's face reddened. "No, but my truck is parked elsewhere and we can save a lot of time if..."

Chapman swore under his breath, lumbered and huffed into the tack room, and came back with a hoof tester. Randy took it and thanked him with his jaw set tight.

The horse flinched several times as Randy moved the instrument around its hoof, crimping it to test for areas of tenderness. With the next squeeze, the horse practically went down on its knee.

Randy looked up at Chapman. "Well, I think the problem is right here."

"You *think*?" Chapman said. "Aren't you supposed to know?"

Randy glared at the man. "It's just a figure of speech. Now here..." He motioned for him to look close and tapped the bottom of the horse's hoof with his finger. "Right here is where the problem is."

"You sure?" Chapman scoffed.

Randy let the horse's leg down gently and sighed. "Yes." He stood back and watched the way the horse put weight on that leg.

"Well," Chapman said. "If you're sure...?"

Randy walked out of the stall past him, getting redder and redder in the face, and had to make a conscious effort to talk to the man in a civil tone. "You're going to have to get your blacksmith to pull the shoe and cut out where I showed you. Let me know when he's coming and I'll drop by to block it for you."

"Why? Why don't you just cut it out? Old Doc Jake would've."

"Oh yeah?" That did it. The hair on Randy's neck bristled. "Well I'm not Doc Jake! And I'm not a fucking blacksmith! Do you understand? So get him to come down here, because if I have to do it I'm going to charge you, and frankly, I'm fed up with your bullshit about your bills as it is!"

Chapman stared, eyes wide, and with his mouth agape.

"All right?"

When Chapman nodded, Randy turned to leave. Chapman hesitated then and reluctantly cleared his throat. "Uh...Doc?"

Randy swung around. "What?!"

"Can I uh..." He motioned meekly to the instrument in Randy's clenched fist. "Can I have my hoof tester back?"

Randy glanced down at it, then shook his head, tossed it to him, and walked away. It wasn't even six-thirty yet. What a way to start the day.

He called Cindy a little after seven from a pay phone at the track kitchen, assured her he'd be home in time to be on the road by eleven, and told her about his truck being towed and all about Dawn.

It hadn't occurred to Cindy that something might have been wrong. Randy often stayed out all night. "Did you make plans to see her when you get back?"

"No, not yet," Randy said. He hadn't even told Dawn he was leaving, and found himself wondering why. Was he afraid of the response she'd give him? No response. Maybe just a casual shrug of her pretty little shoulders, and that's all.

He stopped to talk to several trainers on his way to Kathy Randall's barn, and there, examined two horses. When she offered him a cup of coffee, in spite of having had one or two or three too many already, he said yes and followed her into the tack room.

The coffee was terrible, but his mouth tasted worse. He cupped his hands and breathed into them, then rolled his eyes and made a face. It reminded him of the times he'd slept with Kathy. He frowned at the comparison.

"Well now..."

She was telling him something about one of her horses and he was looking directly at her, but nothing registered. He was thinking about how she always wanted to do it again. 'Do it' being her euphemism and not his, preferring himself to hear a more exact term whispered in his ear. Again? He'd never been able to do it again, ever. Not once in his entire sexual life. Maybe in the morning and again that night, but back-to-back, no. Not even as a teenager, which used to really bother him, until he finally convinced himself without the help of expensive therapy, that any man who said he could, obviously didn't do it right the first time, or was just plain lying.

Kathy offered to drive him to the police station for his truck, which brought him out of his reverie. As they started toward the horsemen's parking lot, she joked about doing him in her pickup. She wasn't kidding though. He knew that and she knew that. And he gave it some thought as they walked along. After all, it's not like they hadn't done it before. Besides, his part was easy. All he had to do was sit there and look nonchalant. But when he climbed into her truck and glanced around, there was Dawn's car, staring at him. And he found himself begging off and putting the blame on the daylight.

By the time he paid his fine, retrieved his truck, swung by his apartment and came back to the track, he had just enough time to make his rounds. He stopped at Chapman's barn last to block that horse's hoof, and waited long enough to see the confirming spurts of blood and pus. Then he gave Chapman several packets of medication and explained the proper dosage and administration.

"Now don't be giving this to any other horse. I'll have it on my records as trainer administered, but only for this horse. You understand?"

When Chapman all but drooled at the packets in his hand, Randy took the time to stress the point even more. "Listen, they're shaking down two or three barns a day. It's not like the old days. So do as I say. Use it all up on this horse and make sure you throw the containers away."

Drawing straws with Tom, Dawn got stuck with the job of holding Son of Royalty for the blacksmith, probably the only chore aside from cleaning Red's stall she thoroughly disliked. And not just Son of Royalty, any horse. Fortunately their blacksmith, Brownie, an animated storyteller and a master at telling jokes, eased the boredom somewhat.

Randy came around the corner of the barn and was just about to call out for her, when he spotted them at the end of the shedrow. As he walked toward them, he hoped either Tom and Ben were around to take over for her, because there was absolutely no way he could leave without getting his hands on her for at least a few seconds. As luck would have it, Dawn was on her own.

"Hey, Doc!" Brownie said, from under the horse without missing a beat.

"Hey, Brownie. What's up?" Randy returned the greeting, but barely glanced at him, looking only at Dawn.

"Did you get your truck?" she asked.

He nodded, smiling as he thought about last night. "I'm driving Cindy home today," he said, and paused. "We're leaving now. She's up by the guard shack calling my parents."

Dawn swished a fly buzzing around Son of Royalty's eyes.

"Her finals are over and she's ready to go home."

Dawn nodded, smiling faintly. "I don't blame her," she said, wishing she still had parents to go home to herself.

Randy had hoped she'd look disappointed, and would've settled for the slightest hint. But she didn't. "Have a safe trip," she simply said. "Tell Cindy good-bye for me."

He'd prepared himself for this kind of reaction, or lack of one. Still, it hurt. "I'll be gone three or four days. Tell Ben that Dr. Raffin will be covering my calls."

Dawn nodded, smiling as she gazed up into his eyes. And there, right there, he thought he saw something. A glimpse of disappointment, maybe even a little regret. But it was enough. He could leave now, and although he would have liked to have kissed her, he simply touched her arm, said good-bye, and left.

Dawn watched him as he walked to the end of the shedrow, smiling to herself and oblivious to several gnats pestering Son of Royalty's ear.

"That Doc's a nice guy," Brownie said, bent over and tapping a nail into a shoe.

Dawn's smile widened.

"Women at the track seem to like him well enough," Brownie added, reaching for his crimper to bend the nails over. "Shit, I think he's slept with most of them."

Dawn's smile stiffened on her face with that remark. It was Tom who came around the corner of the shedrow next. "You're not going to believe this!" he sputtered. "Suzie Strater just shot John!"

Brownie looked up. "No lie?! Where?"

"Right in the ass!" Tom said, laughing and patting his left cheek. "Right in the old ass!"

Brownie put Son of Royalty's leg down and straightened up. "I'll be damned! When?"

"Just now, about a half hour ago. She found him ballin' some chick in the tack room and shot him in the act!"

Brownie started laughing. "Is he gonna be all right?"

Tom nodded and shrugged at the same time. "To hear him carrying on the way he was when they put him in the ambulance, yeah...I guess! It's a long way from his heart."

Dawn stared in disbelief. "How's his wife?" She knew from Tom's constant gossip that Suzie and John Strater were common-law husband and wife. John a trainer, Suzie a jockey. "Is she all right?"

"Her? Oh, she's fine," Tom said, laughing again. "She was kicking and screaming when they put her in the cop car, saying how she'd aimed at his balls and missed and wanted another shot!"

Brownie roared at that. "She swore if she ever caught him again, she was going to shoot him! By God, I guess she meant it."

Again? Caught him again? Dawn shook her head.

"Good thing she can't shoot for shit!"

Tom nodded, wiping his eyes. "And you know what's even funnier? Guess who tipped her off?"

"Who?" Brownie said, trying to guess while still laughing.

"Carol Devey."

"No shit?!"

Carol Devey was the last woman Suzie had caught him with.

"Women scorned," Brownie said. "Women scorned."

"Amen!" Tom added.

Dawn handed Son of Royalty's lead shank to Tom in disgust and walked away, suddenly sick to her stomach. The feeling got worse as the day went on. And that night at her apartment, she ranted and raved from one end of the place to the other.

"Damn it! What is it with men?"

Linda sympathized sadly. Not for Suzie Strater, she didn't even know the woman. But for Dawn, and because of what she'd told her about Randy.

"I don't ever want to see him again! Ever! He's an ass! He's everyone's ass! And he gives his ass and everything else that goes along with it to every woman on the racetrack!"

Linda started to say something, but Dawn had more to say herself. "He'd probably just worked his way down to our barn and it was my turn!"

"Who told you this anyway? Tom?"

"No, Brownie. But I'll bet Tom knew."

Linda sighed. "Who the hell is Brownie?"

Dawn shook her head. "It doesn't matter. Nothing matters. Because I don't want to talk about it any more. I'm just glad I found out now and not later. That way it's over before it begins." She stormed down the hall. "I'll be damned if I'm going to be one of his statistics! Thank you very much!"

Chapter Twelve

Ben had scheduled Beau to work a half mile, thinking if he worked well and came back eager, he'd enter him. Normally by this time of year, he'd have already started several times. The morning was cool and clear as Beau lunged into his feed tub, grabbing a mouthful of oats and throwing them over his shoulder in a ridiculous gesture of aggressiveness.

"Asshole," Ben said affectionately. Throwing his grain like this was an old habit, one that used to aggravate the hell out of him. But seeing as it was the first time Beau had done it since shipping in this spring, today it was almost a pleasure to watch. It was a sure sign of the old Beau coming around.

Another old habit of his was to paw and paw and pile his straw into a mound in the center of his stall. This really irritated Ben, and not so much because of the mess he made of his stall. But because of the way he pounded his leg over and over when digging and digging.

Tom tacked Beau when the time came and Dawn took Red out to the road between the barns to watch for Miguel. She spotted him after a minute or so. He waved, but then he disappeared. Ben walked up to the track. Miguel showed up a few minutes later, and off they went.

Tom often joked about Red having the patience of Job. And he needed it this morning in order to put up with Beau. As hard as Tom tried, and he could really finesse a horse, he couldn't keep Beau from continually pounding and bouncing into Red's shoulder down the backside, practically knocking him off his feet again and again. Tom and Miguel laughed at how obnoxious he was, but along with a great deal of combined swearing through clenched teeth, because this was no laughing matter. If they gave Beau an inch, like the old saying goes, he'd take a mile. And there would go the work, and possibly the race. Not to mention dealing with the wrath of Ben Miller.

The plan was to work the half from the three-eighths pole to an eighth of a mile past the wire. Ben never liked to work a horse to the finish line. He said pulling up there became a habit then. He wanted them running flat out under the wire. As they approached the turn, Tom glanced over his shoulder and at the last possible second, started dropping down on the rail. Beau turned into a bear at this point, and it took everything Tom had to help Miguel hold him.

"You got him?! You got him?!"

It was a good sixteenth of a mile before the three-eighths pole.

"Fuck!" Tom eased Beau's lead free and Miguel sat down on him. Tom galloped Red to the outside rail then, pulled up to watch, and barely had time to catch his breath. Forty-five and four-fifths of a second later, Miguel was standing up on Beau and Tom was clicking to Red to get back around and help pull him up.

As Dawn stood next to Ben by the rail, she was reminded of her first day here. Only today, there were no looks of concern. Miguel was saying something about Beau pulling so hard he was going to have to go check his "Hemm-o-roids." Tom and Ben were laughing. And Beau was dancing and snorting.

It was a scene in her mind, playing over and over. She could hear Ben saying, "This is what the racetrack's all about." It was all in that smile of his. "This is it! It's days like this!" He'd waited on Beau, and waited and waited. And now he was right. The smile on Dawn's face was as wide as Ben's as she walked along with him and tried to appear as if she weren't checking her stride to match his.

"Well?" she said.

Ben nodded.

He was going to enter him for the day after tomorrow.

Since Cajun was running in the fifth race that day, Dawn decided to stay at the track rather than go home and have to come right back at one.

Tom headed out for lunch. "Wendy's or McDonald's?"

Dawn thought for a moment. "Wendy's. And bring me a couple of cookies too."

"The Kids' Meal?"

Dawn laughed.

Cajun didn't need to be iced, though he did have to have a sweat put on his shoulders and back. But that wasn't until about an hour and a half before the race. So, as soon as Tom left, and with all that time on her hands, Dawn lay down on the cot, closed her eyes, and promptly moaned in despair.

She'd told herself she wasn't going to think about Randy, not at all, and yet... She opened her eyes and glanced around the tack room. The tack was clean. The sweat mixture mixed: camphor, Absorbine, iodine, and rubbing alcohol. The bottle was warming in a bucket of hot water to blend and later work its magic. The floor was swept. The bandages rolled.

There was nothing to do. Nothing except close her eyes and sigh and think about Randy some more. There weren't even any manes to pull to keep her mind occupied. Not even Beau, even though his mane could always use a little thinning out, it being so thick and wild it split right down the middle. To pull it now might jinx him. Once a horse was in, according to Ben, it was best to leave him alone. And being somewhat superstitious herself, time on her hands and everything, she thought it best not to tempt the fates.

Tom returned with their food and a bunch of bananas.

"Bananas?"

"For your Beau-Born shits."

Dawn rolled her eyes. Tom laughed. Then here came Barn Kitty, and right after that, Gloria.

"Where's Ben, sweetie?"

"He's at the secretary's office," Tom said.

She was all decked out, dressed from head to toe in white with a really chic lilac scarf tied at her neck, and looked even prettier when it was Tom who had answered and she blushed a bubbly shade of pink. "He is? Oh dear, do you think he'd mind if I came looking for him there?"

Tom gulped down a mouthful of half-chewed burger in an effort to reply to this as well, but Dawn beat him to it. "No. I mean yes. I think he would." She glanced at Tom, who was grinning that grin of his, knowing he would have told her to go on over. "I think he's probably playing cards or something, and when he's playing cards..."

Gloria nodded in understanding. "Well then." She pursed her lips while mulling over what to do next. Tom meanwhile, peeled a banana for Dawn, and nodded for her to take a bite when she just sat there looking at him.

Gloria sighed. "Well, I guess I'll see him later. But do tell me, how's my little Cajun going to run today?"

Tom stretched his legs out and popped a toothpick in his mouth. "He'll win."

"Honest?" Gloria clasped her hands together. "He will?"

Tom nodded with an air of authority. "It'll be like a walk in the park. Picture and all."

"Oh dear!" Gloria said. "My hair. How does it look? I had it done in a different style. What do you think?"

Dawn smiled as she glanced from one to the other. Tom appeared to be assessing Gloria's new hairdo, probably couldn't see any difference, and didn't have a clue as to what to say. She helped him out. "It looks lovely, Gloria. Very becoming."

Tom nodded. "Yes. Very becoming."

"Thank you," she said, fluffing it. "It's less bouffant. It's supposed to make me look younger. Do you think Ben will like it?"

Dawn made sure to answer before Tom again. "I'm sure he will."

"Wonderful. I had it done just for him. But don't tell him, I want it to be a surprise. I have another surprise for him too. You can tell him that. And tell him I'll see him in the clubhouse."

Tom and Dawn looked at one another as Gloria floated down the shedrow, stopping long enough to plant a kiss on Cajun's nose and fuss over him a little, before going on.

Cajun loved attention, even when it came to having a sweat applied. Obviously it didn't matter to him that it was therapeutic, that the heat and the mix of ingredients worked to loosen up his muscles and that the plastic sheet and shoulder blanket put on him after it was rubbed in, made it work even better. He nuzzled Tom affectionately for his kindness, sniffed his leg, his arm, his hair, then Dawn's hair. Applying a sweat was something Dawn left to Tom. She'd tried it once and found the solution too hard on her hands.

"It's a man's job," Tom teased.

"What about gloves? Can I wear rubber gloves?"

"No, it'll eat 'em up." Tom adjusted the shoulder blanket over the plastic sheet.

"Why doesn't it eat up the sheet?" she'd asked.

"Because you're not rubbing it in with it. No friction. Not only that, within minutes there's a layer of sweat to serve as a kind of buffer."

Cajun also needed rundown patches and a patch on the inside of his left hock. The patches first had to be cut to size, then tiny notches made around the edges, so they could conform to the area they were protecting. Dawn made an art form out of it. And even though they came with a peel-off sticky side, in the Miller barn, they were always sprayed with additional adhesive before applying them.

"Better safe than sorry," was Ben's rule, and Tom echoed those sentiments, even when it took ether sometimes to remove them after a race and the smell would get to him.

"An ounce of prevention is better than a whole shitload of pain-in-the-ass cure."

Run-down patches and bandages were always put on at the ten-minute call. If a horse was in ice, this was when he came out. Dawn tacked Cajun and, using a long, thin strip of cloth, tied his tongue.

"Grab the tongue like this," Tom had shown her, pulling the horse's tongue out to the side of its mouth. "Wrap the tie around twice, let him pull his tongue back in place, and tie the string under his jaw."

"Do I make a knot?"

"No." Tom smiled. "A bow."

"Are you serious?"

"World serious," he said. "That's right. Now make sure it's tight."

Not every horse had its tongue tied, only the ones who gave you reason to think they might need it. A horse playing with the bit too much or playing with his tongue all the time, could have trouble when running.

"Poor thing," Dawn had said, looking at that first horse whose tongue she'd tied.

"Poor thing...?" Tom said. "You ain't never seen a horse try and swallow its tongue. *This* is nothing."

"What happens when they do?"

Tom looked at her. "Well, for one, it affects their breathing. Not only that, it panics the shit out of them. You know what that's like? I do. I was with this woman one time, a real go-getter if you know what I mean, and..."

Dawn rolled her eyes and laughed.

When it came time to leave, Dawn locked the tack room and was walking alongside Tom as he led Cajun to the paddock, when she saw Randy's truck. "Damn." She turned to duck between the barns and take the back way, but Tom called out, "Hey, Dawn. Look, there's Randy." Randy saw them, and that was that. No ducking out now. It would be too obvious. Tom would bug her about why and never let up, so she just kept walking.

Randy couldn't take his eyes off her and smiled as she came closer. He said, "Hi." She said, "Hi." And he reached for her hand then, but she pulled away.

"I missed you," he confessed, sounding and looking like he meant it.

"Why is that?" Dawn walked on. "You've only been gone a day."

Randy chuckled, thinking she was kidding. "Do you want to go out for dinner after the races?"

"Sorry," she said, over her shoulder. "Not tonight. I wasn't expecting you."

"Why?" Randy frowned. "Are you and Linda doing something?"

Dawn glanced over her shoulder again without breaking stride. "No, I have a date."

What? Randy leaned back against his truck and crossed his arms. A date? He'd just driven four hundred and fifty miles, one way and then back, because he couldn't stand being away from her, and she has a date.

"I don't believe this," he said to himself, and turned, about to lose it, throwing up his hands and shaking his head, when out of the corner of his eye he saw Ginney walking toward him.

Cajun stood perfectly still in the paddock as Tom and Dawn removed his shoulder blanket and sheet, aside from twitching, and appeared to be enjoying himself. Ben and the valet tacked him. As assistant trainer, Tom could've saddled him, but Ben was avoiding Gloria as long as possible. When he mumbled something under his breath about it, Tom and Dawn both laughed. You'd swear Gloria was a female vampire, Dawn thought, the way he was acting. And yet, it spite of all that, she couldn't help thinking how much better Ben looked since Beau's work. More relaxed. Like the weight of the world had been lifted from his shoulders.

He even joked with Johnny, the young apprentice jockey riding Cajun. "What do you mean, ride him like last time? That race was weeks ago. How can you remember back that far?"

Johnny blushed. "I've only had five mounts since. I remember."

Ben knew exactly how many mounts Johnny had had, having watched every one of them. He also knew he hadn't won any. "Well, did you win on any of these five mounts?"

"No, sir," Johnny said.

"You feel like winning one today?"

Johnny nodded, ready for anything, except maybe the scene in the jocks' room just before he came out; Mastrite and Jenkins popping whatever it is they popped every day and challenging him to join them. "They make holes for you out there," Mastrite had said. "They make you make your own holes." And he and Jenkins had laughed at him when he refused.

"I'm ready," he told Ben.

"Good, then you sit on him like last time. Be patient. Let him tell you when he wants to run, and we'll see you in the winner's circle."

"Riders up!"

Ben had promised Gloria he'd watch the race with her and her lady friends again in the clubhouse, actually not promised but agreed, and started the long trek down behind the ticket booths to the elevator. The last time he'd taken the stairs he'd gotten too winded, too short of breath. It was his nerves, he'd told himself, dreading those women, nothing else. Still...

Dawn jumped up onto the fence, Tom joined her right before the race, and the latch was sprung.

"And they're off!"

Cajun broke well, ran with the pack into the first turn, and laid comfortably fifth or sixth down the backside. Through the far turn, he moved up to take third, and at the head of the stretch he took the lead, and won by five lengths.

"Oh my God!" Gloria and her lady friends jumped up and down, screaming and shouting. "He won! He won!"

"Yes, he won." Ben hurried them to the elevator and got them to the winner's circle and situated just in time. The photographer snapped the picture. Cajun twitched. And the photographer snapped another.

Tom doubled back to the barn for Cajun's halter and shank, while Dawn led Cajun to the spit barn, bouncing and pushing up against her. As she passed the place where Randy's truck had been, she proceeded to tell Cajun what a scuzz Randy was, the biggest scuzz there ever was, and aggravated herself even more when she glanced down the road to see if she could spot him anywhere.

Ben was getting more aggravated as well. Gloria just wouldn't let up. "Remember how you said you loved perogies?"

When Ben nodded somberly, she told him her surprise. "Well, I made you some. Just for you! Potato, prune, cheese, dozens of them, for dinner tonight. Please say you'll come."

Ben sighed. What did he have to say to make this woman understand? What did he have to do? "Of course I'll come," he said. "Meg used to make them for me and I know how much work they are."

Gloria beamed.

"But since you said dozens, do you mind if I bring along a friend?"

Gloria stared. "Why no, I guess not."

"Good." It was a stroke of genius. He wondered why he hadn't thought of this earlier? "What time?"

"Seven?"

"Seven's fine," he said, smiling. "We'll see you then."

Gloria was still somewhat subdued by the time Dawn and Cajun returned to the barn, but lavished him with hugs and kisses. She and her lady friends promised him bushels of apples and carrots. They hugged and kissed him some more, before remembering they hadn't cashed their combined ten-dollar win ticket, and back to the clubhouse they went.

Randy drove by the barn as he was leaving the track, and saw Dawn. She was standing with her back to him, next to Tom, and it occurred to him that he'd never seen her hair loose. It was always in that long braid down her back. He wondered if it would hang loose tonight, all over her date. That thought infuriated him, and he cursed the day he'd ever laid eyes on her. He was glad he'd made a date with Ginney after Dawn had turned him down. He'd screw Ginney tonight, and then he'd feel better.

Dawn ate another banana before doing up Cajun, and as she and Tom and Ben walked to the parking lot, had another. This, as Ben told them about having to go to Gloria's for perogies.

"Oh, so that was her surprise," Dawn said.

Ben shrugged.

"Speaking of Gloria," Tom said. "Did you notice how she didn't smell like a lilac bush today?"

Ben winked at Dawn. "That's because I bought her a bottle of perfume for her birthday. Dawn picked it out."

"Goddamn, old man, you're gettin' smart. You amaze me more and more every day," Tom said. "Who are you taking with you to dinner?"

"Charlie."

"Charlie...?"

"Charlie."

By morning, Dawn had eaten two more bananas, and instead of her usual muffin for breakfast, a cheese danish. Ben was talking to Charlie at the guard shack when she arrived, and from the gist of the conversation, she surmised dinner and the evening had been a success, the perogies delicious, and Charlie smitten.

Dawn linked her arm around Ben's as they walked to the barn, and he told her all about it. Beau was the first to hear his voice coming around the corner of the barn. He stuck his head out and started nickering as usual. Ben glanced down the shedrow to see the rapid succession of heads appearing then, bobbing, whinnying, Cajun included, bright-eyed and twitching. Then came the pawing for breakfast.

Since Cajun had run yesterday and Beau was in tomorrow, training was light this morning. Ben walked over to the secretary's office with Dave a little after nine, and Tom went home. He'd had a date that kept him out all night, he said, pretending to sulk when no one wanted to hear the details. All Dawn had left to do was top off the water buckets and lock up, and she'd be leaving as well.

Luckily she was still there when Gloria arrived with an abundance of apples and carrots. Dawn followed her down to Cajun's stall, but for once didn't have to remind her not to overdo it. One apple and two carrots, and she handed Dawn the rest.

"Save these for later," she said, and walked with Dawn to the tack room. "Sweetie, do you mind if I...?" She wanted to talk. Dawn motioned for her to have a seat and sat down on the cot across from her. "I've tried everything I know. So please, be honest with me."

Dawn smiled supportively.

"I've been a widow too long, and I'm lonely. What am I doing wrong? I thought Ben and I..."

"It's not you, Gloria."

Gloria shrugged, not convinced. "I even wore that perfume he bought me. And honestly, sweetie, between you and me, it was nauseating. I don't think he even noticed."

Dawn smiled, shaking her head.

"His friend Charlie paid more attention to me. Do you know him?" Obviously she and Charlie had never met before, which wasn't surprising considering Charlie worked the horsemen's gate on the one side and Gloria always entered through the owner's parking lot on the other.

"Yes, I know him. He's very nice."

Gloria nodded, apparently agreeing. But nevertheless. "Where did I go wrong? What did I do?"

"Nothing. Believe me, it's not you. It's Meg, his wife."

Gloria shook her head and sighed. "I'm sorry to bother you with this, I must seem so..."

"You're not bothering me."

"It's just that." Gloria stared off. "I have children, grandchildren, friends, dear friends. And yet..."

"Something's missing?"

Gloria looked at Dawn and nodded, tears surfacing. "I'm not trying to replace my husband. I just still have a lot to give."

Dawn reached over and squeezed her hand reassuringly, as Gloria took out a tissue and dabbed her eyes.

"How long has his wife been dead, sweetie?" she asked, and now it was Dawn who felt like crying. Ben was still in such pain. Like her.

"Not long enough."

As soon as Ben started down the shedrow, he knew from the overwhelming scent of lilac, Gloria was there. Her presence was announced, so to speak. He walked in the tack room and sat down at his desk, more at ease around her than ever before. He even teased her about Charlie having a crush on her.

Gloria blushed, saying how it was only her cooking. Dawn and Ben laughed. Gloria left then, and not a minute later as Dawn and Ben were talking, two men walked in and identified themselves as being from the racing commission.

"Mr. Miller, we're going to be inspecting your barn and tack room if you don't mind."

Mind? Ben nodded, thinking what a stupid thing to ask. What would they do if I said I did mind? "No, go right ahead."

Ben never kept drugs at the track. The few if any that he did use, he kept on the farm, and as a result never feared a *shakedown*. Already this month, three trainers had been caught with prohibited substances in their possession. One was suspended, the other two heavily fined.

Dawn went to the ladies room and was occupying one of the stalls in vain, when she heard two girls come in and go over to the sink. "I've never been stood up by anybody before," the one was saying. "The bastard never even called."

"Maybe he had an emergency."

An emergency? Dawn listened.

"Emergency my ass. He could've called. I jumped him this morning when he came to the barn. He said he fell asleep. Big goddamned excuse."

"Maybe that's what really happened, Ginney."

They were running water and obviously washing up.

"Yeah, right! That's why when I said we could just go out tonight then, he said no. No excuse, no nothing, and just fucking walked away."

When the door slammed behind them, Dawn decided maybe the trip to the ladies room hadn't been a complete waste after all. And she was still thinking about the conversation as she walked back to the barn, where who else was waiting for her in the tack room, but Randy.

She hesitated, then walked in past him. "Where's Ben?"

Randy shrugged, and for all practical purposes appeared to be looking through the racing form for something. "He said he'd be right back."

"The racing commission was here."

"Well, they're gone now," Randy said, without looking up. And after a moment, "So uh...how was your date?"

"Fine."

He turned a page. "Where did you go?"

Dawn frowned, shaking her head. "Nowhere really. Just out."

Randy nodded for a second, as if he were giving her answer some thought, then laid the racing form down on Ben's desk and looked at her. "What did you do?"

"Nothing much."

Randy nodded again. "So, who is he?"

"Who?" Dawn repeated. As if it were any of his business.

"Your stinking date..." Randy said, dragging the words out. "Who was it?"

Dawn glanced away, anger building and with an expression much the same as his when she looked back. "What did you do?"

"I slept," he said, glaring, his face getting redder.

Dawn just looked at him.

"Well...?" He crossed his arms and sat back on the desk.

"Well what?" Dawn said, beyond irritated now.

"What did you do? I'm just asking."

"I told you," she said. "Nothing in particular." She started past him, but he stopped her.

"With who?"

"My date! That's who!" Dawn swung around to face him. "What's with the fifty questions? Are you going to ask me next if I slept with him?"

Randy slammed the desk with his hand. "Yes! Because that's *exactly* what I want to know!"

Ben came in behind them. "What the hell's all this shouting about?" he asked, looking from one to the other.

"Nothing," Dawn said, still glaring at Randy.

"Yeah, you're right," he said. "It was nothing."

He walked out and Dawn stormed over to the cot and plopped herself down. Of all the nerve. He's the one that sleeps around, not me. Damn him.

Ben sat down and looked at her. "What was all that about?"

Dawn whisked a hand. "Nothing."

"Well, if it's nothing, then why don't you go after him and straighten it out."

"I'm not going to apologize. I've done nothing wrong. The hell with him."

Ben lowered his glasses and peered at her. "Sometimes it's not important who's right and who's wrong."

"Ben, he asked me if I slept around?"

"He did what?" Ben's eyes widened.

"Well, not exactly. But that's what he was getting at."

"Piss on him then," Ben said, turning and picking up the condition book. They were both quiet for a moment. Then he turned back around. "Are you sure that's what he was asking?"

"No...I'm not sure." Dawn sighed. "He asked me out yesterday and I turned him down."

"Why? I thought you liked him."

Dawn shrugged. "Brownie says he sleeps with every woman on the racetrack."

Ben shook his head. "Gossip," he said, and remembered what Tom had said about him. "I don't take to gossip. Never have and never will."

Dawn looked at him, as close to a father as she had now. "I told him I had a date and he was drilling me about it."

Ben lowered his glasses again. "What do you mean, you told him you had a date? Didn't you?"

Dawn shook her head.

"You lied?"

Dawn hesitated, and then nodded. "Yes."

"Why? Wouldn't it have made more sense just to say no? No, I don't want to go out with you. Why lie?"

Dawn glanced away. "Well, that would've been a lie too."

Ben sighed. He'd thought as much. He'd seen it in her eyes. He also thought he'd seen something in Randy's eyes when the two of them were together. "Forget the gossip, and give him a chance."

"But..."

"You owe him an apology," Ben said, and held up his hand when she started to object. "For lying to him. Nothing else. Just for lying."

When Dawn finally got around to leaving, she stopped at the guard shack to talk to Charlie. He asked her all about Cajun, his habits, his personality and characteristics. He laughed self-consciously when he said it would give him something to talk to Gloria about. Dawn chuckled, and while sitting there with him, she noticed Randy's truck parked between the first two barns.

She told Charlie she'd see him tomorrow and started toward her car, but then changed her mind and walked to Randy's truck instead. The passenger door was locked, so she went around to the driver's side, opened the door, and leaning across the seat, wrote a note on his clipboard.

> *Randy,*
> *I'm sorry. I didn't have a date last night.*
> *And I slept alone. Dawn*

Randy came out from under the eaves of one of the barns, saw her, and hesitated for a second before walking to the truck. He had no idea what she was up to, and found himself approaching slowly so that whatever it was, she wouldn't hear him coming and quit. When he reached the truck, he braced his hands above the door and leaned in as far as he could without touching her. Dawn started to back out then and bumped into him.

"I'm sorry," she said, a little startled but with a laugh. "I didn't know you were there."

"Obviously." Randy leaned across her, read the note, and looked at her. "Why in the hell would you tell me you had a date, if you didn't?" he asked, his face just inches from hers.

"Because you sleep around," Dawn said, as if that alone would explain everything.

"What?"

"Brownie says you sleep around. A lot."

Randy leaned back a little, shaking his head. "So that's what Ben was talking about." Ben had tracked him down a few minutes earlier, saying simply, "Don't assume you and Dawn are alike," then just walked away.

"He told me I owe you an apology," Dawn said, nudging him to let her out.

Randy pointed to the clipboard. "So, is this apology yours then or his?"

"Mine. I'm apologizing for lying to you, and for listening to gossip. Will you let me up? This is uncomfortable."

Randy backed up just enough for her to turn and sit in the driver's seat facing him, and propped his hands on top of the truck, gazing at her.

Dawn glanced away. "So, is it true? Do you sleep with every woman on the racetrack?"

"Every one of them? Sure," Randy said, making it sound ridiculous.

"How about most of them?"

"I don't think so," Randy said, not sounding nearly so convincing this time.

Dawn swallowed. "A lot of them?"

"None that mattered," Randy said, leaning closer.

Dawn started to pull back, but then stopped herself. "Did you have a date with a girl named Ginney last night?"

"Yes." Randy looked into her eyes. "But I didn't go."

"Why not?" Dawn asked, her hand instinctively touching his arm, a gesture of closeness but also an assurance he keep his distance.

"I didn't want to," Randy said. "I thought I did when I asked, but that was only after you turned me down. I thought I'd go out with her in your place, but..."

Dawn smiled. "So you stayed home and slept?"

Randy shook his head. "No, I laid awake for hours. I kept thinking about your hair, and what it would look like loose." He leaned closer to kiss her, but again she pulled back.

She glanced at her watch, trying to hide the rush of feelings inside, wanting him to kiss her but at the same time experiencing a sense of panic. He had her trapped.

"I've got to go. I have the afternoon off, and I'm looking forward to a sauna and a long swim."

"Where do you go?" Randy asked, not quite willing to let her leave just yet, even as he caught sight of the trainer from the first barn looking in his direction, waiting for him.

"At the club. Do you want to join me?"

Randy smiled. "I don't like saunas."

"How about swimming? They have an Olympic-sized pool."

"I can't get out of here before two," Randy said, as he backed up and motioned to the trainer that he'd be right there.

Dawn nodded, disappointed, then cringed, holding her stomach.

"Are you okay?"

"Fine," she said. "I'll be fine. Beau's in tomorrow and my stomach's starting already."

Randy shook his head, smiling.

"Why don't you meet me at the club. I'll sauna first and get done before you get there." She hesitated, searching his eyes, and when he nodded, wrote down the address on the clipboard. "I'll meet you at the pool at two-thirty."

She brushed up against his shoulder lightly when he finally let her out, and started to walk away.

"Wait a minute. What do I bring?"

"Just your suit," Dawn said. "Everything else is provided. I'll tell them at the desk that I'm expecting you."

Chapter Thirteen

Jeremy, the desk clerk at the Arcadia Country Club looked up and smiled as Dawn signed in. She was such a nice person, always so pleasant and cheerful.

"Hi, how are you today?"

"Fine, thank you. How about you?"

"I could be a little better," Dawn said, grimacing as her stomach cramped again. "Who's giving massages this afternoon?"

"Jonathan and Sherry. Would you like me to reserve a time for you?"

"Yes, please, with Jonathan. I'll be having lunch with Linda, so let me know when."

"Of course. Oh, and by the way, she arrived ahead of you. She's waiting in the dining room."

"What?" Jeremy laughed as Dawn went to see for herself. "Oh my God!" she said. "I don't believe it!"

"All right, so I'm early. Big deal!"

"Big deal?" Linda was never ever on time, let alone early. "This is a first! Are you sick or something?"

"No, just hungry. What are you going to order?"

There was no need to look at a menu, they knew it by heart, and most always ordered the same. Soup of the day, salad, and hot bread. Done.

"Randy's coming for a swim later," Dawn said then, and Linda started choking on an ice cube.

Dawn jumped up and patted her on the back. "Are you all right?"

Linda motioned for her cup of hot tea, took two or three swallows, and it finally went down.

"Damn it!" Dawn said. "Don't do that to me. You scared me to death."

"Me?!" Linda shook her head. "Don't do that to you! The last time we talked, you wiped Randy off the face of the earth. And now you sit there like it's nothing and tell me he's coming for a swim. How did this come about?"

"Easy." Dawn sat back down and told her all about what happened that morning, starting with the conversation she overheard, to their argument, to their encounter at the truck, and then inviting him to the club.

Linda liked the part where Randy had a fit and pounded the desk. "Oh my God, he must have really been mad."

Dawn nodded. "You should've seen him."

"You know, I think he really cares for you, Dawn."

Dawn shrugged. How? They hardly knew each other. "Anyway, I figured why not. Remind me to tell Jeremy he's coming. I forgot earlier."

You're so tense," Jonathan said, smacking Dawn's shoulder before kneading and rubbing it. "Relax."

"I am relaxed." Dawn replied, as relaxed as a person could be in his hands. "Ouch, now that hurt." She buried her face against her arm.

"Is something troubling you?"

Dawn chuckled. "You mean besides you?"

Jonathan laughed. "Seriously, what seems to be the problem?'

"My stomach hurts."

"And why is that?"

"I guess because I'm nervous. My favorite horse is running tomorrow."

"Hmph..." He kneaded somewhat more gently between her shoulder blades and then smacked her again. "There you are, all done."

"Thanks," Dawn said, raising her head to scowl at him. "I think."

"You're welcome," Jonathan said, covering her with a sheet. "Let the horse run its own race. Meanwhile, you rest a few minutes and later on have some Chamomile. It's good for the nerves."

Dawn waved, heard him greet his next victim in the room adjacent, and closed her eyes, sympathizing with the poor person. Jonathan's massages were the best. She'd be the first to attest to that, after they were long over. But ask her before or right about now, and it would be, "No way, never. Not in a million years."

When Randy arrived, Jeremy regarded him most suspiciously. "I'm sorry, but Miss Fioritto didn't leave word she was expecting a guest."

"Check with her, please. I assure you, she is expecting me," Randy said, glancing around the lobby.

Jeremy frowned. "I will check with her, but Miss Fioritto never has guests. You're not a reporter, are you?"

"No, I'm not," Randy said, wondering what a reporter would want with her, or for that matter, why this man was giving him such a hard time.

"Hmmm." Jeremy looked Randy up and down, then reached for the phone and dialed. "Jonathan, I'm terribly sorry to bother you, but I need to speak with Dawn Fioritto. There is a gentleman here that says he is a guest of hers." He paused, listening. "Yes, I know she never has guests. That is why..." He paused again. "Oh, I see. Hmmmm." He looked at Randy. "Miss Fioritto is resting. She's uh, asleep."

"Then wake her," Randy said firmly.

Jeremy hesitated, then nodded and got back on the line. "I'm afraid you'll have to wake her. Tell her that a Randy Iredell is here to see her. And call me back, please."

He smiled pensively at Randy as he hung up. "Please, Mr. Iredell, have a seat. Jonathan will call us back as soon as he checks with her."

"It's Doctor Iredell," Randy said, surprising himself with his attitude. And feeling foolish as soon as he said it, he walked across the room, picked up a magazine and sat down. It was then he noticed a large painting on the wall of a man and a woman. The woman looked like Dawn, only older. He dropped his eyes to the plaque below and read their names.

Charles Bask Fioritto
Maria Angelina Fioritto
Founding Father Chairman of the Board

"Holy shit..." he muttered. The resemblance left no doubt. He glanced around the room, shaking his head. With an entire year's salary, maybe, just maybe, he could afford about a month's membership in a place like this. And here was Dawn with a Founding Father. "Jesus."

Jeremy waved to him from across the room and came out from behind the desk. "I'm sorry, Dr. Iredell. Miss Fioritto is awake now, and indeed, she is expecting you. I'll show you to the men's locker room and lounge. An attendant will take you from there."

Randy sighed, stood up and followed him, and was shown into a large room with a bar on the right, showers and lockers to the left. "Kevin, this is Dr. Iredell. Be a dear and show him around the men's area and to the indoor pool. He's joining Miss Fioritto."

The attendant escorted Randy to the other end of the locker room, then stood in waiting as Randy undressed, to fold and hang up his clothes for him. Four men sat opposite them, downing tall drinks as they played cards. Randy marveled, and almost laughed. Ask a middle-class man to play cards in front of a row of urinals and he'd tell you to kiss his ass. For the life of him, he thought he was meeting Dawn at some local health club. And here he was with an attendant folding his underwear. He tied the string on his trunks and motioned for Kevin to lead the way.

They walked down a hall, where Kevin stopped and pointed out a succession of open showers. "They're designed to get you accustomed to the temperature of the pool."

There were two sets of four, one on each side, with plungers, which when pressed, started the cool down. The first one was hot, almost too hot for Randy's liking, the second a little more comfortable. The third was lukewarm, the fourth, a precise eighty-two degrees, the same as the pool. God forbid, Randy thought, that anyone just plunge right in.

"This way, Dr. Iredell," Kevin said, handing Randy a towel and walking with him. "Are you meeting Linda or Dawn?"

It really didn't surprise Randy to hear Linda was a member too, though he did shake his head in wonder. "I'm meeting Dawn."

"Really? She never has any guests, you know."

"So I've heard. But how do you know that?"

Kevin furrowed a wise brow. "I've been on the staff here now for twelve years," he said, and just to prove how much he really did know, he added, "She's a loner. Always has been."

"What else do you know about her?"

Kevin frowned. "You're the one meeting her. Don't you uh...?"

Randy smiled somewhat sheepishly. "To be honest, we just met."

Kevin nodded amiably. This friend of Miss Fioritto's seemed like a nice guy. "Well," he said, thinking out loud. "What do I know? You mean aside from the fact that she's probably one of the richest women in the county, if not the state."

Randy stared. By this time they were at the entrance to the indoor pool. Kevin opened the door. "Miss Fioritto swims from that end," he said, motioning to the opposite side.

Randy shook his head, chuckling. The man was obviously having a little fun with him, but this was too much. "How in the hell do you know which end of the pool she swims from?"

Kevin smiled. "Easy. All the women swim from there. I think it has something to do with the ladies' locker room being on that side."

Randy laughed, thanked the man for his assistance, and spotting Dawn, dove in and swam over to her. She was all smiles as she apologized. "I'm sorry I forgot to tell Jeremy you were coming. Please don't be angry."

Randy put his arms around her and pulled her close. They practically had the pool to themselves. "Did you forget I was coming?"

"No, it's all Linda's fault. She was supposed to remind me right after lunch, and then I fell asleep and..."

"Likely excuse," Randy said.

Dawn laughed. They kissed. And Randy smiled.

"Now what?"

Dawn laughed again. "I don't know. We can race to the end I guess," she said. And with that, she slipped out of his arms, dove under, and got a head start.

It was to no avail. Randy got to the end three strokes ahead of her and swam back and cut her off. They splashed each other then, raced again, and did the back float holding hands, more laughing and sinking than actual floating, until finally exhausted, Dawn pulled herself up onto the side. "I've gotta rest."

Randy stayed in the water, propped his arms on the side, and looked out over the pool. "Tell me about this club."

"What do you want to know?"

Randy shrugged. "It's pretty exclusive isn't it?"

"No more than others. Why? Did you want to join?"

Randy laughed. "Do you ever give a straight answer?"

"Only when I have to."

Randy turned to face her and wrapped his arms around her waist. "All right. How about now then?"

Dawn glanced away and focused on an empty chair. "What is it you want to know?"

"Well, for one, the attendant says you're rich. Very rich."

Dawn shook her head. "Could be he's just repeating hearsay."

"Could be. And could be he's telling the truth. How can you afford this place? It must cost a fortune."

Dawn took a deep breath, trying to think of a fast answer she could give him that would enable her to conceal the truth, and yet... "It's in the trust my father set up for me. He founded the place, and so we, actually me, since they're dead, have a lifetime membership." She sighed inwardly, it was close enough.

Randy pulled himself up out of the water and sat next to her. "I saw their pictures in the lobby. You look just like your mother."

"I know." Dawn smiled. "But I have my father's temperament."

"Your mom is pretty."

"Was. She's dead, remember?"

"That's not what I meant."

Dawn looked at him, his eyes so sincere. "I know. I'm sorry."

Randy leaned close and kissed her gently. "But now that you're in a serious mood."

"I'm not," Dawn said, laughing.

"Either way," Randy said. "Are there any more surprises I should know about, like this club? If so, maybe we can just get them out of the way now."

"No surprises," Dawn said. But judging from the fact that she'd glanced away to say it, Randy wasn't so sure.

"Tell me this then." He hesitated. "Is there anything or anyone that can come between you and me? Anything I should..."

"No, nothing."

"Why is it when you say nothing, I think it's something. What is it with you?"

"I told you. Nothing." She smiled reassuringly. "Nothing else is important, Randy."

Randy nodded, but still wasn't convinced for some reason. They were quiet for a moment, sitting next to one another, touching lightly, and just looking out over the pool.

"Do you have family besides Linda?" Randy asked.

"Yes. Linda's parents, my Aunt Rebecca and Uncle Matt. And my Aunt Maeve. That's all, unless you count Ben and Tom."

Randy looked at her. "The attendant told me you never have guests. Why me?"

Dawn smiled and linked her arm around his. "Because I wanted to spend the day with you. I wanted you asking me all these silly questions."

Randy laughed. "Aw, come on, like you didn't think I'd ask about this place?"

Dawn chuckled. "No, I figured you'd ask. I was just hoping it wouldn't overwhelm you."

Randy leaned close and kissed her, delightfully aware of the softness of her breast against his arm. "I have to say I'm impressed. But overwhelmed, no."

Dawn smiled, gazing into his eyes.

"Would you like to go somewhere for dinner?" Randy asked. "There's an Italian restaurant close to my apartment. The food is delicious."

She nodded. "I love pasta."

"Good. I'll meet you in the lobby. How long does it take you to get ready?" he asked, dreading the wait.

"About fifteen minutes." She stood up, smiling but hesitant from the way he just sat there looking at her. "You're not going to watch me walk away, are you?"

He nodded, motioned for her to go on, and watched her every step, all the way. He dove into the water then, and swam to the other end on sheer testosterone. Tonight she was going to be his and that's all there was to it.

Ben heaved a sigh and smiled. Things were going well for a change. Beau was finally right, no more second-guessing himself. He'd probably win easy tomorrow. Charlie solved his problem with Gloria. And All Together had reached a turning point as well. Fighting everything at first, the bit, the saddle, the night and day, she was finally out of heat and settling down nicely. Yes, things were going well.

He got up and went into the kitchen for something to eat. He wasn't much of a cook, and thinking about that, smiled sadly. The last couple of months of Meg's illness, whenever she had the strength, and sometimes even when she didn't, she made extra meals and froze them. She started marking the dates on the containers then too, something she'd never done before. And when she put them in the freezer, she'd make sure to put the newest ones on the bottom.

Ben reached into the cupboard for a can of potted meat, opened it and set it on the table, then walked back and got some crackers and a can of tomato juice. It would have to do. There was still a frozen container of Meg's lasagna in the freezer. He'd looked at it a hundred times. Once he even took it out, set it on the counter, and lit the oven. But then that would be it. He couldn't do it. He put the container back on the bottom where she had it, and to this day, whenever he opened the freezer, he just looked at it. Meg's lasagna. His favorite meal.

Ten minutes after he ate the potted meat and heavily salted tomato juice, he got indigestion, and went into the bathroom for an antacid. It tasted like chalk.

He'd hauled wood in earlier for a fire in the fireplace and was glad he had, because he was too tired to go out and get it now. It wasn't that cold out; besides he could've turned the furnace on. But it was nights like these he and Meg enjoyed a fire most, the warmth feeling so good on their tired legs.

He remembered how she would sit for hours in her chair by the hearth, knitting or working on her needlepoint. And how he loved to sit next to her and smoke his pipe, listening to the sound of the yarn being pulled through the pattern and the crackle of the fire. A sound so soothing, that it often put him to sleep.

He closed his eyes and could hear her humming, in a dream. She often hummed when she was working, and in a voice so soft, he could still hear the sound of the thread as she wove it in and out. He could smell his pipe tobacco in his dream. He could see Meg with her legs stretched contentedly on the hearth. When she dropped her needle, he reached down to get it for her. "Why thank you, Mr. Miller," she said softly, raising her eyes to his. "It's nice to know you're still looking out for me after all these years."

Randy suggested they drop Dawn's car off at her apartment and go to the restaurant in his truck. Since he was on call, Dawn agreed, providing he promised to bring her home.

Randy grinned. "I may and I may not." He phoned his answering service from her apartment while Dawn wrote Linda a note.

> *Linda,*
> *Went with Randy. We're going for dinner.*
> *Won't be late. My stomach is killing me.*
> *Dawn*
> *P.S. You should see him in a bathing suit!!!*

She left the note on the floor in front of Linda's door and came back into the living room as Randy slammed the phone down. "What's the matter?"

"My pager's been out," he said, pounding on it and wishing he could smash it to pieces.

"Are you sure it's the pager? Maybe it just didn't work when you were at the club. Did you have it in a locker?"

"No, I left it with the attendant. He said it never went off." He pounded on it again, took the battery out, put in back in, and for good measure pounded it once more. "Anyway, I've got to go. I have an emergency. You want to come with me?"

"I don't know. What kind of emergency?"

"The Durans' Queen's Court mare is foaling and apparently having some trouble," he said, as he headed for the door. "We can eat on the way back, if we don't starve first."

"I'll get some fruit." Dawn hurried into the kitchen and grabbed what they had, an apple, two oranges and two bananas, and off they went. In the truck, she peeled an orange for Randy and a banana for herself.

"I should've been there hours ago," Randy said, worrying out loud. "If something happens to that mare..."

"I feel really bad about this."

"Why? It's not your fault. It's the pager's. I've had nothing but trouble with them."

"Maybe you should get a car phone."

Randy looked at her. "Oh sure. I'll get one tomorrow. This may come as a shock to you, Founding Daughter, but they're expensive. Very expensive."

Dawn turned and stared out the window, and it was Randy apologizing now. "I'm sorry. I didn't mean that. Okay?"

Dawn nodded, and peeled another banana. Randy ate half and she ate the rest.

Mr. Duran paced back and forth in front of the mare's stall while his wife stood watch for Randy at the barn door. When his truck turned into the drive, she rushed out to greet him.

"Oh, Dr. Iredell!" she said, panting and trying to catch her breath. "We're so glad you're here! We were just about to call someone else!"

Randy smiled reassuringly. "Well, let's go take a look."

The Durans were new to horse breeding. This was to be their first foal, and understandably they were nervous. Randy was called often to their farm. Mr. Duran jokingly had even started referring to him as one of the family. Randy regretted that closeness now as he looked in at the mare. She was lathered in distress, her enormous sides heaving with each labored breath, and stood pawing.

"How long has she been at this?"

"About three hours now," Mr. Duran said helplessly, to which Mrs. Duran, wringing her hands and clutching them to her chest, added, "Oh, please help her."

As Randy walked into the stall, the mare's knees buckled. She went down with a moan then and laid flat out on her side. Randy squatted next to her and just watched her for a moment. "There now, Momma..." he said, stroking her neck. "There now."

She moaned again, and following that, picked up her weary head and looked at her side. She did this twice, each time rocking her body hard, then lying flat out again.

Randy reached over and turned up her lip to check the coloring of her gums, watched her for another minute or so, then leaned close and listened to her stomach. He thought so. "Let's get her up," he said.

"What?" Mr. Duran gasped. "Shouldn't we leave her be if the foal...?"

Randy stood up shaking his head. "I don't think she's foaling." He motioned for Dawn to hand him the lead shank by the door, and gave the mare's halter a tug. "Come on, Momma. On your feet."

The mare rose slowly. Dawn put the lead shank on her, and Randy examined her. He listened first to her heart, then moved the stethoscope all over her sides.

"Nothing," he said.

"Oh no!" Mrs. Duran cried, her hands to her mouth. "Is the foal dead?"

Randy shook his head. "No, the foal is fine. Moving quite a bit in fact. What I mean is there are no gastric noises. This mare's colicked." He took the shank from Dawn and led the horse out of her stall. "I'm going to give her a light sedative. I can't give her anything stronger at this point, so we're going to have to walk her through this."

Randy administered the injection at his truck, and Mr. Duran started walking the mare around the paddock. She followed along somewhat cooperatively the first couple of laps, but then stopped and tried to go down. Randy rushed up behind her, clapping his hands, and urged her to keep walking. From then on, he stayed close, kicking dirt at her heels and making noise every time she tried to lay down.

Dawn meanwhile, sat with Mrs. Duran on the bench outside the barn. The two of them watched helplessly as Mrs. Duran rambled to keep from panicking. "Dr. Iredell is so very nice. I don't know what we'd do without him. He always comes through for us. One time he had to come out for..."

The mare made another attempt to go down, this time with more determination, and Randy had to resort to kicking her in the rump several times to get her back up.

"Get me a broom."

When Mrs. Duran hurried into the barn for one, Randy looked at Dawn and raised an eyebrow, shrugging as he shook his head, signs she interpreted to mean, rightfully so, that it was possible they were too late.

For the next fifteen or twenty minutes, Randy followed around behind the mare swishing the broom at her hocks, which she didn't appreciate one bit. She kicked at him several times, pinning her ears and glaring back at him. But it served the purpose. She stayed on her feet.

"We've never lost a horse before," Mrs. Duran said, beside herself and sounding close to tears.

"We haven't lost this one yet," Randy said, smiling hopefully. He stood back and watched the horse for a while. "Give her another turn and then let's put her in her stall and see what she's going to do. The sedative should be in her system by now."

Mr. Duran led her inside, but had no sooner turned her loose, when she started circling the stall and pawing again, so it was back out to continue walking.

Randy took turns relieving Mr. Duran. They walked her for another thirty minutes, then put her back into her stall. She didn't try to lay down this time, but it was obvious from the way she kept looking at her sides and shifting her weight from one hind leg to the other, that she was still in a great deal of discomfort. So they led her out to the paddock again.

Randy walked her first, then Mr. Duran, and Randy sat down with Dawn and Mrs. Duran. The poor woman by now was a tired, nervous wreck. "Isn't there anything we can do?"

Randy smiled. "Coffee would be nice."

"You're right," Mrs. Duran said, as if he'd uttered a profound truth. "That's what I'll do. I'll make us some coffee."

When she'd gone, Randy glanced at Dawn, and again there was that look in his eyes that maybe this was an effort in futility. "What are the possibilities?" she asked.

Randy leaned forward, his elbows on his knees and hands in his hair as he spoke softly so Mr. Duran couldn't hear. "Well, if she's ruptured her gut..."

Dawn swallowed hard. "Do you think she's done that?"

Randy sighed and shook his head. "No, but it's hard to tell at this point. If she hadn't been carrying on for so long..."

Dawn slipped her arm around his, and when he looked at her, smiled supportively. "It's not your fault."

Randy shrugged, watching the mare, then nodded and stood up and walked over to give Mr. Duran a break. Twenty minutes or so later, they put her back into her stall and turned her loose. She just stood there.

"What do you think?" Mr. Duran asked.

"Let's leave her be and see what she does."

They walked away from the front of her stall as Mrs. Duran returned with a tray of coffee, cream and sugar, and some butter cookies. As couples, they sat down across from each other on straw bales covered with blankets, with an additional bale between them to serve as a coffee table.

"How cozy," Mr. Duran said, blushing a little with anxiety and most grateful that Randy was still there, in case.

"So what's new?" Randy asked, and they all laughed. He helped himself to a few cookies then, and offered some to Dawn. She shook her head no, which surprised him. It was the first time he'd ever seen her turn down something to eat. And for a while, as long as the mare's stall just beyond them was quiet, conversation was rather lighthearted and pleasant.

When there was a noise, a rather heavy-sounding noise, Randy got up and checked on her. She'd laid down again, but was sedate, and breathing about as normal as her mammoth pregnant girth would allow.

"Do you think she'll be all right?" Mr. Duran asked, walking over and looking in on her now too.

Randy nodded. "I'll stay a little while longer though, just to be safe."

When they sat back down, Dawn handed Randy his coffee, minus the cookies he'd had on the saucer. She shrugged innocently when he questioned her about them, and Mrs. Duran laughed and passed him some more.

This was when Mr. Duran glanced pointedly from Randy to Dawn then back, and Randy realized he hadn't introduced them. "I'm sorry. This is Dawn Fioritto. And this," he said, turning, "as you've probably figured by now, is Mr. and Mrs. Duran."

Dawn nodded and smiled. Mrs. Duran smiled also. But Mr. Duran for some reason, just stared at her, the way one does when trying to place someone. "Any relation to Matthew Fioritto?" he asked.

Dawn smiled faintly. "I have an Uncle Matt," she said, turning and explaining to Randy, "That's Linda's father."

Mr. Duran sipped his coffee, gazing keenly at her over the rim of his cup. "Then you're a Bask-Fioritto?"

"Yes, I am," Dawn said, and to Mrs. Duran, "May I use your..."

"Certainly," Mrs. Duran said. "Come with me."

When they'd gone, Randy quizzed Mr. Duran. "What the hell's a Bask-Fioritto?"

"You don't know?" Mr. Duran waved a hand. "I'm sorry, I forgot. You're new to the area. It's the joining of the Bask and the Fioritto families."

"No shit," Randy said, rolling his eyes, and Mr. Duran laughed.

"Shhhh. Listen." When he thought he heard someone coming, he motioned for Randy to follow him to the other end of the barn. "I want to show you a new horse we just bought."

Randy walked with him to the new horse's stall, and looked in at a flashy, little black colt, flat across the back and mean in the eyes.

"The Basks and the Fiorittos are old money," Mr. Duran said, motioning to the colt as if he were pointing out something in its conformation. "A colleague of mine is her Uncle's attorney. The corporate end. I thought I'd seen her before and maybe that's where. Or maybe it was in the newspaper."

Randy looked at him. "The newspaper?"

Mr. Duran shrugged, motioning to the colt again, and smiled at his wife and Dawn when they returned. "We'll be right there," he called to them. "I'm just showing Randy the colt."

Mrs. Duran nodded, and she and Dawn tiptoed over to peek in at the mare. She was stretched out and snoring.

"The young lady's father and uncle have different mothers," Mr. Duran went on to explain. "I think there was a sister too. Maybe it was in a journal...a recent one, she looked so familiar."

Randy sighed. Normally the Durans and their combined eccentricity was endearing. But not tonight.

"I'll see if I can track it down."

Randy thanked him, though he had no idea why, and turned to walk back, but Mr. Duran stopped him. "Let me ask you. What is she to you?"

Randy swallowed, glancing down the aisle at Dawn, and looked at him. "I think...everything."

"Then for sure I'll make a point of locating that article for you. I think you'll find it interesting."

Randy thanked him again, though again he wasn't sure why, and that's when Mrs. Duran called out, "She's getting up."

The mare nosed around her stall for a few minutes, then walked over to her hay and started eating. She drank a little water after that. Randy assured the Durans she'd probably be fine, and no sooner said, the mare raised her tail and passed some gas.

"Keep an eye on her throughout the night, just to be safe. If she's quiet, leave her alone, even if she's lying down."

Mrs. Duran squeezed his hand tightly. "Thank you. Thank you so very much."

Randy smiled and reached into his pocket for a piece of paper to write down his home phone number. "Call me if there's any change. Don't call my service. My pager's out."

In the truck and on their way, Randy adjusted the radio and looked at Dawn. "Are we still on for pasta?"

Dawn shook her head. "I'm not really hungry anymore."

"What? You, not hungry? I don't believe it. Are you sick?"

"Well, to be honest, my stomach is killing me. Would you mind just taking me home? It's almost eleven and Beau *is* running tomorrow."

"Fine." Randy fixed his eyes on the road. "If that's what you want. Fine."

They rode in relative silence for a few minutes, until Randy's escalating anger got the best of him. He should have let well enough alone. "What's with this Bask-Fioritto thing?"

Dawn looked at him, her stomach cramping terribly. "Would you give me a break?"

"Sure..." Randy said. "Don't talk to me. What the fuck do I care?"

Dawn sighed. A sigh that was to be the last of anything said or implied by either of them the rest of the way.

Randy parked in one of the visitors' spaces in the garage at her apartment, and out of some sense of obligation to the way he was raised, escorted Dawn in the elevator to her floor. But that was as far as he was going to go. She'd already shot him down once tonight. He wasn't going to give her the opportunity to do it again. Stepping out ahead of her, he propped his foot to keep the doors from closing, and glared at her backside as she walked to her apartment. Bitch...

But then at her door, fumbling with her keys, she suddenly dropped her purse and doubled over holding her stomach, and he was off the elevator in a flash and at her side.

"Dawn! What's the matter?"

"It's my stomach, Randy," she said, holding onto him and trying to straighten up. "I told you. It's killing me."

He bent down to get her purse. "Do you still have your appendix?"

She shook her head.

"What did you eat today?"

"I don't know. The same as usual."

When Randy took her keys and unlocked her door, she walked in past him and straight to the couch.

He sat down next to her. "Here, let me see."

"No," she said, and wouldn't let him touch her.

"Dawn..." He pulled her hands away and gently felt around her stomach and her sides. "Does it hurt here?"

She nodded.

"And here?"

She nodded again. "Everywhere." She'd broken out in a sweat, and with the next wave of pain, leaned forward and buried her face in her hands.

"Dawn."

"Go away. Please. Go home."

"No. Listen." Randy hesitated, breaking out in a sweat of his own. "Is there a chance you might be pregnant? Because if you are, you could be..."

"No."

"Dawn?"

"I said no."

He felt the side of her face to determine if she had a fever. "Maybe you're coming down with something."

"No, I think it's the fruit."

"What?"

"The bananas. I think I ate too many of them."

Randy stared. "How many did you eat?" She'd eaten two that he knew of.

"Eleven I think."

"Eleven?"

"Maybe twelve."

"What?" Twelve bananas? Randy started to laugh, but then she looked up and he quickly attempted a very serious expression. "Had I known though," he said, "I could've left you back at the Durans' and..."

Dawn shook her head. "Randy, please. Granted, this may be a lot of things, but certainly not funny. So if you don't mind..."

Randy smiled. "Fine. Are you going to be all right?"

When she nodded, he stood and still smiling, tilted her chin up and kissed her. "Do you have a hot-water bottle?"

"No, just an ice bag."

"You don't need ice," he said, and thinking about how ridiculous this was, he started laughing again. "I can't believe you would eat that many."

"They were supposed to help. Tom bought them for me," she said, in her defense. And this struck Randy as even funnier.

"Now that I can believe!"

Dawn rolled her eyes.

"Goodnight, Randy."

"Goodnight, dear."

Chapter Fourteen

When the alarm went off the following morning, Dawn stared at the clock as if it were a cruel joke. Up half the night with cramps, before any relief whatsoever, it seemed like only minutes ago that she'd finally nestled in for some rest.

Fortunately, once she was wide awake and had made her usual stop at the coffee shop, she started to come around. She stopped to talk to Charlie at the guard shack, then walked on to the barn, and was surprised to find Ben hadn't arrived yet. "Where is he?" she asked Tom.

He glanced at his watch. "I don't know."

Ben was never late. Ever.

"Where could he be?"

"Maybe he's having trouble with his truck."

Ben showed up about fifteen minutes later, complaining about going to three all-night convenience stores before he found what he wanted, and handed Dawn a small brown paper bag.

She looked inside and sighed. It was a bottle of Kaopectate. First Tom and his bananas, and now this.

"Take some now," he said, "and some more in a couple of hours. Read the directions."

Dawn nodded, thanking him, and put the bag in her purse. The morning schedule followed its customary pattern from there. Beau's stall was stripped, while Tom hand-walked him. The horses that tracked filed in and out from bath to walking machine. And along the way, Miguel stopped by with his agent. They wanted to be named on Cajun the next time he ran.

"Johnny rides him," Ben told them.

"I know," the agent said. "But we think we fit the horse better and can give him a better ride."

"Better than what? He win last time out."

Dawn smiled in passing. A race won is always a win to a racetracker, whether it be last year, yesterday, today, or tomorrow. Always in the present. Always in the now. A race isn't won, you *win* it.

Several other agents came by then to check on their respective mounts. Gloria breezed in and out. And Dave arrived bearing donuts.

"Yes!" Dawn beat Tom for two out of the three custard-filled. He got his hand on the third just as she reached for it. They pushed and shoved at each other, laughing and threatening. Ben in turn, threatened both of them. And when this routine had run its course, the four of them sat down with fresh cups of coffee.

Beau meanwhile, pawed and carried on, but was ignored. Any attention would only make him worse.

"How is All Together doing?" Dave asked.

"Good," Ben said. "Training like a pro. At this rate, she'll be ready for the track in a couple of weeks. That's if I can get a stall for her."

"What?" Dave frowned. "With her breeding, I'd think they'd make one for her."

Ben shook his head. "Don't forget where you're at. They don't operate that way around here. Not even if I had Secretariat. It's not the horse, it's the asses you have to kiss over there." He nodded in disgust in the direction of the secretary's office. "And I don't kiss asses."

"No, that's what you have me for, old man," Tom said. "I kiss enough asses for ten barns. Don't you worry, we'll get her in."

They all laughed.

"Politics," Ben said. "Politics."

Dawn walked up to the kitchen a little while later to phone Linda, and got back to the barn as Tom and Ben were leaving to go enter a horse. No sooner had they gone, Johnny stopped by looking for Ben.

"Sorry, you just missed him," Dawn said.

"Shit."

"Can I help you with something?"

"No, I wanted to talk to him about riding some of his other horses."

Dawn towered over the young man. "Don't you have an agent?"

"No," he said, smiling shyly and looking down at the ground.

"Don't you think you should?"

Johnny shrugged. "All the good ones are taken. Sanchez is going to Hollywood Park and his agent said he'd take me on when he leaves, but that's not for a while, so..."

When he stood there and just shrugged again, Dawn started past him. "Well then, if you're going to do this yourself, maybe you should stop by sooner next time."

He followed her into the tack room. "I couldn't. I was galloping horses till the track closed."

"Horses you ride?"

Johnny nodded at first, but then shook his head. "Some. They say they'll ride you, but they always tell you that in the morning."

"Do they pay you to exercise them if they don't?"

"Yeah, right. Every day and twice on Sunday."

Dawn smiled. Johnny wasn't seventeen yet and already sounded like a seasoned veteran. "You want some coffee?"

"Thanks." He poured himself a cup and taking a sip, eyed the box of donuts.

"Help yourself," Dawn said.

"Thanks, but I gotta make weight."

Dawn nodded.

"Will you tell Ben I was by?"

"Sure."

Randy was next to pay a visit, and found Dawn leaning back in a chair with her feet propped on the tack trunk, catnapping.

"How are you feeling?"

She smiled sleepily. "Much better."

He leaned close and kissed her, and when she didn't pull away, kissed her again. "So are we still on for spaghetti tonight?"

"Uh...no, not tonight," she said. "I forgot about..."

He should've known. "Okay, I'll play your little game. Why not? Is your mysterious aunt coming to town?"

Dawn laughed. "No, what I was going to say was, I don't know why I agreed in the first place. I hope it doesn't jinx us. Ben always treats dinner when Beau wins and we always do steaks at The Rib."

"I see." Randy turned to walk out. "Well, have a nice time."

Dawn reached for his hand, stopping him dead with the very lightness of her touch. "I was hoping you'd join us."

"Isn't it a private party?"

"No." She shook her head. "So will you come?"

Randy hesitated, looking at her, and glanced away. "It's not exactly what I had in mind."

Dawn smiled, her fingers tightening ever so slightly around his. "It'll break up early. Ben doesn't like to stay out late, his farm's a good drive from here."

Was there a promise in that? A promise they'd be together? Randy found himself searching her eyes. "You sound pretty sure he's going to win."

"Positive," Dawn said, gazing at him. "Did you hear from the Durans?"

Randy nodded and sat down. "I called them this morning." What's this look? "The mare's fine. No foal." He paused, her expression going right through him.

Tom and Ben returned just then, with Tom talking a blue streak. "The fucking narcs are in the jocks' room arresting them left and right. It's all over the secretary's office."

Randy shook his head. "Who'd they get?"

"I don't know, half of 'em are on one thing or another. Shit, Fred Turner fell off his horse after a race the other day and asked the pony girl, 'Where am I?' Can you fuckin' believe that? And Lucy don't lie."

Ben motioned for Randy to get up out of his chair, and sat down with a heavy sigh. "I sure as hell hope Miguel's straight."

Tom chewed on a toothpick. "Who are you going to ride if he ain't?"

Ben peered over his glasses. "Now how silly is that? You just got done telling me you don't know who got busted, so why would I try to pick out someone now?"

Tom bobbed his head. "Good point," he said, and glanced at Dawn. "Did you eat all your bananas?"

When she nodded, Randy had to look away to keep from laughing. Seeing this, Dawn took him by the arm and headed outside. Ben called after them. "Join us for dinner tonight, Doc?"

Randy thanked him, said he would, and Dawn walked him to his truck. He got in, but left the door open so he could pull her close. She smiled, and with that look in her eyes he thought he'd seen earlier.

"What are you thinking about?" he said. "Right now?"

Dawn hesitated, allowing him to pull her closer. "I was thinking about your facial features."

"What?"

Dawn laughed. "I'm serious. They're perfect."

Now it was Randy who laughed, and blushed as well.

"Did you ever have a beard?"

"In college once. Why?"

Dawn shrugged, turning his face from side to side with her fingertips. "I'll bet you'd look good in one." She kissed him lightly, brushing her lips against his mustache.

He smiled. "What time's dinner?"

"Right after the races. We go from here."

At the call for the third race, Beau was put in the ice tub, and his antics began. He sloshed and splashed, twisted and chewed the shank, and stretched his neck as far as he could to try and chew on Dawn's boots, first one, then the other. Then he sloshed and splashed some more. At the ten-minute call for the eighth, Ben started over to the grandstand. Tom put run-down patches and Vet Wrap on Beau's back legs. He and Dawn took him out of ice then and wrapped the cloth bandages that had been soaking in the tub, around his front legs. The bridle and rinsing his mouth came next, and they headed to the paddock.

Tom stayed out on the track with Red, while Dawn led Beau in, announcing his arrival as they passed the paddock judge. Ben was waiting for them in the fifth stall. He motioned to the jocks' room. "They arrested two of them. It's hard to believe that's all."

Beau took his usual stance, muscles quivering as the valet laid the saddle across his back, and kicked out sharply when his tattoo was checked, not once, but twice this time.

The jocks' room door opened and out came Miguel, uncharacteristically first. He walked straight toward them, nodded to Dawn then Ben, and reached for the reins.

Ben stood back, watching him as he tied the knot. He'd already given him instructions about the race, nothing more needed said. And yet... When Miguel pulled tight on the reins and let them rest on Beau's neck, Ben reached over and picked them up. The knot was tied too far to the one side, the left rein being at least five inches longer than the right. He tapped Miguel on the shoulder. "Look at me."

Miguel turned to face him, but seemed to be looking past him, his eyes glazed over.

Ben waved to the paddock judge, and when he walked over, took him aside. "Find out who's in the jocks' room. I need a rider. Miguel's not fit to ride today."

"What?"

Miguel started to protest, but Ben wouldn't hear any of it. "If you want a scene, fine," he said in an angry whisper. "Otherwise, go back to the room. No, better yet, go to a hospital and dry out." He turned his back to him, Miguel walked away, and Ben looked at Dawn. "The son of a bitch is higher than a Georgia pine."

The paddock judge returned and gave Ben a list of who was left in the room, adding that they all wanted the mount. Ben stared off, thinking, and made a quick decision. "Send me out Johnny."

"You won't get the weight allowance."

"Goddamn it, Jack, I know that! Just get Johnny out here so we can warm up."

By the time Johnny came out the room, still fastening his jockey silks, the other horses were out on the track. Tom came through the paddock entrance astride Red, with an anxious look on his face. Circling from the other end, he came up in front of the stall just as Ben gave Johnny a leg up. He reached for the lead from Dawn and nodded to Ben as he led Beau out.

Dawn took her place on the fence, with Ben standing close beside her. It was three minutes to post as Johnny urged Beau into a slow gallop to warm up. Randy drove up and parked his truck by the track kitchen, got out, and sat on the hood to watch the race. Two minutes to post.

Miguel lay on a cot in the jocks' room, trying to remember how many downers he took, and if he took enough uppers. The narcs had taken the room by surprise. And he, being no exception, had downed the pills he had stashed in his locker, and was clean. All he had to do was remember to throw them up when the narcs left.

"They're at the post! And they're off! Taking the early lead is Beau Born. Second is Bold Kazar, and a length back is Perfect Crime. Followed by..."

The crowd started cheering as Beau lengthened his lead down the backside, running comfortably on his own.

"Approaching the turn, it is Beau Born by five. Perfect Crime is moving up to challenge Bold Kazar for second."

Dawn leaned as far as she could to try to see for herself.

"At the head of the stretch, it's Beau Born out by ten."

Ben glanced at the tote board. The fractions Beau was cutting indicated he should finish drawing away. Easy. But then the pack started to come on.

"In the middle of the stretch it is Perfect Crime taking over second and closing. Beau Born is out in front by six lengths."

"Come on, Beau," Ben whispered. "Come on."

"With a sixteenth of a mile left to go, it is Perfect Crime challenging the leader. Bold Kazar dropping back to fourth. Fox Cleff has taken over third. And as they approach the wire, it is Beau Born and Perfect Crime! Head to head!"

Dawn held her breath.

"Beau Born and Perfect Crime!"

"Come on, Beau. Come on."

Johnny reached down and out with his whip, driving, connecting with each blow, pushing with his hands.

"It's Beau Born and Perfect Crime at the wire!"

Dawn jumped down off the fence and grabbed hold of Ben's arm. "Did he win it?"

Ben shook his head, sounding breathless. "I couldn't tell. I think he held on."

"Ladies and gentlemen, there is a photo for win and place. Please hold all your tickets."

Randy leaned on the rail, watching as Beau passed in front of him, having jumped off his truck to get a closer look at the stretch run. Beau pulled up on his own, at least a hundred feet from Tom and Red. Johnny waited for them, and they turned and headed back to the grandstand. When they cantered past Randy, Tom called to him, "Johnny thinks he hung on!"

Ben and Dawn were out on the racetrack waiting. Beau was the last to return. Perfect Crime's trainer circled his horse in front of the gap, waiting for the numbers to be posted. Ben watched closely as Beau approached, studying his legs as each hoof hit the ground squarely.

The photo sign went dark, and the number five was posted in first place. It was official. Beau Born had hung on to win.

"All right!" Johnny waved his whip, looking up at the stewards' box as Tom led them into the winner's circle. Everyone took their places for the picture. Johnny dismounted then, glancing at Ben before he walked over to weigh in. He looked at him again as he started toward the jocks' room, wanting to say something to him, but knew better, and gave a thumbs up instead. In the jocks' room, Miguel lay on a cot, in a coma.

Dawn headed for the spit barn while Tom took Red back to their barn to get Beau's halter and shank. Ben stopped to talk to a friend for a moment, a trainer called Big Ralph, then headed back to the barn himself. Slowly.

Beau got an extra sudsy soap bath, which he shared with Tom and Dawn. The two of them laughed and joked. Tom did his Mohammed Ali impression, calling Beau the greatest horse of all time, each version slightly different from the last.

"Sharp as a buzzard and swift as a bee."

Randy drove down to the Miller barn and got out of his truck, watching them, well within hearing distance. It would have been nice to be able to join them, but it wasn't allowed. The only time a veterinarian graced the spit barn was when paged, and on record. Emergencies.

Dawn stayed with Beau to cool him out, and Tom walked back to their barn. When he saw Randy, he hailed Beau's tack in triumph.

"Was that fucking close or what?"

Randy smiled and waited until he came closer to ask, "How is he?"

Tom shook his head. "I don't know. He seems..." He glanced over his shoulder. "The way he pulled up had me a little concerned. But then..."

Randy nodded, concerned himself with how he'd eased up coming down the stretch. "Maybe he just ran out of air."

Tom smiled hopefully, and both fell quiet as Ben started down the shedrow. He, too, appeared to have run out of air. Randy shook his hand, congratulating him, and Ben smiled a tired smile, then took his handkerchief out to wipe his brow, and Randy turned to leave.

"You'll be back here in time to go to dinner, won't you?"

Randy nodded. He'd be back within the hour, he told him. Tom headed down to Red's stall to untack him, and came back a few minutes later to find Ben bedding down Beau's stall.

"I'll do that, old man. What the hell?"

Ben shrugged with his back to him, said he was perfectly capable himself, and Tom walked on, grumbling about what a pain in the ass he was. Ben made several trips to the hay room to get more straw, finished, and sat down and mopped his brow again. Tom looked up from cleaning the tack and nodded to Johnny when he appeared in the doorway.

"Ben?"

Ben hadn't realized he was there, and turned as Johnny hesitated. "I want to thank you for naming me on Beau Born. I know he's your big horse, and the confidence you placed in me..." His voice cracked, and he glanced away. He hadn't just won a race, only the second of his career. He'd won on one of the finest racehorses Nottingham Downs had ever seen. A dream come true. "I uh...I just want you to know how much I appreciate it."

"Ah!" Ben said. "He is my big horse and he run big. But I got me a good ride too."

"Thank you." Johnny cleared his throat and hesitated again. "I was afraid they might get to him in the stretch."

Ben's face reddened as he turned and stared at the condition book on his desk. "He came up short, that's all. It's his first time out this year."

Johnny glanced at Tom, an awkward moment of silence following. Ben finally looked at him again, a natural lightweight if he'd ever seen one. Short, a little homely. "What's on your mind, son?"

Johnny drew a deep breath. "I know I'm just a bug and all," he said, referring to his being an apprentice. "But he had trouble in the turn. I know I don't know him that well, but..."

Ben nodded, sparing him. "I know, son. I saw the fractions. I know that horse like the back of my hand. He was stopping." He looked at Tom a second. Tom knew it too. "But you brought him home," he said to Johnny. "And I'm proud of you. You did good."

Johnny smiled, but then turned away, tears filling his eyes, and Ben stood up and patted him on the back. "You're going to be one hell of a jock. I only pray you stay as honest as you are now."

Johnny nodded, and had to clear his throat to speak. "They took Miguel away. He's unconscious."

When Dawn returned with Beau, the first thing Ben asked was how much water he drank?

"One whole bucket and about a third of another."

Ben looked in at him, watching as he circled the stall several times and pawed at his straw. Finally, buckling his knees, Beau laid down and rolled. When he stood up, he shook violently, straw flying everywhere. Then he walked over to his hay rack, tossed his head before rooting into it, and came out with a mouthful. It was then that blood started trickling from his nose. Ben stared as it dropped to the pale yellow straw. That's when Tom saw it. And then Dawn.

"Son of a bitch!" Tom said.

Randy walked up behind them, took one look, and judging from Tom's reaction, surmised Beau had never bled before. As Randy ducked under the webbing to examine him, Tom looked at Ben and shook his head. The old man was white as a ghost. "Well, that explains how he pulled up."

Ben nodded somberly. "And why he almost stopped at the head of the stretch."

Randy took hold of Beau's halter, raising his head so he could look up into each nostril. The hope at this point was for there to be a scratch or a cut responsible. But this was not the case. Though barely more than a trickle, the blood was coming from both sides. Beau was bleeding internally.

Ben drew a breath and tried to think straight. "Do we need to treat him, Doc?"

"No, I don't think so. It's about stopped." He let go of Beau, patted him on the neck, and walked out of the stall. "We'll just keep an eye on him for a few days. He'll give us a sign as to what extent..."

Ben looked at Dawn, and forced a smile as he shook his head and nudged past her into the tack room. "Listen. Come on now. We just won a race. Let's not act like somebody died." He sat down and looked from one to the next as they all filed in behind him. "Today we're winners. And that's what racing's all about."

He stared down at the floor a second. "Do him up, bran mash him, and we'll come back and check on him after we celebrate his win. Go on. Because by golly, he gave us a performance worth celebrating." When he reached into his pocket for his handkerchief, Dawn had to turn and leave.

She walked over to Beau's stall and looked in at him, remembering the first time she'd seen him. He seemed so quiet now, unlike the Beau who came back from a race eager for his bran mash and pawing his stall with impatience. She stroked his neck, more in awe of him now than ever.

In spite of Ben's insistence they get in the mood to celebrate, they remained somber. Ben said he'd ride to the restaurant with Randy, insisted on it in fact, because he wanted to talk to him. And Tom rode with Dawn. It was his first time riding in the Jaguar, so he made a big deal of it, wiping his feet and dusting off his jeans.

"It's kinda cute," he said, patting the dashboard. "Too small to screw in though."

Dawn laughed, and so did Tom, but then they both grew serious again. "Ben's taking this a lot harder than he's letting on," Tom said.

"I know." Dawn glanced at him. "But isn't there something they can give him?" she asked, meaning Beau.

"Sure, there's lots of things, and they all have side effects. Besides, the stuff that's really good, only works for a while, and you only treat the problem, you don't fix it."

Dawn stared at the road.

"Nothing's for sure. And I may be wrong, but knowing the old man like I do, I don't think he'll try any of it. Especially on Beau."

They were quiet for a while, sitting at one light, then another. Dawn glanced in her rearview mirror. "Does Ben look all right to you?"

Tom shook his head. "Don't worry too much about him though. He's a tough old cuss."

"I know," Dawn said. "But I still do."

Tom nodded, looking out his window. So did he.

Inside the restaurant, seated, and coming as no surprise, Ben announced Beau had run his last race. "As of today, he's retired." He'd weighed the options Randy had supplied, back and forth, and always of the opinion, "Think long, think wrong," he was going with his gut reaction. Racing Beau at this stage was not worth the risk. Not with breeding in his future, and the possible consequences.

"He's trying to tell me he's done, and I'm listening. Don't look so sad...it's going to be okay. He went out a winner and that's the way to go. May we all be so lucky."

Chapter Fifteen

Beau was lazily eating hay when they returned to the barn to check on him. It was dark out, and from all appearances, he seemed bored with their being there. Ben and Tom left, and Randy drove Dawn to the horsemen's lot to get her car.

"Finally," he said, putting his truck into park and referring to their being alone.

Dawn chuckled, then saddened. "I feel so bad."

Randy leaned close and kissed her. "Don't. He'll be fine." He kissed her again. "And you'll be fine, and I'll be fine..."

Dawn smiled.

"Let's go to my apartment," Randy said, touching her hair gently as he gazed into her eyes.

Dawn hesitated, her same old defenses surfacing, but now in his arms, found herself agreeing. "Okay. But I need to go home and shower first."

Randy kissed her. "I have a shower," he said, his mouth against hers.

Dawn laughed. "No doubt. But still. Why don't we drop your truck off and go to my apartment so I can shower there. Then we can go back to yours." It sounded silly even to her, but all the same, this was the way it had to be.

"I liked my idea better," Randy said, holding her closer.

Dawn pulled away. "But I need clean clothes, clean underwear."

Randy sat back with an incredulous look in his eyes. "Why? What the hell are you going to need them for? Are we on the same page here?" Angered by her blank expression in response, he threw his hands up in frustration. "My God! I've never ever had this much trouble getting into a woman's pants in my life."

Dawn stared, then quickly, and before he could even move, she was out of the truck and storming toward her car.

Randy got out and chased after her. "I'm sorry," he said, grabbing her by the arm. "Honest, Dawn. I didn't mean it that way." He wished he could take it all back. He'd had her, he could tell by the way she'd kissed him. She wanted him as much as he wanted her. And he'd blown it. "Dawn, I'm sorry."

"Randy, please," she said, and yanked her arm free with such force, it surprised him. He'd barely had his hand on her. "Just let me go, okay?"

"I can't," he said. He shook his head, searching her eyes. "I'm sorry, but I just can't."

Dawn stepped back, then turned around, looked out at the road, and sighed. "Did it ever occur to you, that just maybe we aren't supposed to amount to anything? That maybe it's not in the cards for us."

Randy shook his head, responding honestly, "No, not for a second."

Dawn glanced at him, then stared away again, struggling inside. "I can't agree with your past, Randy. The casual way you regard such..." She trailed off, drew a breath, and turned. "And when you say things to remind me of it, then it's no longer gossip. It's who you are and it happened. I feel like you've got me numbered, and I've just been standing in line."

Randy stepped toward her. "You seem to think you know everything about my past and who I am, and yet I know nothing of yours," he said, desperately trying to establish a defense.

"What's the difference?" Dawn said, starting past him. "We're not going anywhere."

Randy stopped her, forgetting his own cause momentarily. "Why? Is there something in your past I wouldn't be able to handle either?"

Silence.

"I don't get it," he said. "Are you a virgin?"

Dawn sighed and shook her head. "You're missing the point, Randy. You're not even close. Your past is your business. I can even say I don't care. What's done is done. It's what you do from here on in that would..."

Randy swallowed hard, wanting so desperately to be with her, to hold her, to touch her... "You're all I can see, Dawn" he said, searching her eyes. "I can't say what's going to happen. I don't even know where it's headed. I just know you're all I can think about."

Dawn looked at him, the sound of traffic far in the distance. She just looked at him. Then without a word, she turned and reached for the door handle.

Randy gripped her arm to stop her. "Dawn, please. Give us a chance."

Dawn hesitated before raising her eyes to his. He had hold of her arm, but it was a fragile hold, a gentle hold. It would be hard to explain, but it meant everything in the world to her at that moment. This gentle hold he had on her.

He smiled faintly. "We'll do it your way. My apartment to drop off my truck, then to yours, and then back to mine. Okay?"

Dawn nodded. "Okay."

They dropped his truck off as planned. When they arrived at Dawn's apartment, Linda wasn't there. "Make yourself at home. I'll only be about ten minutes, maybe fifteen, so don't panic." Dawn started down the hall. "There's some beer in the fridge."

Randy smiled. "Are you sure I can't...?"

Dawn laughed, shaking her head. "No, you can't join me. And I don't lock the door, I have a phobia about it. So behave and stay out here. Okay?" She waited for him to nod in agreement. "Linda and I have a pact about men in the apartment; it's not allowed that way. So I mean, behave."

"Okay, okay," Randy said, holding up his hands. "I'll be a good little boy, I promise."

He went into the kitchen for a beer, came back into the living room, and walked around looking at the pictures on the wall. Eventually, he ambled down the hall, careful not to go near the room he knew was Dawn's, from the sound of running water. He walked past and stopped at the next one. The door was open so he glanced inside, then marveled.

It was the size of most people's living rooms and had a large canopy bed in the center, the bedspread a yellow silk. The walls, the pillows, and the curtains were also yellow, and even the assorted stuffed animals. There had to be at least fifty of them, all sizes, and perched all over the place. He smiled The room looked like Linda.

He turned and started back down the hall, and as he passed Dawn's door, stopped. For just a few seconds he gave thought to sneaking in to join her. But he didn't want to scare her. He slugged a mouthful of beer. Still, if there were a way to get in there, *without* scaring her...

He waited until she turned the shower off, then called to her. "Dawn, do you have any aspirin?"

"What" she shouted. "I didn't hear you. Wait a minute."

Standing in the doorway, for a split second, he felt guilty. But that passed as soon as she cracked the door and looked out.

"What did you say?"

Having come this far, it made no sense to turn back. "I said, do you have any aspirin? My head hurts." He looked sincere, making no move to enter the room.

"Yes, in here. No, wait a minute. There's some in Linda's bath...no, don't go in there, she'll kill me." She paused, thinking. "Just wait, I'll get you some. Just a minute."

Randy took another swig of beer to hide his smile, and shook his head at his own persistence.

"Come to the bathroom door. Here." Dawn stuck her hand out, waited for him to take the aspirin, and shut the door quickly. "I'll be out in five minutes."

Randy placed the aspirin on the bedside table, and looked around the room, as large as Linda's, but furnished quite differently. It was filled with patchwork quilts. Several of them hung on the walls along with numerous oil paintings of horses. A braided rug covered the floor. The bedside lamps were brass, resembling engineers' lanterns. The bed was a king-size four-poster style, blanketed with a multicolored quilted bedspread. A sweater and a pair of faded jeans were laid out on it. He sat down on the bed and finished the rest of his beer.

"I hit my head," he said.

From behind the door, Dawn asked, "Where?"

"In the kitchen."

"No, I mean where?"

Randy hesitated. "The back of it."

"Is it bad?"

"I'm not sure, I can't see it." He laughed to himself. "The bleeding's almost stopped."

Dawn opened the door and peeked out. "Are you serious? Let me see." She pointed across the room. "Get me my robe. It's on the chair right there."

Randy walked over to get it, careful to keep one hand on the back of his head. When near then, Dawn reached for it, but he held tight. "You don't really need to put this on," he said, "just take a look." He turned his back to her, waiting until she leaned out further, then took hold of her hand and smiled as he gently pushed the door open. Dawn was amazed, even knowing him by now, and shook her head as he let go of her arm and stepped back to look at her.

Digging deep into her Bask-Fioritto breeding, she stood tall, her head turned to one side as she crossed her arms under her bare breasts.

Randy stepped back further, and leaned against the vanity, taking a deep breath as he took a slower look.

"Well now that you've had your fun, get out of here and let me get dressed before Linda gets home." She reached for her robe.

Randy handed it to her, then ran his hand down her shoulder. "Are you sure you want to put this on?" He lowered his eyes again, and gazed back up slowly to hers.

She didn't answer, silent as he started to unbutton his shirt, and shook her head. "Randy, Linda and I have a pact," she said, her voice barely above a whisper as she watched him take his shirt off. "We can't do this." She stepped closer to help him undo the snap on his jeans.

Waking, Dawn reached for the digital clock next to the bed, and had to stare at it a few seconds before she could make out the time. It was two o'clock. She put it down softly, laid back, and gazed at Randy, sound asleep. He had one arm up over the back of his pillow, the other across his chest. Closing her eyes then, she thought about the way he'd made love to her. So slowly...so gently. As if she were breakable china. Whispering over and over, that he loved her.

Sighing deeply, she got out of bed and tiptoed into the bathroom. When she came back Randy was awake.

"Linda's going to kill me. Maybe worse," she said.

Randy pulled her close. "No, she won't. She's not coming home tonight."

"How do you know?"

"There was a note inside the fridge. I saw it when I got my beer. She said she'd be home tomorrow." He glanced at the clock. "Make that today."

"You knew all along, and yet you let me worry."

Randy smiled, tracing his hand down her hip. "You didn't act worried. Besides, it meant more to me that you'd break the pact and take a chance, not knowing she wasn't coming home." He kissed her, then pulled her on top of him.

"Well, I still have to tell her."

"Whatever." Randy smiled. "But in the meantime, would you do something for me?"

"Yes, what?"

"Take that braid out of your hair and make love to me. And take your time."

Chapter Sixteen

Dawn entered the tack room as Ben scratched Beau's name off the training chart and added All Together's. It stopped her for a moment. "At least we don't have to worry about a stall for her anymore," he said. It was final. Tom came in behind her with the latest scoop on the jocks' room bust.

"They only arrested the two, but from what I hear, they confiscated over five thousand dollars in drugs and paraphernalia. It was everywhere I guess. Under the cots, up in the ceiling tile, everywhere. And Miguel's still in a coma."

There, he turned his attention to Dawn. "So, how was the rest of your night? Did Randy score?"

Dawn shook her head in disbelief. Ben scowled at him. Yet he persisted. "What's the big deal? We're talking about a fact of life here. Forget it, I'll ask Randy."

Dawn stared, her face flushing. Would Randy tell him? She wondered. After all, what did she really know about Randy? The kind of person he was. What he stood for.

Tom noticed her reaction, and found himself quickly apologizing. "Hey, I was only kidding. I won't ask."

Dawn walked out past him. Tom turned to Ben when she'd gone, knowing better, and had a fit when Ben just shook his head.

"Jesus Christ! I'm not going to talk to anybody around here anymore. Everybody's so goddamned touchy."

Ben sighed. Tom pouted for hours after this. But all was well when Brownie arrived to shoe a horse. Randy showed up a few minutes later. He checked on Beau first, then walked down to the end of the shedrow, greeted Ben, Tom, and Brownie, and smiled at Dawn. "The Durans' mare foaled," he said. "I thought you might want to ride out with me."

"I'd love to," she said, lost in his eyes and forgetting all her doubts earlier.

"Speaking of foals," Brownie said. "I hear Bud's daughter Ginney's in a family way."

For a moment, a very quiet, still moment, no one responded. They all just stared. Ben broke the silence. "Well, I hope she's getting married."

"I don't know," Brownie said, shrugging. "Hear tell, she don't know who the father is."

Again, silence.

Tom cleared his throat "How pregnant is she?" he asked, his voice sounding odd.

Randy looked at Brownie, awaiting his answer with the same apparent interest.

Brownie laughed, amused at the expression on Tom and Randy's faces. "No more'n a couple of months, from what I hear."

Ben wasn't amused however, nor laughing, and stood shaking his head at Tom.

Randy spoke next. "Less than a couple of months?"

Ben looked at Randy now, and shook his head again.

Tom was staring at the ground and tapping his fingers together, trying to count weeks in his head. Randy, on the other hand, was trying to look nonchalant while doing the same.

"Son of a bitch."

The Durans' foal was a fine colt, chestnut, large and big-boned, and looked a lot like its mother as it hovered close to her side. "She foaled all by herself. We came out to check on her and there he was."

With Dawn and Mr. Duran's help, Randy managed to vaccinate him, dab iodine on the remaining stump of the umbilical cord, and give him a once-over. When turned loose, the foal charged around the stall on wobbly legs, shaking his head furiously and bouncing off his mother repeatedly in the act. The Durans, along with Randy and Dawn, stood outside the stall in awe.

Mr. Duran motioned for Randy to follow him then, and led him down to the end of the barn. Dawn stayed with his wife, both of them oohing and aahing whenever the foal moved, or nursed, or even so much as looked at them.

"I found that article I was telling you about," Mr. Duran said, motioning toward Dawn. "About her family."

Randy gulped. There was something about the way he'd said "family."

"I had my secretary go through some old publications." He pulled it out of his back pocket. "Here."

Randy took it from him, stared down at it a few seconds, then looked up. "That was nice of you. I think."

Mr. Duran chuckled. "Like I said the other day, I think you'll find it interesting."

Randy nodded and tucked it away, feeling a little like a twelve-year old who'd just been handed his first *Playboy*.

"It fascinates me," Mr. Duran said, "her being at the racetrack. It says in the article that she's a writer." He lowered his voice even more. "It doesn't make any sense."

Randy agreed. "A writer?" He glanced at Dawn, his eyes wide. "What does she write?"

"She freelances, I guess, and also writes for the local newspaper. It makes a comment about some feature she did on the racetrack."

Randy shook his head. They walked back then, and he and Dawn left after a few minutes. "Where to next?" Randy asked, motioning at the clipboard.

"It says here, you have to worm a horse at Ridgeway Stables, corner of Route 89 and Ridgeway Rd." She turned the clipboard sideways and read, "Jag is burning oil, check it out." She looked at him.

"Oh yeah, I noticed it this morning when you dropped me off at my apartment. You probably should have it looked at."

Dawn smiled. "Okay, I will." It was nice he'd make note of something like that. It gave her a rather warm feeling for some reason. But in the next instant, she remembered Brownie's news flash and chilled.

Randy reached over and took hold of her hand. "You're quieter than usual today. Even more so. What's going on?"

"Nothing." She shrugged and slipped her hand away. "Just thinking."

Randy glanced at her. "About what?"

Dawn sighed. "About Ginney what's her face."

Randy looked out his window. He'd figured as much.

"Well?"

He glanced at her again. "Well what?"

Dawn hesitated. "Could you be the father?"

Randy shrugged at first and then nodded.

Dawn looked out her window. "So what are you going to do about it?"

"Nothing."

"Nothing? Just like that?"

Randy's face reddened. "Yes, just like that." He raised both hands off the steering wheel. "End of subject."

"That's an admirable attitude."

"Hey look, Dawn. Me and about twenty other guys..." He trailed off, and drew a deep breath. "Let's just drop it, okay?"

They rode to the next three farm calls with little exchanged between them. Dawn wallowed in her thoughts about Ginney and her fatherless baby. Randy could think of nothing but Dawn, her writing, and how it all figured.

"Can you stop at a service station? I need to use the ladies room."

Randy pulled into the very next one, and while waiting, he too thought about Ginney. How stupid of her in this day and age to become pregnant. She said she took birth control pills. Her baby was her problem. Not his. His was in the ladies room, probably hating his guts.

He reached into his back pocket for the magazine. The article was marked. He started reading it, skipping parts as he glanced up repeatedly to see if Dawn was coming. "Oh my God," he said to himself. He skimmed the rest, saw Dawn, and promptly tossed the magazine out the window into the trash.

Dawn glanced at him as she got in. "I take it, it wasn't worth keeping?"

Randy shook his head, about fifteen questions running through his mind, started the truck and pulled back out onto the highway.

"Well...?"

He shrugged. "I didn't need it anymore."

Dawn looked at him. "What was it about?" She'd seen Mr. Duran hand it to him, and couldn't help being curious.

"There was an article in there he thought I might want to read." A millionaire? Why did she lie to me? Underworld connections? "I read all I wanted to."

Dawn nodded. "I don't know how you can do that. I keep everything, especially if someone took the time to save it for me. That's what libraries are for."

Randy laughed. "Yeah, well I file things. I don't have a library. I suppose you do."

"Of course," Dawn said matter-of-factly. "I'm a writer. And it's full of things I've saved."

Randy looked at her. "Is your library at your mansion?"

"The mansion? No, I sold it."

Randy couldn't believe this conversation. "So where is it then?"

"At the apartment."

"Right." Randy pulled off the road and put the truck into park. Now was as good a time as any to get this out in the open. He turned and faced her. "What do you write?"

"Everything."

"Why didn't you tell me that you're a writer?"

"It never came up."

Randy nodded and leaned back. "How did I know you'd say that?" Dawn smiled.

"So what are you doing at the racetrack?"

"I was writing a story for the newspaper and I fell in love with Beau...and Ben, and the racetrack." She paused, recalling, "I was like a little kid at the circus."

Randy smiled. She was so pretty. "When was this?"

"Last year," she said, and looked away.

Randy hesitated. Maybe he was making too much out of this. So big deal, she's a millionaire. The article did say there was never any *proof* of Mafia connections. "Do you see people at the racetrack?"

This question irritated Dawn. She knew exactly where this was headed. "Why don't you just say what's on your mind, Randy?"

"I am." He raised an eyebrow. "I was just wondering. Do you have any friends at the track?" Even the article had referred to her being a loner. "Does it bother you, my asking?"

Dawn sighed. "No. I don't have many friends, if that's what you're getting at, at the track or anywhere else. Lots of acquaintances. That's it. Linda's my best friend." She glanced out her window into the darkness, and edged ever so slightly closer to him then.

"Linda's your cousin."

"She's also my best friend, and if you have a problem with that, then it's your problem. Because that's just the way it is." She glanced out her window again. "Can we go? This road is scary."

Randy nodded, put the truck into drive, and pulled back onto the highway. They rode for a moment without talking. "So, are you writing something now?" Randy asked.

"Yes. I'm working on a novel about the racetrack. I've been working on it since I did the article last year."

Randy stared at the road, the yellow lines a blur. It all made sense now. She befriends a trainer. Rubs elbows with the jocks, agents, and owners. Learns the life from inside out. And now a veterinarian. How else to get that perspective. He shook his head, wondering if it was in the plan for them to screw, or if that was just a fringe benefit of the assignment. "How do you get your material for what you write?" he asked, clearing his throat. "Do you have to do a lot of research?"

Dawn smiled. "Of course you do. Otherwise it wouldn't be believable. Not to mention this being my first novel and..."

Randy nodded. It was all too clear to him now. He knew he was right. And he was pissed. It was a good thing he'd figured it out now, before he got more involved with her. He'd just go along for the ride. Why not? She's beautiful. Who wouldn't? She's not going to hurt me, he told himself, now that I know. But he was hurting already.

Dawn edged over a little closer to him. "Are we still on for pasta?"

Randy glanced out his side window, and looked at her. "Sure," he said, and even managed to smile. "We're only about ten minutes from there now."

As promised, the dinner was outstanding. It was a local mom and pop restaurant, the modest dining area packed with small tables covered with red and white checkered tablecloths. Empty Chianti bottles were used as candle holders, wax dripping down the sides. The pasta was homemade, cooked to perfection, the sauce sweet, and the best garlic bread Dawn had ever had.

"I didn't know they even had restaurants like this anymore. I can see why it's your favorite."

Randy smiled. Now was his chance. "I thought all you Italians stuck together. I can't believe you didn't know about this place."

Dawn stared at him for a few seconds. "I believe your kilt is showing, Mr. Iredell."

Randy's face reddened. He'd certainly had that coming, and never would have said anything in the first place, had he not read that article.

"Are we going to have dessert?"

Randy smiled, lowering his eyes distinctly. "I was counting on it. My apartment's right around the corner."

Dawn chuckled. "Are you insinuating I'm dessert?"

Randy reached for his wallet. "I plan on locking the door behind us and not letting you go home tonight."

"Randy, we've been through this."

Randy stood up. "I know, the underwear. I'm one step ahead of you. There's a K-Mart between here and my place. We'll stop and buy you some."

Dawn laughed.

"I'm serious," he said, leaning down to kiss her.

And he was. In the aisle at K-Mart, he picked out a pair of black bikini panties. "What about these?" he asked, holding them against her.

Dawn shook her head. "I don't like bikini style." She was looking at a plain white pair of briefs and checking the tag to make sure it was 100% cotton. "These will do."

Randy frowned, faked a bored yawn, and reached past her for a red bikini pair with a black heart on the front. "Now here's a nice pair. Let's get these."

Dawn held up the cotton pair. "Really, Randy. These are just fine. I always wear cotton. It's uh...comfortable."

"Comfortable? Who's worried about comfortable? We'll take these."

"And these." Dawn laughed when he stopped and picked up a frilly black bra. "Forget it," she said, and dragged him to the checkout.

His apartment was on the bottom floor of a hi-rise, third door from the lobby. Inside, Dawn toured each room, surprised at how clean everything was, until Randy reminded her that his sister Cindy had just left.

"When will she be coming back?"

Randy headed to the kitchen for two beers. "I'm not sure. She's applied at a local university. She misses her boyfriend too much when she's here."

Dawn nodded and stared at his bed, a waterbed. "What?" Randy said, returning and handing her a beer. "You've never slept on one?"

When Dawn hesitated, as if trying to remember, Randy grew angry with himself for asking. Just the thought of her on a bed other than her own. "Do you want a glass?"

"No, this is fine," Dawn said, and followed him into the living room. Randy turned the television on in passing, out of habit mainly, realized what he'd just done, and was about to turn it right back off, but Dawn stopped him.

"Leave it on. It's *Magnum P.I.*"

Randy shrugged and sat down next to her on the couch.

"This is one of my favorite shows."

Randy stared at the picture.

"You know, come to think of it, you look like him."

"Who?"

"Tom Selleck."

Randy laughed. "Yeah, right."

"I'm serious." Dawn smoothed his hair. "A little younger maybe, lighter hair."

"Right, just like him."

Dawn laughed. "All right, you don't look anything like him."

Randy glanced at her.

"But you do."

Randy shook his head, and downed a swallow of beer. "What kind of men do you like, besides uh..." He motioned to the television.

"You mean looks, or what's inside?"

"Both."

Dawn thought for a few seconds. "I like big men." When Randy raised an eyebrow, she smacked him. "Not that! I mean tall, muscular. And I like mustaches." She turned her attention to Magnum. "I love hairy chests, and lots of hair on a man's arms. Like yours," she said, spreading her hand over his forearm. "And men with blue eyes like yours." She smiled. "And I like a man who's macho enough to cry at sad movies, and who likes little puppies. And red and black bikini underwear."

Randy laughed, kissed her, and then put his arm around her. He hesitated then, not wanting to mess with the mood, that could have even been his opportunity to lead her down the hall. But he wanted to keep her talking. "What about the last man you were with?"

"You mean with, with?" Dawn looked into his eyes.

Randy nodded. "Yes. What was he like?"

"Do you really care about this, Randy?"

He nodded, and sat back, waiting.

Dawn sighed. "Well..." She shrugged, not knowing quite what to say. "He was tall, better-looking than me. And in the long run I guess, he expected too much."

"Like what?"

"Like everything. Marriage. Commitment."

"You weren't ready for marriage?" Randy said, his tone contrary to the anger building inside.

Dawn shook her head. "I didn't love him. I wasn't even sure that I liked him after a while."

Randy swallowed. "Then why in the hell were you seeing him?"

Dawn glanced at him and paused. I think we ought to drop this?" She could see one of these mood swings of his coming on. "Let's just..."

Randy shook his head. "No, it's okay. I want to hear this."

Dawn got up and walked across the room, and sat down in a chair across from him. "It was shortly after my parents died." She stared down at her hands. "I guess I was just lonely."

"And are you just lonely now, Dawn?" Randy asked, his face getting hotter and hotter.

Dawn looked up, smiling faintly. "No, not a bit. I've come a long way since then. Ben and Tom have helped me a lot there." She lowered her eyes to her hands again. "I've been able to work a lot of things out in my head."

"Like what?" Randy asked, taken aback and yet driven by the sudden sadness on her face. "What things?"

Dawn shook her head and glanced at him. "I thought we were talking about Dave. Let's not get into anything heavier, okay?"

"Dave...?" He motioned for her to continue.

Dawn sighed, staring off a second and resigning herself. "Okay, here goes. And then I want to drop it. I don't plan on throwing years of therapy out the window in one evening." She forced a smile, making it hard to tell if she was kidding or not. "When my parents died, there were just too many pressures. I couldn't get away from it. No one would let me." She stood up and walked over to the window, and looked out. "I hate to say it, but I guess I was just using Dave. So, I finally told him I didn't want to marry him and that was that."

Randy cleared his throat. "What did this Dave do for a living?"

Dawn turned and smiled; the strangest things interested him. "He was a stockbroker."

Randy nodded, swallowing hard. "Did you ever write about a stockbroker? Investing and all that?"

Dawn smiled again, then laughed. "As a matter of fact, I did. But I don't think it was one of my best works. Not enough research I guess. I learned a bitter lesson there."

Randy stared. He needn't probe further. When Dawn asked to use the phone to call Linda, he went for another beer. Bits and pieces of her conversation invaded his thoughts. "I broke the pact. Stop laughing, I'm serious. I couldn't help it."

Randy watched her as if he were in a trance, wondering how she could be laughing so easily, when just minutes ago, she looked as though she were going to cry. He wanted to hold her, but he also wanted to turn his back on her. Convinced he was just being used, played with, he would jump at any explanation to sway him otherwise, and was trapped.

Dawn hung up the phone, still laughing. "She doesn't believe me." She wrapped her arms around his neck and kissed him. "She thinks I'm trying to trick her."

Randy pulled her closer. "Do you trick her often?"

"No, that's just it. I never do anything wrong."

Randy smiled, just holding her, loving her in his arms, in his life. "How about we go take a shower. I don't know if I'll ever be able to do it alone again."

Randy lay awake for hours afterward, while Dawn slept soundly beside him. She had been so different this time. Not the fragile woman he'd made love to on her quilted bed. So free, so giving. He looked over at her, sleeping so innocently next to him, when just hours before, she'd fulfilled every one of his fantasies about her. He sighed, wondering if she'd ever been that giving, that demanding with another man. He could almost handle her being with another man, but he wanted to be her first at that.

He dozed for a few minutes, then woke again, haunting himself with thoughts of his own stupidity. How could he have fallen in love with a woman who was using him? He stared up at the ceiling, wondering which chapter of her book he was in.

Dawn snuggled closer and rested her head on his chest. "Why are you awake?"

"I just woke up," he lied.

She mumbled something then, something he couldn't quite make out.

"What?" he whispered. "What did you say?"

"I said, I love you."

He fell asleep shortly after that.

Gloria arrived at the track around ten, with the scent of lilac hovering around her like an invisible halo. She and Charlie had so much in common. He loved flowers, and so did she. He loved to eat, she loved to cook. He liked to pamper her, she liked to be spoiled. She loved to smell his pipe tobacco, and so did he. He was lonely without her, and she was lonely without him. But together, they were happy. In fact they'd spent every evening together since the night Ben introduced them.

"Yoo hoo!" she sang.

Dawn answered from Cajun's stall. "I'm down here, Gloria." She stuck her head out.

"Hi, sweetie. Is Ben around?"

"I think he's up at the kitchen."

Gloria nodded. "And how's Mommy's little Cajun?" she asked, kissing him on the nose. He twitched, and she kissed him again. "I'm going to go track him down, but I wanted to talk to you too, dear. I'd like you to come to my house for dinner tonight. I plan on inviting Ben and Tom, and of course Charlie will be there. And do bring your young man, he is so handsome."

Dawn smiled, just listening as Gloria went on. "It's for a very special occasion. Please say you'll come."

"I'd love to," Dawn said. "But I'll have to let you know about Randy."

"Oh, don't worry about getting back to me, just bring him. I always make enough. We're going to have roast chicken, wild rice stuffing, creamed peas, and bread pudding. They're all Charlie's favorites."

"I wouldn't miss it. It sounds delicious. May I bring something?"

"No, sweetie," she said, already starting down the shedrow. "Just you and your date. And make sure you help me talk Ben into it. You know how funny he can be about..." Her voice trailed off as she rounded the corner. She waved to Randy in passing, coming from the other direction.

He walked along and found Dawn, and sat down in the stall opening, stretching his legs out in the shedrow as she told him about the invitation.

"I'm on call," he said. "Raffin covered for me twice this week already."

Dawn nodded, and wasn't sure if she should push it. He could be so moody at times.

"What's the occasion anyway?"

"I don't know, but I have a feeling it's important," she said, pleased that at least he was giving it some thought.

"Is she rich?"

Dawn frowned. "Comfortable I suppose. But what does that have to do with it?"

"Nothing I guess. I was just wondering," Randy said, thinking, chapter seven...the owners.

Dawn shook her head. "You're complex, Randy. You know that?"

"Me...?" Randy laughed.

"Come on." Dawn crawled over next to him and nibbled on his ear. "She's having roast chicken, wild rice stuffing, creamed peas, and bread pudding."

Randy smiled. "Creamed peas?"

Dawn nodded.

"Okay, you talked me into it. But if I get paged, I'll have to leave."

"Good enough." Dawn kissed him and started to edge away, but Randy wouldn't let her.

"Last night, you told me you loved me."

"I did?" Dawn smiled.

"Yes. So do you?"

Dawn gazed into his eyes. "Yes, I think I do."

"You think?" Randy swallowed. "Last night you sounded sure."

Tom started down the shedrow right at that moment, shouting, "Hey you two!" He stopped in front of the stall and squatted down next to Randy, unaware of his poor timing. "Did you hear about Ginney?"

Randy shook his head, still looking at Dawn with an incredibly hurt expression on his face.

"She ain't pregnant anymore. Probably had an abortion."

Randy turned. "No kidding?"

"It's true. It's all over the track. And frankly, I'm glad. I thought all of us guys would have to go to the claim booth and shake for it before it was all over."

He laughed, and though it struck Randy as funny as well when put that way, he made certain not to even crack a smile, not with Dawn watching his reaction. And here came Ben, who with one look, started mumbling about no one ever working when he left the barn.

"No one." He sat down at his desk in the tack room, winded, and took off his hat to wipe his brow. He'd just made arrangements to have Beau shipped out and All Together shipped in a week from today. He wanted to give Beau a few days of ponying to try and bring him down slowly, while gradually cutting him back on his feed. If he shipped him home now as high as he was, he'd only end up hurting himself.

After catching his breath, he looked down the shedrow and smiled at Randy and Dawn, in the midst of what he would call courting games. He remembered his own courting days, and especially another day, after years of marriage, when he finally talked Meg into a playful romp in the hay with him. How long ago that seemed now. And yet so vivid.

Dinner at Gloria's was a feast, with everyone virtually stuffing themselves. Gloria suggested they retire to the living room for dessert, and Randy put his arm around Dawn.

"Do you know how to cook?" he asked.

Dawn frowned. "No, do you?"

"Not really." He shook his head.

The bread pudding dessert was warm and served with cinnamon ice cream and glazed pecans.

"I have died and gone to heaven," Tom said, and everyone laughed as he helped himself to seconds.

Then came the announcement. "Charlie and I are going to be married," Gloria said. Charlie just beamed. "The date is set for five weeks from today."

As everyone congratulated them, with hugs and kisses and handshakes, Randy, the relative newcomer to the group, watched Dawn in awe. She was so sophisticated, so intent and gracious as she listened to their plans.

"We want you all to be there. We will of course, be married in the parlor. I'm wearing lavender, and do so hope we can find lilac somewhere in season. It's Charlie's favorite flower, mine also. Did you know that?"

Dawn smiled, glancing at Ben and Tom.

"Charlie of course will wear white. It is his first marriage, so I think it's appropriate. Don't you agree, dear?"

Dawn nodded, smiling again.

"My lady friends are wearing lavender too, and will be carrying nosegays. I know they're terribly old-fashioned, but so are Charlie and me." She took hold of his hand. "The reception will be immediately after the ceremony, and of course, it will be in the garden. Oh, it will be so lovely."

Charlie patted her hand, then looked over at Ben. "I'd like you to be my best man, Ben, if you would?"

Ben nodded He'd be proud to.
"Wonderful," Gloria said, and rattled on.

During the drive home, Dawn hummed along with the radio. Randy on the other hand, had gone full circle with his mood again, and had become sullen. He had wanted to go to his apartment, suggesting that to Dawn. But she wanted to go home. She was tired. And she needed a good night's rest. Agreeing without uttering a word, he made a U-turn in the street, and headed in the opposite direction of his apartment.

Dawn moved over closer to him so she could rest her head on his shoulder, and soon dozed, which only added to his mood. At her apartment and just about to get off the elevator, he looked at her.

"Are you going to let me read this racetrack book?"

"Sure. It seems only fair, since you're one of the main characters."

She was teasing, but he had no way of knowing that, and took her much too seriously. "First," he said. "I want to read it first."

Dawn agreed, searching his eyes, and was about to add something else, when his pager went off. He asked to use her phone.

"Come on," she said, and slipped her hand in his. "You can use the one in my library. I want you to see it anyway." She led him down the hall to a spot near her bedroom, where she opened what he'd thought was a closet door.

She stepped back, he entered, looked around, and couldn't imagine it any other way. It was small, probably ten by ten, he estimated, with floor-to-ceiling oak book shelves covering three of the walls. The open wall was papered with burlap, where framed were Beau Born's win pictures. There was a large desk, probably mahogany he decided at a glance, a braided rag rug, and two brown leather winged-back chairs.

"I like it," he said. "It's perfect."

She motioned to the phone, and started out. "Do you want a beer?"

When he nodded, she left. He phoned his service then, jotted down the message, and hung up as he gazed about. On the desk, at his fingertips, lay the manuscript. He picked it up and leafed through it, but laid it down when he heard Dawn coming back.

"Was it an emergency?" she asked, handing him his beer.

"No, not really. A horse I gave a vitamin injection to is having a reaction. I'll have to swing by there on the way home." He looked around the room again. "This is really nice. I thought you were kidding."

Dawn shook her head, and that's when Linda came bounding down the hallway and in to greet them. Randy smiled. She was so unlike Dawn. They were both attractive, but the similarity stopped there. Linda wore a lot of makeup, Dawn wore hardly any. Linda was medium height, Dawn extremely tall. Linda wore her hair short, Dawn wore hers long and braided. Linda was amply built, with larger than average breasts, while Dawn was thin, with small, but what he thought were absolutely beautiful breasts. His mind wandered back to the night before, in his shower, lathering Dawn's hair and sifting it through his fingers, his hands all over her...

"Randy, would you like to join us?"

He smiled, wondering how long he'd been daydreaming, and glanced at Linda as they continued their conversation.

"So what's new with you and Harland?"

"Not much, we had dinner. He just dropped me off."

Dawn chuckled. "Does his cousin still think I'm a devil worshiper?"

"A what?" Randy said.

Linda laughed, told him the story, and even Randy laughed, surprising himself. But all too quickly, his preoccupation with the manuscript returned.

Linda noticed him glancing at it. "Did Dawn tell you you're in it?"

He looked at Dawn. "Yeah, she told me."

"It's great," Linda said. "Whenever I want to find out anything about you two, I just thumb through the pages, and it's all there. Speaking of which..." She turned to Dawn. "I still don't believe any of that crap about you breaking the pact. I don't know what you're up to, but I'm not buying it."

Dawn laughed.

"But just in case. What color are Dawn's sheets?" she asked Randy.

He shrugged. "I don't know."

"See? I knew it. Not only did it never happen, it's not in the book," Linda said, laughing. And out she went.

Dawn shook her head. "She's kidding, Randy. Honest."

Randy hesitated, then reached for her and pulled her close. It's Dawn he didn't believe. "I still want to read it."

Dawn put her arms around his neck and kissed him, then kissed him again, and promptly yawned.

Randy chuckled, and gazed into her tired eyes. "What chapter am I in?"

Dawn yawned again. "Ten or eleven. But really, I'm serious...it's not you."

Randy nodded. "How many chapters do you anticipate before it's done?"

"Twenty or so."

Randy smiled. At least he had some time left. "How explicit do you get with the sex scenes?" he asked, sliding his hands down over her hips and pulling her closer.

Dawn shook her head. "It's a book about the racetrack. Graphic sex has nothing to do with it."

"Does that mean I can get as raunchy as I want, and not have to worry about it being in print?"

Dawn smiled. She could feel him hardening against her. "Yes. I mean no," she said, and reminded him it was time to go. "Now..." she teased, "so I can write all this down."

Dawn had been asleep for hours when the phone rang and answered it only after eight or nine rings, and in a complete fog. "Hello?"

"Dawn, this is Randy. I'm sorry to wake you."

Even half asleep, his voice sounded strange to her. "What's happened? What time is it?"

"It's only four. I have to go home to my parents for a few days. Raffin's going to be covering my calls."

"Why?" Dawn asked, looking at Linda who'd heard the phone, and was standing in the doorway.

"I got a call from my mom. They had a fire, half the house burned to the ground."

"Oh my God," Dawn whispered, gasping. "Are your mother and father all right? What about Cindy?"

"Dad's hands are burned, pretty bad I guess. Mom and Cindy are fine." His voice cracked. "I have to see if I can be of any help."

"Can I do anything?"

"No, but thanks for asking."

"Will you give me your parent's phone number?"

"The phone's out. Mom called from the neighbors."

Dawn motioned for Linda to get her a pen and something to write on, repeating, "Randy, give me the number."

"It's 932-8150, area code 555. I love you, Dawn."

Dawn nodded, swallowing hard. "Give my thoughts to your parents. I'm so sorry."

"I know." Click.

Chapter Seventeen

Several days passed, with no word from Randy, and then a few more. In the meantime, Dawn took her car in to be serviced. Cajun won another race, the only horse in the barn to hit the board; three others were *also-rans*. Tom developed an itchy rash in his groin. And Ben started second-guessing his decision to retire Beau.

Sluggish for days after the race, at first there seemed no doubt. But now, even with having his grain cut and daily ponying, he'd come back to life and refused to settle down. He tore his stall up from dawn to dusk and, from all appearances, through the night as well, squealing, bucking, and charging his webbing. He'd taken to lunging out and trying to bite every horse being led down the shedrow. He even clipped Tom on the calf as he rode past on Red. And now, behind closed doors, he was literally climbing the walls.

"Put him on the walker!" Ben shouted. "Goddamn him!" Beau had every horse in the barn acting up as a result. Tom gave it a try, but couldn't even get him close, let alone hook him on with all the rearing, head tossing, and bucking and dancing Beau was doing. He all but pulled Tom's arm out of its socket twice, and had to be muscled back to the stall.

Johnny came down the shedrow right about then, asking if they had a horse they wanted him to get on, and Ben nodded. "Tack him," he told Tom, referring to Beau.

"What?"

"I said tack him."

Tom sighed, scratched his groin, and shook his head. "All right, but I'll gallop him. Johnny won't be able to hold him." He motioned for Johnny to go get Red. "You can pony me."

Johnny nodded. There was no dishonor for a jock to pass on a tough horse in the morning. They made their money in the afternoon and took enough risks then. Besides, that's what exercise boys and girls were for, stunt doubles so to speak, who usually weighed more and had more strength.

Tom started into the tack room for Beau's bridle and the saddle, but needn't have bothered. Ben changed his mind again. "Forget it! Go get Raffin! Get him to come down here and give him something to quiet him down."

In spite of the tranquilizer, the barn shook for hours from Beau's kicks and thuds. Enough was enough. Ben checked with the vanning company to see if they could ship him out today. They couldn't, but scheduled it for late the following morning.

Dawn was so excited about All Together arriving, she could hardly wait. She'd only seen her once at Ben's farm, and it seemed like ages ago. It also seemed like ages since she'd seen Randy. She walked across the road, stopped to see if the van was coming, and went into the ladies room.

Two young women were standing by the sink. At a glance Dawn thought one of them had been thrown, until she heard the other say, "You can't let him get away with this." The girl's left eye was nearly swollen shut, the flesh a reddish purple. Her friend had been wiping blood from the corners of her mouth, some still dried to her face.

Dawn walked toward them. "What the hell?"

"She's been hurt!"

Dawn stared. She could see that, obviously.

"It was a horse," the girl said, dripping blood from her mouth and dabbing at it with the back of her hand. "I uh...got kicked."

"Ginney, you did not!" her friend cried, in tears. "No goddamned horse did this!"

"Shut up, Julie!" She held a trembling hand to her mouth. "Just shut up! Okay?"

Dawn glanced quickly from one to the other, searching their faces. The swollen eye, the bloody lip, the torn clothing, the pain in their eyes. Even the smell. The scene was all too familiar. Especially the smell. "You've been raped, haven't you?"

Ginney backed up, shaking her head.

"Have you been raped?"

Ginney shook her head again, sucking her breath in. But then the tears in her eyes spilled onto her cheeks, and she nodded.

Dawn turned to her friend. "Go call the police."

Ginney objected, grabbing the girl's arm.

"Go!" Dawn insisted. "Tell them no sirens. Tell them to send a plain-clothes policewoman. Go!" She pulled the girl's arm free from Ginney's grasp and shoved her toward the door.

"No!" Ginney screamed.

The girl hesitated, looking back at Ginney from the door.

"He said he'd kill me! And he will!" Ginney turned to Dawn. "Please, you don't understand. He said he'd kill me. Please don't send for the cops," she pleaded, spitting blood. "It ain't the first time I've been fucked. The whole goddamned racetrack knows that."

Dawn shook her head. "Get the police..." she said, glaring at the friend. "Now!" She turned to Ginney only when the girl left and the door slammed behind her. "Fucked is one thing," Dawn said. "Raped is another." She hurried into one of the stalls, yanked at the tissue and when it only came off in single sheets, tore the role off the holder. She ran cold water on a wad of it, dabbed gently at the corners of Ginney's mouth. "Here, hold this."

Ginney obeyed, numbly.

Dawn ran cold water on another wad, squeezed the excess, and pressed it to her left eye. "Do you know him?"

Ginney hesitated, her chest heaving with each breath. "A little. Oh my God..." She gasped when Dawn dabbed at her battered chin. "They'll say I asked for this. I was coming on to him. But then he got mean and started smacking me around when I told him to stop."

Dawn wiped the dried blood from the side of her face and down her neck, and changed the compress on her eye.

"I know they're going to say I asked for this," Ginney sobbed. "I just know it!"

Dawn shook her head. "No, you didn't ask for this." She gripped her by her shoulders. "And he has to pay. He had no right. No one has the right to do this."

Within minutes Ginney's friend returned with Charlie, panting and in tears. "We called the police. Charlie told them like you said. You know, no sirens and stuff."

Charlie walked over to Ginney, tentatively, and stood back a moment, looking at her face. Then he shook his head and put his arms around her. "You're going to be okay, Ginney. You're going to be okay."

In less than an hour, Ginney, her father, and her friend Julie were on their way. Dawn had stayed with her until the policewoman came, and left only after being assured they were going to take Ginney to the hospital first.

Back at the barn, Dawn sat down outside the tack room, leaned forward, and braced her head in her hands. As hard as she tried to think of only now, what was happening now, the past kept haunting her.

Tom came around the corner of the shedrow, scratching his groin and chewing on a toothpick. "The filly's here," he said. "I just saw 'em pull in." A few minutes later, the van rocked to a stop outside the barn.

She'd definitely arrived. She whinnied and pawed, wide-eyed, tossed her head, and whinnied again. Again and again. As Tom put her on the walker, Dawn stood watching in awe. Next to Beau, she was the most beautiful horse she'd ever seen.

Beau was not to be outdone. He bounced and squealed and jogged all the way to the van, but there, transformed. He walked up the ramp like a pro, backed into the stall without the slightest urging, grabbed a mouthful of hay from the hay net hung to appease him, looked out the window, and that was that.

Ben told the van driver he'd be following him to the farm. The driver closed the ramp and climbed into the cab. Ben stayed until he started the engine, then without a word, turned and walked toward the parking lot.

Dawn noticed him leaving and was about to call to him, but Tom stopped her. He shook his head. "Leave him be. He'll get over it." Tom mucked out Beau's stall, bed it down, and put the filly away. She snorted and sniffed, rolled, snorted some more, pawed the corners over and over, and it would be hours before she settled down.

Dawn met Linda for lunch at the club, told her about the episode with Ginney, careful not to dwell on it, and went on to brag about All Together. Linda barely heard the last part. She knew how hard it must have been for Dawn to involve herself in what took place, regardless of how insignificant she tried to make her part sound.

"Are you listening to me?"

Linda nodded. "Still no word from Randy?"

"No. I can't believe it. Not even a post card. He probably married his high school sweetheart and has three children by now."

Linda laughed. "Dawn, it hasn't even been two weeks."

"That's easy for you to say, you have Harland."

Linda smiled. "That reminds me. I need to talk to you about him. I want to move in with him."

Dawn made a face, teasing. "Did you invite yourself or did he ask?"

"He asked. Honest."

They both laughed.

"A permanent thing?"

"I don't know. To see if we can get along. I'm so set in my ways, and so is he."

"Are you sure about this?"

"No." Linda shrugged. "That's why I'm doing it." She reached for Dawn's hand. "What about you? Are you going to be okay?" She hesitated. "Maybe Randy would like to take my place."

Dawn shook her head. "I don't think so."

Linda searched her eyes.

"So what's your mother going to say?" Dawn asked, diverting the subject.

"Nothing. I'm not going to tell her."

The two of them laughed again.

"At least not until I'm sure."

"Good idea."

Later that afternoon, Dawn ran the stalls and then sat down on the stoop by the tack room to watch All Together. She was the only horse not eating, and stood looking out her stall, first one way then the other. Back and forth.

Dawn smiled, remembering the auction. So many things had happened since then. She wondered how Beau would adjust, and how Ben was doing. He'd looked so sad leaving. Yet so positive, so determined in his decision...which to some was probably a bit drastic. You don't ever fall in love with them, she could hear him saying. She smiled to herself, thinking, yeah right. And it was then, as she looked up, that she noticed Ginney walking down the shedrow.

There weren't any tears in her eyes, but the face was as battered and pained as before. Dawn moved over to make room for her on the stoop and Ginney sat down.

"I uh, want to thank you for helping me this morning."

Dawn nodded, glancing at her.

"They arrested him." Ginney hesitated. "He's denying it though."

Dawn stared straight ahead. "You did what was right."

Ginney cleared her throat. "I wouldn't have done it, if you hadn't come in the john."

Dawn looked at her. "Are you okay? Did they treat you all right at the station?"

She nodded. "Yeah, they did. They took me to the hospital first. The nurses were really nice. I'm glad you told them to come in an unmarked car. I couldn't have gone in an ambulance or cop car."

Dawn smiled, touching her arm. "You'll be okay."

Ginney shrugged and then nodded. "I'm not sure what's next. You know, with him." Her voice cracked, and she looked away, her chin beginning to quiver.

Dawn hesitated. "You said you knew him. How well?"

"Well enough to be afraid of him. I'm gonna come and go with my dad." She glanced at Dawn, shaking her head. "I found out he's out of jail already. He's an exercise boy from Chicago. I've only known him for a few weeks."

Dawn nodded, and the two of them just sat there for a moment. Ginney stood then, turned, and self-consciously extended her hand. "My name is Ginney Meyers."

Dawn took her hand and gripped it gently, rising also. "I'm Dawn Fioritto."

Ginney bit her trembling bottom lip. "I'm glad to meet you."

"Me too."

They stood looking at one another a moment.

"Well, I gotta go. My dad's waiting for me at the barn." Ginney swiped a tear trickling down her face. "Thanks again for helping me."

Dawn nodded, watched her walk away, locked up, and went home. A letter was waiting for her in the mailbox. Unable to wait, she opened it and read it in the elevator.

> *Dear Dawn,*
>
> *Dad's hands are bad. I'm helping him and my Uncle rebuild the house. The neighboring farmers are helping too. Cindy's fine. My mom cooks all the time. Nobody's allowed to go hungry. I've talked to Raffin several times, he says all is well at the Miller barn. I hate to write. And for the life of me, I lost your unlisted phone number and I can't remember it. See you soon.*
>
> *Love, Randy*

Dawn unlocked the door, walked in, sat down on the couch, and read it again. This time she sighed. It was a nice letter, but he could've said more. She dug into her purse for his parent's phone number, dialed it, and hung up when she got a recording. It was still out of order. Resigned, she walked down the hall, into Linda's room, and sat on the bed and watched her pack.

"Are you taking any of your stuffed animals?"

Linda smiled sadly and shook her head.

"Not even Wittle?"

Linda laughed, then noticed the letter. "Who's it from?"

"Randy."

"Really?"

Dawn handed it to her, and reaching for Wittle, hugged the stuffed animal to her chest. Linda glanced at her and smiled. "I hope this means he'll be coming home soon."

Dawn shrugged. "If it doesn't work out with you and Harland, are you going to come back?"

Linda looked at her, with tears suddenly welling up in her eyes. "Oh Dawn...I'm really going to miss you."

Dawn nodded, her too.

"Why does it have to be this way?"

Dawn smiled. "Don't feel bad. We'll probably see more of each other now."

"Promise...?"

"Promise."

The next few days passed quickly. Dawn kept herself busy, and on the third day of Linda's new living arrangement, they met for lunch. With Linda so happy, it only made Dawn lonelier. Linda coaxed her into trying Randy's parents' phone number again. It rang, but no one answered. "At least it's working again," Dawn said. "I'll try him later."

Randy poured a cup of coffee and sat down next to his mother at the kitchen table. "Who was that?"

"I don't know, I didn't get to it in time. They hung up. Probably wrong number."

Randy sipped his coffee. "I think I'll head back tomorrow." The repairs on the house were almost completed. "Uncle Jimmy says he and Joe can finish up the siding and..." He hesitated. "What do you think?"

"I think you should. You've stayed too long already," she said, her smile showing the love and pride she felt for her first and only son. "I hope this hasn't hurt your practice."

Randy's father came into the kitchen and sat down across from them. His hands were still bandaged, but as of this morning, his fingers were exposed and healing well. "It feels good to be able to move them," he said, with a barely concealed wince when he tried to wiggle them.

Randy's mother smiled. "Randy's going back tomorrow."

His father nodded. "And it's high time," he said, and with his next breath, choked up. He rose and walked over to the sink, with his back to them. "You've been a great help, son. I don't know what we would've done if you hadn't been here." He sniffed loudly, then walked back over and put his arms around Randy, careful with his hands. "Yeah, it's time you got back to your work, and your own life."

Randy stared at the table, trying to swallow the lump in his throat, and couldn't. He nodded.

"Yep, it's time." His father sat back down across from him and glanced at his wife. "It's also time you tell us about Dawn."

Randy looked up. It was the first time he'd heard her name in weeks. It sounded strange, especially coming from his father. Dawn. He'd thought about her often, non-stop actually, but purposely avoided talking about her. He didn't want to give the impression he would rather be with her, and not here where he belonged. "What about her?" he heard himself saying, and sounding defensive. The mere mention of her name brought back all the old insecurities.

"Cindy tells us you've been seeing her pretty regular." His father watched his eyes. "So does this mean I'm going to get grandchildren out of you yet?"

Randy laughed. His father never quit. The eternal, underprivileged, having never been and still waiting, grandfather to be. "I was seeing her before I came home."

His mother smiled. "What's she like?"

Randy looked off, quiet for a moment. "She's beautiful, Mom...absolutely beautiful." He paused, smiling. "She's got hair down to here." He put his hand behind his back. "And she's got the greenest eyes I've ever seen."

His parents smiled. "I hear she's pretty tall," his father said.

Randy chuckled. "Yeah, and stands that way too." He tilted his chin, to show them how. "She's really something." He paused again and glanced at his watch. And when he looked at his mother and father again, waited for a sign. His dad nodded, and that's all it took. He ran up the stairs to pack.

Chapter Eighteen

Dawn couldn't sleep. Ben had scheduled All Together to work out of the gate three-eighths of a mile with two other horses. Today. She grew tired of lying awake staring at the ceiling, and got up and went into the kitchen to make a pot of coffee. She sat down in the living room to wait and listened to it perking. The apartment was quiet, too quiet lately. She turned the radio on, but couldn't find a station she was happy with, and turned it off. She'd showered last night, but hadn't washed her hair, so to kill time, she decided to wash it now. Four cups of coffee later, she left with her hair still damp and hanging loose to dry.

Randy had just taken a five-and-a-half mile curve, commonly called a detour. He'd had been making good time up until then with the hopes of getting to Dawn's apartment before she left for work. Not anymore. He glanced at his watch and headed for her favorite donut shop instead. With a little luck, he'd catch her there.

Dawn paced back and forth in front of the counter, unable to make a decision. Blueberry or cranberry? Cinnamon? What? Randy parked two spaces down from the Jaguar, got out and walked over next to it. From where he was standing, he couldn't see her. The windows of the shop were fogged from the ovens.

Dawn started out the door and saw a tall, bearded man leaning against her car. She stepped back, the blood draining from her face, and glanced at the clerk, about to alert him, when suddenly she did a double take. A truck. She opened the door. "Randy...?"

He smiled, shaking his head as he watched her walk toward him. Her hair was down, not in the braid, and hanging loose on her shoulders. When she reached him, he took the coffee from her, put it on the hood, wrapped her in his arms, held her tight and swung her around.

"I love your beard! I almost didn't recognize you!"

Randy put her down, leaned back to get a good look at her, and threaded his fingers through her hair. "And I love your hair. When did you start wearing it this way?"

"I didn't. It was still wet when I left. I'm going to braid it when I get to the track."

Randy bent down to kiss her. "God, I missed you."

Dawn nodded, the past few weeks fading away in his arms. "When did you get back?"

"Just now." He picked her up and swung her around again, watching her hair. "You are so beautiful."

Dawn laughed. "Put me down, you're making me dizzy. Come on, let's sit in the car. I want to hear all about your family." Inside, they each took a sip of coffee. Randy told her about the fire then and how it started, and about rebuilding the house.

"The hard part," he said, "was all the rewiring. It shorted everything. It all had to be done over."

Dawn listened intently, her attention averted only when she couldn't stand it anymore and had to touch his beard again. Touch him. Randy kissed her, and then kissed her again.

"Okay, so what's been going on here?" he asked.

Dawn smiled. "A lot. Linda moved in with Harland." Randy raised his eyebrows at that, but Dawn seemed not to notice. "Beau's at the farm and All Together's at the track. Ben is really pleased with how she's doing. Oh, and you were right, the Jaguar was burning oil. I had it tuned up and it's running super." She paused to take another sip of coffee. "Ben doesn't look well to me, but he gets mad when I ask him anything about it. Charlie and Gloria's wedding is just a few weeks away." She paused again. "And I have really, really missed you. I called your house yesterday but no one answered."

Randy smiled. "My mom did, but you'd already hung up. I had a feeling that was you. It was right after that when I decided to leave. I finished up what I had to and drove through most of the night."

"So your mom and dad are all right?"

Randy nodded. "They're fine. Dad's hands are going to be sore for a long time, but basically he's okay. That reminds me, I forgot to tell you, Cindy's getting married next weekend."

"You'll be going back then?" Dawn asked, her disappointment obvious at the prospect of his leaving again so soon.

Randy smiled, loving the look in her eyes. "Yes, and I was hoping you'd go with me. I want you to meet my parents, I think."

Dawn laughed. "I promise I'll try not to embarrass you."

Randy smiled and traced his fingertips down the side of her breast. "Can you take the morning off?"

"Not on your life. I can't. Didn't I tell you? Ben's scheduled All Together for a work out of the gate with several other horses."

Randy just looked at her, then glanced away. You should've known better than to ask, he told himself. You're not first in her priorities. Ever. And never will be.

Dawn sensed his mood change and started rambling in an attempt to head it off. "Cajun won and had two seconds since you left. Son of Royalty's in tomorrow. And you should see Charlie, he is so nervous about the wedding. While Gloria..."

Randy interrupted her. "What about you, Dawn? What have you been doing?"

She sighed. "I've been writing and eating a lot of Chinese food. That's about it."

"Oh?" Randy sat back. "And how's the precious book coming?"

Dawn hesitated and chose to ignore his tone. The best thing to do, she decided, was to get going before it got worse. "I'm having some trouble with it, writer's block I guess." She leaned over to kiss him, though he hardly warmed to it. "With you gone, what did I have to write about?"

Randy glanced away again, doing a slow burn, and looked back only when she touched his arm. "I really do love your beard, but right now, I have to go." She frowned when all he did was open the door and turn to get out. "Are you going straight to the track? Maybe you can catch her work."

Randy shook his head. "No, I'm going to go home and shower and maybe take a nap. I'll see you later." As he drove to his apartment, he argued with her in his mind. Back and forth. At one point, he cursed her so vehemently, he smacked the steering wheel and startled himself when the horn sounded. Apparently, he'd fallen asleep.

After the allowed time to clean up breakfast, the horses' feed tubs were pulled, and training began. The walkers as usual were done first, two horses tracked then, and were bathed and cooled out. One ponied. He got a bath too. And Dawn was glad to be busy. Every time she thought about All Together's upcoming work, her stomach started turning flip-flops. Finally the time came. Johnny was due any minute.

"Whew! Talk about hustling ass," Tom said. "I've been working my chapped balls off. You'd swear it was a race. The whole damned track's talking about it. We ought to charge admission."

Dawn smiled and stroked All Together's forehead, as she stood in front of her stall and held onto her reins. She was tacked and ready to go. Randy came down the shedrow then and walked right past her as he and Tom greeted one another.

"Hey, Doc. You're back."

Randy shook Tom's hand, smiled, and glanced at Ben as he rose from his chair.

"Good to see you back," Ben said. "How are things at home?"

"Everything's fine."

"House all back to normal?"

Randy nodded. "Just about."

Tom motioned to Dawn. "Yeah, well she ain't been the same since you left."

Randy glanced at her, then followed Ben into the tack room. Tom, never one to let anything pass, ambled over to Dawn. "Odd how Randy didn't say hi to you, don't you think?"

"I saw him earlier," Dawn replied, regretting it as soon as she said it.

"I thought as much." Tom nodded knowingly, and headed out to the road between the barns to see if Johnny was coming.

Randy talked to Ben a moment and was just about to leave the tack room when he noticed Ginney walking toward Dawn and calling her by name. He backed up, stared, and sat down next to Ben, then looked out again, as if he couldn't believe his eyes. He touched Ben on the shoulder, pointing to them, but Ben just shrugged. He never cared for the Ginneys at the racetrack and wasn't too thrilled with Dawn's involvement with the girl, noble as it was, and was keeping his opinion to himself.

Randy crossed his arms and sat back, listening.

"We're working one of my dad's colts with her," Ginney said, reaching up to straighten All Together's forelock. "Goddamn, she's pretty."

Dawn smiled. "Has the colt run before?"

"Last year as a two-year old. He win all three races. But then he popped osselets so we pin-fired him and sent him home. He was shin-bucking too."

Randy stared at the floor in amazement, face in his hands, elbows on his knees. What gives? They're talking like they're old friends.

"How's he doing this year?"

"Good, real good. This'll be his third work. Dad's schooling him out of the gate to see how he'll behave. He was a real son of a bitch last year." There was a momentary silence, before Ginney said, "I go to court Friday."

"You're going to be fine," Dawn assured her.

"I'm scared shitless."

"Do you want me to go with you?"

"Thanks, I'd really appreciate it." Ginney smiled and then shrugged. "Well, I guess I'll see you up at the track."

Randy rose to his feet and rubbed a tense ache in the back of his neck. He'd just heard the whole conversation, and still it didn't make any sense. Dawn and Ginney friends? Dawn, who worried about clean cotton underwear, and Ginney, who most of the time didn't wear any.

"Ben, what's this all about?" he asked, practically whispering.

Ben glanced at him. "Ginney was raped."

Randy just stared a few seconds, then leaned closer. "What's that got to do with Dawn?"

Ben shook his head. "You're going to have to ask her that," he said, thinking about how if Randy were his son, that now might be the time to sit him down for a good talking. It was obvious he was uncomfortable because of his relationship with both Dawn and Ginney. But he decided to remain quiet, thinking Randy just might learn more by stewing a bit.

"Johnny's here!"

Ben gladly accepted a ride up to the racetrack in Randy's truck. Dawn chose to walk; she was too nervous, and followed the filly. Randy knew he should probably start making rounds, but decided if it waited this long, it could wait a few more minutes. He wasn't about to miss this.

Tom was right. It was an event.

Dawn stood on the bumper of Randy's truck, bracing herself by holding onto his shoulder as she strained to see. The gate was at the end of the track, in the gap at the head of the stretch. Ginney and her father stood close by, along with thirty or forty other trainers and grooms anxious to watch.

The first horse loaded easily, All Together was loaded next, then Bud Meyers' colt. The colt went in quickly, banged his chest against the padding at the front of the gate, reared, and was brought back down by one of the gate crew.

"Spring the latch..." Dawn whispered, squeezing Randy's shoulder even tighter.

Ben shook his head. "Make her stand." She'd been schooled thoroughly in the gate on the farm, but had a nervous streak in her. "Make her stand."

All Together pulled back, digging in with her hind legs as she tossed her head, connecting hard with the side-bars again and again.

Randy glanced at Ben. "She's a bitch."

Ben nodded.

One of the men on the gate crew jumped from stall to stall, calling out names, banging on the gate with his feet, making as much clatter as he could, while another banged on the poles in the back. Noise, noise, noise, that was the purpose. Prepare them for anything. More noise. Then all of a sudden, everything got quiet, eyes focused straight ahead. All Together stared and froze. The latch was sprung, and the bell sounded.

From out of the gap, it was hard to tell who broke on top, since they were coming directly at them. All Together was running in a weaving pattern, bumping the horse on the left before going back to bounce off the colt to her right. She did this at least twice. But by the time they got to the main track, she'd settled down, started running straight, and it became a horse race. The three ran in a tight pack.

The horse on the inside appeared to have the lead as they dropped down on the rail, passing the sixteenth pole. Johnny was riding low, his head barely visible behind the filly's large neck. At the wire, the horse on the rail started to drop back, while the colt fought to stay within a length of the lead. Johnny clicked to All Together, waving his whip before he tapped her with it and she pinned her ears, shied a little and then dug in. When Johnny stood up on her at the seven-eighths pole, she was four lengths in front of the colt. The third horse was three lengths behind him.

Ben was grinning from ear to ear as he looked at Dawn and Randy. Dawn pounded lightly on Randy's back, knowing better than to display too much excitement, following in Ben's footsteps. She leaned to look at Ben's stop watch. Thirty-four and three-fifths seconds.

Bud Meyers walked away in disgust over his horse's performance, Ben got back in Randy's truck, and Dawn and Ginney headed toward the barns. "I love it!" Ginney said, in a low voice so her father wouldn't hear. "That was Dad's best colt, and the filly outran him."

Dawn noticed Randy standing by his truck looking at her, realized she should've said something before just walking away, and waved. He shook his head and got in behind the wheel.

"This is unbelievable," Ginney said, again keeping her voice low. "Dad hates fillies. He calls them cunts. He says they're always too busy horsin' to amount to anything. Says they're common." She glanced ahead. "I think he hates women, period. Sometimes I think he hates me."

Dawn looked at her. She didn't say anything; she just looked at her, and Ginney nodded. "It's a fact. Ever since mom left him for some jock a few years ago. He hates them. We're all alike, he says. We're all cunts. Hell, if I didn't know how to clean a stall, he probably wouldn't have me around."

Dawn frowned. "Come on, your father wouldn't have you around unless he cared."

"You kidding? He doesn't trust a fucking soul. He wouldn't let anyone but his own daughter work for him. Besides, he don't pay shit!" Ginney laughed and shook her head. "Like I said, mom did him in when she left."

"Do you ever see your mom?" Dawn asked. All Together was almost to the gap, Johnny was smiling in their direction. She smiled back and turned to Ginney.

"Yeah, once..." Ginney said, her voice saddening. "She wanted money."

"Did you give it to her?" Dawn asked, having a feeling what her answer would be.

"Yeah." She headed toward her barn, but stopped to look over her shoulder. "I gave her everything I had."

Tom, astride Red, led All Together and Johnny off the track. And was pumped. "Did you see her? She yanked the balls right out of those two colts! Shit, they're probably little peas rolling around back at the quarter pole!"

Dawn laughed, but didn't appreciate Tom's humor half as much as Johnny. He'd been laughing so much, he had tears in his eyes. All the jocks liked Tom. He was a living legend. Ain't no horse too tough for Tom. And he was funnier than hell.

Johnny jumped off then and hopped onto the running boards of Randy's truck as it passed by so he could talk to Ben. His youthful eyes were big as silver dollars. "Did you see her? Did you see her?"

Ben laughed. "Yeah, I saw her."

"She ducked in and out all over the place at first. But once she took to running..."

Ben nodded, listening.

"You're gonna let me ride her, aren't you, Ben?"

"I'd planned on it. I want to take all the weight I can get."

"But I'm about to lose my bug."

Ben looked at him and smiled. The kid had been winning races left and right lately. "Well in that case, I'm going to have to think about it then."

Randy spent the rest of the morning trailing around behind Dr. Raffin, holding instruments, retrieving supplies, and just plain feeling useless. Though he was thankful to have several farm calls to make, he called and scheduled them for the following day.

Driving toward the Miller barn, he caught a glimpse of Dawn as she was almost to the stable gate. He pulled up next to her. "Were you going to leave without letting me know?"

Dawn was taken aback with his tone. Damn him and his moods. "I thought you'd be busy, or I would've checked in."

Randy shook his head and drove off, then stopped, and backed up. "So where are you going?"

Dawn was in a mood now. "Home."

Randy put the truck in drive again, trying to think fast. "The filly worked good."

Dawn brightened. "She really did, didn't she?"

He nodded.

"Thanks for coming back to see her."

"I wouldn't miss it for the world," Randy said, adding foolishly, "If I hadn't, you probably would never speak to me again."

Dawn shook her head and walked on. "Is that the only reason you came back?"

"No," Randy said, keeping up with her. "I mainly came back to see you, not that you've had any time for me." He hated the tone of his voice, feeling like a love-sick teenager begging for a date. But damn it, he wanted her. He *wanted* her. "I was hoping we could get together. I'd like to come over."

"Suit yourself," Dawn said.

Suit yourself...? What, he thought, is this a one-way thing? "Hey, don't let me put you out. Never mind, I don't want to come over now anyway." He drove on, pulled past the guard shack, and out onto the highway. "Fuck her!" he said. At the light, he glanced at his clipboard. "Okay, Mrs. Richmond. Here I come."

The woman hovered on Randy's every move, even followed him out to his truck, and especially liked it when he had to lean in to put supplies away. With his body angled to one side, his shirt hiked up, exposing his bare muscled abdomen and all this dark luscious hair.

"Would you like some lunch?" she asked, in a sultry voice. "Mr. Richmond is at the office and I'm all alone, except for some mute-like servants who see nothing." She slipped her hand under his shirt and ran it across his back.

Randy reached up to close the compartment door, which afforded her the opportunity to duck under his arm. She pressed up against him, arching her thigh between his legs.

Randy smiled. "I've got a full afternoon. I'm sorry. Maybe some other time."

Mrs. Richmond wrapped her arms around his neck, moving her breasts back and forth across his chest. "I'll make you anything you like."

Still smiling, Randy gave it some thought. Certain parts of his anatomy gave it equal thought. Why not, he said to himself. Mrs. Richmond pulled his face to hers, kissing him as she detected the stirrings of his interest, and ran her hand down the front of his pants.

Dawn was just about to order up Chinese when the intercom buzzed. She pushed the button. "Yes?"

"Dr. Iredell to see you. Shall I send him up?"

"No."

The attendant covered the phone, for Randy to respond, and came back with, "He says it's important. It's about a Ginney Meyers."

"Okay, fine. Send him up." Dawn ran across the room to look in the mirror, stared at her reflection, and drew a deep breath before she opened the door. "I thought you weren't coming over."

Randy just stood there a moment. Her arm blocked his entry. "Are you going to let me in?"

Dawn stepped aside, taking him in entirely with her eyes as he walked past her. "So what's this about Ginney?"

"I just figured it out," Randy said, "and came over to see if I'm right. She's a character in your book, right?"

Dawn closed the door. "What?"

"In your book. She's just one of your characters, one of your many characters."

Dawn watched him as he sat down and crossed his arms, then walked over and sat down next to him. "No, she's not a character in my book. Not really."

"What is it? No, or not really?"

Dawn sighed. "You can't write a book about the racetrack without a Ginney, is what I meant. But it's not actually her."

"Someone a lot like her?"

"I don't know. I'm not sure yet."

"Are you using her for research?"

Dawn stood up. *Using* her? "You know, I'm getting tired of you drilling me all the time. If it's not about my book, it's about my money. Honestly, Randy, I don't like you sometimes. In fact, most of the time lately."

Randy's face reddened, embarrassed that she would think he was interested in her money. "I haven't been around lately, in case you've forgotten."

"Forgotten?" Forgotten? "No, I haven't forgotten." Dawn looked at him and sighed. "I missed you terribly, though right about now, I'm not sure why." She sat back down next to him and reached for his hand. "Please don't do this..."

Randy just looked at her.

"Let's start over."

Randy smiled faintly. "From where?"

"From where I said I loved your beard."

Randy laughed and pulled her close. "You mean this morning, when I told you how much I loved your hair before you put it in that stinking braid."

Dawn leaned back, frowning.

"I'm sorry. It's just that it's so beautiful. I can't understand why you braid it all the time." He pulled her onto his lap. "Undo it," he said. And it was then, Dawn noticed something.

She sat up. "Since when did you start wearing Vanderbilt cologne?"

Randy stared. "What?" This was a new expression, one he hadn't seen on her before. He'd found her weakness. "What do you mean?"

Dawn got up off his lap and took a step back. "You smell like Vanderbilt cologne."

Randy glanced away, looking guilty. But instead of feeling caught red-handed, he wanted to jump up and down and shout. She was jealous and he was loving it. It was the first time she'd shown any signs of being possessive, of caring. "I don't know what you're talking about."

"Right." Dawn shook her head and turned and walked to the terrace, her back to him as she stared out into the night. Every time she started to feel really close to him, he reminded her he was only playing a game. One he was good at. She wondered how many times he'd played already that day. She looked at him, perhaps to see if she could tell, to see it in his face. And there he sat, pretending to be innocent. It couldn't have hurt more if she were watching him in the act.

Randy stood up and walked over then, feeling he'd allowed enough time to sufficiently irritate her. "I was at Richmond's today for a farm call," he confessed. "And she was coming on to me."

Dawn swallowed hard, thinking back to the time she'd gone there with him. "And?"

"And nothing," Randy said, in earnest. "That's it."

Dawn searched his eyes, believing him. "I knew she wanted you. It was so obvious."

Randy put his arms around her, relishing the feel of her body against his.

"Have you been with her before?" Dawn asked.

Randy stared, hesitating. He wasn't ready for that, nor was he ready for the instant turn-off of the jealousy. He shook his head in disbelief. How foolish to have thought she was jealous in the first place. Had he forgotten he was the one being used? "No, I haven't been with her before, not that I haven't thought about it. But her husband was always there. This was the first opportunity," he added, sounding disappointed with himself for not following through.

"So why not today? Why didn't you?"

Randy gazed into her eyes, helpless to look away. "Because it wasn't her I wanted."

Dawn warmed in his arms. "How did you say no?"

"What?"

"Mrs. Richmond. How did you turn her down?"

Randy turned her loose and stepped back. "What, do you want to write it down?"

Dawn laughed. "No, I was just wondering. You know, like what she said, what you said."

Randy shook his head and laughed. "Well she didn't exactly come right out and say let's screw, if that's what you mean." Jealous? Yeah, sure. "She just kept rubbing on me." He drew her close to show her how. "She rubbed my leg and stroked my back. Then she told me her husband was gone, and..."

Dawn looked distracted all of a sudden.

"What?"

"I just thought of something. Wait, I do have to write it down." She pulled free and headed down the hall. "If you want a beer, get it."

Randy stood watching her in amazement. "Write what down? What Mrs. Richmond did?" He laughed at the way he'd said Mrs. Richmond. He'd almost screwed Mrs. Richmond. He felt like Dustin Hoffman. "Come on, what are you writing down?"

Dawn called something to him from the library, which he couldn't quite make out, and did as she initially suggested. He helped himself to a beer. "Where's mine?" Dawn said, glancing up from the typewriter when he joined her.

Randy stared. "I didn't know you wanted one, here."

Dawn shook her head, typed out another sentence, backed up, corrected it, and got up to get one herself. "I'll be right back."

Randy almost insisted she take his, that he'd go get another, but he wanted to see what she'd just typed. He stepped aside, waited a second or two, and sat down at her desk.

"His good looks far outweighed his lack of breeding," she'd written, "his strength giving in only to his childlike enthusiasm. I was taken by him the moment I laid eyes on him and had to have him, if just for a short time."

Dawn came in and looked over his shoulder.

"Who's this about?" he asked.

"A horse."

Randy slugged a mouthful of beer. He didn't believe her. "What's his name?"

Dawn shrugged. "I don't know. I haven't thought of one yet."

Randy downed the rest of his beer and turned to face her. "What made you think to come in here and write this now?"

"Who knows?" Dawn said. "Sometimes I think and think and think, and nothing comes. And then I don't think about it, and it pops into my head."

Randy nodded. What did it matter, he only had a short time. "I thought it was about me," he said.

Dawn laughed. "Why? Because of the good looks?"

"No." Randy blushed.

Dawn glanced at the page. "I probably should have said conformation."

Randy looked at her. She'd leaned close. "Correct it tomorrow," he said, and Dawn smiled, gazing into his eyes.

He had more urgent things on his mind at the moment. "When Linda moved, did she take the pact with her?"

Dawn laughed, a gigglish laugh. "We're on our own."

"Good," he said, reaching for her.

Dawn's eyes widened. In here?

"Turn out the light."

Much later, Dawn woke and glanced at the clock. "Randy, your truck. Wake up, it's past ten."

Randy wrapped his arm around her and tucked her back in. "It's in Linda's parking space, go back to sleep."

Dawn sighed and burrowed next to him, then turned slightly. "You know the whole time you were gone," she said, "when you were at your parents..." She trailed off, turning back.

"Yes..." Randy nuzzled her neck, wrapping his arms tighter around her. "Go on."

She hesitated and shook her head softly.

"Dawn please, come on. Finish what you were going to say."

When Dawn remained silent, Randy propped himself on one elbow and turned her to face him. "Tell me, goddamn it," he said, his voice a whisper. "I want to hear it, whatever it was. I need to hear it. Tell me..."

Dawn hesitated still, but only for a second. "I love you, Randy. Tom was right. I wasn't the same without you."

Randy smiled, gazing into the sleepiness of her eyes. "And I love you too, Dawn. God help me, I do. Just don't break my heart, okay?"

Chapter Nineteen

Ginney was standing in front of one of the stalls, talking to Dawn, when Randy started around the corner of the barn, well within hearing distance.

"Do you think they'll bring up my friggin' reputation?"

Dawn drew a breath and sighed. "Legally, it has nothing to do with it, but I'm sure it'll come up in some way at one point or other, so count on it. Go in there expecting it, and it won't catch you off guard."

Ginney nodded. "God, I'm glad you're coming with me."

"What time is the hearing?"

"Two."

"All right. I'll have to go home and change, but I'll meet you back here at one-thirty."

Randy approached them. "Good morning."

Ginney smiled and walked past him, waving over her shoulder to Dawn as she left.

Randy leaned against the doorway of the stall. Dawn was brushing Son of Royalty. He motioned to the horse. "He's got your hair color."

Dawn looked at him and laughed. It was close. Son of Royalty was liver chestnut, a shade quite similar to auburn.

"So what's going on?" Randy asked, glancing in the direction Ginney had taken. "What was that about?"

Dawn shrugged. She didn't want to talk about it.

"Something to do with the rape?"

She nodded.

"How do you figure in this?"

Dawn hesitated. "I don't know. I just offered some help."

"I see. Do you have experience in that field, rape counseling?"

Dawn shook her head. Oh, this man and his quirks. "I don't think there's a woman alive who can't relate to what Ginney's going through. If you want to call that experience, then suit yourself."

Randy crossed his arms. "Did you ever write about anything like that?"

Dawn buried her face against Son of Royalty's neck. "Hide me," she said. "It's the FBI." And Randy laughed.

"All right. So what are we going to do tonight?"

Dawn shrugged. "I don't know, what do you want to do?"

Randy smiled, a very definitive smile, and Dawn chuckled. "That's fine, but first I thought we might go to the club."

"What time?"

"Five or so. I'm going with Ginney at two, but it's a preliminary, so I don't think it'll take long."

Randy glanced at his watch. "Let's make it more like six."

Dawn confirmed that with a kiss and went back to brushing Son of Royalty. "Do you have a lot of farm calls?"

"No, not that many. But I have a pin-fire to do here first."

Dawn cringed. Pin-firing in her opinion, was a cruel operation. It was a quick fix when a long layup was pending.

"I'll see you around six, okay?"

Dawn nodded, and stuck her head out of the stall when he started to walk away. "I'll either be at the pool or in the sauna. And don't worry, I'll make sure to tell Jeremy you're coming."

"Name?"

"Virginia Meyers."

"Citizenship?"

"American." Ginney's voice cracked.

"According to the report filed on your medical examination, you showed evident signs of sexual intercourse with multiple contusions of the labia, vagina and cervix. Also on the report, you had multiple contusions on your face and right arm, and a laceration on the upper lip. Is this correct?"

Ginney nodded.

"Is this correct?" the judge repeated. "Counsel, would you advise your client to verbally answer all questions."

When Ginney's lawyer nudged her arm, Ginney cleared her throat, close to tears. "Yes, that's correct."

Dawn moved uncomfortably in her seat.

The judge proceeded. "You are aware the accused has pled innocent to the charge of rape and assault?"

Ginney was silent, until her attorney whispered something to her. "Yes, your honor."

"Has your attorney informed you of all circumstances and options available to you?"

Ginney looked at her attorney. He nodded. "Yes, your honor," she said.

"And is it your wish to proceed?" the judge asked.

Ginney didn't have to look at her attorney this time. "Yes, your honor. It is."

Out in the hall afterwards and in a hurry, Ginney's attorney glanced at his watch. "There, now that wasn't so difficult, was it?"

Ginney shrugged, visibly trembling, as Dawn stared critically at the man. She'd taken an instant dislike to him in the courtroom. Not only had he been late, he obviously had not spent any time beforehand to prepare Ginney in the least.

"Does it get any easier?" Ginney asked.

Her attorney shook his head. "I'm afraid not. It gets worse." He glanced at his watch again. "I'll be in touch. I've got to run." He started down the hall. "I'll be contacting you in a few days."

Dawn called after him, waited until he stopped, and approached him. He glanced yet again at his watch, sighing impatiently. "Yes?"

Dawn didn't mince words. "I trust you'll prepare her better for the next phase."

The man stared. "Yes, and your name again?"

"My name is not the issue here," Dawn said. "All I'm asking is for you to pay a little more attention."

The man's mouth hung open as she nodded curtly and walked away.

"What did you say?" Ginney asked. "What did he say?"

"Nothing. I just had a question," Dawn replied, seething inside. "Come on, let's go get some coffee."

"Coffee? How about a beer?"

Dawn smiled. They chose a pub a block from the courthouse, and sat at a table in the corner. "Jesus, fuck...I had no idea," Ginney said, referring to the proceedings.

"Don't worry. You'll be okay."

Ginney rolled her eyes and downed a mouthful of beer. "What a day."

Dawn smiled, agreeing, and for a second or two, they both stared into their glasses. Ginney raised her eyes. "Are you seeing Randy?"

Dawn hesitated. A raw nerve. She didn't like discussing her relationships with anyone, let alone with a woman who'd slept with the same man. "Yes. I am."

Ginney nodded agreeably. "He's a good fuck."

Dawn gasped. "Ginney!"

"Well he is," Ginney said, shrugging and without the slightest catty intent. "What's the big deal?"

Dawn shook her head and sighed, glancing away and then looking back to shake her head again.

"Wanna compare notes?"

"No..." Dawn said, and in spite of herself, laughed. Ginney had an almost child-like expression on her face. It *was* no big deal to her. "You know, you and Tom ought to get together."

Ginney snickered. "Ought to? We do. At least three times a year. And when it comes to fucking..."

This really got them to laughing, so much so, several people from the bar, glanced in their direction.

"Stop!" Dawn sputtered, whispering. "Enough."

They both laughed still, then finally wound down. It was then that Ginney got very serious. "I didn't mean anything about Randy. When it came to me and him, I was just a convenience. He sorta made that clear." She shrugged. "He's looking for more out of life, not somebody like me. More like you. Someone with some class."

Dawn stared, and then lowered her eyes to the table. Ginney was being sincere, she *didn't* mean any harm. But her comment about Randy's ambitions struck a cord. "Why do you do it, Ginney? Why do you sleep around?"

Ginney sat back and crossed her arms. "Dad says it's in my blood. Says I take after my mom, the slut."

Dawn shook her head. She was tired of hearing this already. She could only imagine how Ginney must feel after years of it. "He's been pretty hard on you, hasn't he?"

Ginney shrugged, hesitated, and nodded. She took a drink then, put the glass back down and wrapped both hands around it, holding on. "Shortly after my mom left, Dad caught me jerking-off Timmy Dobbs."

Dawn stared, not exactly the kind of comment one responds to.

"He was working for us at the time. It was his birthday." Ginney laughed to herself, but it was an agonizingly sad laugh, a solitary laugh. "I was giving him his present. He wanted to fuck. But believe it or not, at sixteen, I was still a virgin." She looked into Dawn's eyes for a moment, perhaps for confirmation Dawn believed her, and continued. "Dad wasn't supposed to be back for a while. And there I was...with my hands full. Dad fired Timmy, called me a whore, and here I am." She held her arms out. "Living up to it."

Dawn shook her head.

"At first I started sleeping around to get back at him. He could have trusted me you know. I think I wanted to get back at my mom too. But then I got to liking it. At least when I'm getting fucked, I know exactly what's going on."

Dawn leaned forward. "But, Ginney..."

"I know." Ginney laughed ironically. "I know what you're going to say. I'm only hurting myself. And don't think I haven't tried to change, because I have. Lots of times. I'll be with someone and I'll think, it's gonna to be different this time. This one's gonna care. I go out of my way for them. But in the end, it's always the same. When it's over, it's over. And all I know is that I've been fucked."

Dawn shook her head, again about say something, but Ginney stopped her. "Dawn, you don't know what it's like, to only be wanted when they can't have someone else. And damn, I'm easy." Her voice cracked. "They don't even have to try. I'd do almost anything for a hug." She raised her glass to her mouth. "Corny...huh?"

"No."

Ginney cleared her throat. "I almost hate sex now. I do. I wish I could be a nun."

Dawn hesitated. "You could change, you know."

"How in the fuck...?"

Dawn smiled. "Well, you could start by not saying fuck so much."

"Sheeettt!"

"That too," Dawn said, and they both smiled.

"Don't you ever swear?"

"Sometimes," Dawn said. "Out loud even."

The two of them laughed. It was getting time to leave. Dawn paused to reflect. "You...a nun?"

Ginney nodded. "I look real good in black."

Five miles away, in a hospital room, Miguel opened his eyes. His wife and mother were sitting in chairs on both sides of his bed. "Can I get sometheeng to eat?" he said. His wife hugged him, then went running for the nurse, while his mother fell to her knees, clasping her hands together as she whispered thanks to her God.

Dawn ran into Linda at the club, talked to her a few minutes in the locker room, and headed for the sauna. When she found it too crowded, she went to the steam room instead. A few minutes later, someone came in and sat down next to her.

"How have you been, Dawn?"

She glanced over. "Just fine, Dave."

"I've missed you."

Silence.

The door opened. Two people left as one entered, barely visible through the murky steam.

"My family misses you too."

Dawn smiled. "Give them my regards," she said, rubbing her ankles.

"I will." Dave paused. "What have you been doing with yourself lately?"

"Nothing much." Dawn stood up to push the nozzle on the wall, and blasted herself with a spray of cool water.

"Are you still playing groom at the racetrack?"

Dawn sighed and sat back down. "Every day."

When she leaned forward, rubbing her neck, Dave seized the opportunity. "Here, let me do that. I assure you, I haven't lost my touch."

Someone off in the corner sighed heavily.

"So, still seeing your veterinarian?"

Dawn hesitated responding. "Yes."

"I hear he's been a guest here. Are you sure that's wise? We are different than most folks. Surely you haven't forgotten that?" Dave said, still rubbing her neck and shoulders.

"You needn't worry yourself over it."

"I'm not worried. By the way, I hear Linda moved in with Harland. Match made in heaven, don't you think?"

Dawn nodded. "Seems to be." There was a lot to be said for a club as close-knit and private as this place. But there was nothing private once inside. She leaned back against the wall, forcing his hands away.

"It must be lonely living by yourself. Especially the nights," Dave said, his voice lower.

"No, not really," Dawn said. She stood up and started toward the door. "I have my veterinarian, remember?"

Dave mumbled something like, "Bitch," when she'd gone, and two more people got up and left.

Randy looked out over the pool. It was more crowded today, at least ten or twelve swimmers. Spotting Dawn at the far end, he dove in, swam to her, and was greeted with a kiss and a warm smile.

"Did you just get here?" It was almost seven.

"No. Kevin showed me to the steam room."

Dawn draped her arms around his neck. "I thought you didn't like the steam room," she said, thinking if he'd been there with her, she'd have been spared Dave's company.

"The sauna. I hate the sauna. I love a good steam bath." Randy wrapped his arms around her waist. "I love a good sweat."

Dawn kissed him and smiled. The man oozed sex out of his every pore. "Good, next time we can sweat together. It's coed."

"I know."

Dawn smiled, and then soured at the sound of a familiar voice to her right.

"Where are your manners, Dawn? And shouldn't you be controlling yourself?" It was Dave in all his pompous glory, extending his hand to Randy. "Controlling herself has always been a problem. The name's Dave. Dave Winchester."

Randy shook his hand, and would have responded with an introduction of his own. But Dave beat him to it. "Dr. Iredell I presume? Unless Dawn has taken to entertaining all her suitors now at the club."

Dawn let go of Randy's neck, let herself sink to the bottom, and without surfacing, swam away.

Randy laughed.

"Yes, she is something," Dave said, staring in her direction as if reading Randy's mind. "We'd be married right now, if it weren't for her getting cold feet."

Randy glanced at him, then looked at Dawn again across the pool, and had to force himself to keep from laughing. She was in well over six feet of water, and apparently doing a hand stand. All he could see was her toes.

"Surely you've noticed that tendency in her?"

Randy shook his head. "Can't say that I have." He felt a little sorry for the man. It was obvious he was still hung up on Dawn, and fishing.

"Well then, what have you noticed?"

Randy hesitated. Now the man was irritating him. Big time. He repeated the question out loud. "What have I noticed?" He watched Dawn as she pulled herself up out of the pool and sat on the side. "Well there is that tremendous appetite of hers..."

Dave nodded smugly. No news flash.

"For oral sex," Randy added.

Dave's eyes bulged.

"Yeah," Randy said, nodding and crossing his arms as he glanced at Dave. "I guess that would be it. And perhaps I have you to thank for that. Thanks," he said then, almost as if it were an afterthought as he patted Dave on the shoulder. "Nice meeting you." He dove in and swam to Dawn.

Later, as they were walking to the parking lot, she asked Randy what they talked about. Randy laughed, and didn't know whether to tell her or not. He told her.

"What? Are you crazy?"

"Hey, the guy pissed me off."

Dawn laughed. "That's no reason to go and tell him..."

"Yeah, but you should've seen his face."

"No thanks."

Ben sat down on the bench outside his main barn at home, in full view of the paddock, and watched Beau as he trotted up and down the fence line. He smiled to himself, thinking about how much Meg loved this farm. And how much he loved it. How proud he was to have built it for him and her. Home. When it came time to die, he wanted it to be here.

Beau romped back and forth again, confined, and obviously not liking it one bit. In a few more days, Ben planned to turn him out in the north pasture, allowing him the time to gradually get used to the clover. The last thing he needed at this stage, was for him to colic or founder. Watching him, he could remember the day he was born, wobbly-kneed and still wet from his mother. He knew even then he'd be a runner. "Mark my words," he'd told Meg. And it was true. Beau never let them down. "Yep, you belong here ole boy," he said. "Just like me. This is your home and you're home to stay." He laughed at himself then. Dawn and her incessant talking to the horses had rubbed off on him. At his age yet. Talking to a horse. And now talking to myself.

Across town, Tom was in a quandary, and talking to himself as well. "This is fucking scary," he said, his pants down around his knees and examining his rash. There is something really wrong here. It covered his entire groin area, all the way down to the tip of his penis. "I think it's time to go see a goddamned doctor."

He pulled his pants up, so lightheaded he had to sit down. He hated hospitals, he hated doctors. Just the very thought of them. Maybe he should give it a few more days. He nodded emphatically. Yeah, a few more days. If it doesn't go away by then, "Then I'll go see a doctor." What a load off his mind.

Miguel had an aversion to doctors and hospitals as well, and wanted out, wanted to go home. Dr. Martin was somewhat sympathetic.

"Maybe tomorrow. You came very close to dying. It's a tricky game tempting death."

Miguel nodded, true. Yet... He had a family to support, wife, children, mother. A life to live. "I will not play that game again." He crossed himself and glanced at his wife. "No mas."

Dr. Martin smiled. "Muchas gracias. I'd rather make my living removing tonsils and giving vaccinations any day. Thready pulses give me the creeps."

Dawn and Randy ate at Burger King, and stopped on the way to her place to pick up some ice cream. "Chocolate or vanilla?"

"Vanilla. No, let's get fudge ripple."

Randy laughed. Fudge ripple it was. Inside the apartment, he locked the door behind them. "This is going to be great. I can't believe it."

"What?"

"I'm not going home, I'm here for the night, and it's understood ahead of time. I don't have to finagle my way into your bed, there's no pact. We have food." He held up the ice cream. "We don't need showers. We don't need underwear."

Dawn laughed, squealed when he reached for her, and ran down the hall. Randy chased after her, grabbed her, and they fell onto the bed together, where they undressed in a fit of giggling. Sweater, jeans, underwear...and ultimately, the braid in Dawn's hair. Off came the rubber band.

"Randy, wait. Wait," Dawn said, right about the time Randy got serious. "We didn't put the ice cream away."

Randy stared, then got out of bed and extended his arms. "Do you see me? Do I look like a man who cares about ice cream at the moment?"

"Uh, no..." Dawn said, smiling. "But you will later, I think."

Randy shook his head and laughed. "I'll be right back." He went into the living room, picked up the ice cream and started toward the kitchen, but then a devilish thought crossed his mind, and instead of putting it away, he got a spoon. As he started back out, the front door opened.

Linda gasped. "Randy!"

He glanced into the kitchen for something to conceal himself with, backing up and holding the ice cream strategically. Then tearing a few sheets of paper towel off the role, which would have to do, he left the ice cream and walked down the hall, shut the door behind him, and sat on the bed. "I don't frigging believe this. Linda just walked in on me."

"What? Where?" Dawn sat up.

"In the living room," Randy said, shaking his head. "Do you have any idea..."

Dawn got out of bed and put on her robe. "I wonder why she's here?"

"Like I care," Randy said. He pulled back the bedspread, punched and fluffed the pillow, and laid down and yanked the covers up over him. "Son of a bitch."

Linda sat on the couch with the container of ice cream in her lap and spoon in hand.

"What happened?" Dawn asked, sitting down next to her. "Why are you home?"

"We had a fight. He's a maggot."

Dawn glanced back down the hall. "Do you want to talk about it?"

Linda contemplated the fudge swirls. "I don't want Randy mad."

Dawn took the spoon and helped herself to a mouthful. "He won't be mad. He's probably asleep."

Linda chuckled. "You sure? He didn't look sleepy when I saw him."

Dawn laughed. "So what did you and Harland fight about?" she asked, passing the spoon back.

"Well first off..."

It was after three before Dawn crawled into bed with Randy. When the alarm went off on his side at a quarter to five, he was so dead to the world, she reached across him and knocked it off the table. That woke him. He half opened his eyes and laughed, and had to fumble around and find it to finally turn it off.

Dawn sighed. "Why me?"

Randy laughed again and tucked her in his arms. "What time did you come to bed?"

"I don't know," she said, warm and cozy next to him. "Around three."

"Why don't you go back to sleep and go in later. I'm sure the Miller barn can get by without you for one morning."

"I can't," Dawn mumbled. "I'm committed. I'm dedicated. I'm tired."

"You're crazy."

"That too."

They lay quietly in each other's arms a moment, breathing softly and cuddled.

"Randy...?"

"Hhhmmmm."

"Let's not fight, okay?"

Randy hesitated, and turned her to face him. "What would we fight about?"

"I don't know." She shrugged, and had to swallow a lump forming in her throat. "People fight about weird things."

Randy shook his head.

"Just promise me, okay?"

"Okay."

Chapter Twenty

Randy leaned against the bathroom counter and watched as Dawn braided her hair. She was going to be a little late, but wasn't rushed, and certainly hadn't rushed a few minutes earlier, much to his delight.

"I'll stop and have coffee and donuts with you, then go home so I can get some clean clothes."

Dawn smiled. "Which reminds me. I have to go shopping for something to wear to Cindy's wedding, and should probably get something for Gloria's while I'm at it. Are you all set for the big events?"

He nodded, trickling his hand down her shoulder. "Yes. For Cindy's, I'm wearing a tux. I was fitted for it before I came back."

"What about Gloria's?"

He leaned over to kiss her neck. "Suit...right?"

She nodded.

"Then I'm all set."

"What color?" she asked, gently nudging his hand away when he tried unzipping her jeans.

"Gray," he replied, and frowned. "Do you want to know the brand name?"

"No, but I was hoping it was blue." The color of his eyes. She stepped back out of reach. "But gray is fine. Do you have a blue shirt?"

He shook his head and smiled. "Yes dear, I do."

Dawn leaned close to kiss him, careful to hold his hands. "Let's get going. It's almost six."

Tom appeared to be waiting for her as she rounded the corner of the shedrow. He was. "Hey, Ben...Dawn's late," he sang. "Very, very late, because she probably had a date."

Dawn laughed, and then shook her head when Tom stopped to scratch himself. "You're obscene. You know that?"

"I can't help it," he said. "It itches like hell. Not to mention what it's done to my sex life."

"So go see a doctor."

Tom stopped scratching. "Why? It'll go away. You just wait and see."

With all the horses in the barn scheduled to walk that morning, it would have been a breeze had it not been for the soaring temperature. With it well above eighty before ten, Dawn claimed even her eyelashes were sweating.

Ginney came down the shedrow fanning herself with an old racing form, just as Dawn finished up raking. "Do you want to go to Mario's with me?"

Dawn wiped her brow. "Where's that?" she asked, thinking it must be a restaurant.

"Mario's Hair Salon. It's across the street in the mall. I need a respectable look for the trial. Something really boring, my attorney said. I was hoping you'd come with me on the road to prim and proper."

Dawn laughed. "What time's your appointment?"

"I don't have one. It's not needed."

Dawn hesitated, giving it some thought.

"It's air conditioned," Ginney said, still fanning herself.

"Okay, you talked me into it. Just let me lock up. Tom and Ben have already gone." She took about three steps and stopped. "Maybe I'll get mine done too."

Randy pulled into the barn area shortly after two and was surprised to see Dawn's Jaguar in the parking lot. He reached for the *overnight* and scanned the list of horses scheduled to run today. The Miller barn didn't have anything in, so why was she here? He drove down to check, but it was locked up tight. No Dawn. He glanced at his watch. He had about forty-five minutes before he had to start running medications for tomorrow's entries. So he eased down into the seat, leaned his head back, and closed his eyes.

Ginney's voice woke him. He sat up and looked at her. "What the hell happened to your hair?"

"I got it cut," she said, twirling around in the shedrow. It was styled shorter than most men's. "It's supposed to look boring."

Randy nodded. "Well, I'd say you accomplished that. Where's Dawn?"

"She's in the feed room. She got hers done too."

"What?" Randy stared, then buried his face in his hands. If she cut her hair, I'm going to die. "Right here and now," he said to himself.

"Randy..." Dawn called to him.

"No." He couldn't bear to look.

Dawn laughed. "Randy, come on."

He shook his head.

"It's really pretty," Ginney said.

"Oh, and do you think yours is pretty?" Randy asked, still refusing to uncover his eyes.

"Yes."

"Then I really don't want to look."

Dawn shook her head. "Randy, you're being silly. You're going to have to look sooner or later. Come on, you're going to like it, I promise. Aren't you the one always complaining about my braid?"

Randy sighed. He'd obviously complained once too often. "Go in the tack room and I'll walk in and see it. I need to prepare myself," he said, laughing now as well. "Go on."

Dawn played along, but no sooner had she and Ginney gone into the tack room, Randy started his truck and drove away. "He's crazy," Ginney said, and Dawn agreed.

"Totally."

Randy had every intention of going back after a few minutes, but it didn't work out that way. Chapman waved him down. "I got a horse that was cast," he said, in that way of his. "He needs attending."

Randy sighed and headed in that direction. Though not an emergency in itself, a horse cast means that either when rolling or lying down in its stall, it ended up too close to the wall and unable to get back up. Most horses right themselves without harm, aside from a momentary panic. But some wind up injuring themselves in the process.

Chapman's horse proved the latter. He required stitches on the outside of his right knee and some preventive measures to head off infection and swelling. By the time Randy made his way back to the Miller barn, it was after five. He knew Dawn would be gone already, but checked anyway just in case, and was about to head over to her apartment for a few minutes, when he was paged to the stable gate.

The message was from the Durans. Randy phoned them from the pay phone at the guard shack.

"Oh, Dr. Iredell, we're just frantic. It's the foal. He won't nurse, and his manure just runs out of him."

Randy assured Mrs. Duran he'd be there within half an hour. He hung up and damned himself for repeatedly forgetting once again to get Dawn's unlisted number and then for not being able to remember it in the first place, and wondered if it was a Freudian thing, as he started out.

Meanwhile, Dawn ordered Chinese food, went down to get it, and returned in the doldrums to her apartment. How could Randy get angry with her for having her hair done, when her changing it was entirely for him? To think, she'd subjected herself to the whole smelly two-hour process for him, for this. She looked in the mirror. Damn him. *I was perfectly happy with my hair the way it was.*

Randy finished up at the Durans' and again was making his way to Dawn's apartment, when his pager went off. He stopped at the first pay phone he came to, got the number and dialed. The call was from an elderly man whose horse he said was, "In a mighty bad way. Colic, I suspect."

"Can you keep him walking till I get there?"

"No, I can't get him up, and I've no strength."

Randy feared as much from the sound of his voice. "I'll be there in about twenty minutes."

Upon arriving at the farm, Randy estimated Mr. Turner to be at least seventy-five years old, if a day, weathered and kind, and frail.

"This way," he said, shaking Randy's hand before leading him down the aisle of the barn. "I appreciate you coming out so soon."

Randy smiled and followed. The barn was empty, except for one cow and the horse, who lay lathered and failing. Looking in at him,

Randy thought about the old vet-school adage, "As long as they're breathing, there's still hope." It didn't apply here. This horse was a goner.

Though there was no real reason to examine him, Randy went through the motions anyway for Mr. Turner's sake, then stood back and shook his head.

"Give it to me plain and simple."

Randy nodded. "There's nothing we can do for him, except maybe help him along."

The old man paused. "Let's do it then."

Randy went to the truck and came back with the lethal injection. Mr. Turner was crouched by the horse, tenderly wiping the green mucous from the horse's nostrils with a worn handkerchief.

Randy drew a deep breath, hesitated, and walked in and stood next to them. "Why don't we try and get him up, outside maybe. At least in the aisle."

Mr. Turner shook his head. "No, I'd like it done here." He stroked the horse's face, his voice quivering. "This has been his stall now for more'n nineteen years."

Randy nodded and knelt down beside them. The horse blinked twice, once when Randy inserted the needle, and again when he removed it. He drew his last breath a moment later. Peacefully. "His name was Rudy," the old man said, with a catch in his throat. "I won't have any more."

He followed Randy to the truck. "I do appreciate you coming out so quick." He glanced back at the barn. "I don't get out as often as I used to, or I maybe could've caught him sooner today. When I came out to feed, that's how I found him. I'll bury him in the morning."

Randy nodded sympathetically and closed the back of his truck.

"What do I owe you, Doc?" Mr. Turner pulled out a leather change purse attached to a chain hanging from his belt.

"Twenty eight for the injection. I've got another call in the area...a mare foaling," Randy said, which was a lie. "So I'll waive the farm call."

While Mr. Turner counted out the money, Randy glanced around the farm again. Though well-kept, it had the tell-tale signs of hardship, all too familiar to him. A battery charger next to a tractor. The chicken coop empty, the barn siding painted but rotting, that one cow, a meager corncrib. He glanced at Mr. Turner, the old man's dungarees looking as though they'd been washed a thousand times.

"Here." Randy really didn't even want to charge for the injection, but knew better than to insult a proud farmer. Mr. Turner handed him the twenty-eight dollars, then reached in for two more. "This is for some coffee and a sandwich. I feel bad you coming out at this hour."

Randy smiled. "Thank you. A sandwich sounds pretty good right about now. I appreciate it." He shook the old man's trembling hand and left, saddened and depressed. On the way to his apartment, he thought about the farms back home, his parents, Cindy's wedding, and Dawn's hair...lying on a floor in some beauty shop.

Morning chores at the Miller barn were done by nine, but it would be a long day for them. Son of Royalty was in the fifth race and Too Cajun the last. Shortly after ten, Ben asked Dawn if she wanted to go for breakfast.

"Breakfast?" This was a first.

"Come on," he said. "I'm buying."

Dawn frowned, wiping her hands on her jeans as she walked along with him. When they were almost to the stable gate, she gave in and looked down the road between the barns for Randy's truck. "Do you want me to drive?" she asked Ben.

He shook his head. "I could probably get in that car of yours, but I don't think I could get out."

Dawn laughed. They both waved to Charlie, and at the restaurant, scanned the menu.

"Just coffee," Ben said, handing his to the waitress.

Dawn stared. "I thought you were hungry."

"I never said that."

Dawn opted for coffee as well. "Okay, so what are we here for?"

Ben drew a breath and sighed, scratched the back of his neck. "It's time for my typical trainer-owner speech." He hesitated, fretted. "Only it's tough with you, because I think of you like family, the daughter Meg and I never had."

Dawn smiled. "I love you like a second father."

Ben nodded, then cleared his throat, not knowing where to begin.

"Ben, just say it."

"All right. You've seen the way I am. When I train, I call all the shots. Which is why I don't run a big public stable. I'm not good at doing things any other way than my own."

"And?"

"And, we'll be running the filly soon. You have to trust my judgment."

"You know I do."

"No matter what?" he emphasized. "It's a business, Dawn. It takes business decisions from the head, not from the heart."

She nodded. "I know."

"If I decide she's a pig, then she's a pig."

"Okay." Dawn shrugged. "But she's not. Is she?"

"No." Perspiration dotted Ben's forehead. "But promise me. You understand? I don't want any problems later." He looked into her eyes. "All right?"

Dawn nodded.

"Good," he said, reaching into his pocket for some change. "Let's get back to the barn."

Dawn stared. "We haven't had our coffee."

"We can have coffee back at the barn."

Randy left his truck running and walked down the shedrow calling out for Dawn.

"She ain't here," Tom yelled from the feed room.

Randy followed the sound of his voice and found him in the corner, his back to the door and his hand in his pants, scratching himself.

"Jesus Christ! What the hell are you doing?"

"Know anything about itches, Doc?" Tom asked. "It's driving me nuts. You know, around the balls."

"It's probably crabs," Randy said, laughing. "But you'd better stop scratching like that, you look like a goddamned pervert."

"Go ahead and laugh, but this ain't funny." Tom rubbed an irritated area under his armpit. "I got this stuff everywhere now."

Randy raised an eyebrow. "We could put a good sweat on you; that may take care of it. Course, I'm not sure what size your pecker would be afterwards." He ducked when Tom swung at him, and started back down the shedrow. "Seriously, stop scratching it. You're only going to make it worse."

Dawn and Ben returned to the barn area shortly after Randy left, and ran into Miguel and his agent making their rounds. Dawn walked on when Ben stopped to talk to them.

When she reached the tack room, Tom was sitting at Ben's desk, staring helplessly at Ginney, who was in tears.

"What happened?"

Tom held his hands out. "I don't know. She was waiting for you...and then just started to cry."

Ben appeared at the door, took one look, mumbled something about going to the secretary's office, and Tom tagged along after him.

Dawn sat down next to Ginney. "What's wrong?"

Ginney shrugged, tried to swallow her tears. "My dad and I had a fight. He threw me out. He said he never wants to see me again."

"He probably didn't mean it. You know how people say things they don't mean when they're fighting."

"No, he really meant it this time," Ginney cried, too emotional to realize how contradictory that sounded. "He really did."

Dawn stared, pausing for a moment. In her opinion, Ginney might actually be better off without her father in her life, judging from what she'd told her about the man. "What did you fight about? Not the trial, I hope?"

"No." Ginney sniffed and wiped her nose with the back of her hand. "He wanted me to clock a horse you're running today."

"Son of Royalty?"

"No, the Cajun one. Too Cajun."

Dawn lowered her eyes, staring. "Gloria would die."

"No, he won't claim him. Not now. I told him he was a dink, the son of a bitch." She wiped her face again. "I hate him!"

Dawn sighed. "No, you don't."

"He hates me."

Dawn shook her head. "I can't believe any father would hate his daughter."

Ginney chewed hard on her trembling bottom lip. "I'll bet he hates me even more for taking this rape thing to trial."

Dawn shook her head. "He took you to the police station, didn't he?"

"Yes, but..." Tears flooded Ginney's eyes. "Oh God, I'm such a fuck up."

"No, you're not. Listen to me. Ginney..."

Ginney sniffed and swallowed.

"You're not. Now come on. Let's figure out what you're going to do."

Ginney sat back in an attempt to compose herself, and drew a deep breath. "I can get a room at the Horsemen's Efficiencies up the block tomorrow. I called them. Can I stay with you tonight?"

Dawn stared, thinking of Randy, the quiet apartment, no Linda. "Maybe you can stay at Randy's till then. I haven't seen him yet today, but we can ask him."

"What?" Astonishment flashed across Ginney's face.

"Oh no," Dawn said. And from the way she said it, they both laughed. "That's not what I meant. Randy will be with me."

Randy turned down Mr. Turner's driveway for the second time in as many days, and parked by the barn. He hoped he wouldn't offend the old man, but he just couldn't see him tearing down that stall himself. He could hear the pounding of a hammer. It stopped as he walked inside. Mr. Turner straightened up slowly and looked at him.

"Doc?"

Randy smiled. "Hope you don't mind me stopping by, but I need a favor."

The old man braced himself against the stall wall, a faint smile etching his face. "Oh? What can I do for you?"

Randy swallowed, hesitating. "Well, you can let me help you tear that stall down and get your horse out for burying."

"You don't say." Mr. Turner pulled a handkerchief out of his back pocket and mopped his brow. "And how will that help you?"

Randy tried to think fast. He'd come up with a few plausible reasons on the way, but something about the wisdom in the old man's eyes made them seem ridiculous now. "Uh...I just came from a call." He sighed dramatically upon saying this, trying to imitate his father. "This guy was a real ass. You know, the kind you'd like to deck." When Mr. Turner nodded, as if he knew the type, Randy gathered momentum. "So I figure, seeing as I was in your area and knew you had this job to do, I might work off some of my anger. Put it to good use, so to speak. It beats kicking my truck door."

Mr. Turner smiled. "Now I don't believe any of that horse shit for one minute. You came back here to help an old man because you didn't think he could handle the task."

Randy stood quiet, unable to think of anything to say to the contrary, and finally just nodded.

Old man Turner shook his head. "Well, if you're hell bent on helping, there's a crowbar over there." He motioned. "Just don't be getting in my way."

Randy smiled, pushing up his shirt sleeves as he walked over to get it.

"And, Doc...?"

Randy turned.

"Thanks."

Randy nodded, sized up the crowbar, and went to work.

Chapter Twenty-One

As soon as Ben returned from the secretary's office, Dawn reported what Ginney had said about Bud Meyers' interest in Too Cajun. Gloria arrived no less than five minutes later, enveloped in lilac, and oozing praise for her baby, who twitched and nodded in agreement with everything she had to say.

Dawn stood at her side, smiling, an equally appropriate response for whatever Gloria said, but was concerned. Ben had assured her that if Ginney told her father Cajun was a dink, he probably wouldn't go for him. Still...

"Just don't say a word of this to Gloria. God almighty."

The next few hours passed quickly. At the running of the fourth race, Tom started over with Son of Royalty. Dawn stayed at the barn with Cajun. A sweat had already been applied to his shoulders and back, and he was covered with a plastic sheet and shoulder blanket.

Randy stopped by, glanced into the tack room, and called out for her.

"Down here," Dawn said, poking her head out Son of Royalty's stall. She was just finishing bedding it down.

Randy jogged to where she was, and couldn't believe his eyes. "You didn't cut your hair!" He ran his fingers through it. "It's beautiful. Why did you tell me you cut it?"

"I didn't." Dawn laughed. "Though they did cut some of it. I had it permed. It's called a lioness."

Randy turned her completely around, fluffed it, and kissed her. "I love it!" He pulled her close and kissed her again. "Boy, am I glad I didn't shave off my beard now."

"You wouldn't?"

"I was going to, just to spite you. Sort of my version of *The Gift of the Magi.*"

Dawn shook her head and smiled. "Why didn't you come back yesterday? I missed you."

"I'm sorry. I tried. Several times in fact. But I just kept going round in circles. One farm call after another."

Dawn stepped back and crossed her arms. "Was one of them the Richmond's?"

"No." She's jealous, really this time, he told himself. I can see it in her eyes. "I did have to go to the Durans' though. The foal had the scours."

"Is he all right?"

Randy nodded. "I had to put a horse down too. It was sad. It was the old man's only horse."

Dawn gazed into his eyes. "Bad night, huh?"

Randy shrugged. "I could've used a woman's soothing touch in the end."

Dawn raised an eyebrow. "Any woman?"

Jealous again. Randy loved it. "I didn't mean it that way. And please, give me your phone number again. I had no way to get a hold of you."

Dawn found comfort in how he'd said that, and smiled. "Can Ginney stay at your apartment tonight?"

"What?" Jealous...? Yeah, sure. "You want me to screw her too?"

Dawn frowned. "No, I wanted you to stay with me."

Randy shook his head, about to say something, but Dawn shushed him and walked down to the end of the shedrow to listen for the ten-minute call.

Randy followed her. "Why does she need a place to stay?"

Dawn heard the announcement and turned to face him. "Her dad kicked her out."

"Again? Why?"

Dawn hesitated, uncomfortable whenever she was reminded of just how familiar the two of them were. "I'm not sure, but I'm going to ask him."

"I wouldn't mess with him, Dawn."

She walked past him. "I'm not going to. I just want to talk to him."

Randy turned, watching her. "So, is Linda still at the apartment?"

"No, they made up."

"Good. Can I nail the door shut?"

Dawn laughed. They made plans to meet at six, and Randy walked to his truck, glancing back to comment again about how much he loved her hair. "It's just beautiful," he said, already imagining how it was going to feel against his bare skin. Everywhere.

Dawn stood in the road between the barns and listened to the race being called. The sounds came and went whenever the wind changed directions. She could have sworn she heard Son of Royalty's name repeated several times at the end. A few minutes later, and still out on the road, she watched as Tom approached the turn-off to the spit barn. She held her breath, hoping, hoping, and sighed disappointedly when he kept on coming.

He held up three fingers. "We got beat just a neck for all of it." At the barn, he dismounted Red and smacked him on the rump to send him to his stall as he led Son of Royalty down the shedrow.

The ease with which he did this always amazed Dawn, all in one fell swoop. She helped him take off the bridle and put on Son's halter. Son dragged him to the water bucket then and gulped down what Tom allowed him to safely drink.

"Do you want help bathing him?" Dawn asked.

"Nah." Tom chewed heartily on a toothpick and grinned. "Wouldn't want you to mess up your new hairdo." He stopped long enough to scratch himself and off they went.

Dawn checked on Cajun and following that, cleaned Son's bridle and bit. When Tom returned, she scraped off Son of Royalty, gave him another drink, and Tom hung him on the walker.

"What a team," Ben would say.

Tom headed to the kitchen then, while Dawn kept an eye on Son and Cajun. She leafed through a magazine, but got bored with it. Son of Royalty drank two more times before having his fill. Dawn leafed through the magazine again, and walked up and down the shedrow, stopping to talk to each horse in passing. She removed Son's cooling sheet, let him walk another five minutes or so, then put him away, and decided to run stalls.

When Tom returned, she was once again leafing through the magazine. "I mixed the feed," she said, glancing up at him.

Tom smiled. "Did you fool them?"

She nodded. "I used all the extra water buckets and didn't make a sound."

Tom chuckled. "Well good for you. I'll go run stalls."

"I did them already."

"What? What the fuck?" Tom stood, bobbing his head. "Do you think you're the only one bored around here? What am I supposed to do now?"

"I don't know. But I do wish you'd quit scratching."

Finally, after what seemed like an eternity to Dawn, it was time to head over to the paddock with Cajun. "Go on," Tom said. "I'll catch his stall and throw the feed in and meet you over there."

As usual, Cajun stood like an old pro in the paddock, aside from his constant twitching. But Ben was fidgety. "Bud's clocking him," he told Tom.

Tom just looked at him. Dawn just looked at him. Neither dared so much as move or glance left or right. It was as if nothing had been said, but the realization was in their eyes.

"Fucking wonderful," Tom muttered under his breath.

Ben forced a smile as Johnny approached. His instructions to the young man were brief. "He's as fit as he'll ever be. It's all up to you now." If they were going to lose him, Ben wanted the win.

Johnny nodded.

"Riders up!"

Ben wouldn't even attempt the long trek to the clubhouse elevator. It took a lot less these days to make him winded. Add that to the possibility of losing Cajun to a claim and the prospect of Gloria's ensuing reaction, and his chest was thumping already.

Where was his blood pressure medicine? He checked his pocket. He must have left it at home.

Dawn and Tom were on the fence with only a minute to post time when he finally joined them.

"You okay, old man?"

Ben scowled at him.

The horses were being led to the gate, so close they could smell the sweat and lather, and almost hear the horses' hearts beating.

The first four loaded easily, Cajun being one of them. But the fifth, a large chestnut, balked and reared. It was then, and probably caused by the commotion of the gate crew forcing this horse into position, that the number two horse started acting up. His jockey came flying out the back of the gate, landed squarely on both feet, and immediately started limping.

A moment of temporary chaos followed. The number two horse was unloaded, examined, declared fit to run, and it was announced there would be a late rider change. The horses already loaded were backed out, the jock was helped off the racetrack, and the riderless horse was led back to the paddock to be resaddled.

Tom and Dawn jumped down off the fence support and turned to Ben. He shook his head and motioned to Cajun. Johnny was circling him behind the gate along with all the other horses delayed, but Cajun was the only one calm and collected, and gazing around as if he was thoroughly enjoying himself.

"Gloria probably thinks he's looking for her."

Dawn and Tom chuckled.

The drama ended then. The two horse reappeared. It loaded in turn, without incident this time, and the latch was sprung.

"And they're off!"

It was Cajun's race from start to finish, an easy pace, no early speed in the race, and a comfortable lead at the head of the stretch. He won by three lengths.

Ben and Tom just beamed. They knew he could run all day, and he proved them right. "How sweet it is!"

Gloria was ecstatic and Charlie as proud as can be. They assembled in the winner's circle, had their picture taken, and Tom and Dawn headed toward the spit barn. It was then Ben caught a glimpse of the paddock judge. He hustled Gloria and her entourage on their way.

A claim *was* dropped. The paddock judge wouldn't say who, but it came in too late and was disallowed. Ben relayed the information to Tom back at the barn.

"No shit? Now what?"

Ben shrugged.

"Did you tell Gloria?"

"No, and I'm not about to. I told Charlie."

Dawn returned from the spit barn with Cajun a little while later and learned the news as well.

"I don't like that man," she said.

Ben smiled, reminding her that this was in fact how they had acquired Cajun. But it didn't matter, not to her at least. "I still don't like him."

Randy walked in as Ben and Tom were discussing where to run Cajun next, and shook his head at Tom. He was scratching again.

"Hey, if you're not going to go see a doctor, let me at least go get my magnifying glass and a pair of tweezers and take a look at it for you."

"Fuck you!" Tom said, and the three of them laughed.

"Seriously..." Randy warned.

"I know, I know," Tom said. Eventually he was going to have to go. But just the thought of it. "Maybe tomorrow."

Randy sat down on the cot to wait for Dawn and yawned. "So Bud went for him, huh?"

Ben nodded. News traveled fast on the backside.

"What are you going to do?"

"Punt," Ben said. They laughed again, and Randy closed his eyes. Dawn all but startled him a moment later.

"Have you seen Ginney?" she asked, walking into the tack room.

He stared. "No. Why?"

"We're going to have to go find her before we leave."

Randy got up and followed her out. "Why? Why do you worry about her?"

"I don't know, I just do. Come on. Do you know which barn's theirs?"

Randy nodded, motioned for her to get in the truck, and climbed in behind the wheel. "You know, I don't think she'd worry about you like this."

"Maybe not," Dawn said. "But that's really not the point here, is it?"

Randy shook his head. "I wish you wouldn't have anything to do with her. She's nothing but trouble."

"Oh?" Dawn looked at him. "Is that why you never had anything to do with her?"

Randy held up his hands and wisely chose to drop the subject.

Bud Meyers could be heard screaming at Ginney from two barns away. Dawn slipped her hand in Randy's as they started down his shedrow.

"I told you I want you out of this barn! And out of the house!"

"I will leave! I just wanted to talk to you!"

"Fuck you! You lied to me! That horse could've won walking!"

"I didn't want to lie to you!"

"Yeah, right!" Bud Meyers pointed vehemently behind her. "Because you got more goddamned loyalties to her!"

Ginney turned.

Dawn glanced from the man to Ginney. "We're going now. Are you coming?"

"Yes." Tears streamed down Ginney's face. "He won't listen anyway."

Bud threw his hand up. "That's right! Go shack up with them! You sons of bitches!"

Ginney swung around. "I'm not shacking up with them or anyone else! And don't call her names! She's not like me!"

"She's not?! She's whoring around with him, isn't she?"

Randy started toward him, but Dawn grabbed his arm, held tight. "We're not the issue here. Ginney is. Don't."

Ginney ran past them, sobbing.

"That's right!" her father yelled. "Go on! You're just like your mother! A slut!"

Randy turned to leave, but Dawn stood perfectly still, glaring at Bud Meyers. And still glaring, she approached the man. "Make no mistake about this," she said, her voice barely above a whisper, face to face. "Because I don't plan to repeat myself."

Bud opened his mouth to object.

"You're a sick man, and you're allowing that sickness to destroy your daughter. You say Ginney is a slut. Well, I say you made her that way. And none of this, I mean none of this, phases your ex-wife one stinking bit!"

She turned from Bud's stunned expression, and took about two steps toward Randy before swinging back around. "And make no mistake about this either. You ever call me a whore again, you will live the rest of your life regretting it. I promise you."

As she took Randy's hand, he was amazed. Amazed she'd confronted Bud like that. And amazed that Bud listened. But what amazed him most, was when she'd reached for his hand, his was trembling with anger. Hers was perfectly calm.

Dawn nudged Ginney to move over and got in next to her, while Randy walked around to the driver's side, frowning at the seating arrangement.

Ginney was still crying. "God, I hate him."

Dawn nodded, glancing at her. "Do you want to go get something to eat?"

"I need a drink."

"Sounds good to me," Randy said, agreeing, but feeling awkward and being careful to sit as close to his door as possible. "Where to?"

They went to the bar at The Rib, the jam-packed racetracker owned and frequented establishment across the street, where Ginney wasted no time. "Rum and coke and make it stiff."

"Beer," Randy said. He looked at Dawn; she nodded. "Two light drafts."

Ginney wiped her eyes with a napkin and drew several deep breaths to try and compose herself. "So, what did you say to my dad anyway?"

Dawn shrugged. "Nothing really. I just..." She shook her head. "Nothing."

Randy leaned back as the waitress put their drinks down and just marveled as he looked at Dawn. Nothing? He thought about what she'd said and the tone of her voice. "Make no mistake about this." Such power, such confidence. So, so sure of herself. Bud Meyers never stood a chance. No wonder he listened.

When Ginney excused herself to go to the ladies room a few drinks later, Randy had to ask. He leaned close to Dawn and gently pushed her hair back off her cheek as she stared down at her hands. "Dawn, what you told Bud. Could you do that? Would you?"

Still focusing on her hands, Dawn nodded slowly, her voice taking on that same menacing tone. "In a New York minute."

Randy turned her face toward his, and stared into Bask-Fioritto eyes for the first time. He swallowed hard, with no doubt whatsoever about what Bud Meyers had seen in them.

By the time they stood up to leave, Ginney had consumed six rum and Cokes, and Randy seven beers. Dawn had spent the entire time nursing two drafts and eating five bags of tortilla chips. As they started out, Bud Meyers rose from the far end of the bar. Dawn feared another confrontation between him and Ginney, but Bud said he just wanted to talk.

"What about?" Ginney asked defiantly.

Bud hesitated. "I want you to come home."

Dawn glanced from one to the other, then at Randy. She hadn't realized until now, but he was as buzzed as Ginney.

"You gonna yell at me again?" Ginney asked.

"No. Where's your car?"

Ginney turned to Dawn then Randy, who just shrugged. He had no idea. And Dawn stepped closer. "Ginney, are you sure you want to go home? Because you don't have to."

"It's okay." Ginney staggered a little. "Dad don't hurt me. He just yells at me."

Dawn stepped back out of the way. "Her car's still in the horsemen's lot. It's locked."

Bud nodded, but wouldn't look at her, and took Ginney by the arm to lead her out.

Dawn walked with Randy to his truck, and smiled when he stopped at the door and just stared. "Do you mind if I drive?" she asked.

"Your car?"

Dawn shook her head and reached into his pocket for his keys. "No, your truck. I'll leave my car at the track."

Randy bowed and raised his hands. "Anything you say, Princess Fioritto."

Dawn laughed. "Do you get crazy when you're drunk?"

"I'm not drunk."

"Right." Dawn unlocked the passenger door and watched in amusement as he poured himself into the seat. "You're slurring."

"I aaam not."

Dawn smiled and kissed him. "I think you need to eat something."

"Fine...show the wave."

Dawn shook her head and laughed. "On second thought, maybe we ought to just go home. Heaven forbid someone should see you like this."

Chapter Twenty-Two

Randy spent the following morning regretting the night before. He couldn't remember even leaving The Rib, let alone how he got to Dawn's apartment, and nursed a hangover until well past noon. When he finally finished morning rounds and made his way to the Miller barn, Dawn was just about to leave and added to his anguish.

"How are you doing?" she asked.

He shrugged. "I think I'll make it."

"I wish I could say the same."

"Why?" Randy frowned. "What do you mean? You were fine."

Dawn started past him into the tack room. "I have cramps."

Cramps? Randy turned. Stared. Again he tried to remember. "I don't suppose we uh...?"

Dawn chuckled. "Last night? No."

Randy sighed. Wonderful. Cindy's wedding was only three days away. No sex now and none then. He followed Dawn inside. "Wait a minute. *Cramps* as in getting my period? Or cramps as in I already got it?"

Dawn laughed. "Already got it." She shook her head, sat down on the cot to make a list, and smiled at him when he sat down next to her. "Of all days too. I'm meeting Linda for lunch; then she and I are going shopping."

Randy nodded, wallowing in his self pity.

"Do you need anything?"

When Randy just looked at her, Dawn laughed. "From the mall," she specified. "From the mall."

Randy shook his head.

"Then leave, so I can lock up." She made one last notation and folded her list. "I have to go by and see Ginney before I leave. Did you see her this morning?"

"No..." Randy said, refusing to budge. "Nor did I care to look."

Dawn frowned. "Randy, come on. Don't make me sorry I waited for you."

Randy looked at her, registered what she'd just said, and smiled. This was a first. "You waited for me?"

Dawn reached for his hand and pulled him to his feet. "Yes, now come on, or I'm going to lock you in here."

"Fine with me. Just make sure you let me out in five or six days."

Dawn laughed and in a very uncharacteristic show of affection, hugged him. "What do you want to do tonight?"

Randy sighed and brushed his lips against her hair. "I don't know." With this, they made plans to do nothing, absolutely nothing, except maybe Chinese food and television, and then went their separate ways.

When Dawn walked under the shedrow of Bud Meyers' barn, she could see Ginney at the other end holding a horse for her father, who was swearing up a storm while trying to dab ointment on a cut on the inside of one of its hind legs. Dawn motioned she'd wait for her up at this end. After a few minutes, Ginney walked down.

"All that, and wouldn't you know the goddamned thing rubbed it right off."

Dawn smiled. "So how is everything?"

Ginney hesitated. "Okay."

"Okay...?" Dawn searched her eyes.

Ginney nodded, then shrugged. "It's weird. He never said anything last night, but this morning we talked. I mean, we actually talked."

Dawn acknowledged this apparent rarity with supportive silence as Ginney continued. "He's trying to see things from my point of view. Of course, that means I have to try and do the same. Me and Mom have embarrassed him a lot."

Dawn studied her face and smiled.

Ginney laughed then. "You know, he thinks you're a witch. It's true. A real live, honest-to-God witch. He says there's something about your eyes." Both of them laughed. "He really believes it too. He's been knocking on wood all morning."

Linda surprised Dawn by being on time again. She'd already ordered for both of them and was drinking her second cup of coffee.

"Is this going to become a habit?" Dawn teased.

"Perhaps." Linda smiled. "I love your hair! When did you get it done?"

"The other day. Randy likes it too, though he wouldn't even look at it at first." She relayed the story to Linda, who at first laughed and then in the very next instant started to cry.

Dawn shook her head. PMS. They both suffered from it in varying degrees. Nothing to be alarmed about. "Okay, you're crying because...?"

Linda shrugged, wiped her eyes, and shrugged again. "It's just that it's so obvious how much he cares for you."

"And...?"

"And Harland's asked me to marry him."

Dawn smiled, pretended to be surprised, and sat back. "This is a sad, sad day."

"I know." Linda laughed, still tearful. "I'm so happy, I can't stand it. Something's going to go wrong. I just know it."

"Nonsense," Dawn said, reminiscent of her mother, and invoking immediate thoughts of her. Haunting thoughts. She quickly changed the subject. "Eat up. We've got shopping to do. And you know how I love shopping."

Linda smiled. Dawn hated to shop, and as the afternoon wore on, hated it more and more. "I look like a football player," she said, referring to a dress with huge shoulder pads, which she couldn't get out of fast enough. "Forget this."

Linda was growing weary as well. She turned to Miss Diane, the woman who'd been fitting them both for years, top floor at Saks. "I think we're losing her."

"Not to worry. I have been saving the best for last." She disappeared and returned with two outfits, a pale green silk dress, crisscrossed and draped elegantly at the shoulders, and a three-piece winter white cashmere suit.

"Yes!" Dawn tried them both on. The always-necessary alterations were pinned; hips, waist, and hem lowered. And they were all set. Both outfits would be tailored and delivered within two days. When Randy arrived at the apartment, Dawn was sound asleep on the couch. The lobby attendant had to buzz twice before she answered.

"Sorry, yes. Send him up."

He was due well over an hour ago and looked exhausted. "What happened?" she asked, letting him in.

"I was meeting with Raffin. We're going to make an offer to buy out Jake's old partner." He wrapped her in his arms, savoring the length of her body against his, and kissed her, then kissed her again. "How late are they open downstairs?"

"They're closed."

"Oh great. Do you feel like going out?"

Dawn shook her head. "When you were late I went ahead and ordered up two of the specials." She glanced into the kitchen. "All we have to do is microwave them."

Randy smiled, laced his fingers through her hair, and held her a moment. "Which reminds me." He turned and walked to the phone to write down her number, once and for all, and having taken out his wallet, put a twenty-dollar bill on the table.

"What do I have to do for that?" Dawn joked.

"It's for dinner. But let me see how much more I've got?"

"Not enough," Dawn replied, laughing. "What do you want to drink?"

"Coke, if you have it. I'm on call."

"Again?" Dawn said from the kitchen.

"And tomorrow too. I'm going to be gone this weekend, remember."

Dawn nodded. "So what's this about buying out Jake's partner?" When she handed Randy his Coke, he popped the lid and took a long thirsty drink.

"Raffin and I have been kicking it around since..." He trailed off, didn't want to say since Jake's death, and took another drink. "We're just finally getting around to putting a proposal together."

Dawn placed one of the meals into the microwave, closed the door, set the timer, and looked at him. "This is really strange, I never thought of you as having a base here. Are you sure you want to do this?"

Randy looked at her. "What do you mean?"

"Set down roots here, with your family being so far away."

Randy stared, felt a lump forming in his throat. "Dawn? Did you think I was just passing through?"

Dawn shook her head, staring as well now. "No, I just..." She shrugged, seemingly nonchalant, and turned her back to him, watching the turntable in the microwave go round and round.

Randy touched her arm, and when she wouldn't look at him, put his Coke down and pulled her close. "What *did* you think?"

"I don't know. I'm not sure. I guess I thought this was just a residency. That you'd be here only until..."

Randy swallowed hard, gazing into her eyes. The timer went off then, but he refused to let her go. "If that's the case, then what did you think was going on here? Between you and me?"

Dawn shook her head. What could she say? This was only temporary. They were temporary. "Randy, forget it. Okay? I didn't mean anything."

"Fine." Randy hesitated, then smiled tentatively and kissed her. "If you say so. But I'm here to stay, Dawn. I want you to understand that."

"I do." Dawn nodded, steadied her trembling bottom lip before it gave her away, and turned to finish heating their dinners. "I hope you like shrimp."

When they were seated in the living room in front of the television, Dawn asked casually, "Why are you interested in buying Jake's practice? What's the appeal?"

Randy chewed and looked at her. "The appeal?"

"Yes. Is it the business aspect that...?"

Randy smiled. "No, not at all. That part I dread. But then again so did Jake, which is why this is so ideal. He'd literally removed himself from the daily operation of the building and the small animal end over the years. Half the time I picked up supplies from his house."

"So you would be...?"

"Strictly large animal. Not that I don't like cats and dogs," he added, smiling. "Or that there isn't any money in it."

Dawn looked at him.

"I just don't like being inside all that much."

Dawn nodded. "So how does Dr. Raffin figure in?"

"Well, he feels the same way. He prefers large animal. But with all the developments going up in his area, it doesn't seem to be the direction he's headed. He wants out."

"And so you two are going to...?"

"The basic proposal is this. His booming small animal practice for Jake's hospital and the large animal end."

"It sounds reasonable to me."

Randy agreed. "There's only one snag. The twin brothers who want to buy in with Lenore."

"Lenore?"

"The small animal vet at Jake's."

"What's the snag?"

Randy chuckled. "Their uncle's an attorney. You should see some of the fine print."

Dawn smiled. "For instance?"

"Well, territory stipulation for one."

"Which you agree or disagree with?"

"Disagree. I wouldn't actively go in and recruit their patients. I don't want them. But at the same time, I don't like people telling me what to do, or where I can or can't go. The point of being your own boss is to be your own boss."

There were other considerations as well. Randy scooped up the last of his fried rice and explained about the size and benefit of Jake's building as opposed to Raffin's; Jake's was owned outright by his estate, Raffin's was under a mortgage, and Jake's also offered the most room for expansion.

"What would you do about large animal surgery in the meantime?" Dawn asked, if in fact they bought out Jake.

"The same thing he's been doing for years. Anything other than a standing operation gets sent to Ohio State. Which is why we'd want to build as soon as possible. We're figuring it in the loan package."

It was then his pager went off. He phoned the answering service right away and was promptly put on hold. He looked at Dawn. "So what do you think?"

Dawn shrugged.

"What? What's the problem? Does this mean you have to rewrite some of your book?"

Dawn rolled her eyes. Him and this fascination with her novel. "At least two chapters."

"I'll bet," Randy said, believing her and turning as the operator came on the line. "What do you have for me?"

As he jotted down the information, Dawn gathered their plates and took them into the kitchen. Randy hung up the phone, studied the name and address for a moment trying to place the person, and looked up when she returned. "Do you feel like coming with me?"

Dawn paused, and shook her head. "Not tonight. I'm still not feeling all that great."

Randy teased her with a smile. "You do look a little pale."

"Thank you." Dawn leaned her head against his chest, nestled in his embrace, and found herself listening to the steady, familiar beat of his heart. "Are you going to come back?"

Randy smoothed her hair. "If you want me to."

She did. Desperately.

"Are you going to wait up for me?"

"Uh..."

Randy laughed. "Then you'd better give me a key."

"Good idea." There was an extra set in the desk. "Here. This one's to the garage door, and this one's to the apartment."

Randy took them both and as she looked up at him, searched her eyes. "Are these mine to keep?"

Dawn hesitated, but only for a second. "Yes," she said. "Put them on your key ring."

When Randy returned several hours later, Dawn rolled over in bed, focused on him, and smiled. "Everything okay?"

He nodded. "Shhh. Go back to sleep." He sat down on the chair next to the bed, took off his shoes, and quietly went into the bathroom. The ensuing sound of the shower reminded Dawn of a distant ocean, the waves coming and going with the apparent turns and motion of his body...the spray pulsating his massive shoulders and strong back. The length of his arms. His muscular legs. Harder and harder. Again and again. Then softer. And softer. More distant and further and further away.

Randy crawled into bed next to her, tucked her snugly into his arms, and kissed her good night. The blankets were nice and warm. She was nice and warm. "I love you," he whispered.

"I love you too."

Dawn left for the racetrack in the morning without waking him, and a little after eight walked up to the guard shack to make a phone call. She hung up when she saw his truck turn in off the highway. He stopped for his messages and then drove up next to her.

"Calling the weather?"

Dawn smiled and leaned in to kiss him. "No, I was calling you to make sure you weren't still sleeping."

Randy yawned. "You should've woke me when you got up."

"I figured you needed to sleep, you got in so late."

Randy shrugged. "It goes with the job. Speaking of which." He glanced at his watch. "I've got a ton of farm calls this afternoon, so I'm going to be late again, but let's do something besides Chinese. I'll stop for a pizza."

Dawn smiled, agreeing, and started to walk away. "I'll pick up some beer."

"Wait a minute," Randy took out his wallet. "Here, and while you're at it, pick up some pepperoncinis. You know, the little hot peppers. They're..."

"I know what they are. Anything else?"

Randy handed her a ten-dollar bill and then a five. "Yes, get some Oreos."

Dawn laughed and kissed him again. "I'll see you later."

Tom was scratching himself when she returned to the barn.

"Jesus! Enough is enough. All right?"

"I'm sorry. I can't help it. But I do think it's getting better."

"Right." Dawn sighed. "Where's Ben?"

"He went up to the kitchen with Miguel and his agent."

Dawn headed for a bale of straw to bed down the filly's stall. "Do you think Ben'll ride him again?"

Tom flicked a toothpick toward the muck bin and popped another one in his mouth. "Probably. You know what he says about not taking things personally."

Dawn glanced back at him and shook her head. "*Stop scratching*!"

"Shit!" Tom cupped his hands. "I don't even know when I'm doing it anymore."

Dawn sighed in exasperation. That a grown man, particularly one as rough and tough as Tom, would be afraid to go to a doctor, amazed her. "What's the big deal?"

Tom shrugged, and in a rare moment, grew rather serious. "Listen. I don't want a man touching me there. All right?"

Dawn shook her head. "Then go to a woman."

Tom gasped. "What? And have her see me when I'm not at my best? Not on your life."

Dawn laughed. He was hopeless. "Have you tried putting anything on it?"

"Yeah, lots of things. They only make it worse. It's driving me crazy. And I'm so goddamned tired of washing everything. I keep..."

"Wait. Maybe you're allergic to your soap."

"No, I've been using it for years."

"I mean your laundry soap."

Tom shook his head at first, then stared. "Holy shit!" His eyes lit up. "I bet that's it!" He grabbed her by the shoulders, hugged her, and took off down the shedrow. "Do Red's stall for me!"

"What?! No!"

"And tell Ben I'll be back later. I've got laundry to do."

Dawn laughed. "Use Ivory Snow."

"Oh baby, I will," he sang. "From my head to my shoes. Ooh, ooh, ooh ooh ooh, I got a new attitude...."

Ben laughed as well when Dawn relayed the message and sat down in the tack room with a heavy sigh. "I was allergic to a certain shaving cream once. I walked around for days looking like Meg had slapped me up one side of the face and down the other."

Dawn smiled.

"Well, let's hope that's what it is." He took out his condition book. "So what time are you and Randy leaving tomorrow?"

"Around noon. Our flight's at one."

Ben nodded. "And you'll be back when?"

"Late Sunday." Dawn glanced over his shoulder to see which page he was looking at in the book, and whose name he was penciling in. "Why?"

Ben glanced at her and grinned. "Just wanting to know how many days of peace and quiet I'm going to have."

Dawn laughed. "Don't let Tom change anything."

"Don't worry. Nothing'll change."

When Randy arrived at Dawn's apartment that evening, she had all the drapes pulled and the stereo playing softly. "Lord, it looks like a dungeon in here." He put the pizza down and walked over to the terrace. "You're missing an awesome storm coming with these curtains closed."

"I hate storms. And they're drapes."

"Yeah, well I love them. Dark clouds, whistling wind, the snap of lightning."

"And let's not forget the rattling of wood, the creaking of windows. The lights going out. Wires down. Sirens off in the distance." She turned the music up louder.

"Come here," Randy said, twice before she relented. "Now tell me that isn't beautiful?" A distant lightning bolt lit up the clouds in spectacular hues of red and orange.

Dawn shivered in his arms. "Even so, it's still a storm."

Randy kissed her neck. "How many times did you see the *Wizard of Oz*?"

Dawn laughed. "Go ahead, make fun of me." She cringed from the sight of an aggressive streak of vertical lightning. "At least ten or eleven times."

"Well, if I promise to keep the wicked witch from stealing your shoes, can we keep the curtains open?"

"Drapes, Randy. They're drapes."

Randy laughed. "Come on, let's eat."

Dawn placed her back to the storm, only to jump repeatedly with each thunderous boom, and moved her chair so she wouldn't have to see the reflection of the lightning.

Randy just shook his head.

Eventually she relaxed a little and thought about tomorrow. "What are your parents like?"

Randy reached for another piece of pizza. "Oh, average I guess."

Dawn smiled.

"You'll like them. Don't worry."

Dawn nodded. What concerned her was if they would like her. She could see them saying, "Excuse me. What did you say your last name was? Isn't that the name of...?"

"Dawn?"

"Yes." She looked at him.

"I'm serious. You'll like them. Okay?"

"Okay." She passed him another napkin when he motioned for one. "I wasn't sure of a gift for Cindy, so I'm just going to give them money. All right?"

Randy shrugged. "Not too much I hope."

Dawn smiled, ignoring the implication, to a point. "No, it'll be the appropriate amount. I've consulted my social secretary."

Randy laughed. "Are you all ready to go?"

"Yes." Her dress had arrived and everything else was laid out. "Are we still going to meet here at noon?"

Randy nodded. "I've got an appointment with Raffin and the lawyer at ten-thirty, so I should be right on time."

Dawn studied his eyes. It looked as if he had a thousand things running through his mind. "All Together's scheduled to work out of the gate again. It's set for eight. Do you think you can make it?"

"I'll be there," he said. His pager went off then. A few minutes later, he was kissing Dawn good-bye. It was after one when he returned, and this with his pager beeping in the elevator. He phoned the answering service from Dawn's living room, and smiled as she emerged from the bedroom rubbing her eyes.

He hung up, gazing at her. "You are so beautiful."

Dawn walked like a zombie in his direction. "You don't have to go back out again, do you?"

"Sorry...but yes." He tilted her chin and kissed her. "Don't worry, I'll be back."

Dawn gazed into his tired eyes. "Are you all right? Do you want some coffee?"

He shook his head. "I'll get some at the corner. Come on, I'll tuck you in." He lifted her up into his arms and carried her down the hall, laid her down gently and kissed her, then kissed her again, lingering this time. "Sleep tight," he said, touching the side of her face and securing the blankets around her. "I'll see you in a little while."

He never returned. When the alarm went off, Dawn stared at his side of the bed, showered, and left. The crowd for All Together's last work was meager compared to the one assembled for the show today. And no one would leave disappointed. She stood a little better this time, was first out of the chute, worked a blistering 44.1 for the half mile, and galloped out five eighths in 56.2. Of the four horses she'd worked with, the nearest one at the finish was at least six lengths back.

Randy had gotten there right as she broke and just shook his head when Ben showed him the times on his stopwatch.

He looked at Dawn and smiled. "I'm about half a minute behind schedule."

Ben walked on.

"Did you get *any* sleep?" Dawn asked.

"No, none."

"What happened?"

Randy yawned. "Well, the last one was an Arab stud horse that fractured its hock."

"Oh no. Is he going to be all right?"

"Yeah, it's the owners I'm worried about. If it scars, they'll either die or sue me."

"Incorporate," Dawn said. "Quickly."

Randy laughed. "I'll see you at noon."

Dawn called after him. "Randy?"

He turned.

"Do your parents know I'm coming?"

Randy laughed. "Relax."

"Well? Do they?"

"Yes."

"Are you sure?"

"Positive."

Chapter Twenty-Three

Dawn and Randy arrived just in time for their flight, and settled into their seats. "God, I'm glad you're with me," Randy said, smiling. "Just don't go to sleep. That one stewardess keeps looking at me."

Dawn chuckled. She'd leaned her head back, eyes closed, and now opened one facetiously. "So I've noticed. I'll have to have a talk with her."

Randy laughed. If she could only be jealous just once. Just once. It would make his day.

The stewardess in question stopped to serve them. "What can I get you?" She smiled at Randy.

"Well, I don't know," he said, seizing the opportunity to *make* Dawn jealous. "I'm not really sure."

The young woman smiled modestly, as if being addressed by a movie star, an idol, and giggled, actually giggled as she went through the selections.

Dawn marveled.

"I think I'll have a Coke," Randy said.

The stewardess handed him a plastic glass filled with ice cubes, and a warm can of Coke, blushed, and looked at Dawn.

"And what would you like?"

"Mineral water," Dawn said. "Please."

The stewardess hesitated. "Uh...we don't..." She glanced over her shoulder to the front of the plane, the first class section, and turned back to Dawn, whose expression never wavered. "I'll see what I can do."

"Thank you," Dawn said.

When the young woman walked away, Randy smiled at Dawn. "How do you do that?"

"What?"

"That power thing you do?"

Dawn laughed. "I asked for a mineral water, Randy, not the moon."

"I know, but still..."

Dawn thought of her mother, a woman never refused anything, for as long as she'd known her, for as long as she'd lived. Ask, and ye shall receive. Until the day she died.

Randy gazed at Dawn apprehensively. "Are you all right?"

Dawn nodded and stared out the window.

"You don't get motion sickness, do you?"

Dawn shook her head. "We're sorry, Miss Fioritto," she could hear a strange voice from the past saying. "When the plane went down..."

"Dawn?"

She looked at Randy. "I'm fine. I'm just thirsty."

Randy nodded, and turned to look for the stewardess, to tell her to hurry, to insist she hurry, and use all the charm he had. My God. He'd just remembered. Her parents died in a plane crash.

"How long is the flight?" Dawn asked.

"An hour and a half," Randy said, covering her hand with his. "Hang in there."

Dawn nodded, staring at the wing tip.

Hurry, please.

Arriving on time and without incident, the two of them were disembarking when Randy spotted his father and waved. "Dad!" His father greeted him with a hug, and stood back, smiling as he turned to Dawn.

"Dad, this is Dawn Fioritto. Dawn...my dad, also known as Randy."

Dawn smiled. "It's nice to meet you."

"And it's nice to meet you too." Mr. Iredell nodded, held up his scarred hands apologetically, no hand shake, and motioned to his left. "Baggage is that way."

As Randy retrieved Dawn's leather tote and the overnight bags, his father observed the ease in which the two got along, the way they looked at one another. And frankly, how beautiful Dawn was, even more so because of the way she gazed at his son.

"Did mom make a lunch?" Randy asked, as they headed for the truck and the hour and fifteen minute drive home.

"You betcha."

She'd packed a feast. Cold pork-loin sandwiches on homemade bread, two with mustard and two with mayonnaise, just in case. Randy chuckled, she'd cut the crust off one of each. And four still-warm apple fritters, two sandwich Baggies of potato chips, several soft drinks and two Strohs.

"Go ahead. Those are all for you two. I ate while I was waiting for the flowers."

Dawn, sitting in the middle of the two men in the cab of the truck, handed a mustard sandwich to Randy and helped herself to an uncrusted one with mayonnaise.

Randy didn't say anything, but never recalled her eating mayonnaise before. He smiled. She was such a lady. Which is exactly what his father was thinking at that moment. Poised, and so prim and proper.

"So what do you two have in common besides horses?" he asked.

Dawn and Randy looked at one another. They just looked at one another, and then they both smiled. "I guess that's it," Randy said. "What else is there?"

His father laughed.

"How's Mom?"

His father sighed. "Oh, she cries a lot. Women amaze me. Why do they cry over weddings?"

A momentary silence caused Dawn to glance from one to the other. This was obviously intended for her to answer. She swallowed and shrugged slightly. "I don't know, I guess it's because it's a beginning, but also an end."

Mr. Iredell nodded. "All right, then why don't men cry?"

Dawn smiled. "Well, some of them do. By the same token, a lot more of them get choked up at the beginning of the World Series. The singing of the anthem. The first pitch. It's the same thing. A beginning and an end, with everything on the line."

Randy stared in amazement. "Now you talk! Apparently I just haven't asked the right questions."

Dawn and Mr. Iredell laughed. "So then," he said, changing lanes. "I hear you're a writer. What do you write about?"

Randy anticipated her reply as intently as his father. "I'm writing a novel. It's about the racetrack. By the way." She turned to Randy. "Ben's going to enter All Together next Sunday if everything goes all right."

Randy nodded.

"Is this horse in your novel?" his father asked.

"No," Dawn said.

Randy looked at her.

"Not exactly."

Randy shook his head and sighed. Not exactly. Someone like her, he heard her say, knew she'd say, as his mind wandered. It's fiction. Fiction, fiction, fiction. Yeah, right. Don't think about it, he told himself. She's in your world now, and there's not a typewriter in the house. Don't give it another thought. At least try not to.

The Iredell farm was precisely the way Dawn had pictured it, rambling and white, Spic-n-Span clean, and productive. There was even a welcoming committee of dogs, just as she'd imagined. An old Lab with a white muzzle, a hyper Golden Retriever, and a small terrier mix, friendly and not much bigger than a Chihuahua, but with a big-dog strut.

Dawn leaned down to pet them and looked up as two women appeared outside a screen door on the side porch. She wondered which one was Randy's mother. Randy took her by the hand to introduce them.

"Mom.... Aunt Helen.... This is Dawn."

The two women smiled. Up close, they looked alike except for the tears welling up in the one's eyes. Randy's mother embraced Dawn. "It's so nice to meet you," she said, and stepped back, fumbling for a tissue in her apron pocket.

Randy laughed. "Jesus, Mom!"

Aunt Helen grinned and reached for Dawn's hand. "Don't mind her. I think it's something in the water."

The next few hours were hectic with last-minute preparations. The bride and groom's families were providing the meal for the reception, and food was coming from three different houses. The Iredells were responsible for the main dishes, cabbage rolls, sausage, rigatoni, and scalloped potatoes. The groom's family was making the salads and casseroles. And a team of aunts, uncles, and cousins were furnishing the desserts. Dawn was grateful for something to do. Her job was to slice the six dozen rolls and eight loaves of bread. Some of the loaves were still warm, which proved a challenge. But she had gentle hands, Liz, Randy's mother said, "and did a fine job." At five o'clock, right on schedule, the back of Mr. Iredell's pickup was loaded and on its way to the VFW Hall.

Cindy showed Dawn to her bedroom, jokingly referring to it as her "old bedroom" as of that night, and Dawn sat down on the bed. She could hear Mary Lou and Anne talking in the bathroom next to them. She'd met so many people downstairs, it was hard keeping all their names straight, but Mary Lou she remembered well. There was something about the way she'd kept staring at her and then looking away conspicuously whenever Dawn glanced in her direction.

"With just one bathroom," Cindy said, "we'll have to take turns getting ready."

Dawn smiled. "That's okay. I'm quick." She laid back on the bed and ran her hands over the chenille spread, bare in spots in a comfortable way. "I love this house."

Cindy nodded, and sat down next to her. "I'm going to miss it." She looked around with nostalgia already in her eyes, sighed, then stood up and shook her head. "But not the fact that there's only one bathroom. Mary Lou, hurry up!" she shouted, and headed down the hall to pound on the door. "You've been in there for an hour already. Come on!"

Dawn reached for a pillow and closed her eyes, thinking about the living room downstairs, how cozy it was, the furniture all Early American, the fireplace large and smoke stained. In fact, to her, the entire house was cozy, even the utility room with all the boots, gloves, and jackets and a stockpile of wood. She imagined what it was like for Randy to grow up here, a little boy, Christmas mornings, the first day of school...

Mary Lou sat down hard on the bed. "I'm sorry. Did I wake you?"

Dawn smiled and sat up. "No, not really. Is it my turn?"

"In the bathroom? No," Mary Lou replied, pretending to be enthralled with the gloss of her own fingernails. "Anne's still in there."

Dawn glanced at her watch.

"Cindy tells me you're a writer and that you have racehorses. Is that how you met Randy?"

"Yes," Dawn said, glancing at Anne as she came through the doorway. "But actually I only own part of a racehorse."

Anne smiled, having taken an instant liking to Dawn. "Was it love at first sight?"

Dawn chuckled. "No." And fortunately there was no time to elaborate, which would have been awkward under any circumstances, let alone under this Mary Lou's watchful eye and eager ears.

Cindy appeared in a crisis. "My hair! Of all days! See what you can do with it," she pleaded to Anne.

Mary Lou glanced at Dawn. "Anne's a beautician," she explained. "Maybe she can do something with your hair too."

Anne frowned at her for saying such a thing. "Are you crazy? Her hair is beautiful. I wish it were mine."

Dawn glanced in the mirror. The main reason she'd always preferred to pull her hair back in a braid, was that there was so much of it, which was never more evident than now with the perm.

"I can dress it up if you want," Anne said, motioning for Cindy to sit down at the vanity. "I have plenty of time. I'm all ready. All I have to do is put my dress on."

Cindy and Mary Lou laughed. "She's never been on time in her life," Cindy told Dawn. "Her mother was three weeks late delivering her and she's been late ever since."

"Yeah, well not today." Anne nudged Cindy's hand out of the way and picked up a comb. "Everything's under control."

Dawn took her turn in the bathroom and while she was gone, became the subject of discussion. "So what do you think of her?" Cindy asked.

Anne smiled. "I like her. And it's pretty obvious why Randy likes her."

Cindy nodded. "He's crazy about her."

"She looks rich."

Mary Lou disagreed. "She doesn't look rich to me. Just plain."

Anne looked at her and frowned in disbelief. "Plain is not the word I'd use to describe her, not unless that's the latest term for tall, thin, and rather beautiful."

Dawn returned a few minutes later, dressed, and with her hair all but dry. Anne fussed over it eagerly, still bragging about having everything under control. Cindy slipped on her Victorian wedding gown of satin and lace. Anne zipped her up, and it was time for the veil. This was when Cindy's mom and Aunt Helen appeared in the doorway.

"Oh my..." Liz muttered. "My little girl." Of course, she started crying again, and that made Cindy cry. Aunt Helen scolded them both, but had tears in her eyes as well.

"Now, now..." she said. "Let's make sure we have everything. Something old, something new, something borrowed, something blue."

Cindy's mouth dropped. "What?"

Anne glanced from Cindy to her mom and plopped down on the bed. "Some maid of honor I turned out to be. I knew I'd forget something. I forgot everything."

Aunt Helen laughed. "Let's not panic." She looked at Cindy. "Your dress is new. That leaves..."

"Like I said, everything," Anne moaned. "I knew it. It was too good to be true. We're going to be late."

Dawn observed the mounting anxiety, all eyes darting around the room, and touched her neck. "I have my mother's..."

Everyone looked anxiously at her.

"What?"

"Her blue diamond," Dawn said, removing her hand from the pendant. "It's old, and it's blue. And you certainly may borrow it."

"Oh, Dawn," Cindy sighed. "I'd be honored. If you don't mind."

Aunt Helen rushed over to help Dawn unclasp it, squeezed her shoulders warmly, and with great care and reverence, put it on Cindy. "There," she said. "All set. Now let's get going before we *are* late."

They arrived at the church ten minutes early. Dawn hadn't seen Randy since he'd left in the truck with the food. Marvin, Cindy's husband-to-be, had offered his home for the men to shower and change, and Randy had hoped to be able to take a nap, even if it was just for a few hours.

Dawn looked around the tiny church, enchanted with its stained-glass windows and the rainbow of light dancing on the rows and rows of sturdy oak pews. Cindy, Anne, and Mary Lou were hurried into one of the Sunday School rooms, while Dawn and Aunt Helen were ushered to a pew up front. Liz was escorted alone and with formality, as all those gathered smiled and nodded and acknowledged the tears in her eyes. Her baby was getting married.

The organ sounded the prelude to the wedding march as the groom, his best man Steve, and Randy took their places to the right of the altar.

Dawn leaned close to Aunt Helen. "Isn't he handsome?" she whispered.

Aunt Helen nodded. Randy turned then and smiled. And the music changed with hesitation and a succession of beats. Mary Lou started down the aisle first, then Anne, both of them dressed in fluffy pink gowns and carrying pink and white carnation bouquets.

"Please remain seated," the Reverend Van Cleff announced as the bride appeared on the arm of her father, to be escorted down the aisle to the man who was to be her husband.

The ceremony was brief, yet elegant, in a no-nonsense Presbyterian sort of way. The receiving line following included both sets of parents, the bridal party, the bride and groom, two deacons, and the minister and his wife, who stood at the door.

Aunt Helen took hold of Dawn's hand to introduce her. She in turn offered her best wishes, greetings, and congratulations. Randy kissed her and whispered, "I love you," in her ear. She smiled and went outside with everyone to shower Marvin and Cindy with rice. Then it was off to the VFW.

Dawn was seated next to Aunt Helen again, Liz and Randy Sr. to her left. The family table, it was dubbed, and every time the expression was used, Dawn experienced a feeling of warmth, but also sadness. There would be no wedding for her. No mother and father to look on with approval. Not hardly. She was living a lie, and to enter into a marriage under those circumstances would be a travesty.

Mary Lou sat across from Randy at the bridal table and took every opportunity to touch him, engage him in conversation, and monopolize his attention. Dawn appeared not to notice, even when Mary Lou would laugh out loud and say, "Oh, Randy..." in the most annoying way. But notice she did.

Her mother had taught her early on how to hold things inside, not to ignore them, for that wasn't healthy. Just to not let it show. Hold your chin high. Rise above it. Don't let it get to you. Smile.

"Champagne?"

"Yes, please."

There were toasts for health, happiness and prosperity from the best man, amidst the clanging of silverware demanding the bride and groom kiss. Trust and longevity from Randy. More kisses. And a tribute to just about everything else from Anne, who quite relieved to have gotten through the day without any major snags, even toasted, "Being on time. What an occasion!"

The food was served buffet style from both sides of the table, and each dish was as delicious as the next. The band played as people filed back and forth to the dessert table and the first polka brought most everyone to their feet. Dawn found herself dancing with numerous uncles, cousins, old classmates of Randy and Cindy's, and the father of the groom.

Randy remained with the wedding party, participating in pictures, toasts, more pictures, and more toasts, all the while trying to keep an eye on Dawn, who seemed not to miss him at all. She was dancing with someone else each time he looked, and twice he saw her waltzing with Doug Hathaway, someone he never liked much and now liked even less. Well, at least she wasn't bored, he told himself. But did she have to look like she was having the time of her life? She was laughing. What on earth could Hathaway be saying that could be that amusing?

When the band took a break, Dawn excused herself and went to the ladies room. It was a busy place. Anne made her way up next to her at the vanity.

"Having fun?"

Dawn nodded, smiling. "Yes, but I don't think I'll be able to walk tomorrow. I can't remember dancing this much."

Mary Lou appeared and leaned close to the mirror to inspect her eye makeup. "You and Doug Hathaway do make a cute couple."

Dawn stared, ignoring the innuendo while trying to place which man she was referring to. With the band playing so loud, names blended with the beat. "You mean the one that...?"

Anne intervened while compulsively fluffing Dawn's hair with her pick and adjusting the comb. "He's the one that always steps on your feet, wears enough Canoe to float a battleship, and talks about his vacation in Las Vegas."

Dawn laughed. "Oh, that one!"

Mary Lou laughed as well, in spite of herself. "He took that vacation over five years ago. To hear him talk, you'd swear it was yesterday."

Anne headed into one of the stalls then, complaining for all the world to hear about having to hike her dress up to her chin just to pee, and Dawn chuckled.

"Randy and I were childhood sweethearts, you know," Mary Lou said, right out of the blue and sounding just a wee bit tipsy. "For years. And pretty seriously if you know what I mean."

Dawn gazed at her with a somewhat indifferent expression. Not coming as much of a surprise, at least that information explained the attitude. "Really?"

Mary Lou nodded, and applied a very heavy coat of crimson lipstick, which she then blotted on a paper towel three times. "Yep, me and him were something else."

Dawn smiled. What was there to say?

Anne emerged, washed her hands, and the three of them zig-zagged their way through the crowd to the door. Randy was waiting for Dawn in the hallway. He grabbed her hand and pulled her close, his eyes glistening from the champagne.

"I missed you," he said, kissing her.

Dawn laughed and tried to step back a little. He was holding her much too close. "Have you been smoking?"

Randy nodded and kissed her again. "Steve, Marvin's best man handed out cigars. We really hammed it up for the pictures."

Anne smiled and waved over her shoulder as she edged past them, but Mary Lou held her ground. "I was telling Dawn all about us," she said.

Randy glanced at her and frowned. Just then someone shouted, "Single men over here. It's garter belt time!"

"Quick!" Randy said. "Let me go!"

Dawn laughed, shaking her head as he darted around the corner. And with a heavy sigh, Mary Lou walked away.

Aunt Helen motioned from across the room for Dawn to hurry to where the single women were assembling for the tossing of the bouquet. But Dawn very discreetly turned the other way and appeared not to see her waving with such fervor.

Randy caught the garter. Mary Lou the bouquet.

The photographer linked them together for more pictures, even had them kiss for one, and the band picked up where they'd left off with another polka. It turned into one of those dances where one constantly switches partners.

Randy didn't care to polka. He actually wasn't much of a dancer, and found himself on the sideline, watching Dawn and smiling. He hadn't even had a chance to tell her how beautiful she looked.

The bride and groom slipped out some time between eleven and eleven fifteen. There were shouts and hoots when the band leader made the announcement. And then the evening started to wind down. Randy put his glass on the bar and headed across the floor to dance with Dawn. But Doug Hathaway beat him to it. His mother and father appeared at his side. "Well, what do you think?" Liz asked.

"I don't know, Mom. I don't think it could've been any better."

Liz nodded proudly. "Thanks to everyone."

Randy agreed, still watching Dawn.

"You could always cut in, you know," his father said, glancing at him out of the corner of his eye.

Randy laughed. "Oh no." He wouldn't give Hathaway the satisfaction.

"Then allow me."

Randy played innocent observer as his father intervened, and smiled at the tender way Dawn gripped his father's arms.

"So..." Mr. Iredell said. "Are you having a good time?"

Dawn nodded and smiled. "Very. It was a beautiful wedding."

Mr. Iredell glanced at his son across the room. Randy was shaking his head, wondering what his father was saying. "So you two are quite an item, I take it."

Dawn smiled. "I don't know about that," she said. "But I do love him, if that's what you mean."

Mr. Iredell grinned. "Precisely." When he gave his son a nod, Randy straightened his tie and walked over to dance with Dawn, for the first time all evening.

The last dance of the night.

It was two forty-five before they got back to the house and just after three when Dawn curled up in Cindy's bed and fell asleep. Not a sound could be heard throughout the house when she woke at seven and tiptoed to the bathroom, wide awake. She brushed her teeth and tiptoed back to Cindy's bedroom, opened the curtain and looked outside, then sat down on the bed and saw the note Cindy had left for her on the dresser. Wrapped inside, was her mother's necklace.

> Dawn,
>   *Thank you. I was honored to wear your mother's*
> *blue diamond. I hope you are a keeper. Randy says he*
> *thinks you're going to break his heart. Please don't.*
>   *Love, Cindy*

Dawn folded the note and lay her mother's necklace on the night stand. She thought she heard a soft tap on the door, and crept over, quietly cracked it open, and when no one was there, lowered her eyes and smiled. There was a cup of steaming hot coffee on the floor, heavy on the cream, just the way she liked it. She picked it up and took a sip, sugared to perfection.

She closed the door, put on a pair of jeans and a sweater, finished the coffee and went downstairs. The kitchen was empty, but the coffee pot was full, so she helped herself to another cup, and when she heard some activity outside, walked out to investigate.

Randy was coming from the barn with his dad.

"Morning!" Mr. Iredell said, waving.

Dawn waved back.

The dogs ran up onto the porch and milled around her. She petted each one, making a big fuss over them, and smiled at Randy as he started up the steps. "Thanks for the room service," she said, and he nodded.

"I knew you'd be up." He kissed her and smoothed a lock of hair off her face.

His father walked on into the house, the dogs trailing behind him, and Dawn and Randy sat down on the porch swing.

Randy steadied it with his feet.

"This is nice." Being here felt like a different world to Dawn. It *was* a different world. And one soon full of delicious aromas emanating from the kitchen.

"Breakfast."

The rest of the morning and afternoon went much too fast for Dawn. She and Randy had taken a long walk. He gave her the grand tour. Practically every tree and rock sparked a different childhood memory or story. He explained which part of the house had to be rebuilt after the fire, how his mom had insisted it be done exactly the way it was before, minus the droop in the kitchen floor. And Dawn laughed. Then they hiked to Randy's favorite hill. A "phenomenon" he called it, with a slope so upright it felt as if they were literally standing as they laid in the grass and stared up at the meandering forms of the clouds.

"It's so quiet," Dawn said. No planes, no jets, no sounds of any traffic, just the gentle rustling of the leaves and the distant lowing of a cow.

It was here, amidst "his" heaven on earth, that they made love for the first time in a week. Hidden in the reeds, and on his own turf, Randy couldn't help thinking this. Slowly, gently, without a care in the world. Later, hand in hand, they walked back.

Dinner was roast chicken, stuffing, mashed potatoes and gravy, corn put up from the garden, and angel food cake with strawberries and real whipped cream. Afterward, while Dawn helped with the dishes, Randy went out to the barn with his father to give the pigs a going over. Then they packed to leave.

Soon they were fastening their seat belts and settling in for the flight back. Dawn closed her eyes as their plane taxied to the runway, remembering the warm embraces from Randy's parents and how they made her promise to come back real soon. She smiled and gripped Randy's hand, thinking about Aunt Helen and the wedding, the dancing, the polkas, and the white farm house already miles behind them. It would be dark by the time they landed.

Chapter Twenty-Four

The following morning it poured and poured and never let up. No lightning or thunder, just rain. But it was a deluge. The shedrow was a mess, the horses restless and itchy, and for the first time since anyone could remember, the track closed early for training. Word had it, the stewards considered it too dangerous.

"They're gun shy!" Tom shouted over the din, referring to the horrendous spill in the third race the day before. "Dawn, give me that bucket!"

Dawn had to scrape the ten pounds of mud stuck to the bottom of her boots first, then trudged her way down, and she and Tom did their best to wipe off Red before he put him in his stall.

"What happened?" Dawn asked.

"They're not sure," Tom said, following her into the tack room for a cup of coffee. "Three of the horses had to be put down, one right on the track, and two more hauled off. You should've seen the gawkers."

Ben glanced up from reading the racing form and nodded in disgust. It was something that never made sense to him, how people'll flock down to the fence to see something like that.

"That poor mother fucker couldn't even stand," Tom said, as he thought of the one that had to be put down immediately. "They held up a tarp, and people were still trying to see. What the fuck do they want to see anyway?"

Dawn shook her head.

Tom turned and noticing Barn Kitty, laughed. "Hey, little puss puss." He leaned down and picked him up. "You look like a drowned rat." He wiped him dry with a towel, the cat meowing mournfully the whole time, then launched him onto the top saddle. Barn Kitty glared down at him, flicking his paws. "Don't mention it," Tom said, and laughed again.

Dawn fixed them both a cup of coffee, handed him his, and sat down next to him. "Did any of the jocks get hurt?"

He nodded and raised his cup, his way of saying thank you, and continued. "Yeah, two." He identified them, but their names didn't ring a bell with Dawn. "Johnny got banged up too, but he was checked out and released. Kincaid is the one that's serious I guess. Only I hear, they can't operate on him because of some illegal substance they found in his blood."

Dawn shook her head.

Tom explained how the accident happened. He'd ponied a horse in the race and saw it firsthand from the quarter pole. "The horse behind Johnny clipped heels with him, bobbled, and a horse run up on him. That jock fell off; I think it might've been Kincaid. Another horse tried to jump over him, he was half up and half down, and ended up rolling him like a bowling ball. Then his jock fell as well. And after that it got really ugly."

Dawn shuddered.

Randy stopped in right about then, but didn't need to hear about the accident. He'd just come from treating one of the gruesome survivors, whose future at this stage was questionable, and he was on his way out for a full day of farm calls. He asked Dawn if she could come help him, but she said she was meeting Linda, and walked with him just outside the tack room to explain.

"She paged me."

Randy nodded. "I know, I heard. What's up?"

"I don't know, but she's never paged me. She says it's really important, otherwise..."

Randy gave her a quick kiss and ran through the rain to his truck. "It's all right. I'll see you later."

"What do you want to do?"

"I don't know," he yelled from behind the wheel. "Why don't we cook hamburgers or something."

"What?" Dawn stared through the rain. "I don't have hamburgers."

Randy laughed. "I'll bring a grill and buy some."

"Are you serious?"

Randy waved.

Dave Bacardi arrived with donuts and Tom repeated the story. This time it wasn't just one illegal substance found in Kincaid's blood, but two. He gave Dawn first dibs on the donuts to show how grateful he was for her curing him of his itch. "It was the soap powder, you genius you!" She helped herself to two of the three custard-filled. And then came the lightning and thunder.

Dawn glanced up as Linda approached the table, started to smile, and changed her mind. "What's the matter?"

Linda sat down and shook her head. "You're not going to believe it."

"Okay, try me."

Linda hesitated, searched Dawn's eyes, and fought back tears. "It's my mom and dad."

Dawn swallowed hard. "Are they...?"

"Oh, God...no," Linda said, apologizing. "It's not that. I'm sorry." She'd been so wrapped up in her own feelings, she never thought... "They're fine. It's just..." She clasped her hands in a helpless gesture. "They've separated."

"What?"

Linda nodded. "Can you believe that?"

Dawn shook her head. "No. Why?"

"Are you ready for this? Mom's seeing someone."

"What? Are you sure?"

"Yes. She told me herself. She says she's in love."

Dawn just stared a moment, then glanced around the club dining room, and leaned close. "Does Uncle Matt know?"

"Oh, yeah," Linda said. She took a big drink of ice water.

"And...?"

"I don't know. It's like he doesn't care."

"Does he know the guy? Is he...?"

"In the business? No."

Dawn nodded, uncertain if that was good news or not.

"He's a cabbie."

"What?"

"A cabbie. That's all he does. He drives a cab."

Dawn just sat there, then crossed her arms on the table and sighed. "I don't understand."

"Well, it's quite simple," Linda said, mimicking her mother's love-struck voice. "Her car broke down, it had to be towed, she took a cab, and that was that."

"Wow." Dawn sat back and just shook her head again. She didn't know what to say.

"And there's more. Harland's had him checked out. He's a recovering alcoholic and in debt up to his ears. He's after her money, that's all there is to it."

"Now wait a minute." Dawn disagreed, but fell quiet as the waiter approached the table. When the man left with their selections, she leaned close again. "I don't think in all fairness to your mother..."

Linda held up her hands.

"I'm serious. Now listen. All right?"

Linda shrugged.

"There's always two sides to a story."

Randy wasn't kidding earlier. He arrived with hamburger meat, buns, Ketchup, mustard and pickles, barbequed potato chips, and a portable tabletop gas grill, which he set up on the terrace. "It was on sale," he said. "Do you have garlic salt?"

Dawn stared. "I don't know."

Randy laughed. "Do you want to check?"

Dawn went into the kitchen and returned with a container and a frown. "Well, I found some. But..." It was half full but hard as a rock.

Randy popped the lid and held it up to the light. "This'll do." He pried it loose with the end of a fork and sprinkled it onto the already sizzling burgers. "What's the matter with you?" he asked, sitting down next to her on one of the two chaise lounges.

Dawn hesitated. "My Aunt Rebecca and Uncle Matt have separated."

Randy looked at her a moment. "So that's what Linda wanted to talk to you about?"

She nodded. "I can't believe it. They've been married for twenty-nine years."

Randy glanced at the burgers. "What happened?"

Dawn shrugged and then sighed in a manner that made it obvious she didn't really want to share this with him. "Apparently she's seeing someone else."

Randy didn't say anything.

"According to Linda, he's a cabbie."

"A what?"

"He drives a cab."

"I see," Randy said. "The low-life fucker."

Dawn looked at him. "That's not what I meant."

"What's the point then?"

Dawn stared. The point? Maybe she didn't have one. But if the man were in the business, even remotely related...

"Let me guess," Randy said. "Linda thinks he's after her mom's money."

Dawn raised an eyebrow, went to shrug, but nodded instead. Linda's mom didn't really have any money. In fact, Dawn wondered if her Aunt realized that, and she was sure Linda wouldn't know either, for that matter.

Randy got up to turn the burgers. "So, are they going to put a contract out on this guy, or what?"

Dawn glanced at him and shook her head. "A contract?"

Randy laughed. It was funny. But then again it wasn't. "Did anyone check this guy out? Maybe he can be bought off?"

Dawn reached for the potato chips. "Let's hope not."

Randy looked at her.

"Apparently he's heavily in debt."

Randy shook his head. This was unreal, and yet they were actually having this conversation. Something occurred to him then. They were having a conversation, and though it wasn't exactly about her, it was about her family, and that was progress, even if the subject matter did annoy him.

"Where do you want to eat, inside or out here on the patio?"

"Let's eat out here on the terrace," Dawn said. "I'll get the plates. What do you want to drink?"

"Beer," Randy said, and couldn't resist asking, "What's the difference between a terrace and a patio?"

Dawn glanced over her shoulder at him. "I don't know. Why?"

"Just wondering."

Dawn returned with something else on her mind. "I wasn't sure if I should tell you or not, because I don't think of it as any big deal, but Wednesday's my birthday."

"And you're just telling me now?"

Dawn smiled. "I told you it's no big deal. I don't even know why I'm telling you now, except that if you found out and I didn't tell you, you'd probably..."

"Get mad? You're damned right I would. We're supposed to be a couple here."

"And we are," Dawn said. "Look, we're eating at home."

Randy laughed, put a burger on her plate, and fixed one for himself.

"This is delicious," Dawn said.

Randy smiled. "Anyone can cook a burger, Dawn."

"Not like this," Dawn said. "You've done something amazing with the garlic."

Randy shook his head, and for a moment they just looked at one another. "So how old are you?" he asked, and remembered asking her this before.

"Twenty-seven," she said.

"Hmph." They *were* making progress. "So what do you want?"

"For my birthday? Nothing."

"Right. I'll think of something."

"Randy..." She waited for him to look at her. "Do you know what I would really like."

"What?" he said, taken by the sudden seriousness in her eyes, the sadness.

"I want things to stay the same. I don't want anything to change. Can you give me that?"

Randy nodded. "You got it."

For the next few days, Dawn hardly saw Randy, as he was on call. "It's the full moon," he kept saying, every time he started out again for yet another bizarre emergency. "Light a candle or something. I need to get some sleep."

Ben was in a bit of a mood himself. "Where the hell's my condition book? Goddamn it, I had it right here!"

Dawn searched for it. Tom searched for it. Ben searched for it again.

"Give him yours," Dawn whispered to Tom.

"I tried. He wants his."

Dawn rolled her eyes and ducked under the webbing of the filly's stall to make herself scarce. "Hide me," she said to All Together, hanging on her neck and hugging her.

Ben continued to rant and rave. "Why can't a person put something down and have it be where he left it?"

"Maybe you didn't put it down, old man. Maybe you left it at home."

"Are you trying to tell me that I don't know what I'm doing? That I'm senile? Don't you start!"

Tom threw up his hands. "Oh, give me a break."

"I'll give you a break."

Dawn drew an exasperated breath, sighed, and stuck her head out of the stall. "Do you want me to go get you another one?"

Ben looked at her. "No. I want the one I had."

Dawn turned back to All Together.

"Besides, we still have three more horses to track."

"It won't take me five minutes," Dawn said.

"Fine!" Ben decided. "It won't be the one I had, but..."

Dawn walked to the secretary's office and picked up not one, but three condition books. As she turned to leave she saw Bud Meyers. He was standing with another man at the far end of the counter and were both staring at her, apparently watching her every move.

Bud said something to the man and the man shook his head. "There's no such thing as a witch. You're crazier than a loon."

Dawn walked across the room, knowing they were still watching her, and at the door, stopped and just stared back at both of them.

Bud looked away first, then his friend, who held on a little longer, and Dawn walked out. "I told you," Bud said. "Did you ever see eyes like that? That woman's a bona fide witch."

Dawn heard Randy's voice in the tack room and walked into a waiting assembly of Ben, Randy, Ginney, and Tom.

"Surprise! Happy Birthday!"

Dawn shook her head and looked at Ben with realization. "You set me up."

He grinned, his condition book in hand.

"And you," she said to Randy, who just smiled. "You said you wouldn't tell anyone."

"Come on, come on," Tom insisted. "What's the difference? Open your gifts."

Dawn sat down on the cot, drew a deep breath, hesitated as she glanced at Randy, and began opening the first one. "You guys really didn't have to do this."

"That's from me," Tom said, motioning for her to get on with it.

Dawn smiled. "Did you wrap it yourself?"

He laughed. "Just open it." He'd gotten a little carried away with the tape.

Dawn finally was able to lift the lid, and sat there smiling. "It's my favorite," she said. Chantilly cologne. "Thank you."

"There's something else, under it," Tom said. It was a small package.

Dawn opened it carefully as Ginney, Randy, Ben and Tom looked on. "Oh, Tom..." It was a pair of tiny gold horseshoe earrings.

"I told the lady you had little ears and that you weren't big on jewelry."

Dawn gazed into his eyes. "They're perfect." She reached for his arm, he leaned down, and she kissed him on the cheek. "Thank you."

He shrugged, speechless for a change, pointed to his cheek and then at Randy to emphasize the kiss. Ginney handed over her gift.

"Really, you guys didn't have to do this," Dawn repeated, shaking her head. She looked at Randy. He was standing in the doorway, arms crossed, smiling.

Ginney wrung her hands anxiously as Dawn opened the box. "Oh my," Dawn said, and held it up. It was a hand-tooled leather belt with her name on it. "This is beautiful."

Ginney nodded. "Just don't ask what I had to do to get it so fast. Just kidding."

Dawn smiled. "Thank you."

"It's reversible," Ginney said, showing her. It fit perfectly.

Ben's gift was next, and the heaviest. She shook the box and smiled, thinking about his mood earlier. "I can't believe you set me up like that."

Ben laughed.

Dawn placed the box on her lap and proceeded to open it. "Oh, Ben." It was a brand-new bridle, one thoroughly and painstakingly treated with neatsfoot oil, which he'd taken hours to do himself last night, and it had a brass nameplate on the face strap engraved with All Together's name. "It's beautiful." She passed it around, gave Ben a hug, and turned to Randy.

"I'll give you mine later."

Dawn smiled.

"What do you mean later?" Tom teased. "You trying to say it would embarrass us?"

Randy shrugged, smoothing his beard, and everyone laughed. Then Ginney produced the cake she'd hidden on the medicine shelf. "The first one I've ever baked, so I hope it's good." They each had a piece with a cup of coffee, and then it was back to work.

With Cajun running in the fourth race that day, as usual Gloria arrived enveloped in lilac to lavish him with hugs and kisses. Charlie had maneuvered his day off to accompany her for the event. Cajun was running in a starter allowance race, so there was no threat of him being claimed. Their wedding was this weekend, only three days away. And everyone, as Charlie said, "was on cloud nine."

Gloria oohed and aahed. "Is my Cajun going to win today?"

Cajun scrunched up his nose, which Gloria declared a gesture meaning yes, and Ben shook his head and laughed. The race was two miles, and he had a good chance, but... "Don't count your chickens before they hatch."

"Oh, pooh," Gloria said. "If he says he's going to win, he's going to win."

Charlie laughed and said he wasn't about to disagree. And just then, as Gloria was patting Cajun's neck and Cajun jerked slightly, Ben noticed something. A lump.

He grabbed hold of Cajun's halter and looked closer. It was about halfway down his jugular vein.

"What is it?" Charlie asked.

When Ben touched the surrounding area, Cajun jerked and tried to pull away. He looked at Cajun's eyes, and stepped back. "Dawn?"

She came around the corner from the feed room. "What?"

"Did you eat here or go out?"

Gloria turned anxiously to Charlie. "What's the matter?"

"I went to Wendy's," Dawn said.

"Shit!" Ben muttered, and then, as if he needed to double check himself, he looked at the lump again.

"What is it?" Gloria asked frantically.

"I'm not sure," Ben said. "But I think someone's gotten to him."

"What?!" Gloria gasped, covering her mouth with both hands.

"Charlie," Ben said, walking past them and implying Charlie explain it to her. "Dawn!"

Dawn came back around the corner.

"Go find Tom," Ben said. "Check the kitchen."

Dawn stared.

"Go on," he said, and explained why. "And tell him to go to the secretary's office and get the track vet over here."

Gloria started to cry, and even harder when Ben tried to reassure her Cajun would more than likely be all right.

"More than likely?" she sobbed.

Ben held up his hands, looked at Charlie, and walked out onto the road between the barns. Dawn returned a few minutes later, said she'd found Tom, and it wasn't long before he returned as well. "Fuck!" was all he said. The track vet was right behind him.

Procedure was followed to the letter. Cajun was examined and found less than responsive, blood was drawn, questions were asked, and upon the track veterinarian's order, Cajun would be scratched from the race.

"What happens now?" Gloria asked Charlie, wiping her eyes and clinging to him.

"Well." He lowered his voice. "First of all, Ben and Tom'll have to go before the stewards."

"Why? They didn't do anything?"

"You know that, and I know that. But until an investigation proves otherwise..." He hesitated. Gloria was looking back at Cajun. "A horse is in the trainer's care."

Gloria heaved a heavy sigh. "My poor little baby."

Johnny showed up at the barn right after Gloria and Charlie left. "What happened? They just announced Too Cajun as a late scratch."

"Someone fucking got to him," Tom said, and raised his hands when Ben looked at him. "Hey, it's probably all over the goddamned track by now anyway. What difference does it make?"

"Is he all right?" Johnny asked, looking in at Cajun.

"Yeah, fine, fine," Tom said. Cajun had probably been given Acepromazine or a similar tranquilizer just to take the edge off. The blood test would tell. "He'll just be twitching in fucking la-la land for a while." He reached up and patted Cajun on the forehead. "I've been there, old buddy. I know where you're at."

Cajun stared at him in a stupor.

"Yep, I've been there," Tom said, and walked away.

Johnny followed Ben down the shedrow. He hadn't been the jock named to ride Cajun today, because he was still recuperating from the spill he had on Sunday, but was campaigning ahead. "I start riding again tomorrow. The doctor says I'll be as good as new."

Ben nodded.

When Ben walked into the tack room, Johnny lingered outside, fidgeting. Ben looked at him.

He cleared his throat. "Miguel's agent says you're riding him on All Together Sunday."

Ben shook his head. "I haven't even talked to Miguel's agent." He sat down at his desk. "All right?"

Johnny nodded, lowered his head, and just stood there.

"Look," Ben said, when finally acknowledging that Johnny wasn't going away. "If you're up to snuff by this weekend, you'll ride her. There's no question. But if you're not, you won't. It's as simple as that."

Randy was late again, a pattern Dawn should have gotten used to by now, but hadn't. She hugged her sides as she stared down at the street, wondering where he was. She wanted to talk to him about Cajun, get his opinion, have him say in that pragmatic way of his, "It's nothing, it happens, he'll be all right." She glanced at her watch. Seven forty-five.

She decided to try writing for a while, got through two terribly contrived paragraphs about racetrack grievances, read them out loud, made a face, crumpled the page, and threw it in the trash. The information was good, factual, but her heart wasn't in it. She wished she could write ahead, write about what happened to Cajun, and how it made her feel. But that wasn't how she wrote, and being relatively new at novel writing, she didn't want to fall out of line. She put another piece of paper in her typewriter and whimsically started writing about the ice machines that were always empty by seven every morning, and the mad scramble to get enough if you had a horse in that day.

She got in the groove. Security is one thing, as were run-down barns and insufficient lighting, but ice, that was another. She laughed to herself. And hot water. Ice and hot water. Where would a horseman be without them? She crumpled and tossed this page as well.

About an hour passed. She glanced at her watch and thirsty, decided to have a beer. When she opened the refrigerator, she found a note from Randy. "Hang in there," it read. "I'll be home soon."

When the phone rang a little while later, she thought it would be him, but it was Linda. "Oh my God, I'm so sorry! I can't believe I forgot your birthday."

Dawn walked over to the window and looked out. "Well, it's not like it's a big deal."

"But it is! Maybe I'll come over. Are you busy? What are you doing?"

"I'm waiting for Randy. He's planned something really special he said, but he's a little bit late. You can join us if you want."

"No, I don't want to spoil anything. What about tomorrow? Can you meet me for lunch?"

Dawn paused, trying to remember if they had a horse in tomorrow. "You want to meet at the club?"

"Where else?"

Dawn laughed. "I'll see you then."

She stretched out on the couch, stared up at the ceiling and sighed. "Where is he?" It was almost nine. She rolled onto her side eventually, let her one arm dangle to the floor, and within a moment or two of just lying there, started tapping out "Hang On Sloopy" into the carpet. "Sloopy, hang on."

Randy arrived a few minutes later, with his right arm in a cast.

"What happened?"

He sat down, rested it on his lap, and pointed to where it was broken. "I got kicked."

Dawn sat down next to him. "Why didn't you call?"

"I tried, just before they took X-rays, but the phone was busy." He leaned over and kissed her. "Then it was back to the examining room, to wait for them to put the cast on. I was ready to walk out and do it myself at that point. Finally the doctor showed up. And here I am."

Dawn touched the cast. "Does it hurt?"

"A little. At least it was a clean break."

"Who kicked you?"

"That little black shit of Durans'. I never saw it coming."

Dawn gazed thoughtfully at him. "Are you hungry? Did you eat?"

"No. You?"

She shook her head. "Do you want to just eat Chinese? We don't have to go out; they're probably still open."

He nodded. "Here, there's some money in my pocket," he said, and laughed when Dawn pretended to be leery of reaching in and getting it herself.

"Do you want a beer or something till I get back."

Randy smiled. "I can get it. Go on, hurry before they close."

Dawn got the last two sweet-and-sour pork dinners they had, and was turning to head back upstairs when Lin Chu, the man behind the counter, handed her a tiny wrapped box.

"Your friend, Randy, drop this off. He say to give to you when you come down."

Dawn thanked him, smiling tentatively, and walked away in a fog.

"Missy Fioritto?"

Dawn turned. "Yes."

"Happy Birthday!"

"Thank you." Dawn made her way to the elevator, boarded, put the dinners down, and fumbled with the wrapping paper on the gift. "Oh no...oh no," she muttered, when it became obvious that it was a ring box. "Randy, no..."

She swallowed hard, opened the card first, and read it.

> *Dawn,*
> *Nothing has to change.*
> *Love, Randy*

She opened the box, tears welling up in her eyes, and pressed it to her heart. It wasn't an engagement ring as she'd feared, but an anniversary ring. Sixteen diamonds set in white gold. She removed it carefully, her hands trembling, and smiled.

Randy was standing by the terrace, looking out into the night when she returned. "Well," he said. "Do you like it?"

"Yes," she said softly. "It's beautiful."

"Does it fit?"

"I don't know."

He walked over and took it from her, put it on the ring finger on her left hand, and looked into her eyes. "Do you understand what I'm trying to say with this?"

"I think so," she said, her voice quivering.

Randy shook his head. "I don't want you to think it. I want you to know."

"Then you're going to have to tell me what it means, Randy."

He leaned down and kissed her. "It means I'll play it any way you want, Dawn. But I want you to understand I'm playing for keeps."

Dawn nodded, her bottom lip trembling.

"Happy Birthday," he said. "Now let's eat."

Chapter Twenty-Five

Randy talked Dawn into helping him with farm calls Thursday afternoon. She had lunch with Linda first, hurried home to change, and climbed into the truck. He'd been instructed to use his broken arm as little as possible, awkward as it was, but that didn't, and wasn't stopping him.

"It's never going to heal, Randy," Dawn said, when they'd done seven calls with three more to go. "I'm sure you're supposed to be resting it."

"I'll rest it tonight," he said, and smiled. "I'll lay flat on my back and leave everything up to you."

Dawn laughed. "What would it take to slow you down?"

"A lot more than a broken arm," Randy said. "A hell of a lot more."

The last appointment proved a challenge; tubeworming a Trekaner stallion standing over eighteen hands. Randy couldn't maneuver the tube with his right hand and had to use his left, which meant holding the solution in a bucket higher than the horse's head with his right. Dawn wasn't tall enough, although she tried. The farm manager and the groom were much too short. The son attempted to stand on a step ladder, but this only spooked the horse, who held his head up even higher. So Randy struggled to do it himself, and in the truck as they were leaving, asked Dawn if she had any aspirin.

She shook her head. "No. And I have no sympathy for you."

Randy looked at her. "None?"

She smiled and gently laid her hand on his cast. "None," she said, and curled her fingers in his. "I think we passed a drugstore just up there. Stop and I'll run in and get some."

Randy nodded. His hand was trembling. In fact, his whole arm was trembling. Throbbing. After the aspirin, which he downed with a root beer, they drove to Ben's farm since they were in the vicinity, so Dawn could visit with Beau.

"Do you think he misses me?" she asked Randy, as they pulled down the drive.

Randy glanced at her. "I'd miss you."

Dawn smiled. "So what you're saying is...?"

"I'm saying yes, he probably misses you."

Dawn shook her head, still smiling. Randy didn't believe horses cared much for people one way or the other. Feed them and take care of them, they like you. If someone else feeds and takes care of them, they like them. They'd discussed this before. Dawn disagreed, and appreciated his tactful reply.

Beau jogged over to the paddock fence when she climbed up and called him, and stood with his head resting in her lap while she, as Ben would say, "talked nonsense" to him.

"Do you think he's happy?" she asked Randy.

He shrugged. "He'll be happier come this breeding season."

Dawn laughed. Ben came out to join them. "He looks a little lost, doesn't he?" he commented to Dawn.

She nodded.

"I sure hope I did the right thing."

"You did," Randy said, matter-of-factly, and Ben noticed his arm. "What happened to you?"

Randy explained, grimacing when he said he actually heard the bone snap, and Ben shook his head. "I got kicked in the chest once trying to load a horse in a trailer. I broke two ribs and bruised a kidney. I hate hospitals."

Randy nodded sympathetically.

"The worst part was they needed a..." He glanced at Dawn. "A specimen. But nothing was working, if you know what I mean. So what do they do? They go out in the waiting room and get Meg, and asked her if she could help me." He laughed. "God, I loved that woman! She told them that when I got good and ready I'd go, and to leave me alone and stop badgering me. Like what was she supposed to do to help me?"

"Well, she could've whistled," Dawn said, and they all laughed.

"Did you two eat yet?"

Dawn and Randy shook their heads.

"Come on then, I'll whip us up something."

As soon as the overnight for Sunday came out, with All Together entered and *no boy* named to ride her, a horde of agents descended upon the barn. Ben had left it open purposely because he wanted to watch Johnny ride this afternoon, to be sure he was up to snuff before deciding. He also wanted to watch Miguel, who was scheduled to ride three today, with two of them back to back.

"All things considered, Mr. Miller," Miguel's agent insisted, following him down the shedrow, "Miguel is the best choice to ride her. After all, he lost the big horse when you sent Beau Born home, and he's been very loyal."

"Loyal?" Ben stopped dead in his tracks, the hair on the back of his neck bristling. This had been a rough morning, what with going in front of the stewards, faced with a fine and having to file an appeal. "I'll tell you what. I ain't never seen such a fuss over a goddamn maiden in all my life. But if I decide to ride Miguel, and if you don't piss me off once and for all, I'll come looking for you. All right?"

Miguel's agent nodded and left as quickly as possible.

"A little hard on him, wouldn't you say, old man?" Tom said. "He's just doing his job."

Ben shrugged, tipped his hat to wipe his brow, and sat down with an exhausted sigh. Why did everything seem to take so much energy these days? He glanced down the shedrow when something caught his eye, and promptly buried his face in his hands.

It was Johnny. "Why didn't you name me on the filly, Ben?"

Ben drew a deep breath, hesitated, and looked up. He liked this kid, he really did. Still. "I don't appreciate having to explain myself, son. I told you the other day how it is, nothing's changed."

Johnny steeled his youthful jaw.

"I want to ride you, you have to know that. You've been with us on that filly from the start. But you know as well as I do how strong she is."

Johnny turned to leave.

"Now wait a minute, goddamn it!" Ben said. "You asked and I'm telling you!"

Johnny glared at the ground and slowly raised his eyes.

"She's a tough horse to ride, that's the bottom line. And I won't put you up on her unless you're a hundred percent. She's going to be looking around, she's going to be nervous, she's going to be a disaster waiting to happen, and I need one hundred percent. Okay?"

Johnny nodded. "Okay."

Dawn met Linda for lunch again. "See, I told you we'd be seeing more of each other once you moved out."

Linda laughed, in a much better mood than the last couple of times, and seemed to be handling her parents' separation a little better. It was a rather unusual separation anyway, as Uncle Matt was still at home, occupying the east wing.

"Maybe they'll get back together."

"Maybe."

"I've got to run."

Gloria and Charlie's wedding was at six that evening, with the reception immediately following, and Dawn had to go back to the track to run stalls and feed, get home and shower and dress and be ready by five, so Randy would have time to shower and change. Hopefully he'd be on time today. He'd promised. And all was well until about five-fifteen, when he still hadn't arrived.

"Come on, Randy," Dawn moaned, looking out the window into the street. "I hate being late." She turned when she heard a key in the door and let out a sigh of relief. He was all ready to go, and looked so gorgeous in his gray suit and blue shirt.

"I was running late and decided just to shower and change at my place." He lowered his eyes slowly down to her feet and back up. "Wow..."

Dawn blushed.

"Turn around," he said.

"Randy..."

"Come on."

Dawn held her hands out and twirled around, curtseyed, and laughed.

"You're beautiful, Dawn. That's all there is to it."

"I'll get my purse," she said, and glanced back over her shoulder. "Did you have any trouble getting your coat on over the cast."

He nodded. "It barely fits." The phone rang then, and Dawn motioned she'd be right back and for him to answer it.

"Hello."

"Why yes, hello. Is this Dawn Fioritto's?"

"Yes. Who's calling?"

"Matthew Fioritto."

"Just a minute." Randy handed Dawn the phone when she returned. "It's your Uncle Matt."

"Uncle Matt. Hi. How are you?" she said, and listened. "Yes, yes, that was Randy."

Randy traced the back of his hand down the side of her breast, felt the softness of her curves under the cashmere.

Dawn smiled and pushed his hand away, then turned, and listened more intently. "Why?" she said. "Why so soon? I thought. Okay. I'll talk to you then. Yes, I'll tell him."

Randy studied her eyes as she hung up. "What was all that about?"

"Nothing," she said, clamming up in that same way she used to. "He uh...says he's looking forward to meeting you."

Randy shook his head. "I hate when you do this, Dawn."

"What?" Dawn asked, knowing full well what he was referring to. "It was nothing."

"Oh really? Well, you didn't see your face. It was like somebody died, so don't tell me that."

Dawn sighed, and when Randy looked away, put her arms around his neck. "Randy, please."

He shook his head.

"I love you," she said.

He looked at her.

"Some day I'll tell you all about it, okay?"

He just looked at her still.

"I promise."

He mellowed a little, enough to lean down and kiss her, then kissed her again.

"Come on, let's go," she said, and he nodded, smoothed the front of his pants, and off they went.

Gloria was radiant in her lavender dress, and Charlie very distinguished in his white tuxedo with tails. Gloria's matron of honor wore lavender also. And Ben donned a white tuxedo as well. The house and patio had been decorated with boughs of lilac *alstroemeria* and baby's breath, and the surrounding garden was a late summer mass of fragrance and color.

It was a unique ceremony in more ways than one. There were readings of poetry; Gloria's eight-year-old granddaughter read *Words of Love* by Eliza Dunn in the most precious little voice. Solos were sung, one a cappella, and one with only the distant accompaniment of an acoustic guitar.

Gloria and Charlie each said their vows, which they then repeated upon changing positions, Gloria to the right, Charlie to the left, to signify equality. Their wedding rings were identical, except for their size. And Charlie was not only granted permission to kiss his bride, Gloria was told she may also kiss her groom.

The newlyweds insisted the evening's festivities be called a celebration. "One can't give their own reception. Come! Celebrate with us!" Lavish bowls of peeled fruit were placed at each table, along with chilled bottles of champagne and Catawba grape juice. Finger sandwiches were served, paté and caviar and imported creamed cheeses. The salads were layered with slices of Bermuda onions and Valencia oranges. Raspberry sorbet to cleanse the palate followed. Then the main course of rare beef tenderloin, parsleyed potatoes, green beans almondine. And dessert: three-tiered petit-fours in the shape of individual wedding cakes.

"Do you think it would be all right if I take my jacket off?" Randy asked Dawn, when the evening was pretty much coming to an end.

Dawn nodded. "Is your arm sore?"

Randy shook his head and took off his jacket. "No, it itches."

Ben sat down with them a little while later, complaining about the length of the ceremony, saying his legs fell asleep standing that long, and that he was getting a headache from all the flowers.

Tom laughed, the perfect gentlemen as he'd been charming the daylights out of the single woman sitting next to him, a distant cousin of either Gloria or Charlie. He couldn't remember which, but she sure was pretty.

"He's got her eating out of the palm of his hand," Randy whispered to Ben. And Ben just shook his head. Tom never ceased to amaze him. By the end of the evening, he went home with her, and at her suggestion.

Ben came back from the secretary's office winded, and sat down to catch his breath.

"So," Tom said. "Who'd you name on her?"

Ben just stared for a moment.

"Johnny or Miguel?"

Ben hesitated. "Martinez."

"What?!" Tom did a double take.

"You heard me, Martinez. He's in for the stake."

Tom shook his head, about to say something, but Ben stopped him. "I wasn't pleased with Johnny's riding yesterday. He put his stick away and went to hand riding the last sixteenth. It cost him the race. A horse got up just in time to nose him out."

"Okay. So..."

Ben held up his hand. "I'm not saying the filly has to win. I just want to make sure I get a strong ride to the wire."

Tom sat down and sighed. He felt bad for Johnny. This filly was going to run big, there was no doubt about it. "You could've ridden Miguel."

"No, I watched him ride in both the third and the sixth. He's not right either. And then he scratched off his last mount in the seventh." Ben paused, hoping he'd made the right decision. "And where were you yesterday? You'd have known all this if you'd watched the races."

Tom laughed. "I was buying a suit, remember? Don't show up if I didn't have one. Isn't that what you said? Well, I had to go buy one. And shoes. I had to buy fucking shoes. I'm all set for weddings and funerals now too for that matter, so there."

"And you looked so nice," Dawn said, in passing.

Tom bowed gallantly. "At your service."

Dawn laughed and walked away.

Ben called after her.

"Dawn?"

She turned.

Ben drew a breath. "Fernando Martinez is going to ride the filly."
"Who?"
"Fernando Martinez," Tom said. "He's in from Arlington for the stake. He's big time."
Dawn stared.
"He's ridden some of the finest colts and fillies in this country," Ben added. "He's a strong rider and knows young horses. He'll do just fine. All right?"
Dawn shrugged. "All right." She glanced in at All Together, who was pawing at the back of her stripped-down stall. "Does Johnny know?"
Ben nodded somberly. "Yes, I told him." The fact of the matter was, he'd walked halfway across the backside to tell him himself, before he heard it from anyone else.
"And?"
Ben hesitated, remembering the look of disappointment on Johnny's face. "Like I said, it's not a personal decision."
"Right." Tom wasn't disputing that. "So how'd he take it."
"Oh, I'd say personally."
"Wonderful," Tom said. "I got Son of Royalty tacked for him. He probably won't even come down."
Ben shook his head. "He said he'd be here."
"Yeah. Well, we'll see."
Johnny arrived no more than five minutes later, right about the time Dawn started hiccuping.
"Hold your breath," Tom said.
"I tried."
"How's your stomach?"
"Fine. Why do you ask?"
"Just wondering."
Dawn stared at him. "You don't think...?"
What? Tom smiled. That her hiccups started because they were running the filly? Her latest nervous tick. Just like her going back and forth to the bathroom when Beau was in. Dawn hiccuped again. And again. And again. And all through the rest of morning chores.
"At no time, when we have something in, is the barn to be left unattended on the day of the race," was Ben's remedy for what had

happened to Cajun. "You take turns going to eat, whatever. But someone has to be here at all times, and visible."

"Pizza," Dawn said, looking at Tom at the mention of food.

"Everything but anchovies?"

She nodded and hiccuped. "Whose turn is it to buy?"

"Mine," Tom said, and left.

Dawn parked herself on a chair just outside the tack room and read the racing form for All Together's race. The filly was the only first-time starter. Six of the nine-horse field had placed second in their previous starts. One horse in particular had finished second four times already. Any one of them could win. And yet, All Together was the odds-on favorite, based on her three recorded "black letter" works, which only meant she'd worked the fastest at that distance of any horse training on that particular morning.

Dawn smiled, recalling the time Ben tried to sneak a work in on her, a practice frowned upon by the racetrack clocker. "All Together, 37.2..." he said over the tiny speaker phone by the rail. At this point in her training the man could spot her a mile away from his glass booth above the clubhouse. "Nice try, Ben. Do you want fined?"

She remembered Ben laughing. He hadn't thought he'd get away with it. Dawn looked in at the filly, sulking in the back of her stall, not at all pleased with being drawn, and obviously having no idea why. She was in the seventh race and had hours to go. Dawn felt sorry for her. And worried. And hiccuped.

"Poor All Together," she said soothingly.

The filly pricked her ears, stared hopefully, for food perhaps, then lowered her head and continued sulking. Dawn found herself sympathizing with Gloria's line of thinking. What would one little carrot hurt? Half an apple?

"A lot," she could hear Ben say in her head. "Leave her alone. It's time she earn her keep and it ain't all a piece of cake."

A piece of cake. That sounded good right about now. One of Gloria's petit-four wedding cakes. Hiccup.

When Randy stopped by before leaving the track, Dawn convinced him to stay and have pizza first.

"How'd you get the hiccups?" he asked, leaning over her and kissing her long and hard.

"I don't know, but I've had them all morning. I've tried everything." Hiccup.

Randy nodded. "Well, so much for my cure," he said, referring to the passionate kiss. "Maybe we ought to find an empty stall."

"Oh, I'm sure that would do it," Dawn said, and laughed. "Why didn't I think of that?"

"Because that's my department."

Tom returned then with pizza in hand and an ice-cold six-pack of Coke. It came as no surprise when Barn Kitty showed up a few minutes later.

"Hey there, little puss puss." Tom fed him a pepperoni and smiled when he stood on his hind legs to take it out of his hand.

Randy shook his head. "You shouldn't be feeding her like that. I can only imagine where all she's been."

"Hey, probably some of the same places I'd go," Tom said, chuckling. "Besides, *she* happens to be a he and us guys have to stick together. It's a cruel world out there."

Randy smiled. "I guarantee you, she's a female."

Tom stared. Not this renegade cat. He leaned, tried to see for himself. "You can tell that from sitting way over there. Goddamn, Doc! You're good!"

"Not hardly." Randy laughed, then wolfed down the rest of his pizza, and glanced at his watch. "She's a calico. All calicos are females."

Tom shook his head. "I'll be damned." He fed the cat another piece of pepperoni. "How's come she never has kittens?"

Randy shrugged. "She's probably spayed."

"By who? She's a stray. Who would spay her?"

"I don't know. Why are you asking me?"

Tom shrugged. "Well, you know everything else."

Randy and Dawn laughed.

Barn Kitty worked her way over to Dawn, got two pieces of pepperoni there, and set her sights on Randy.

"Forget it," Randy said.

The cat meowed.

"I said forget it."

"Randy..." Dawn admonished.

Barn Kitty begged with her paws, and when that didn't work, rolled onto her back and begged some more.

"Look at this act," Randy said.

Tom and Dawn shook their heads.

Randy stared stubbornly, a contest of sorts to see how long this cat would continue, and found himself taking a good look at her eyes. "Hmph." he said, and picked her up.

"What?" Tom said. "What's wrong with her?"

Randy turned her face from side to side. "She's blind in her right eye. Watch this." He eased his other hand around the back of her neck and waved it up and down. Nothing. The cat never even blinked. The eye wasn't cloudy, no evidence of infection or injury. It was just blind. "I'll be damned." He fed her a piece of sausage, purposely offering it to her from her blind side, and watched as the scent brought her around to where she looked at it first with her good eye, then took it gently from his hand. He noticed something else. The whiskers on her blind side were longer than the ones on her left. It amazed him. Mother Nature at work.

The ten-minute call for the first race sounded then, and he put the cat down, gulped the rest of his Coke, and kissed Dawn good-bye.

"Wait a minute!" Tom called after him when he started to leave. "Is she all right?" he asked, looking worriedly at Barn Kitty.

"Yeah, fine." Randy said. "What do you want, a bill?"

Tom laughed. "Fuck you! Come here, little puss-puss."

Ben had debated and debated over whether or not to school the filly in the paddock the past couple of weeks. It was allowed with permission from the paddock judge, a dry-run so to speak. But he'd decided against it. He told Tom they'd just take their chances. The truth of the matter was, he wasn't up to it, and was simply hoping for the best when the time came.

Consequently, with both he and Tom knowing anything could happen, even with a young horse that had been schooled, the plan was for Dawn to stay with Red out on the racetrack, and for Tom to handle the filly in the paddock.

It was a good thing. She reared, she kicked, she bucked, cow-kicked, and tried to go through the wall, and ultimately had to be tacked while walking. It was the only way to get along with her, keep her moving. She danced and pranced and tossed her head, dazzling the crowd that hung over the railing three deep just to get a glimpse of her, and she put on a show.

To make matters worse, when they finally got the saddle on and went to put on the overgirth, it proved too small.

"Shit!" the valet said.

When he returned with another, she started her act all over again. Ben was exhausted by the time Fernando Martinez emerged from the jocks' room. "The filly is headstrong," he told him, his chest heaving hard with each breath as the two of them stood watching Tom lead her around the paddock. "And likes to go to the front."

"She work good, huh?" Fernando said, more a statement than a question.

Ben nodded. "Calm her down, don't fight her, and let her go."

Fernando smiled. "Jesus, is she a big mother."

Ben nodded again, breathlessly.

"Don't worry, Meester Miller. I get her there."

"Riders up!"

Dawn's hiccups vanished as mysteriously as they began, about two minutes to post time. She climbed up on the fence and looked to see if Randy's truck was parked by the kitchen. It was. She squinted. He was sitting behind the wheel, with his head down. Probably writing something on his clipboard, she thought, and smiled.

Ben walked down to join her. The two of them exchanged anxious glances, and looked at the tote board. The filly was three to five. Ben shook his head. He'd seen horses, a lot of them in fact, that would work well in the morning and not amount to a hill of beans in the afternoon when it counted.

He wiped his brow. They had a lot of money in this filly. And a lot of hopes and dreams.

Johnny appeared from seemingly nowhere, nodded at Ben, and jumped up onto the fence support the other side of Dawn. "I was going to watch this from the room, but I couldn't stand it."

Ben smiled, but his eyes were on the gate. The horses were being loaded.

Dawn glanced at Randy's truck. He'd gotten out and was sitting on the hood.

"And they're off!" the announcer said, and immediately following, "Moving up to take the early lead is All Together!"

Dawn reached down and gripped Ben's shoulder; in her mind, flashed the memory of the day they'd bought her. The morning, the afternoon, the evening. A blur amidst the distant thunder of pounding hooves.

"Final Bend is running second, and back two lengths is..."

Dawn gripped Ben's shoulder even tighter.

"Coming into the far turn and lengthening her lead, is All Together."

"Come on, filly," Johnny said. "Come on, bring it home."

Dawn laughed, giddy as she watched. She gasped then. Through the turn and four lengths in front, All Together went wide, almost to the middle of the track.

"And as they turn for home, Final Bend has taken over the lead."

"What?" Ben said, unable to see. "What'd she do?"

"She went wide," Johnny said. "Wait! Wait! She's coming back on." He strained to see. "Yeah! She's back in front."

"Come on, Momma," Ben said, seeing her now, about a half length in front. "Come on."

"Come on."

"Come on."

"As they cross the finish line, it is Alllll Togetherrr!"

"Yes!" Johnny shouted. "Yes!"

When he and Dawn jumped down and hugged each other, even Ben couldn't contain himself. "She run big!" he said, his eyes wide. "Damn, she run big!"

The three of them headed for the winner's circle.

Tom had a grin from ear to ear as he and Red led All Together and Martinez on their way back to the grandstand. "Did you see her?" he yelled to Randy. "Did you see her?"

Randy nodded, laughing.

Martinez saluted the stewards with his whip as Tom slid off Red and walked the filly into the winner's circle. "Do this quick," he told the photographer, the filly at this point pushing hard up against him. "Stand back, stand back!" he warned, as she kicked out and just missed one of the valets walking by. "Watch it!"

The photographer snapped the picture, Martinez dismounted, and everyone backed clear out of the way as Tom turned the filly around. "Is she pumped or what?" he said as All Together tossed her head, danced, and gnawed at the bit. "Jesus Christ!" He motioned for Dawn to get Red, and yelled that he'd meet her at the spit barn.

Dawn nodded gratefully, picked up Red's reins where he'd been ground-tied, and followed at a safe distance behind. Ben waited for Martinez to weigh in and walked with him to the jocks' room. This would be the only time he'd have to talk to him. Johnny tagged along.

"She a nice filly," Martinez said, shaking his head. "I mean nice filly. She strong."

Ben nodded. "What happened up in the turn?"

"She look around. She run so easy, she look at the crowd."

Ben laughed as Martinez stopped to shake his hand. "Thank you, Meester Miller. She be all right," he said, "I tell you. And when I read about her, I remember it was me who popped her cherry."

Ben nodded and gave Johnny a pat on the back. Johnny smiled and followed Martinez into the jocks' room, and Ben began the endless walk to the backside, in seventh heaven.

Randy drove down to the barn, watched from that distance as Tom and Dawn attempted to bathe All Together, who was being totally obnoxious, and felt so helpless, he decided to finish off her stall.

"What are you doing, Doc?" Ben asked, arriving as Randy was just finishing bedding it down.

Randy shook his head. "I don't know," he said, especially considering how his arm ached at the moment. Ben smiled. He didn't know either, but was grateful. Tom returned to the barn first, and about fifteen minutes later, Dawn and All Together returned.

The filly was as calm as could be at this point, and already a little muscle sore. "Here, bring her here," Tom said, and motioned under the light. He and Ben and Randy looked at a cut high on the inside of her right hock, agreed it was nothing to worry about, and Dawn put her away.

"Lord," she said, and sat down for a rest.

The celebration at The Rib that night was loud, boisterous, and contagious. "Did anyone get the time of the race?" Ben asked. "What did she run?"

Dawn shrugged. She never paid attention to details like that, Ben always did. And Tom never even looked. "Hey, I had my hands full," he reminded everyone.

Ben nodded and laughed. He could find out in the morning paper, but in the meantime. "I can't believe I never even looked. I don't know how fast she ran."

Bob, a fellow trainer walked by the table right about then with his wife Blanche, congratulated him, said she'd run it in 1.09 and 4/5, shook Ben's hand and walked on. And Ben just marveled. She'd broke her maiden running just four fifths of a second slower than Beau's best start. "Jesus!"

"She can bookit now, I'm telling you," Tom said, and they all laughed.

Ben grew serious then. He didn't want to, he didn't mean to, it just happened. Tears welled up in his eyes and he just shook his head.

Dawn covered his hand with hers, and he looked at her and smiled through his tears. "I'm a lucky man," he said. "A lucky man."

Randy put his arm around Dawn.

Ben took out his handkerchief, wiped his eyes, and sat back. "Most trainers would give everything they had for just one good horse. I've been fortunate to have had two, and now three." He hesitated, struggling to maintain composure. "Most men search all their life for the right woman, I had mine for most of my life." He looked at Dawn. "And now I have you." He smiled. "I thank God for the day you walked into my life."

Dawn bit at her trembling bottom lip, nodded, and swallowed hard.

"And I've got the best friend a man could hope for," he said, turning to Tom. "And you..." He looked at Randy. "I seem to have acquired you."

Randy smiled, but with a choked-up lump in his throat as well. Tom had to wipe at his eyes; he had big tears trickling down his cheeks.

"Yes," Ben said. "I'm a lucky man."

It was a moment they would remember forever.

Chapter Twenty-Six

Dawn and Randy had just gotten home and undressed when his pager went off. He phoned his answering service and was told there was an emergency at the Durans'. "Oh great," he moaned. Not only was he beat, his arm was killing him.

"What is it?" Dawn asked, as he hung up.

"It's that black colt that kicked me. Apparently he's laid his ass open on a nail."

Dawn cringed. "Do you want me to come with you?"

Randy glanced at his watch; it was nine-fifteen. "You don't have to, I can manage."

"Are you sure?"

Randy nodded. "Not unless you want to?"

Dawn smiled. "Well, if you weren't wounded..."

"Is this pity?"

Dawn laughed.

"Never mind, I'll take it. Come on."

As usual, Mrs. Duran was in hysterics by the time Randy arrived, and rushed out to the truck before he'd even turned the engine off. "Oh, Dr. Iredell, it's such a mess. I'm sure he's lost most of his blood."

Randy tried to put her mind at ease. "Well, let's go take a look. They have quite a bit of blood, you know."

Mrs. Duran smiled a hopeful, tense smile in response, took hold of Dawn's arm, and led them into the barn. "We don't know how it happened, but his stall is all torn up."

Mr. Duran motioned helplessly to a splintered pile of wood in summary of the situation. "He's really done it this time."

The colt was standing in the middle of the stall, ears pinned, and swishing his tail furiously at the steady stream of blood dripping onto his hock from a large, gaping wound on his hip. He also had blood trickling from his nose and a crusted area of blood, manure, and sawdust on his shoulder. Randy stared into the colt's eyes, his broken arm throbbing all the more at just the sight of him, and sighed. "Well, I'm sorry to say, nothing looks life-threatening."

Mr. Duran laughed nervously, relieved, and at the same time rather embarrassed to be such a constant bother to this nice young veterinarian. "How's your arm, Doc?"

"Not too bad," Randy said, and motioned to the colt. "Let's get a twitch on him." Dawn followed him out to the truck to help him gather the instruments and supplies he needed. He cautioned her repeatedly about being on guard in the stall, and couldn't seem to stress it enough. "Stay to the right of me," he said, half-smiling but deadly serious. "I'll shield the blow."

Randy and Mr. Duran twitched the colt. Then Randy administered a large dose of antibiotics first, mainly to get it out of the way, and he and Dawn went to work. "Crank it tighter," he said, of the twitch, as he prepared to clean the wound. "Tighter."

"I got him," Mr. Duran said, and Randy looked at him. They'd been here before.

"Tighter."

Randy cleaned the wound; Dawn helped as much as he'd allow her. He was so concerned about her standing too close to this time-bomb of an animal, it was almost a hindrance. And finally, as sterile as he was going to get it, he blocked the surrounding area, cut some of the ragged tissue away, inserted a drain, and began suturing. He'd push the needle in and start it through the other side, and Dawn would pull it the rest of the way and pass it back. The two of them worked together to tie each knot, around and through, pull, snip, and had the routine down so pat by the time they were done, Randy had to smile. The shoulder wound was next.

This one wasn't so bad. It only required cleaning with a disinfectant and antibiotic topical ointment. "Hang in there," Randy told Mr. Duran, who was still cranking on the twitch for all he was worth. Randy peered up into the colt's distorted nostrils, saw only a small cut, motioned for Dawn to leave the stall, and had Mr. Duran slowly release the twitch. The two men backed out then, and Mr. Duran quickly pulled the door shut.

"He's such a mean little shit," Mr. Duran said, heaving a huge sigh of relief at being done with him for the moment.

The colt charged the door.

"He's not mean," his wife said. "He's just a little mischievous."

Mr. Duran laughed at that, as all four of them jumped with a start, when the colt kicked the wall.

"We should cut him," Randy said.

"What?" Mrs. Duran gasped.

"Geld him." Randy gathered up his instruments, wincing each time he moved his arm the wrong way. "It might settle him down a bit. How's he bred?"

"Nothing out of nothing," Mr. Duran said. "The wife here fell in love with him at the sale though and..." He glanced at her. "She said he was cute."

Randy laughed. "Oh, he's cute all right." He reminded him of a Black Angus bull, seeing red. "Cute as hell. I'll stop back by tomorrow and check on him. You're going to need a supply of antibiotics."

Dawn offered to drive, and Randy gratefully accepted. She felt even sorrier for him since he was literally cradling his broken arm with the other because it hurt so much. She suggested since they were much closer to his apartment, that they go there instead of back across town to her place.

"What? No white cotton underwear?"

Dawn laughed. "I'll wear the red bikinis."

"You're on," Randy said.

Morning chores were moving along right on schedule, in spite of Dawn's tardiness. She'd allowed Randy to sleep in after he'd tossed and turned all night. One more stall and she could rake the shedrow and take a coffee break. She grabbed the muck basket and pitchfork and was in full swing when she heard Tom shout her name. Dave would be arriving with donuts any minute now and she wanted to get to them first.

"What?" she called back, still working. "I'm in Lady's stall."

"Dawn! Come here!"

She peeked out of the stall, expecting to have to dodge a loose horse, and saw Tom standing in the doorway of the tack room. Ben was behind him, red in the face and coughing.

Tom turned, a look of horror in his eyes as he shouted again. "Dawn!"

She ran down the shedrow, but by the time she got there, Ben had stopped coughing and was slumped over his desk, his arm dangling limp at his side.

She and Tom stared, just stared, for the briefest of moments. "Oh my God! Was he choking?!"

"I don't know!" Tom shook his head. "I don't know! No! He wasn't eating! How could he choke? Hurry! Go get help!"

Dawn bolted around the corner of the barn and ran into Gloria coming the other way. "It's Ben!" she gasped. "Something's happened to him!" She grabbed her by the arm. "He was coughing and now he's not moving!"

Gloria stepped inside the door, assessed Ben's condition in a glance, and immediately checked his pulse. "Get the ambulance!" she told Dawn. "Quick!"

Dawn ran up to the gap, dodging horses, people, a truck that just missed her, and stood gasping for breath when she located the attendant. "Barn fourteen!" she said. "It's Ben Miller! He's collapsed!"

A crowd of people had gathered outside the tack room by the time she returned, and she had to push through them. She stood at Tom's side and stared frantically. Gloria had put a quilted wrap under Ben's face, his head turned to one side. His eyes were closed, his mouth gaped as she hovered over him...her hand on his wrist, her eyes on her watch.

The ambulance attendants came in, Gloria gave them some numbers. Their voices were muffled and distorted to Dawn as she stared at Ben's lifeless arm. She turned her attention to the one attendant, thought he said the words "possible stroke." She looked at Gloria.

"Step back please," one of the men said to her and Tom. "Step back."

A stretcher was brought in, positioned so they could lift Ben onto it, and they wheeled him out.

"No one survives a stroke at his age," Dawn heard someone say. "No one." She and Tom followed Gloria to the ambulance.

"I want to go with him," Dawn said to one of the attendants.

The man looked at Gloria, who shook her head and took Dawn aside. "You can't help him in there." She gripped Dawn's shoulders and turned her face so she would look at her. "Listen to me. What you can do is help him here, and when you're done..." She motioned for Tom to intervene, Tom pulled Dawn back, and Gloria climbed into the rear of the ambulance. The attendant nudged them out of the way so he could close the doors.

"I'm sorry," he said.

Sorry? Dawn looked at him, watched as he got in behind the wheel.

This can't be happening, she thought. This *can't* be happening. She and Tom stared as the ambulance slowly turned around, made its way to the stable gate, and pulled out onto the highway, its siren screaming.

The crowd dispersed.

Tom rushed to finish the last stall and put the horse away while Dawn hurried to start the oats. She spilled a whole scoop all over the floor, swore out loud, and nearly burst into tears. "Forget it! Let's go!" Tom told her. "We can clean it up later. Come on!" They locked up and ran to the parking lot.

"Where's your car?!" Tom gasped, looking around.

"Oh God! It's not here!" She'd come with Randy straight from his apartment. "Where's your truck?"

"Fuck! By the secretary's office. Come on!"

Charlie yelled after them. "You call me, all right? Do you hear me? Call me!"

Tom shouted he would, and he and Dawn ran all the way to his truck. "Shit!" Tom said, banging the steering wheel when finally they were on their way and caught the first light. "Shit!"

It was only a ten-minute drive, tops, to Charity Hospital, but seemed an eternity. He honked his horn. "Move it! It doesn't get any greener!" he shouted, as soon as it changed from red. He jumped the curb to get around this car, sped into the lot designated for emergency room parking, and he and Dawn hurried into the building.

Gloria was sitting in one of the chairs in the waiting room, alone. "Good, good, you're here," she said, looking up with tears in her eyes.

"Is he...?" Tom shook his head, glanced away, and swallowed hard. "What did they...?"

Gloria tried to smile to reassure him, to reassure Dawn. "I don't know. We're just going to have to wait."

Time passed slowly. The wait seeming endless, though the hands on the clock hardly moved. Unable to sit any longer, Tom started pacing back and forth across the waiting room, stopping every three or four trips to look through the window of the door that led to where Gloria said they'd taken Ben.

A nurse approached Gloria. "Does Mr. Miller have family?"

Gloria looked at Tom and Dawn. Tom hesitated. "Just us," he said. "How is he?"

The nurse shook her head. "I'm sorry. The doctors are still with him."

Tom watched the woman walk away and sat down between Gloria and Dawn. "God, I hate this. Why won't they tell us anything?"

"They will, dear," Gloria said. "As soon as they know something."

Tom glanced away, looked at Dawn, and then leaned forward, propping his elbows on his knees and his face in his hands. "I'll tell you what," he said, visibly trembling and his voice shaky. "If he dies, then I'm glad he went the way he did. His wife suffered."

Dawn touched his arm, leaned her head against his shoulder to try to comfort him, and they sat there like this for a moment. Then she was the one who got up and started pacing. It had been an hour and a half already. She stared through the window down the hallway.

Tom picked up a magazine and started to leaf through it, only to end up throwing it to the floor. One of the nurses looked up from behind her desk, and he picked it up and laid it on the table.

Two young men came into the emergency room, one of them holding a bloody bandage to his head. He was hurt on the job, he told the secretary, and she handed him a form to fill out.

A hearse pulled up outside, and a man and a woman, double doors swinging open, guided an empty stretcher into the waiting area. "Oh my God!" Dawn said, and Tom rose to his feet.

They heard a name then. It wasn't Ben's, and the two of them all but collapsed into their chairs next to Gloria. "I can't stand this," Tom said. "I'm going to fucking go nuts."

A nurse looked up and frowned at him. He held out his hands; what did she want him to say? It was the truth. The three of them, Gloria, Tom, and Dawn...sat watching as the hearse attendants were directed down the hall and returned with a covered body, and a grieving family.

"You'd better call Charlie," Tom said. "Not that you have anything to tell him, but you better call him anyway."

Gloria nodded and walked to the pay phone.

"What about George?" Dawn said. George was Ben's farmhand.

Tom looked at her, nodded, and walked to the phone next to Gloria's. Dawn watched them both, focused on their actions. Gloria was dabbing her eyes with a handkerchief; Tom had his one hand braced on the top of the phone booth, shoulders squared, and was shaking his head. She turned then and looked out the glass doors into the parking lot, staring at a row of white cars, staring, staring, until they blurred into one.

Tom walked back and sat down next to her. Gloria returned a few minutes later. And again, they waited. A young doctor and an elderly man in a three-piece suit and shiny black shoes walked by, the sounds of their footsteps echoing off the walls long after they'd disappeared down the corridor.

"This sucks," Tom said, and approached the nurse's station. "Does anyone want to tell us something. I mean, come on. Enough is enough. There's someone we care about back there, and no one's telling us a goddamned thing."

Two nurses scowled, but the one standing to their left sympathized with him. "I'll go see what I can find out."

"Thank you," Tom said, his voice trembling. "Thank you."

As he sat back down between Gloria and Dawn, Gloria smiled sadly. This scene was far from new to her, she'd been on both sides of the nurse's station. Doctor, the family wants to know. They want to know. And then, yes, I'm his wife. I see, a stroke. Massive stroke. Brain dead. His organs? Yes, of course. Complete heart failure. I understand. Widow. I am a nurse. I am a widow nurse.

"Dr. Martin, please report to emergency. Dr. Martin, please report to emergency."

Tom leaned his head back and closed his eyes, thinking about the remark he'd made to Ben about being all set for funerals, and remembered the way Ben had laughed.

Randy came through the door, quickly glanced around, found them, and walked over. Dawn instinctively rose and fell into his arms. He held her tight, met Gloria's eyes, whose expression said the outlook wasn't good, and turned to Tom.

"We don't know a thing," Tom said, clearing his throat.

Randy nodded, smoothed Dawn's hair, and looked again at Gloria. "I understand you rode over with him. Do they suspect a heart attack or...?"

"No, they believe he's had a stroke."

Tom started to move over then, to allow Randy to sit next to Dawn, but Randy shook his head. He motioned to the nurse's station. "I'll see if I can find out anything."

"Good luck," Tom said.

Randy approached the nurses and for all his size and good looks, he didn't get their attention until he rested his broken arm on the counter.

"Can we help you?"

"Yes," he said. "Mr. Miller. We'd like to know how he's doing?"

The one nurse hesitated. "I'm sorry, but..."

"I know. I'm not asking for any information you're not allowed to give me." He leaned a little closer. "Tell me though, what time was his arrival?"

Both nurses checked their records. "Ten-twelve."

Randy glanced at his watch. It was almost two. "Who initiates the death certificates?"

The nurses stared. The paperwork started with them.

Randy figured as much. "Then is it safe to say...?"

The elder of the two nodded.

Randy thanked them and walked back.

"Well?" Tom looked up.

Randy hesitated, thought of how to word this. He didn't want to give them any false hope, in the event... "They couldn't say, but I think as of now, he's still hanging in there."

Dawn and Tom stared, Gloria nodded, and it was Randy who paced back and forth from this point. Again and again. He stared down the corridor, remembering a time long ago, a hallway just like this one. He was just a child then, but recalled it in his mind as if it were yesterday. The sounds. The smells. Doctors walking through the swinging doors to tell his father that his wife was going to be fine. "But we lost the baby, Mr. Iredell, and had to do a complete hysterectomy."

Randy could still see the look on his father's face, the pain, the anguish, the way his throat tightened when he tried to swallow. "You can go in now if you like, but leave the children here."

He remembered Cindy laughing and giggling for the nurses, too young to know what was happening. And he remembered holding on tightly to her stroller, afraid to let go. How does one *lose* a baby? Dear, God, don't let me lose my little sister.

Randy walked over and sat down next to Tom.

"Fuck this," was all Tom said, his head back and staring, and Randy nodded.

About five minutes later, the nurse Tom had appealed to, returned. "The doctors are still with Mr. Miller, but will be out to talk with you all as soon as possible."

She looked weary saying this, and Dawn took that as a bad sign. "Is there a chapel?"

The nurse nodded. "Down that hall and to your left, second door."

"Thank you." Dawn glanced at Gloria, Gloria nodded, and the two woman rose together. Dawn reached for Randy's hand, and he and Tom followed.

The chapel was small, eclectic, four narrow pews on each side. An altar, a kneeling board, tapestries on the walls, carpet on the floor, a table and chairs, and well lit.

Dawn sat in one of the back pews; Gloria walked up front to kneel down and pray, Tom genuflected, made the sign of the cross and sat in the second row, and Randy stood just inside the door.

Charlie arrived a few minutes later, touched Randy's arm reverently, then Dawn's shoulder, and on the way to Gloria, gripped Tom's hand to keep himself from falling. "Oh, God..." he said, as he knelt down next to his wife.

Word from the doctor when it finally came was the proverbial mixture of the good with the bad. Dr. Martin motioned to the table and chairs and they gathered around him. "Mr. Miller has had a stroke, but is alive, stabilized, and we have run several tests." He focused on each of their faces. "He's being transferred to the intensive care unit, and he is on oxygen support and a heart monitor."

Dawn shivered.

"I'm telling you this to prepare you for the tubes and all the equipment." He glanced at everyone and settled on Dawn; this had to be a daughter, from the look in her eyes. "In about an hour, you may take turns, two at a time, to see him. But only for a few minutes."

Gloria cleared her throat. "Is he conscious?"

Dr. Martin nodded. "Yes."

"Can he talk?"

"Yes, though his speech is affected. It's very important he not try to talk too much."

Gloria nodded. "Any other apparent damage?"

Dr. Martin hesitated. "Some paralysis naturally, but as to the extent..." He left this in the air. "As I said, we'll know more later. ICU is at the back of the West End. I suggest you all get a cup of coffee or something to eat, and give the staff time to get him settled in." He stood up to leave, knowing the question on all of their minds, seeing it in their faces, and addressed it before walking out. "Our concern now is recovery with no setbacks. This stroke he survived." He looked at Dawn again. "The next forty-eight hours will be crucial. I wish I could tell you more, but at this time it would only be speculation."

They went to the hospital cafeteria as a group, one of three groups gathered there that day. And though no one was hungry, they all opted for coffee and grilled cheese sandwiches.

The conversation was grim. "I wish we knew more," Dawn said, sipping her coffee and putting her cup down, only to pick it right back up again.

Gloria shook her head. "I wish I knew less. I know too much about strokes. They can be devastating."

"You mean he'll get worse?"

"No, sweetie. What I meant was, well..." Gloria paused. "Complications. But let's wait and see. Think positive."

Finding ICU by following the signs and arrows, they were pointed to a lounge area and asked to wait. Permission to go in to see Ben came about fifteen minutes later. Tom and Dawn went in first, and found the warning that Dr. Martin had given them totally inadequate.

Ben looked small in his sterile bed, small and helpless, and pale. He was on oxygen, his breathing labored, had an IV needle in his arm, electrodes taped to his chest, a catheter, and was surrounded by a stockade of beeping, flashing machines.

"Five minutes," a nurse said cautiously.

Dawn nodded, reaching for Tom's hand as the two of them edged closer to Ben's side. "Oh, Jesus..." Tom said, shaking his head at seeing this mountain of a man reduced to this.

Dawn touched Ben's arm gently. "Ben... Ben, it's Dawn. Tom and I are here. Ben, can you hear me?"

Ben struggled to open his eyes. "Dawnnnn. Tommm."

"Yes," she said, tears flooding her eyes. "Yes."

He focused on her and then Tom.

The nurse intervened at this point. "I'm sorry," she said, watching the monitor. "You'll have to leave now."

Dawn looked at the woman as if she were from another dimension.

"I'm sorry," the nurse repeated. "I'll come out and let you know when you can come back in," she added, hovering over Ben as the monitor beeped faster.

Gloria, Charlie, and Randy stared anxiously as they returned. "He said our names," Dawn said, her voice cracking. "Didn't he?" she asked Tom, needing assurance that it really happened.

"Yes," he nodded, looking away as he bit at his bottom lip. "He knew us right off."

Everyone laughed then, a giddy laugh, when Charlie called Ben a tough old fart, and for a moment it seemed like everything was going to be okay. "They made us leave though," Dawn said, "because of something on the monitor. They'll come out and let us know when someone can go back in."

"How does he look?" Gloria asked.

Dawn shook her head. "It doesn't look like Ben," she said, and broke down. "I'm sorry."

Randy pulled her close and she buried her face against his chest. "It's all right," he said. "It's all right."

Tom stood struggling with his own emotions, glanced at the door and then at the clock on the wall. "I'm going to go feed," he said. "I'll be back."

Dawn turned, wiped her eyes. "Do you want me to...?"

"No, you stay here," he said, and was gone.

"Dawn, I'm going to have to go too," Randy said, tilting her chin up and kissing her lightly. "I got paged while you were in with Ben. Hopefully I won't be long."

Dawn nodded. "I'll be here."

Randy kissed her again. "I know."

Dawn sat down with Gloria and Charlie to wait for word from the nurse, and caught herself rocking back and forth, an old habit of hers that signaled disaster.

Help me, help me, help me, she kept saying inside her head. Help me, help me, help me. I don't want to do this.

About a half hour later, Gloria and Charlie were allowed in to see Ben. "Five minutes," the nurse said.

The first thing Gloria noticed was Ben's coloring, or lack thereof, and the extent to which the right half of his face slackened. Charlie stood like a soldier at her side. "Ben, Charlie and I are here," she said, gripping his hand gently. "You get lots of rest, you hear. Rest is what you need right now." Charlie nodded in agreement, tears trickling down his face.

"Hang in there, Ben," he said. "Hang in there."

The nurse motioned it was time for them to leave.

Dawn heard them coming. "Did he speak to you? Did he know you?"

"No, dear, he's asleep," Gloria said, dabbing her eyes with her handkerchief. "But that's good," she added, in response to the sudden look of alarm on Dawn's face. "Rest is what he needs."

The vigil continued. Forty-five minutes later, Dawn and Gloria were allowed back in. But only for a minute, the nurse cautioned. Ben appeared weaker to Dawn, his face more stricken, his lifeless arm swollen.

"Ben..." Dawn said, leaning down to whisper to him, compelled to wake him, to hear him talk, to assure her he would be all right. If *he* told her, then she would believe it. "Ben, it's Dawn." She smoothed his hair back off his forehead, the way he always wore it. "Don't you dare give up. Do you hear me? Don't you dare give up."

Gloria felt as helpless as an outsider. As Ben opened his eyes and looked at Dawn, the one side of his face quivered as he tried to speak. And yet she felt honored to witness the bond between this gruff old man and this proud young woman.

"Dawnnn...?"

"Yes," Dawn said, gripping his hand. "It's me. Gloria's here too. Charlie's outside, and Tom went to feed."

Ben focused on the two of them, then closed his eyes, and without being told, albeit for the accelerated monitor, Dawn and Gloria stepped back and exited quietly.

"See, he recognized us, didn't he?" Dawn said to Gloria in the hall.

"Yes, dear. He did," Gloria said, and wished she could be as encouraged. Too often she'd seen this type of behavior lead to hopes soon crushed. A last hurrah. Or worse. Paralysis, years of suffering, dependency, decline, and ultimately distance. "He definitely did."

Over the next few hours, they were allowed in periodically to see him. Ben was asleep the entire time. And Tom talked Gloria and Charlie into going home. They both looked so tired.

"Dawn or I will call you if there's any change."

When it was just the two of them, Dawn asked how things were back at the barn.

"Okay," Tom said, and searched his shirt pocket for a toothpick. There was none. He took off his hat, dragged his fingers through his hair, and crossed his arms. "Ginney left a note on the tack room door, said to page her if you need her."

Dawn nodded. "Is the filly all right?"

"Fine," Tom said. And there they sat, the best of friends, but for the moment, too polite and feeling like strangers in an alien world.

Dawn noticed bruises up and down Ben's arms when they were allowed in to see him again later, and a different rhythm in the way he was breathing. His coloring was worse as well, grayish, and around his mouth, almost blue.

Neither Tom nor Dawn could think of leaving the hospital after this visit, and took to pacing again, in turns. "He looked so much better earlier."

"I know. I know."

"Are you hungry?"

"I don't know. Are you?"

They decided to go get something to eat. It would kill time if nothing else, and were gone when Randy returned. The nurse informed him of their whereabouts, and also of Ben's condition.

"No change."

Randy nodded and stared down the corridor.

"So how'd you break your arm?" the nurse asked.

Randy smiled. "I was kicked by a horse."

"I'll bet that hurt."

Randy shrugged.

"I take it you're a trainer also then, like Mr. Miller."

"No, I'm a veterinarian," Randy said, glancing at his watch. "Do you mind if I wait over there?" he asked, thinking if he could sit down and rest his arm a moment, it might stop throbbing as much.

"No, go right ahead," the nurse said, and just then Randy's pager went off.

He needn't ask. The nurse pressed down on an open line and handed him the phone. He thanked her, phoned for the information, and hung up and glanced at his watch. "Would it be all right if I see Mr. Miller for a moment?"

"I'll check," the nurse said, and when he was allowed, showed him the way. "He's sleeping, so I wouldn't wake him."

Randy nodded, stood at Ben's side, and for the first time in a long time, prayed. When Dawn and Tom returned, she was given the message that he'd been there, had seen Ben, and would be back as soon as possible.

Evening blended into night; the shift change came and went, Ben's heart beat slower and slower as new faces hovered over him, and with each hour, more and more sirens sounded from the streets below.

It was after one in the morning before Randy was able to make his way back, and found Dawn and Tom asleep. The overhead lights in the waiting room had been turned off, leaving only a small table lamp. Dawn was curled up in a large chair, her head resting on the arm. Tom was sprawled in the chair next to her with his head against the wall. Randy sat down across from them, stretched out his legs, drew a breath, and sighed. He rubbed the side of his neck, then leaned his head back and closed his eyes.

He listened to the sounds around him, the shuffling of feet as they passed, the buzzing of phone lines, the whispers of the nurses, the beeping of monitors. He opened his eyes, looked at Dawn, then stretched his legs out further, slouched down in the chair, rested his head back and drifted off to sleep.

He dreamt he burned Dawn's book, page by page, in a huge bonfire. She was angry with him and appeared in a smoky cloud, her eyes black, her mouth red. As she spoke, she drooled blood. "How dare you kill my book. You have killed me and everyone in it. Look what you've done to Ben."

Randy woke in a sweat, his heart pounding rapidly as he looked around the room. Dawn and Tom were still asleep. He glanced at his watch, forty-five minutes from the time he'd sat down. He ran his fingers through his hair, got up, and walked to the nurse's station to ask about Ben.

"Guarded," the nurse replied. "Would you like some coffee? There's some down the hall."

"No thanks," Randy said. "I think I've probably had one too many already tonight. I'm having nightmares."

The nurse smiled and he walked back to the waiting area. It wasn't long before he was asleep again.

Dr. Martin looked at the clock, made note of the time on the chart, and placed it in the slot at the foot of Ben's bed. Knowing the family were still here, having seen them when he passed in the hall, he walked into the waiting room, glanced from one to the next, all asleep, and sat down for a much-needed rest himself. It had been a long day, a difficult day. It was never easy losing a patient, and today he'd lost two. One in surgery, the other in a coma. He rubbed his eyes, leaned his head back and stared across the room, noticed the thermometer in Randy's pocket, and looked at Dawn. Such a pretty woman, plain, sort of, but in a nice way. So tall and slender.

He thought about his wife, his ex-wife as of two-thirty this afternoon, and imagined her thin and tall, and not in bed with his best friend, and closed his eyes.

A nurse walked by, backed up, then walked on, smiling. Dr. Martin was asleep. A little past four Randy stirred, woke, and in moving about in his chair, woke Dr. Martin, which in turn woke Dawn and Tom.

"What time is it?" Tom cleared his throat.

"Four-twenty," Dawn said, squinting at her watch.

Dr. Martin sat up, rubbed his eyes, and smiled apologetically. "I'm sorry. I didn't realize how tired I was. I stopped by to tell you about Mr. Miller, and well, I guess I fell asleep."

"How is he?" Dawn asked.

"Well, he was stable a few hours ago. Let me go check on him. I'll be right back."

Randy stood up and stretched, as best he could with the hindrance of the cast. Dawn watched him, still trying to fully rouse herself as she ran a brush through her hair.

"Good news," Dr. Martin said, rejoining them. "Mr. Miller is doing well. I won't say 'as well as can be expected,' because I hate that expression." He smiled. "Almost as much as I hate the ones about dying of old age or natural causes."

They all smiled. Tom even laughed a little. A doctor wouldn't joke like this if Ben were still critical. Would he?

"Anyway," Dr. Martin continued. "I think you should all go home and come back later, much later. Mr. Miller needs his rest, and so do I for that matter. I've scheduled more tests for him later today, so please. Go home."

They all decided to get breakfast and then go straight to the track. Showers would have to wait.

"I'd kill for a toothbrush," Dawn said, as they passed the gift shop doors, locked tight. Inside were rows and rows of them.

They stopped at the first open restaurant they came to, ate heartily, and lingered over a second cup of coffee. Tom popped a toothpick in his mouth, helped himself to three or four more, which he slipped into his pocket, and sat back.

"I feel a lot better about this today," he said. "I think he's going to make it."

Randy agreed, to a certain extent. "I think the fact that he's made it this long is a good sign."

"I hope you're right," Dawn said. "I was just thinking about that song, the one about what a difference a day makes. Two days ago we were on top of the world. And yesterday, our world practically fell apart."

Tom nodded, and stared off. "I hope the training chart's marked. I think he wanted to run Cajun on Friday."

Dawn sipped her coffee. "If he didn't, Tom, you know how he thinks. It'll be all right."

Tom looked at her. "Let's hope so."

Chapter Twenty-Seven

"We've got two to track," Tom said, looking at the training chart. "And his condition book's marked too, so that won't be a problem for a while."

Dawn nodded in agreement as she gazed over his shoulder, and thus started the morning routine; walkers first, horses that trained next, baths for those that needed them, and finally grooming and doing them up. Randy stopped by as they were winding down.

"Can I help?"

"I've got to go enter," Tom said. "Dawn has two horses to do up and we're done. We would've been finished by now, but every time I turned around someone was over here asking about Ben."

"Who's left to do up?" Randy asked, turning to Dawn.

"All Together and Branden."

"All right, I'll do the filly, you do Branden," he said, ducking under the webbing. He had a full schedule of farm calls today and needed to leave right away if he was going to get to them all. He had been dragging earlier, but had gotten his second wind. He dropped Dawn off at her apartment, told her he'd see her at the hospital later or at home, kissed her good-bye, and took off.

Ben was by no means out of the woods, but at least today, he looked more like himself, because of the expression in his eyes. And Dawn found comfort in that. She hugged him as best she could, careful of all the tubes and cords, and pulled a chair up next to his bed.

He smiled a crooked smile and just looked at her.

"Tom entered who you had marked. He'll be here in a little while."

"Good," Ben said, with a great deal of difficulty.

"Don't try and talk, it's okay."

Dr. Martin walked into ICU then, picked up Ben's chart, nodded to Ben, and smiled at Dawn.

"Do you want me to leave?" she asked, standing.

"No, you're fine," he said, scanning the notations from the first shift duty nurse. "Well now."

Dawn squeezed Ben's hand.

"Mr. Miller, Ben. I'm Dr. James Martin. I've been on your case since yesterday. I even spent part of the night with this young lady here. I feel like family," he said, joking.

Dawn liked the man instantly, though she didn't remember much about him from yesterday or early this morning, and probably couldn't even recall his hair color, if asked, which was coal black.

"So, Ben..." Dr. Martin said, pausing to again glance at the chart. "Why is it that since you're on a prescribed medication for hypertension, there was no evidence of it in your system?"

Dawn looked at Ben.

"Did we forget?"

"Yesss," Ben said.

"I see." Dr. Martin nodded. "Well, there's no sense me scolding you at this point. You've paid the price. Let's just see what we can do to get you well, so you never forget again."

Dawn smiled.

"You've had a stroke, Ben," Dr. Martin said. "Plain and simple." He laid the chart down on the bed and looked Ben in the eye. "You're having a little trouble talking, and there's some paralysis on your right side, but it could've been worse."

Dawn patted Ben's hand to reassure him, and he turned slowly to look at her.

Dr. Martin glanced at the heart monitor. "For the next few days, you're going to get a lot of rest; then the work begins. I'm being frank with you, Ben. I'm not known for my bedside manner, ask my wife," he said, and laughed. "It's lucky for you that you were found so quickly and got in here as fast as you did. It may have saved your life. I want you to remember this when we start therapy, because it's not going to be easy. Do you understand?"

Ben nodded as best he could.

"All right." Dr. Martin clapped his hands together. "I'm off then to make someone else's morning."

"Dr. Martin," Dawn said. "Could I speak to you a moment?"

"Of course." He started out the door, implying she follow him. "I could use a cup of coffee."

Dawn had to practically jog to keep pace with him. They ended up in the staff lounge at the end of the hall. "Cream?" he asked, pouring her a cup.

Dawn nodded, and spooned in the sugar herself.

"Have a seat."

Dawn sat down across from him, the only two in the room aside from one other physician in the midst of a phone conversation about the stock market, as best Dawn could surmise.

She sipped her coffee, stalling, and almost choked on it. "How can you drink this? It tastes like Mercurochrome."

The doctor laughed. "Oh? Do you drink Mercurochrome?"

Dawn smiled, excused herself to add more cream, and sat back down.

"Better?"

She nodded.

"So what can I do for you?"

"I'm not sure. I guess I just want to know if what you told Ben is the whole story."

Dr. Martin took a drink of his coffee. "At this point, yes." He looked at her, took her in. "You are his daughter?"

Dawn smiled. "Not really," she said, and let it go at that. "You mentioned therapy."

He nodded. "He'll need two, three months of it at least."

"Would that be done here?"

"Depending on his insurance. This is the best place." He explained the basics of the process. Dawn thanked him, asked a few more questions, and drank only enough coffee to be polite. "Thank you for your time."

Dr. Martin smiled. "You too, Miss uh...?"

"Fioritto," Dawn said. "Dawn Fioritto."

Dr. Martin shook her hand. "It's a pleasure to meet you." Definitely, he said in his mind.

Dawn returned to ICU, stayed with Ben as long as the nurse would allow, then met up with Tom in the hall.

"How is he?"

Dawn motioned to the waiting room and they went in and sat down. "He looked a little better today. Dr. Martin's encouraged also."

Tom nodded thoughtfully. "So what happens now?"

"Well, I guess in a couple of days, therapy."

"What?"

Dawn stared. "I know." It seemed too soon.

"Boy, they don't waste any time, do they?"

Dawn shook her head. She had reservations also. It was just yesterday he'd almost died. And as if to emphasize that fact, in came a family of three, in tears, and obviously waiting for word on the fate of a loved one.

Tom couldn't handle it, and walked out into the hall. Dawn followed. "Are you all right?"

He nodded. "Dave didn't come by. I wonder why he didn't come by."

Dawn looked at him. "He doesn't come every day."

Tom shrugged. No consolation.

One of the nurses at the desk got their attention. "You can go in now," she said, and held up her hand to indicate the cautionary five minutes. But they weren't with Ben thirty seconds, when they were asked to leave because of something going on with the patient in the cubicle next to him.

"Code blue."

Ben listened, motionless.

"What's going on?" Ben tried to ask the nurse, his words a slur.

"It's all right, Mr. Miller," she said, watching his monitor. "It's all right."

He shook his head, tried to ask again, his heart racing faster and faster. He wasn't deaf. He could hear. "What's going on?"

The nurse left and came back with a syringe to inject into his IV. "You must relax, Mr. Miller. Relax."

Dawn and Tom meanwhile had left the hospital with plans to meet when it was time to feed and come back again that evening.

Dawn spent the afternoon with Linda at the club, dropped her things off at her apartment, and before she knew it, she and Tom were back at ICU. The bed next to Ben's was empty.

And Ben was in a mood. He tried to tell them that Gloria and Charlie had come by, but couldn't remember whether it was in the morning or afternoon. Tom and Dawn didn't care which, but it mattered to Ben, and apparently a great deal. His mouth wouldn't cooperate, his face felt stiff and empty, and he'd only found out, just minutes before, that he had a catheter in him.

"Miss..." The nurse advised they leave when she saw how frustrated he was getting. "I'm sorry."

"That's okay, we understand. Ben, we'll be back," Dawn said.

"No. Go home," he insisted, angry with the world and mad at himself. "Go home."

Dawn looked at the nurse and smiled apologetically. "Believe it or not, this is good," she said, referring to Ben's temperament.

"Easy for you to say." The nurse chuckled.

Tom and Dawn went for a cup of coffee, waited for word, and were allowed back in around five-thirty. Ben was in a somewhat better mood, but tired easily. He listened to what Tom had to report, nodded, and closed his eyes.

"We'll see you tomorrow," Dawn said, and Ben looked at her, thinking they'd just arrived.

"The man died," he said. "Next to me. He died."

Dawn nodded, tears clouding her vision. "I'm going to ride out and see Beau in the morning. Okay?"

"Okay."

He shook Tom's hand then, and Tom walked out and headed straight for the elevator.

"Tom! Tom!" Dawn grabbed him by the arm.

He pressed the button and looked at her. "I can't handle this. All right?"

"All right. I can't either, but..."

Tom banged the elevator button harder, stared and then looked at her again. "He's not going to pull through, is he?"

"Yes," Dawn said. "He is. Dr. Martin said it's natural to go through this. It's just a phase."

Tom shook his head. "Fine. When he gets better, I'll come back. Meanwhile, I'm outta here. I'm gonna go get laid. Okay?"

"Okay." Dawn paused, then laughed. "If that's what it takes."

Tom stepped back, ran his fingers through his hair, sighed, and leaned against the wall. "You want to go get something to eat?"

Dawn nodded, and straightened the fold on his collar. "Sure. I wouldn't want you out on the prowl on an empty stomach."

Dr. Martin walked down the hall as she and Tom boarded the elevator, and wished he hadn't missed her.

Randy arrived a few minutes later and was allowed a short visit. Dr. Martin glanced up at him as he approached the bed. "Hi there."

Randy smiled, nodded, and looked at Ben. "How are you doing?"

"Finnnee," Ben said.

Dr. Martin agreed, and in saying so, stepped closer to Randy and scrunched up his nose.

"Horse shit," Randy said, explaining. "It's been one of those days."

Dr. Martin laughed, made a notation on Ben's chart, and left them alone. Ben was glad to see him and had something he wanted to say.

"Take care of Dawn."

Randy shook his head. "You're not going anywhere."

"Just take care of her. Please?" Ben drawled.

Randy nodded.

Ben dozed then, just that little bit of talking had drained him completely. It was difficult thinking, but sometimes if he closed his eyes, everything became clearer. "I'll see you later, Randy," he said.

"What did you say, Mr. Miller?" his nurse asked.

He looked at her, Randy was gone. He'd actually been gone for some time. "Nothing," he said, and drifted again. He didn't know if it was night or day, it didn't matter one way or the other. "Nothing matters," he said, unable to feel the passing of his own urine. I'm just laying here, and can't even spit. There's probably a machine that can do that for me too. Meg, I'm glad you're not alive to see me now. I can't piss on my own again. I can't do anything. Move your legs I tell myself. Move your legs. And I just lay here. I just lay here.

"Ben..." Gloria hovered over him. "Ben, what is it? Are you in pain?"

Ben opened his eyes and stared at her through the blur of tears. "This is no good. I don't want this."

Gloria cupped his hand in hers. "Ben, you're going to be just fine."

Ben shook his head, and looked at Charlie. "I'm sorry," he said, when he saw his best friend standing there in tears as well. "It's going to be just you now."

"Oh no," Charlie said. "They're going to be getting you up and around any day now."

"That's right," Gloria emphasized. "So none of this talk now. You hear?"

Ben nodded and wiped at his eyes with his good hand, laden with an IV, two identification bracelets and a finger monitor that looked like a clothespin. "What time is it?"

"He's always asking that," one of the nurses said, snickering as if it were the most ridiculous question she'd ever heard.

Ben asked again. "What time is it?"

"Seven-fifteen," Gloria said. "I'll bring you a clock tomorrow." She scowled at the nurse. "This way you can remind the nurses when their shift ends."

Ben laughed, actually laughed, and when they'd gone, lay there enveloped in the aftermath of lilac cologne. He laughed again, to himself this time, and started remembering. The tack room, he'd gone in there to sit down a minute, to catch his breath. He started coughing then and thought he was coming down with a cold. Pneumonia maybe, because his chest hurt. Then that godawful smell of lilac, enough to take his breath away, but with the effect of smelling salts.

"Ben..."

"Ben..."

"What?" He opened his eyes.

"How about a little broth?"

"Broth?"

"It's time," the nurse said. "We've got to get you back on your feet."

Randy just missed Dawn at her apartment, according to her note. She'd spent part of the afternoon with Ginney at her trial-briefing, ate Chinese, and had left an extra dinner waiting for him on the kitchen counter if he wanted it, and she'd see him later. He shook his head. Why couldn't she have waited just a few more minutes? What was the big hurry? It's not like there were regular visiting hours in ICU. Damn her.

As luck would have it, at the hospital, they missed each other again. Apparently she'd just left. But he had a nice visit with Ben, was able to stay with him a little more than ten minutes, and ran into Dr. Martin in the hall.

"Well, hello there."

Randy smiled, they shook hands, and since both were going to the elevator, they walked along together, discussing Ben's condition.

"He's doing well. I'm quite pleased," Dr. Martin said. "A little progress every day is all we can ask for." Randy nodded, the elevator opened, and they boarded. "The family visiting often has been good for him."

Randy nodded again.

"How about animals?" Dr. Martin asked. "Does it matter?"

Randy shrugged. "Cats and dogs mainly, yes. Although in some cases..."

Dr. Martin smiled. Some families had adverse effects on humans as well. "But that doesn't seem to be the case here," he said, fishing. "Particularly when it comes to Dawn."

Randy stiffened. "Dawn?"

"Yes." When the elevator stopped on the second floor and the door opened, Dr. Martin hesitated getting off. "Tell me, I know she's not his daughter, but..."

Randy looked at the man.

"Perhaps a daughter-in-law? Married to the cowboy?"

Randy shook his head. "No. They're just friends."

Dr. Martin smiled, grinned actually, and got off and looked back. "So she's unattached?"

What's with this guy? Randy's eyes hardened. "I don't know. You'll have to ask her that."

"Thank you, I will," Dr. Martin said, still smiling as the doors closed.

Randy stared, and got off at the first floor, shaking his head. The son of a bitch. Why the interest in Dawn? Well, actually why not? But why? He walked to the pay phone thinking about her. Did she appear unattached? Was it in her eyes? Her manner? Bad enough he felt so insecure about their relationship, particularly since she hadn't had one minute for him in the last couple of days, regardless of the reason.

He let the phone ring at least ten times, hung up, and walked out to his truck. If she's not home, where is she? Unattached? Why didn't he just say, yeah, she's attached. She belongs to me, okay?

Why? He berated himself. Because she *doesn't* belong to you, that's why. And no one knows that more than you. He wanted to drive to her apartment, forgetting all this, be there when she got home, from wherever she was, and make love to her. His heart ached, literally ached, and it scared him. She doesn't belong to you. It's just a matter of time. He thought about her novel, his part in it, and since she wasn't home, considered going to her apartment and reading it until she got there, ask her once and for all and insist she tell him the truth. Instead, he started the truck and drove home. If she missed him and phoned him, then it would be a different thing.

Dawn meanwhile, arrived home, expected Randy at any minute, and after an hour or so, became concerned. She didn't think he was on call tonight, but perhaps she was mistaken. She phoned his answering service to be sure, and was right initially.

"Thank you," she said, and hung up. So where is he? Maybe he stopped at the hospital, she decided, appeased for the moment. But as time wore on, she found herself worrying and wondering again. Where could he be?

She phoned his answering service a second time, left a message for him, and really started to get concerned. Even if he'd swung by the hospital, he would have been here by now. The hospital. What if Ben's condition had worsened? What if...?

She looked up the number, was patched through to the nurses' station, and was informed Ben was asleep and hadn't had any recent visitors. She thanked the woman and hung up.

"I'll give him fifteen more minutes," she said. Then she was going to panic, because obviously something has happened to him. If not, he would have called.

She heard from him about half an hour later.

"Where are you?"

"I'm home. Why? Where were you?"

Dawn paused. He sounded different. "I was at the hospital, then Tom and I went and got something to eat. I thought you might show up at The Rib, but you didn't, so I left."

"I thought you had Chinese."

"I did, earlier." She paused again, trying to figure out his attitude. "What are you doing at home?"

"Oh..." Randy slurped a long drink of beer. "Sitting on my patio. Which reminds me. What's the difference between a patio and a terrace?"

Dawn laughed a little. "I don't know. Why?"

"Just wondering."

"Are you all right? Have you had dinner?"

Randy nodded, as if he could see her, and gazed at the pink stains on his fingertips. "I had some pistachio nuts. A lot of them I guess. Hold on, I'm going to get my dictionary."

"Randy...?" Too late, he'd put down the phone, and came back on.

"All right, we'll do this alphabetically. Patio first."

Dawn shook her head and laughed.

"Patio, an inner court open to the sky, a recreation area that adjoins a dwelling. Hmph." He leafed ahead to find terrace. "Terrace, a flat roof or open platform, balcony or deck. Wait a minute, that's no difference? What's the difference? What if I lived on the second floor?" He stared above his head. "His is the same as mine."

Dawn went for her own dictionary. "It's all in the interpretation."

"Uh huh," Randy said. "I see. Interpretation." He flipped the pages but Dawn beat him to it.

"To understand according to individual belief."

Randy took another swig of beer and looked around for the rest of the six pack. He was down to one can. "Well now," he said, "here's something to contemplate." He lined up the empty beer cans on the patio table next to him, made sure they all faced the same way, and thought about his college days. "At this rate, I could very well be drunk. Or at this point in my life, would that be intoxicated?"

"Intoxicated," Dawn said, and read the definition. "To make drunk, to excite or elate."

"Well then that's it, I'm drunk," Randy said. "Because I'm not having a good time."

Dawn put her dictionary away, a tremendous wave of depression washing over her. "Why didn't you come over, Randy?"

"Why weren't you home?" he said.

Dawn picked up the shirt he'd had on yesterday, which he left flung over the side of the couch, and covered her legs with it. "I had to go see Uncle Matt."

"Oh really? And how is old Don Corlione?"

Dawn tensed.

"I know," Randy said, popping the tab on his last beer. "Some day you'll tell me."

"I'll talk to you later."

"No, wait a minute...here's a good one. Listen to this. Your name means to 'begin to be understood.'"

Dawn sighed. What on earth brought all this on? "My name means nothing, Randy," she said. "It's just a name." Click.

Randy stared at the phone. "Well, you bitch." He dialed her number right back, but it was busy. He couldn't believe it. "She hung up on me," he said out loud, as if there were someone around to hear him. "She hung up on me."

He downed the rest of his beer and just sat there for a moment, doing a slow burn, then dialed her number again. No answer. "Goddamn her. Who does she think she is?"

"Dawn Fioritto," he could hear her saying. "What's it to you?"

"Nothing," he said, and went in and crashed on the couch, where over the next few hours he dreamt one bizarre dream after another. He didn't know his own name in one, and kept asking everyone what it was. In another, he saw Dawn and Dr. Martin traveling in a covered wagon across the desert. Dawn was wearing a fur coat and Dr. Martin a white jumpsuit with huge bellbottoms. He was whipping the horse, and Randy was summoned to heal the animal, but the horse was dead. As Randy reached to pet the horse's neck, it turned into a sow, a large sow. And he woke up.

He thought of calling Dawn, but it was almost morning. Besides, he felt like he was going to be sick, decided to stay put, hoping the nausea would pass, and fell back asleep.

Randy avoided the Miller barn until he finished the morning rounds, having taken that long to muster up the courage to apologize to Dawn.

"She just left to go over to the hospital," Tom said.

Randy nodded, a bit relieved since he still didn't know what he was going to say, and feeling really foolish for his behavior. "Do you guys have anything in?"

"Two," Tom said.

"All right, I'll see you later. Tell Dawn I was by." He walked toward his truck, stopped, and looked back. "What kind of mood was she in?"

"Okay, I guess," Tom said, shrugging. They'd been pretty busy all morning. "Why?"

"No reason," Randy said, and left. Couldn't she at least have been a little depressed? He passed Ginney between barns, backed up his truck and called to her. "What are you doing this afternoon?"

Ginney walked over to talk to him. "Probably hanging around here. Why? What's up?"

"I could use your right hand."

Ginney laughed. "Aren't you a little past that stage?"

"Yeah," Randy said, laughing as well. "What I need is some help." He and Raffin agreed they both needed assistants, but with their trying to buy Jake's practice, they couldn't afford any right now.

Ginney hesitated. "Does Dawn know you're asking?"

"No, but she has two horses in and couldn't help anyway."

Ginney shook her head. "I don't want her mad at me."

"Why would she be mad? Come on, I'm not asking you to go screw. I just need some help. Come on."

Ginney stared in the direction of the Miller barn, gave it some thought, and finally relented. "All right. But if she fucking gets mad at me, I'm not ever gonna talk to you again. Okay?"

Randy smiled. "Okay. But trust me, she's not going to get mad."

Son of Royalty finished second, and Branden a distant fourth. Both horses came back fine, cooled out well, were done up. And Tom and Dawn fed.

"Did you and Randy have a fight?" Tom asked, right out of the blue when they were locking up.

"No, not really."

Tom looked at her.

"Why?"

"I don't know. He said something funny earlier."

"When?"

The two of them walked to the parking lot. "When he stopped by."

Dawn kept her reaction from showing, though she certainly would like to have been informed of this earlier, and changed the subject. "Do you know anything about Ben's hospitalization? Which plan he has."

Tom shook his head. "You want me to find out?"

"No, I'll do it. I'll see you at the hospital."

Randy and Ginney returned shortly thereafter, pulled in next to Ginney's car in the parking lot, and sat talking a minute. "I can't tell you how much I appreciate your help," Randy said. "I owe you."

"No, that's okay. It was fun." Ginney glanced around. "Dawn's car's gone. She's probably at the hospital."

Randy nodded. Probably. He paused. "Do you and she ever talk?"

Ginney looked at him. "Yeah, asshole. Lots of times."

Randy laughed. That's not what he'd meant. "I mean really talk?"

"You mean about you?"

Randy shrugged. "That, and about herself."

"No." Ginney thought back to the morning Dawn found her in the ladies room, remembered her compassion and understanding of what had taken place, and felt sure that Dawn must have gone through the same thing at one time. "I'll tell you what, if you wanna talk about owing somebody, I owe her. If it wasn't for her." She turned, getting choked up, and stared out the window for a moment. "She's going to the trial with me, you know."

"I know." Randy looked at her, studied her expression. "Most women would shy away from something like that, don't you think?"

Ginney smiled. "Dawn's not most women."

Randy nodded. "You got that right."

Ginney got out and looked back in at him. "I'm warning you, Randy. If she gets mad at me, I'm going to hate you."

Randy smiled. "She won't. She won't even care." He thought about going to the hospital, but had a message at the stable gate to phone Raffin. His assistance was needed in surgery. He'd go to

Dawn's apartment when he was done and apologize, he told himself. There was no sense phoning her; he knew she wouldn't be home. So it would have to be later.

Tom and Dawn were allowed a full half hour visit with Ben, who listened intently and asked questions and gave comments as best he could. He was concerned about the status of his appeal to the racing stewards. Tom told him they'd put it on hold for the time being.

"Hmph," he said, in that familiar, cynical way of his, and Tom laughed, teasing.

"So don't be in a hurry to get well."

Ben smiled a lopsided smile. "No, that's okay. I want out of here."

"All in due time, Mr. Miller," a nurse in passing said. "All in due time."

Tom thought he and Dawn might go get a bite to eat afterwards, but Dawn had other plans. "I'm going to try to track down Dr. Martin. I think I'll have him paged."

Tom looked lost. "Do you want me to wait?"

"No, you don't have to. I'll see you tomorrow."

Dr. Martin returned her call within minutes, said he was about to leave for the day but would answer any questions she had, and suggested they do it over dinner. "I'm starved," he said. "Where would you like to go?"

Dawn hesitated. She'd assumed he meant the hospital cafeteria. "Uh..."

"Where do they have good steaks? This eating out is new to me."

Dawn said The Rib had good food, and since she didn't have to go there alone now, which she would never do, it seemed as good a place as any. "I'm not sure where it is," Dr. Martin said. "So I'll meet you in the lobby and follow you there." Which he did.

They sat themselves at a table to the back, away from the bar, where it was quieter and they could talk. Dawn wanted to hear all about the options on Ben's therapy, wanted to discuss a controversial program she'd read about using electrodes. And Dr. Martin, "James...please," he said, wanted to talk about life in general, and starting over.

It made for good conversation, but then again, Dawn was a good listener. He recommended traditional therapy. "Mr. Miller is a very strong man for his age. As long as we keep his blood pressure under control, I think he'll do just fine."

He talked about his son Jimmy. And displayed a bitterness against the legal system. "I understand I get him every weekend from now on. Some stranger in court gave me that right."

Dawn studied his eyes, deep set but distinct with dark lashes and heavy brows. "Is your wife a good mother?"

He nodded, and smiled apologetically. "I'm sorry. Of course she is." He didn't mean to mislead her. "She was just a lousy wife," he added, and the two of them laughed.

"What does she say about you?"

Dr. Martin grew serious and shrugged. "She says I'm a good doctor."

Dawn nodded. That said volumes. Ginney and her father entered the restaurant then. Bud walked on, and Ginney approached the table. "Hey, what's up?"

"Not much," Dawn said, and introduced them.

"James," Dr. Martin insisted again. "Please. It's nice to meet you."

Ginney nodded, smiling, and looked warily at Dawn. "Is Ben all right?"

"Oh, he's fine," Dawn said, thinking that was what the look was about. "Isn't he?"

Dr. Martin smiled. "Yes. Or at least he will be, if we can get him to cooperate." He studied Dawn's friend, noticing how different the two were.

"Did you and Randy have a fight?" Ginney asked.

"No." Dawn shook her head. "Why?"

"He was asking me about you earlier, and it seemed like... Well, never mind. It was nice meeting you, Dr...I mean, James. I gotta go. I don't want Dad getting a head start on me."

James stood as she left the table, sat back down, and in through the door came Randy. One look and his eyes hardened. He knew she was here; her Jaguar was parked right out front. But he'd figured she was with Tom or maybe Ginney. He never expected Dr. Martin. But then again, he asked himself, why should you be surprised?

He walked straight to their table. He'd be damned if he was going to ignore them or be ignored. Dawn looked up as he neared, and Dr. Martin rose to shake his hand.

"How nice to meet up with you again. As you can see, I took your advice and asked her myself," James said, as congenial as could be. "And well, here we are."

"I see that."

Dawn stared, swallowed hard. What advice? What were they talking about?

"Well, if you'll excuse me," Randy said, glaring at Dawn.

Dawn lowered her eyes to the table as he walked away, James sat back down, and Randy joined Bud and Ginney.

"He seems like a nice guy," James said. "Uh, how long have you known him?"

"Apparently not long enough," Dawn said. "Or perhaps too long."

James looked at her. Admittedly, he wasn't the most intuitive person in the world, but even he could see there was something between these two. But it didn't make any sense. After all, he'd asked the man about her. "I'm sorry."

"Don't be," Dawn said. "It has nothing to do with you."

Randy sat watching them from across the room. He'd been hungry when he came in, but had lost his appetite. This Martin guy didn't waste any time. The son of a bitch. And where was his commitment from Dawn? Didn't that ring he gave her mean anything?

Apparently not. Dr. Martin and Dawn stood up to leave, causing the hair on the back of Randy's neck to stand on end.

Ginney glanced over her shoulder, looked at Randy, and shook her head. "You're fucking up big time, Randy. I mean it."

Randy looked at her, thought about setting her straight, letting her know she was being used too. They were research for a novel, nothing else. Dr. Martin was probably no more than that either. But instead, he just shook his head and stared across the room. Dr. Martin was paying the bill.

"They're just talking about Ben," Ginney tried to tell him.

"Yeah right," Randy said.

And then they were gone.

Chapter Twenty-Eight

Randy had a smile pasted on his face late the following morning when he showed up at the Miller barn. He knew Dawn would be there since Cajun was running in the first race, wanted desperately to see her. But for all practical purposes, his appearance suggested he was just checking in.

"Am I needed for anything?"

Dawn shook her head, ducked out from under the webbing of Lady's stall, and headed for the tack room to get her grooming bucket.

It pissed him off, her ignoring him like this. "Uh..."

She stopped and turned, looked at him. "What?"

Randy spoke without any forethought. "I have to come by and get my things. If you're not home, I'll just leave the key."

Dawn nodded and stared. This was it; he was moving on. If she had any doubt last night, with that reference to his supposedly telling James to ask her out, on top of the way he'd behaved the night before on the phone...it was gone now.

"Fine," she said. "I won't be home this afternoon. Perhaps you can do it then." She didn't want to be there. It would kill her. It was taking everything she had not to break down and cry now. She turned and walked into the tack room and waited until she heard him start his truck and drive away before she crumbled onto the cot.

"Sweetie," Gloria said, entering a moment later and witnessing her rocking back and forth, arms folded and hugging her sides. "What's the matter?"

Dawn shook her head and forced some composure. Focus, she told herself. Focus. "Oh, it's just one of those days."

Gloria sat down next to her and put her arm around her. "And it's no wonder, the pressure you've been under. There, there now. It's okay."

"I'm sorry," Dawn said, wiping her eyes with her trembling hands. "I'm sorry."

"Don't be," Gloria said. "I've just come from the hospital, and Ben is just fine. It's all just a matter of time. He'll get better, you'll see."

Dawn nodded, sniffed, picked herself up, and went through the motions of the day. Cajun ran second. Tom said he should've won. Gloria was thrilled anyway. At least no one had snuck in and drugged him this time. "Winning isn't everything," she said. And Tom and Dawn visited Ben afterwards. Dawn drove home exhausted, saw that Randy's things were still there and crawled into bed.

During the night she thought the phone rang. She answered it, and it was Randy. He told her he loved her and she hung up. He didn't love her. It was all a dream. Lies.

A creature of habit, she stopped at the donut shop on the way in. Then remembering the morning Randy surprised her there, how excited she'd been to see him, she berated herself all over again for being so taken in.

The training schedule was light, but for some reason, they were still walking horses at ten o'clock. Finally, the last were put away and Tom headed over to enter All Together. Dawn raked the shedrow, first one way then the other, back and forth, back and forth, in her customary herringbone pattern.

Randy came around the corner, hesitated, and watched her from the end of the barn. As hard as he tried, he just couldn't stay away. He'd spent the whole night trying to make sense of what was going on between them, and why, and was still fighting his profound fear of being used. What else could explain her attitude?

She didn't care.

She just didn't care.

He walked toward her. "Dawn."

She swung around quickly, his voice startling her, and split her lip when she ran smack dab into the side of Son of Royalty's face, who'd chosen that precise moment to hang his head out of the stall. "Oh my God!" she gasped, her hand instinctively going to her mouth, then realizing how dirty it was, and now with blood all over it.

Randy rushed to her side. "Here, let me see," he said, reaching to turn her face so he could look.

"No!" She pushed him away, wiped her hand on her pants, stared at the grime and blood, and started backing up. "Oh my God!" she said, blood dripping from her mouth and not knowing what to do with it. The taste. "Oh my God!"

Tom started down the shedrow then, took one look, and turned on Randy. "What the fuck's going on here?"

Randy glared at him. "Yeah, like I'd hit her?" He tried again to get Dawn to let him look at her mouth. It was bleeding quite a bit. "She ran into the side of the horse's face."

"Shit!" Tom said. "Let me see."

"No!" She didn't want him touching her either. She backed away from both of them, quickly rolled her sleeve, pressed the clean side hard against her mouth, and headed for the ladies room.

Tom called after her. "I'll go get some ice. You hear me? Come right back," he said, as if this were suddenly all his fault. And Randy walked away.

Dawn saw Randy in passing over the next few days, but neither made an effort to acknowledge one another. Randy visited Ben at odd times, when he was sure she wouldn't be there, and was careful to have an excuse ready if Ben ever asked why they weren't together.

Ben didn't ask, not that he didn't notice. He may have had a stroke, but his mind, now that he was no longer sedated, was as sharp as ever. Randy and Dawn both had that lost look in their eyes, and never once even mentioned the other's name.

"How's therapy?" they'd both ask, smiling.

"You're looking stronger." Smiling.

"How's your appetite?" Smiling.

"You've got good coloring." With more smiling.

Yet the look in their eyes.

"I'll see you later."

"I'll see you later."

"I'll see you later."

Even Tom. "Stay at the barn," Ben told him. All Together was running today, and he wanted her watched like a hawk.

"What we need is to pad her stall," Tom said.

Ben nodded. He'd seen glimpses of that side of her even at the farm. When she wanted her way, she flat wanted her way.

"I'll see you later."

Randy had to stop by the Miller barn to give Branden a *jug* of vitamins and electrolytes. Tom thought maybe if Dawn held the horse, she and Randy would talk. But no such luck. It was all business, though in Tom's opinion, Randy had at least made an effort.

"I don't know what's wrong with you, Dawn," he said, when Randy had gone. "I don't even think you two know why you're fighting anymore."

Dawn looked at him. "Yeah, well that's where you're wrong, Tom. Because we're not fighting. It's just over, okay?"

"No," Tom said.

Dawn started past him. "What's it going to be, pizza or burgers?"

"Burgers," Tom said. "And don't change the subject."

Dawn shook her head. "Since when are you an expert on relationships?"

Tom stared, visibly hurt by that, and Dawn found herself quickly apologizing. "I'm sorry."

Tom shrugged. "Why? It's true. What do I know?"

Dawn sighed. "Are you trying to give me the hiccups? Is that what this is all about? Do you want me worrying? Do you want me to be a basket case? Do you want me beating a path to the ladies room?"

Tom smiled. "Boy, those were the days, weren't they?"

Dawn shook her head. "A lifetime ago."

The filly was in the eighth race, and as the afternoon wore on, she got increasingly wound up. Dawn pulled the manes of every horse in the barn, to kill time. Everyone except All Together's, that is, who she wouldn't dare attempt, even without Ben's rule, for fear of being trampled, kicked, or bitten, given the filly's agitated state. As a result, she never had a chance to worry about herself, or have it manifest into a tic or nervous ritual. Finally, the ten-minute call was announced. All Together was tacked, Tom mounted Red, and off they went.

The filly was unbeatable, and all business once she left the gate. It was in the paddock that she put on a show, and in the post parade and even at the gate. She broke on top, led by a length down the backside, ears pinned, and finished eight lengths in front and widening.

"A walk in the park," Tom said.

The photographer's good memory cautioned him against getting too close when snapping the picture in the winner's circle. Everyone swung wide after Johnny jumped off, beaming, and Tom turned the filly around. Dawn followed them to the spit barn, leading Red who, sweating up a storm, kept rubbing his left ear against Dawn's arm until she scratched it for him.

"You big baby," she said affectionately, and grew quiet as they passed the spot where Randy's truck would always be parked for the race. "He's gone," she told Red, who wanted scratching again. "I guess my number was up."

The filly was obnoxious to bathe, pushing, kicking out, tossing her head, swishing her tail, and dancing back and forth in place. Eventually she started settling down. Tom rode Red back to the barn then, saying how he was too tired to walk, and later he and Dawn commiserated about running her, and what it took out of them.

"She exhausts me," Dawn said, stretched out on a bale of straw, arms sprawled. "I can't move."

Tom nodded. "We've got to get some help, before you get hurt."

Dawn raised her head and looked at him. "Don't be doing that just on my account. I'll be all right; just get me some oxygen."

Tom laughed. "We need some help anyway. What with my ponying and saddling and entering, and going back and forth to the hospital. Shit, I ain't never been so tired."

Dawn smiled, and got up and looked in at the filly, just as gentle as could be now. She clicked to her, and the filly came over and nuzzled her face.

"I've known women like her," Tom said.

Dawn chuckled. "Spare me."

"Okay. But they were all winners too."

Ben insisted they go out and celebrate. "My treat." He wanted it just like before, even though he couldn't join them. "Call Randy," he said.

Dawn hedged. "Uh, I think he's busy."

"Page him then," Ben said, and looked at Tom. "Leave a message." He reached for the phone with his good hand, passed it to him, and that was that. Dawn could've said something at this point, and probably should have, she thought. But she didn't want to spoil the moment for Ben.

Tom apologized in the hall. "What was I going to do?"

"Nothing." Dawn eased his mind, said it didn't matter one way or the other, that it was no big deal. "He probably won't come anyway." She invited Dr. Martin before they left, phoned Ginney at the racetrack, who phoned right back and said she was on her way, and they were all seated when Randy showed up.

He walked to the men's room, washed his hands, and thought about walking right back out the front door. Originally when asked to join them, he'd said yes because he knew Dawn would probably be in a good mood, and maybe, just maybe, they would talk. He hadn't expected Dr. Martin, though he should have known, he told himself. Or Ginney either for that matter. So now what?

He dried his hands, combed his hair, smoothed his beard, picked up a drink at the bar, and sat down in the chair saved for him, directly across from Dawn.

She smiled at him, a smile he'd seen before, one usually directed at a stranger, then turned and continued her conversation with Ginney. "What did you say this was again?" she asked, referring to the tall icy refreshments they were drinking.

"Iced tea. Long Island Iced Tea."

"Hmph." Dawn took another long sip through her straw. "It's delicious."

"What's it taste like?" Tom asked.

Dawn shrugged. She wasn't sure. "Tea, I guess."

Tom sniffed it, opened his eyes wide, and they all laughed. Dawn smiled at Randy again, that same indifferent smile, and he sat back and crossed his arms.

I know every inch of you, he was thinking, like the back of my hand. And yet I know nothing about what's going on in your head.

Nothing. He lowered his gaze, noticed she was still wearing the ring, and thought about the day he'd bought it, the hope he'd felt, the promise. And about the other night, when at two in the morning he phoned her, and how she hung up on him.

"Your order, please."

The meal was delicious, generous helpings of sautéed mushrooms smothering steaks grilled to perfection, mounds of sour cream piled on baked potatoes, strawberry shortcake with banana whipped topping. And for Dawn and Ginney, plenty of Long Island Iced Tea.

Tom kept the conversation going, and in his usual rare form. He had everyone laughing, even Randy on occasion, who, in spite of his calm exterior, sat seething and totally preoccupied with all the attention James was lavishing on Dawn. One small comfort was that he appeared to be paying an equal amount of attention to Ginney. Still, each and every time he put his arm around Dawn, Randy had to fight back the urge to yank him across the table and throttle him.

When it was almost nine, Randy glanced at his watch. He could leave now and not have it look as if he was bailing out because he was uncomfortable with the situation. But then he noticed something. He wasn't sure at first, because she hid it so well, always so in control. But it was a fact. Dawn was getting a little tipsy, more frequent laughs, rather talkative. She even at one point referred to something that happened between them on a farm call, and looked right at him as if nothing had changed and they were still together.

The sliding doors between the restaurant and the dance floor were pushed open and the weekend band began to play. They weren't very good, but they were, "Family," Momma Leone told them in Italian, as she passed between the tables urging everyone to get up and dance.

Dawn smiled, said something in Italian in return, and Momma Leone cupped Dawn's face in her aged hands, squeezed gently, and walked on.

Randy marveled at such a sweet exchange, and apparently James was moved as well. "Would you like to dance?" he asked Dawn, much to Randy's chagrin.

"Certainly," she said, and she and Ginney laughed when she stood up and had to sit right back down again because the room was spinning. "Oh Jesus."

"Here, lean on me," James said, helping her to her feet and wrapping his arm around her waist.

Randy watched as they walked to the dance floor, and absentmindedly picked up a butter knife and started flipping it back and forth.

Tom took it from him, frowned, and nudged him. "Man, what's the matter with you? You gonna put up with this?"

Randy looked at him.

"Go for it."

Ginney smiled drunkenly, echoing his sentiments. "Yeah, go for it."

Randy glanced from one to the other, sat there and stewed a moment, and finally stood up. When Dawn turned from James she found herself in Randy's arms, so warm and strong, and so very familiar. Even the shape of his cast.

"Hi," she said, and he laughed. She was shit-faced. Dawn Fioritto, founding daughter. "Have we met?"

"Several times," he said, and she nodded and looked away.

"I think I'd better go home now." She turned and headed for the table, maneuvered her way through the chairs, and reached for her purse. "I'm going to go home now," she said, and looked around for the door.

Ginney nodded. "I think I should go too."

"Can you drive?" Dawn asked. "Are you all right?"

James rose then, observing the two, and offered to drive them both home.

"Thank you," Dawn said, and stared at her keys as if she didn't know what to do with them now. Randy reached over her shoulder and took them from her. "I'll take you home, come on."

"No," she said, and shook her head. "I don't want to go with you. I don't even know you," she said in a bitterly sarcastic tone. "I hate you."

Randy glared at her, the feeling mutual right about then.

"Give me my keys."

Randy shook his head.

"Hey listen," James said, glancing at Tom for help, who just shrugged, offering none. "I'll take them both home, and you two can continue this tomorrow when you're both in a little better mood. All right?"

"No, there is no tomorrow," Dawn said. "He'll be busy."

Randy shook his head in disbelief. Me? Too busy for her? It was always the other way around.

"Let's go," Dawn said, forgetting all about her keys, as she and Ginney linked their arms around James's. "I'll see you in the morning, Tom. Okay?" she said, glancing back at him over her shoulder.

"Okay." He nodded, waving, and then looked at Randy as if he couldn't believe Randy was going to just stand here and let her walk out.

Randy shook his head; this woman had shot him down just one too many times. And yet... "Dawn," he heard himself saying.

She turned. The band was playing a song she'd never heard before, and sounded far, far away. "What? What did you say?"

"I said I love you."

Dawn stared at him, just stared, and reached out her hand.

"No more games, Randy."

He shook his head. "No more games."

Randy woke to the sound of running water, looked beside him for Dawn, and closed his eyes. She was in the shower. He could hear her mumbling, and after a while, got up and went in to check on her. She was still in her jeans and bra from last night, when any movement whatsoever nauseated her. And apparently she wasn't in much better shape even now.

A forceful spray pelted her head and body.

"Dawn, this water is cold."

She looked at him through the cascade streaming down her face. "It is? I thought so."

He adjusted the temperature. "Do you want some help?" he asked, referring to her clothes.

"No," she said, wearily, and then, "God, what do they put in those drinks?"

Randy smiled. "I'm going back to bed. Call me if you need me."

Dawn eventually turned the water off and sat on the edge of the tub, peeled off her clothes, which she left in a heap, dried off, and put on her robe. She made her way to the chair on the other side of the bedroom, held onto the windowsill for balance as she eased herself into it, and dug her toes into the carpet, for fear of falling off the face of the earth.

She looked at Randy, traveled the contour of his body under the sheet with her eyes, and wondered if they'd talked. She couldn't remember. The sound of his breathing was comforting. When she closed her eyes, it sounded like the wind. The words to a sonnet came to mind then, but vanished in an instant. And she fell asleep.

Randy woke her at the usual time, and offered her two options. "Stay home or get dressed."

"Let me think," she said.

He hoped she'd stay home. She'd be captive then, sleep it off and be here when he returned so they could talk and get it all out in the open.

"I promise," she'd said last night, and he'd relented, because with the most solemn look on her face, she also said she loved him. "On my honor." And for once he believed her.

"Well?"

"Help me braid my hair," she said.

Randy knelt down beside her and smiled.

Tom had something new to razz her about, and never let up. As the morning dragged on, Dawn found herself growing more and more agitated with him.

"Good, you're mad," he said. "The juices are flowing. Now it's time to eat."

Dawn looked at him. At this particular moment, she didn't care if she ever ate again. "Maybe tomorrow."

Tom laughed. "It'll be worse then. You gotta do it now. Here." He used a napkin to tear off a piece of donut, the way she always did, and handed it to her. "Eat."

She took it from him, groaned, and put it in her mouth.

"Chew," he said, demonstrating. "That's it. Okay, a little more. Now swallow."

Dawn shook her head and smiled.

"So." He took a sip of coffee and sat down next to her. "I take it you and Randy made up."

Dawn shrugged. "I think so."

"Well, it was about time," Tom said. "I can't stand everything falling apart."

Dawn looked at him. "It's not like it was your fault."

"Whose fault was it then?"

Dawn stared, took another bite of donut after he handed it to her, and forced herself to chew. "I don't know. Maybe it was yours."

"Yeah right." Tom laughed. "Blame me."

When it was close to eleven and Randy still hadn't come by the barn, Dawn phoned Linda and made plans to meet at the club. They whiled away the afternoon as they brought each other up to date on what had taken place over the last few days. Tom had said he'd feed, so Dawn went on home, and was pleasantly surprised to find Randy's truck parked in the garage in Linda's spot. She wondered how long he'd been home.

He wasn't in the living room or in the kitchen, so she walked down the hall, and found him stretched out on the bed on his stomach, feet hanging over the side, and apparently sound asleep. She tiptoed up next to him and leaned over to see his face. That's when he grabbed her and pulled her onto the bed next to him.

"Where have you been? I've been waiting for you for hours!"

Dawn laughed. "You have not. Your engine was still warm."

"So what," Randy said, and planted a series of sloppy kisses all over her face. "A minute, an hour, what's the difference?"

Dawn smiled. "My worrying about where you were and being late is what started all this."

"Not really," Randy said, and smiled. "But speaking of which..."

Dawn tried to pull away but he wouldn't let her. "Not until you tell me we're going to talk like you promised."

Dawn nodded.

"Okay," he said, releasing her and getting up to walk across the room and sit down. "Where do we start?"

Dawn sat up and looked at him. "How about the dictionary?"

Randy flushed, somewhat embarrassed to be reminded of that. "How about your novel?"

Dawn sighed. Not this again. "Do you want me to stop writing it? Is that what this is all about?"

"No. Why? Would you?"

Dawn stared.

"I didn't think so."

"Randy..." She looked at him. "If I asked you to give up being a veterinarian, would you do it?"

"No. It's what I do. It's my job."

"Right. And writing's my job."

"What about the racetrack?"

"So I have two jobs. What's your problem with that?"

Randy hesitated and shrugged. He didn't know. "I guess it's because you're writing about the racetrack."

Dawn shook her head. She didn't understand why that should bother him. "You still don't think I'm writing about you, do you?"

He stared.

"Randy! I told you, it's not you."

"I know. Just someone like me."

Dawn sighed.

"Are you writing about a doctor now too? A doctor not exactly like..."

"No. No, no, no," she said, over and over again. "No." Then she glanced at her watch, and did something that took Randy totally by surprise. She started unbraiding her hair. He watched her, silently, watched as she separated the strands, and then shook it loose and wavy onto her shoulders.

He wet his lips with the tip of his tongue, still watching her, watched as she reached for a pillow and laid back, watched as she unbuttoned her blouse and looked at him.

"Is there something you want?" he asked, lowering his eyes down over her.

"Yes," she said. It was the first time ever between them that she'd initiated their lovemaking.

"Go all the way then," he said, wanting her to undress completely. Wanting to watch. To sit there until he couldn't stand it anymore. Every inch of her...his. And there was no more talking.

Chapter Twenty-Nine

Ben was glad to see Dawn and Randy together again, and asked them who they thought they were fooling all the other times.

Dawn smiled. "Apparently no one."

"So what are you two up to?"

Dawn shrugged. "Oh, just dinner and then going home."

Ben nodded and looked at Randy. "Dr. Martin wants to talk to you."

"Me? Why?"

"I don't know. He said to have the nurse page him. And that it had nothing to do with me."

Randy could guess, and it wouldn't surprise him. James struck him as a basic up-front kind of guy. And sure enough, when Randy had him paged and the two men met in the lounge at the end of the hall, it was about Dawn, and quite direct.

"I asked you about her, Randy, and you set me up. Why?"

Randy apologized. "I don't know. But the day you asked, and the circumstance surrounding everything... I didn't know what to say. Dawn makes me a little crazy sometimes."

James nodded. "I can see that."

"Again, I'm sorry." Randy smiled. He liked this guy. "Trust me, telling you I didn't think Dawn was attached was not something I enjoyed doing. It's just that there's times I really don't know where I stand with her."

"She is a bit of a puzzle, isn't she?"

Randy looked at him.

"I talked to Ginney about her, who by the way is rather nice herself. She sobered up fairly well after a little fresh air. We went for coffee. In fact, we sat at the coffee shop for most of the night. Talk about a life, one could write a book about it."

Randy smiled. "I think somebody already is."

"Oh?"

Randy laughed, as if he were just kidding.

"So is everything all right with you and Dawn now?"

Randy nodded. "For the time being."

Now it was James who laughed. "You're right. She does drive you crazy. Why all the conflict?"

"I don't know, maybe because we come from two different worlds."

James sympathized. "I know the feeling. My wife and I, ex-wife I mean, were planets apart."

"Thanks for the encouragement," Randy said.

"Any time," James replied, and laughed again. "You might need it."

Randy studied him, smiling. "What's that supposed to mean?"

James shrugged. "Do you know who she is? Who her family is, to be more specific?"

"Yeah, I know," Randy said, and couldn't help adding, "Do you want to hear how I really had my arm broken?"

James stared. "You're kidding, right?"

Randy grinned. "Maybe. But I'd stay away from her if I were you."

Ben meanwhile, complained to Dawn about the way the nurses fussed over him. "They never leave you alone, ever. They even wake you from a sound sleep to find out if you're comfortable. I'm serious." And his therapy was going well, even by his account. "I won't do that damned occupational therapy though. I'm a horse trainer, I told them. I don't need to learn to play with building blocks."

A nurse smiled at Dawn, shrugged, and Dawn smiled back. Ben could be difficult at times, but seemed to have a point there. "How about speech therapy?"

Ben looked at her. "Why? I can talk. I hear myself."

Dawn laughed, feeling all was right with the world. She and Randy stopped at the racetrack afterwards, so he could check on a horse he'd treated earlier, debated about where to eat and stopped at a restaurant neither had ever been to, only to be greatly disappointed. They were both still hungry when they got home, and ended up eating the rest of the Oreos, stale by now, with milk.

"I think one of us ought to learn to cook," Randy said.

Dawn agreed. "When will you find the time?"

Randy laughed, wrestled her for the last cookie, split it in half, and fed it to her.

"Speaking of time. I don't know if I told you or not, but Uncle Matt and Aunt Rebecca are having a pre-engagement, engagement party for Linda and Harland."

"A what?"

Dawn smiled. "I think it's to give some semblance of family continuity and spontaneity."

Randy looked at her and laughed. "Oh, by all means then."

Dawn laughed as well. "I'm serious, so we're going to have to shop. Okay?"

"Okay. But how many horses am I going to have to worm to pay for this?"

Dawn chuckled. "No gifts, not at this one," she said. "But you do need a dinner jacket."

Randy did a double take.

"Sorry, but it's going to be formal."

"When?"

"Next Saturday."

"That's kind of soon, isn't it?"

Dawn nodded. "Like I said, they want it to appear casual and spontaneous. And you have been curious about my family, so..."

Dawn and Randy literally "slept" together over the next few days, and nothing else. That's how hectic Randy's schedule was, and day three, Dawn had cramps.

"Didn't you just have a period last month?" Randy asked, dramatizing the situation when he finally got home at a somewhat decent hour.

Dawn snuggled in bed next to him. "Tom hired a new groom today. His name's Fred."

Randy tucked his arm under her pillow. "How's he working out?"

"Okay, I guess," she said, sleepily. "Did you see Ben?"

"No, I never got a chance. How is he?"

"I don't know; I'm not sure. He said he fell in therapy."

"Oh, wonderful. Did you talk to James?"

Dawn yawned. "Yes. He said these things happen sometimes, but that he'd look into it."

Randy moved his arm, and then moved it again when it still wasn't comfortable. Two more days and the cast would come off. He could hardly wait.

"He wanted to be a jockey," Dawn said.

"Who?"

"The new kid, Fred. Tom's going to let him pony."

Randy smoothed her hair, and moved his head closer to hers on the pillow. "Shhhh," he said softly, always feeling guilty whenever he came in at night and woke her up. "Go to sleep."

Ben had better news the following day, and though somewhat embarrassing, he told Tom and Dawn anyway. His catheter had been removed. Tom and Dawn gave him a round of applause. He blushed. And with this out of the way, Tom went over the training schedule with him.

"I think Branden needs to be turned out. He's sour."

"Did you tell Dave?"

Tom shook his head. "He's not gonna listen. He thinks he just got a bad ride last time out."

"Tell him."

Tom scratched the back of his neck and then crossed his arms. "It'd be different if you were telling him, Ben. He has no reason to believe me."

"He has no reason not to believe you. Tell him."

There was more optimism today regarding Ben's condition, and Tom and Dawn were still there when he got the news. "You're being moved to another floor." A regular room.

Ginney was waiting for Dawn at the barn when she and Tom returned. "You're not going to believe it. They postponed the trial again. I don't believe this."

Dawn stood looking thoughtfully at her.

"And you know what else? Someone called the house this morning and told me to fucking back off or else."

"What?"

Ginney nodded. "This is scary! I know who it is. Who else would know to call my house that early?"

"Did you recognize the voice?"

"No." Ginney shook her head. "I didn't have to."

"Did you call your attorney?"

"Yeah, that's when he told me about the trial."

"What did he say?"

"He said it could be just kids, pulling pranks."

Dawn stared in disbelief.

"I told him I was scared, and he asked me if I wanted to drop the charges?"

"What?"

"He said he would understand if I wanted to, and talked about how humiliating the trial was going to be, and..."

Dawn shook her head. "Come here." She took Ginney by the arm and led her into the tack room and sat her down. "What do you want to do? What do you want?"

Ginney stared at the floor and shrugged. "I don't know. I honestly don't. Sometimes I wonder if it's worth all the trouble. I *was* a slut. Who's going to give a shit if the first time I say no, some bastard won't take no for an answer?"

Fred, the new kid, started into the tack room. Dawn gave him a look, and he backed out. "Sorry."

"Listen," Dawn said to Ginney. "You do what you want. It's your life. But I for one care, and a lot of other people do too."

Tears sprang to Ginney's eyes hearing this, and the two of them just sat there a moment. "Fuck 'em," Ginney said. "Fuck all of them. I'll just get an unlisted phone number."

Dawn smiled. An attorney with some backbone wouldn't hurt either, she thought. She related the story to Randy when he stopped by the barn on his way to farm calls, and asked him to phone someone for her once he got off the track. It was post time for the first race, and as was the rule, all the phones on the backside were turned off to prevent any booked betting activity.

She wrote down the name and number on his clipboard. "Tell him I need to talk to him, the sooner the better."

"Why? Who is he?"

"My attorney."

Randy nodded, and looked around. "So where's the new kid?"

Dawn glanced over her shoulder. "I don't know. He was just here. We're not running till the seventh."

"Where's Tom?"

She didn't know where he was either. "Someone paged him, and he hasn't been back." She didn't think much about it at the moment, but started getting concerned after a while. Just about the time she really started worrying, Tom returned.

"Where have you been?"

"The hospital."

"Is Ben all right?"

"Yeah." He sat down to catch his breath. "But the shit's hit the fan."

"What? What are you talking about?"

Tom looked at her. "Have you been paying for Ben's physical therapy?"

Dawn just stared, an admission of guilt if he'd ever seen one, and Tom nodded. "Well, the old man found out. And he's pissed. He wants to see you. Now, he said."

Ben was in his new room, sitting in a chair next to a bed facing the window when she got there. She smiled tentatively at his roommate, who seemed to be expecting her from the expression on his face.

"Ben?"

He turned and looked at her. "Tell me," he said, without hesitation. "How did you come about deciding to pay for my therapy?"

"I'm not paying it," Dawn replied, gripping the leather strap on her shoulder bag. "I'm just supplementing it."

"Don't quibble with me. It's the same thing, goddamn it!"

Dawn swallowed hard. "I wanted you in the rehab program here. Dr. Martin said it was the best in all of northeast Ohio."

"But *you* don't decide for me. I'm an old man, a cripple," he emphasized vehemently as he grabbed his weak leg. "But it's still my life, and I pay my own way. I'm not dead yet!"

"Ben, I'm sorry. I didn't want to upset you. I just wanted you to get better, and I wanted you to have the best care."

Ben glared at her. "You should've come to me about this."

"But..."

"No," he said. "Me and Meg have always paid our way and I won't tolerate strangers and outsiders telling me what to do every moment of my life. I don't need charity!"

Dawn stared and took a step back. The reference to charity didn't bother her, that was just Ben, but outsider? Outsider? She steeled her eyes and raised her chin. "Are you done?"

Ben didn't answer, too angry and too choked up to utter another word. Dawn turned and walked out. Tears streamed down Ben's face, as a moment later he started pounding his leg, once, and then again, and again, and again, harder and harder. His roommate rang for the nurse.

Dawn drove around for hours, thinking, agonizing, and finally headed home. She pulled into her parking place at five thirty-five, turned the key off, but stayed in the car. It was so quiet, a kind of cocoon away from the traffic, the world, a place to hide. A vacuum. Inside her head she could hear a soft roar, then pounding, a pulse, throbbing. Her steering wheel became her focus, and for some reason, seemed too small, and after that, the seat next to her, the wrong color. She felt as if she were sitting in a car that wasn't hers, and quickly got out.

Randy came home about an hour later and found her in the living room, lying on the couch, and staring up at the ceiling. He bent down to kiss her, and showed her that his cast was off. She smiled.

"I really wanted to do it myself," he said. "But they wouldn't let me."

Dawn sat up and looked at him, cleared her throat. "Does it hurt?"

He nodded. "A little. But I'll make it."

She smiled. "Hold me," she said, and he pulled her to her feet and wrapped her in his arms.

"You're shaking. Are you all right?"

She nodded. "I'm okay. It's probably just my period."

"Have you eaten?"

"No, I was waiting for you."

Chinese was their choice. Randy went down and got it, and a short time later, the intercom buzzed. "A George Meredith to see you, Dawn," the security guard said.

"Send him up." George Meredith was her attorney.

Randy opened the door, showed him in, and the two introduced themselves. Randy was rather surprised to see the man. "When I called your office today, they said you'd be out of town until tomorrow."

"I got back early, and came right over," George Meredith said, smiling as he turned to Dawn. "Dawnetta."

Dawn gave him a hug and a kiss on the cheek, and motioned they sit down to talk. "Can I get you a drink?"

"Yes, please. Scotch."

Randy glanced at her, for some reason expecting her to ask him to get it, but she walked to the liquor cabinet close to the kitchen and prepared it herself. "Ice?"

"No, thank you."

When they were all seated, George Meredith in a chair, Dawn and Randy on the couch, George sipped his drink, set the glass on the table, and got right down to business. "What can I do for you?"

Dawn explained Ginney's situation as delicately as she could, the gist of it at least, and George took notes.

He glanced up to comment on the frequent postponements. "That's not unusual."

"I know that," Dawn said. "But what I think *is* unusual is that her attorney seems to be trying to convince her to drop the charges."

George made a hmmm sound, and kept on writing. "Why do you think that is?"

When Dawn hesitated responding, George Meredith glanced up again, waited, and then looked at Randy.

"Ginney has a bit of a reputation," he responded, and felt bad saying it.

Another hmmmm. "Still?" he asked, meaning now.

Randy shook his head, and so did Dawn.

"Was she indeed raped?"

"Yes," Dawn said. "There were medical reports."

George Meredith made a few more notations, asked Ginney's attorney's name, and closed his note pad. "Just so you know, even though legally it's not supposed to be an issue, this young woman's reputation is going to surface in one way or the other."

"What about the man's?" Dawn asked.

George Meredith smiled. She'd made her point, and one well taken, by both men in the room. "We'll see what we can do." He finished his drink, rose and shook Randy's hand, kissed Dawn on the cheek, and said he'd be in touch.

Randy was on call and a little while later had to go out, returned, and got another page just after four in the morning. "Do you want me to put on the coffee?" he asked Dawn, kissing her good-bye. She'd be getting up soon herself.

"No, that's okay. I'm not going to go in; I don't feel well."

Randy felt her forehead to see if she had a fever, none. "What's the matter?"

"I still have cramps. Would you stop by and tell Tom," she said, quickly adding, "not that I have cramps, please, but that I won't be in."

Randy smiled and kissed her again. "Well, at least we know you're not pregnant," he said, referring to her menstrual agony.

"Right." When he left, Dawn lay in bed thinking about what he'd said, and then back to something years ago that her doctor had said. Not to her, but to her parents, outside her room at the hospital. Bits and pieces of hushed conversation. "The cervix is damaged. No, she'd not in any pain at the moment. We have her heavily sedated. But as for the future and her ever bearing children…"

"Dr. Adler. Dr. Adler."

"We'll talk later."

Dawn woke at nine, got dressed, and headed for the club, where she would spend the day, trying to pretend she didn't have a care in the world. Linda was there for a while, so was Aunt Rebecca, and Dawn was back home at five when Randy returned.

She looked at him from her chair in front of the television. "What are you watching?" he asked.

"*Donahue*," she said, and slipped her hand in his as he leaned down to kiss her. "How's everything at the track?"

He sat down on the couch and rubbed his arm. It hurt worse now than when he'd had the cast on. "Okay, I guess. Tom says you didn't come back for the race yesterday."

Dawn looked at him. "Fred was there to help."

Randy nodded. "He says you and Ben had a tiff."

"No, that's not correct. Ben tiffed, I was tiffed at."

"Did you go see him today?"

Dawn shook her head, and rather indifferently, in Randy's opinion.

"Are you going to?"

"No."

Randy studied her expression. "Ever?"

When Dawn just looked at him, Randy found himself feeling sorry for Ben...and for himself. After all, if she could turn her back on a man who'd seemed most important in her life, where did that leave him?

"Tom says you were paying his bill, part of it at least."

"Tom talks a lot."

"Is it true?"

Dawn nodded and sighed. "I honestly don't see what the big deal is. I have the money and Ben doesn't. I know for a fact all of the available cash he had went into buying All Together, and I pushed that, remember? I thought this was the least I could do."

Randy listened and nodded, thinking of something else Tom said, and how as soon as he'd said it, how he'd tried to cover it up. "How much of All Together do you own?"

Dawn turned off the TV. "Half," she said.

Randy stared. That was obviously the truth. "Why did you lie to me before?"

"Because before, it wasn't any of your business."

Randy smiled. She hadn't said that sarcastically, so it didn't offend him. Still... "So why tell me now?"

Dawn looked at him, hesitated. "Because I love you, and I don't like lying to you."

Randy leaned over, kissed her, and gazed into her eyes. "Wait a minute. Does this mean you didn't love me then?"

Dawn smiled and shrugged. "Sorry. I hardly knew you."

Randy laughed. "Not even a little?"

When Dawn shook her head, Randy pretended to be crushed, and then had another question. "How did you pay for her? With this uh...trust of yours?"

"Yes."

"Some trust."

Dawn looked at him. "I'm an only child."

Randy nodded and glanced at his watch. "I have to go back to the track in a little while. Do you want to stop and see Ben?"

Dawn shook her head and glanced away.

"What about the track? Why don't you ride with me and we'll get a pizza on the way back."

Dawn agreed to go, but not because she was hungry. She missed All Together. No one would be at the barn this late, and she could check on her.

As they drove there, Randy kept thinking about Dawn's attitude. "Are you sure you don't want to stop and see Ben?"

"Positive."

Hmph. This was hard for him to take; how she could turn her back so easily? She never ceased to amaze him, but even so, this didn't seem like her. As a result, though he swore against it, he started thinking about the book again. All those old doubts and fears resurfaced.

Ginney was walking to her car in the horsemen's lot when they pulled in, waved her arms to stop them, and rushed over, talking so fast, Dawn insisted she stop, take a breath, and start over.

"You're not going to believe this."

Dawn nodded, that part she'd understood.

"I just got off the phone with my attorney. I had a message to call him and came up as soon as the phones were back on. And boy did his story ever change. I got a new trial date, and this time he guarantees me it won't be postponed." She leaned against the truck, her heart beating so fast, and had to catch her breath again. "There's more." She fanned her face with her hand. "Someone in the media, he said, has picked my case out for some reason, and they're gonna do a three-part special on it for the six o'clock news. Can you believe this?"

Dawn smiled.

"At first I thought, wait a minute, I don't want to be on the six o'clock news. What the hell? Everyone'll know then. But my attorney says this'll work to my benefit. Everyone watching will make everyone pay better attention. I'm gonna get him. Can you believe it? I'm gonna get him!"

Randy sat there and shook his head in utter amazement. George Meredith, it had to be. Yet Dawn never let on, the two of them talking as if this were some sort of divine intervention. His mind wandered. The book. The stinking book. The vested interest.

"I'm meeting James for dinner. Do you guys want to join us?" he heard Ginney saying after a while.

Dawn declined. "Not tonight, maybe some other time."

Ginney smiled. "Tom said you weren't feeling well? You okay?"

Dawn nodded and thanked her for asking. "I'll be all right."

"He said Ben's not feeling well either. Must be something going around."

"Must be."

"I want to read something you've written," Randy insisted later when they were home.

"Something recent?" Dawn asked, knowing he was referring to her novel, and knowing he knew she wasn't going to let him read it until it was finished.

"It doesn't matter," he said. "Anything."

Dawn smiled. She'd left him watching the news and had come into her library to write, her sanctuary. She walked to one of the book shelves and handed him a magazine. "There's an article in here, though the subject may not interest you."

Randy sat down and looked for the right page. It was a women's magazine, the kind sold at the supermarket.

"I think it's one of the best things I've ever written," Dawn said, sitting down at her desk and watching him. "If not the best."

Randy began to read. It was a story of a young woman facing the decision of whether or not to have an abortion. A woman who one minute was brave and angry, and the next frightened, unsure, and clinging to her mother. Randy couldn't stop reading. It had such compassion, such feeling. Twice it brought a lump to his throat, this story about a stranger, as the procedure was enacted. The lights in the examining room, humming slightly and ricocheting a glare off the stainless steel sink to the doctor's left. The sounds of the instruments as they were placed on the tray next to the woman's trembling thigh. The twitch in her knee, the muffled sob in her throat. When he finished the last paragraph he himself could've cried.

Jesus, he said in his mind. He glanced over it again, and looked at Dawn. She was still typing, and had been, though all present sound had been blocked while he'd read. "This is good, Dawn," he said.

She looked at him.

"You're one hell of a writer."

Dawn smiled sadly and thanked him. "Tell me that when you read this book."

Randy nodded and studied her eyes. "This person, is she real?"

"Of course, she is. She's everywhere," Dawn said. "It happens every day."

Randy hesitated. "How do you feel about it?"

"Do you mean, am I pro-choice?"

He nodded.

"Yes." Dawn asked him the same thing then, remembering back when they heard Ginney was pregnant. "What about you?"

Randy stared. "I don't know," he said, and glanced at the magazine again. "How do you get into somebody's head like this?"

"You just do. I can't explain it. It's what makes a writer, I guess. You don't judge, you can't judge. Because you become them."

Randy shook his head, quite taken by her explanation, and got up and walked over to see what she was typing.

"The filly loaded without incident and stood quietly while the rest of the field was ushered into the gate. The bell rang and the gate doors slammed open....."

"Well?" Randy said, leaning over her shoulder.

Dawn looked at him and smiled. "Well what?"

"Come on." Randy stared at the page. "Keep going. Does she win or not?"

Dawn nudged him to move and sat back, crossing her arms. "I don't know. I haven't decided yet."

Randy shook his head. "Give me something else to read then."

Dawn motioned to a shelf behind him. "The blue book, yes, the third one. That one right there."

Randy opened it and sat down. It was a book of children's stories. "Rubbie Rubbles," Dawn said. "Story eight. I wrote it in my junior year in high school. It got published through a young author's contest."

"You've been writing that long?"

Dawn nodded, went back to typing, and Randy started reading. A smile spread across his face, which Dawn noticed, then he chuckled, and after that he started laughing.

"Do you mind?" she said.

He smiled. "This is funny." Rubbie Rubbles were cousins of the Adrenalin Frenalins, invisible little creatures who attached themselves to people in need, sometimes giving off an odor as a means of protection.

Dawn typed a sentence and sat staring. Randy didn't notice she'd stopped until he finished the story, laughed again, and looked at her. "What?" he said.

Dawn shrugged.

"Tell me. What's the matter?"

"What time is it?" she asked.

Randy looked at his watch. "A little after ten. Why?"

"I have to call Ben," she said, picking up the receiver and dialing the phone. She held her breath, waiting for Ben to answer, not knowing exactly what she was going to say, and got the switchboard operator instead.

"May I help you?"

"Yes. Can you connect me to Room 409B? I know it's late, but..."

"I'm sorry, we can't forward calls after ten. You'll have to call back in the morning."

"That'll be too late," Dawn insisted.

"Please hold," the woman said, and a moment later came back on the line. "I have checked on Mr. Miller's condition and can tell you that he is listed as satisfactory. Please call back in the morning."

Dawn put the receiver down and sat thumping her fingers on the desk as Randy observed.

"Did you ever sneak into a hospital before?" she asked.

"No, not lately," he said, facetiously. "It's not the sort of thing I do often."

"Oh, come on," Dawn said, the wheels spinning inside her head. "How hard can it be? No one stopped us when we were there before."

"That was a different floor. Besides, what's the hurry? Why not just wait till tomorrow?"

"I don't know; I can't. I've got to talk to him tonight. Are you coming with me?"

Randy laid the book down. "Do I have a choice?"

"Yes. Do you want to hear them?"

Randy shook his head. "No. But I'm going on record as saying this is a dumb idea."

"Duly noted," Dawn said, and off they went.

"Do you have a plan?"

"No." They entered through the emergency room doors and sat down quickly. Dawn took hold of Randy's hand and looked around the waiting room. Too many memories. Too many. She started rocking back and forth slowly, and Randy touched her leg to get her to stop. She frightened him when she did things like this; it was weird.

"Listen," he said. "If anyone asks, I thought I broke my arm again, but it feels okay now, so I'm not sure. Okay?"

Dawn nodded. "Okay." It was a busy night. There were people everywhere. They blended in.

"Now what?"

Dawn stared at the elevator directly across from the emergency room desk. A nurse was handing out forms to a man hobbling on one leg. "Is it your foot?" the nurse asked.

"No," Randy said in his mind along with the man. It's his knee. He could tell by the way the man was holding it.

"It's my knee."

Dawn squeezed Randy's hand, the elevator had stopped, a bell sounded, and she wanted to be ready in case... A nurse got off. Dawn sat back, then quickly decided to go for it, and pulled Randy to his feet. Five steps. That's about all it would take.

"Just a minute," a voice behind them said.

They both froze.

"Where are you going?"

Dawn turned, thought frantically. "To the ladies room. I looked and couldn't find one on this floor, and..."

"Down the hall." The nurse pointed. "To your left."

Dawn thanked her, and she and Randy pivoted in that direction.

"I told you this was a bad idea," Randy mumbled.

"Which patient are you with?" the nurse asked.

"Uh..." Dawn motioned that she really had to go bad, but that she'd be right back, and Randy followed, nodding and apologizing to the nurse for taking her away from her duties. He smiled and smiled and smiled, practically walking backwards, bounced into the wall at the corner, apologized to the nurse again, as if he'd run into her, and turned and chased after Dawn.

"This is so stupid," he whispered, catching up to her.

Dawn looked at him. "Why? What's the worst that can happen?" she asked, and didn't wait for an answer. "There! Stairs!" She tiptoed as fast as she could, opened the door, dragged Randy in with her, and leaned back against it to get it to close quicker. "Let's go," she said, and started up the stairs.

"Wait!" Randy grasped her arm and pulled her back. With her hair all loose and wild, her eyes all lit up, her voice husky and cheeks red, she looked so sexy. "Kiss me," he said, and she laughed.

"You're crazy."

"Kiss me anyway," he said, and covered her mouth with his. "Again," he said, and picked her up, wrapped her legs around his waist, and pressed her against the wall. "Once more."

Dawn laughed. "You're sick, Randy. You know that." She kissed him hard, wriggled out of his arms, grabbed hold of his hand, and up the stairs they went.

Panting by the time they reached the top, Dawn peeked out the door, and ducked back in. "Damn!"

"What?" Randy smoothed her hair.

"The nurses, they're all there."

"Good. Let's go home."

Dawn shook her head. "Not after coming this far. They can't stay there forever." She waited a minute and peeked out again. "They're gone, come on."

"Are you sure we're on the right floor?"

Dawn hesitated, looked at him, and Randy smiled and nudged her. "Go." They hurried down the hall, to the right, made the turn, got to Ben's room, and were just about to congratulate themselves, when they came face to face with a nurse on her way out, and not at all happy with this late encounter.

"What do you think you're doing here?"

"I have to see Mr. Miller," Dawn said, looking over her shoulder at Ben's side of the room where the curtain was pulled.

"Patients need their rest. That is why we have rules and visiting hours," the nurse said, in a firm but hushed voice as she edged them back toward the door. "How did you get up here?"

"The stairs," Randy said, pointing to the hallway.

"We'll only stay a minute," Dawn pleaded. "Please..."

Ben recognized her voice and called to her. "Dawn? Dawn, is that you?"

"Yes." Dawn implored the nurse with her eyes. "Just one minute. I promise."

The nurse scowled at her, then at Randy, and finally relented. "One minute, and that's all."

"Thank you," Dawn said, and hurried around the curtain to see Ben. Randy started after her, but the nurse blocked his way.

"Don't ever do this again. Do you understand?"

Randy nodded, thanked her again, and Dawn hugged Ben tightly. "I'm so sorry," she kept saying. "I'm so sorry."

"Me too." He held her tenderly and patted her back. "Me too."

"I just never thought..."

"It's all right. It's all right." He glanced at Randy and wiped his eyes. "I shouldn't have jumped on you like that, but you were wrong."

"I know." Dawn leaned back and looked at him. "I just..."

Ben handed her a tissue and smiled. "Don't do anything like that again, okay? And when I can't make my own decisions, bury me. All right?"

Dawn nodded. "What about your therapy? Do you want me to...?"

Ben shook his head. "It's taken care of. I have a supplemental policy that picks it up."

"I'm sorry. I didn't know."

"And you didn't ask."

Dawn nodded, corrected, and Ben smiled at Randy. "Go on home now, go on," he told them, and Dawn kissed him on the cheek.

Ben looked into her eyes then. "I didn't mean..." he said. "What I said when..."

"I know," Dawn smiled. "I'll see you tomorrow." She waved to his neighbor, apologized for waking him, stopped to thank the nurse again, and she and Randy walked down the stairs and out into the coolness of the night.

"Now what?"

"I don't know. Are you tired?"

"Not really."

"Good."

Chapter Thirty

It poured. The backside was a muddy, rutty mess. All Together was in the eighth race. And Dawn was a wreck. If only she could rake the shedrow. Routine, routine. She needed her routine. She stared into the sky, begged the rain to stop, wiped her face, and told Fred for the tenth time this morning to leave the filly alone.

"I'm not bothering her. I'm just talking to her."

"Leave her alone."

Tom heard them. "Goddamn it, Fred. Leave her the fuck alone. Here." He took a twenty dollar bill out of his wallet. "Go get us a pizza. You want pizza?" he asked Dawn. She nodded. "The works, no anchovies. And a six pack of Coke. Understand? Coke. Cold ones."

Fred smiled. He was such an easy-going kid, Tom and Dawn instantly felt guilty for jumping on him. If it just wasn't for that annoying habit of his of not listening, of daydreaming all the time, and of not taking anything seriously. They liked him in fact. He had a way with horses. He just never knew when to back off. Red had even lost patience with him, and would pin his ears whenever he so much as heard his thundering voice.

All Together charged her webbing, squealed, and kicked and bucked. Then squealed some more.

Tom trudged his way past her to the tack room, scraped his boots at the door as best he could, and Dawn followed suit. "How do you think she's going to run?" The filly had never run on an off track before.

Tom fixed a cup of coffee, tasted it, and handed it to Dawn. "Who made this? You or Fred?"

"Fred," Dawn said, tasting it herself and shuddering at how strong it was.

"Tell him not to make anymore, okay?"

"You tell him," Dawn said, and they both shook their heads at their reluctance. Dawn sat down next to him, and asked again, "Well? Do you think she'll be all right?"

Tom sighed, propped his elbows on his knees, held his coffee cup in both hands, and stared at the floor. The filly had worked in the mud, and worked well. And with the way she was built and her nicely cupped feet, there was no reason why it should give her any trouble.

"Tom...?"

When he just shrugged, she looked at him, watched the way his eyes fluttered as he sipped his coffee, how bloodshot they were. How his hands trembled. My God, she thought, how long has he been like this? She noticed his hair then, longer than she'd ever seen it, and touched his face with the back of her hand. He needed a shave. "Tom?" She'd never known anyone more meticulous about his appearance than Tom, not even Randy, who was rather fussy himself. Or proud. "Tom, are you all right?"

He looked at her and shook his head. "I want a drink," he said. "I want it bad."

Dawn swallowed hard and put her arm around him, leaned her head on his shoulder, and the two of them just sat there like this for a moment.

"I don't know what I'm gonna do. I'm so tired of fighting it. God, I'm so tired," he said, his voice cracking. "This is no way to live."

Dawn searched his eyes and shivered, having felt this desperation herself.

"Every fucking day," he said. "I just can't take it anymore."

"No," Dawn said. "You can take it! We'll get you some help. You've probably been trying to do this alone, and you can't do it alone."

Tom looked at her and shook his head. "Oh, God...Dawn, you're so naive." His voice cracked again as tears filled his eyes. "There isn't anybody that can help me. I can't be helped. I want a drink because I'm a fucking alcoholic, and that's all there is to it."

"No." Dawn combed his hair back behind his ear with her fingers and kissed him on the cheek, as tears of her own trickled down her face. "That's not all there is to it."

Fred came around the corner then, calling out for one of them. "My car won't start, Tom. Can I use your truck?"

"Oh Jesus." Tom reached for a towel to wipe his eyes, threw Fred his keys before he had a chance to come in, and dumped his coffee in the shedrow. "I'll be back in a little while," he told Dawn.

"Tom...?"

He held up his hands and walked away, leaving Dawn feeling helpless, able to do nothing but stand there and watch.

"What's wrong with him?" Fred asked.

"You," Dawn said.

"Me?"

"Yes, you're driving him crazy," she said, and smiled as if maybe she were kidding. "Just go get the pizza, okay?"

"Okay," he said, and reached up to pet the filly.

"And leave her alone."

Fred laughed. "Jesus, you guys gotta lighten up."

"Pizza," Dawn said. "Go!"

By noon, the sun was out.

Dawn was relieved not to have to handle All Together in the paddock, and never appreciated Fred more. He was lanky but strong, and though infatuated with the filly, never let her get the best of him. "Quit that," he kept saying, "now quit that," as the filly danced round and round. Tom tacked her, Fred kept her walking, and Tom hurried out to where the ponies were assembled and got on Red just in time as the post parade emerged. Fred handed the filly over to him and headed for the five-dollar window to make a bet.

"Dawn, can you lend me some money?"

"You should've asked sooner. Does it look like I have my purse with me?"

Fred laughed. "I'll be right back."

Dawn climbed up on the fence, hiccuped and thought, oh God, here I go again, but only hiccuped that once. She looked for Randy's truck; he pulled up and parked at the last minute. When Fred climbed up next to her, she made him switch sides. The race was a flat mile. She didn't want anything blocking her view. The horses upon loading were so close she could see that familiar look in the filly's eyes, the way she kept tossing her head, Johnny adjusting his goggles again and again until they were set.

"And they're off! Taking the early lead is Allllll Togetherrrr."

She'd broke from the five hole and was three wide going into the first turn, half a length in front, before dropping down on the rail at the three-quarter pole, and made it look so easy. From there, she just lengthened her lead. The announcer called the positions for the rest of the field, as if they were two different horse races. And the filly finished seven lengths in front, going away.

"Holy Mackerel!" Fred shouted.

"Ladies and gentlemen, we have an unofficial new track record for the mile."

"What?" Dawn darted her eyes at the tote board. "Oh my God!"

Fred jumped up and down. "What a horse! What a horse! I knew she'd run big!"

Dawn laughed and looked for Randy; he flicked his lights off and on, and she laughed again. Then, she and Fred hurried to the winner's circle.

"Congratulations!" came from everywhere as they weaved their way through the crowd. "Congratulations!"

The new track record of one minute, thirty-five and one fifth seconds, was declared official as Tom dismounted Red and led the filly into the winner's circle, dancing, tossing her head, and kicking out at her muddy tail, still half-tied in a knot.

"Did you see how wide she was in the first turn?" Tom yelled to Dawn, beaming as he struggled to keep the filly on all fours. "Jesus! I asked Johnny, what, were you taking her to the kitchen for a fucking omelet!"

Johnny laughed, eyes big and round as he did his best to help control the filly, while waving his whip to the stewards and repeatedly looking over his shoulder at the tote board to see the new track record flashing.

The photographer snapped the picture quickly, Johnny dismounted, and Tom warned everyone to stand back as he turned the filly around. She was still doing battle with her tail. He handed her over to Fred on the track and Fred walked her to the spit barn as Tom and Dawn followed with Red.

"I can't wait to see Ben's face!" Tom said to Randy as they passed. "A fucking new track record!"

Randy nodded, smiling, and winked at Dawn. "I'll be back around six," he told her, and she waved, the two of them saying just about everything else with their eyes.

The filly pulled her usual stunts at the spit box. Dawn was happy to take Red and leave them behind. She hosed him off and wiped him down, gave him a drink and hung him on the walker to dry, and did both their stalls. He was put away by the time Tom returned.

"Is she all right?" Dawn asked.

Tom nodded. "They're coming now. I thought she was going to *tie up* there for a while." Tying up is a condition most common in fillies, Dawn had learned early on, where they develop back spasms over their kidneys and refuse to move. "She's fine, though."

Ben was so anxious he could hardly sit still, and kept glancing at the clock Gloria had brought him, on the table next to the bed. He could always call the secretary's office to find out how the filly ran. They'd probably tell him, under the circumstances. But he didn't like owing anybody a favor.

Finally, Dawn and Tom and Randy came in, and all he needed to do was look at their faces. "Hot damn!" he said, and slapped the arm of his wheelchair. "She win, huh?"

Tom nodded. "How about a new track record?"

"You're kidding."

When Tom shook his head, Ben looked at Dawn and Randy. Both were nodding. "How fast?"

"One-thirty-five and one."

"Jesus!" Ben sat back, listening as Tom related the race from start to finish, the wide, going-to-the-kitchen turn and all, and Ben laughed. "What'd Johnny say?"

"He said the going was better out there. The track was hard as a rock after that rain. Down inside was where it was cuppy."

A nurse entered the room. Ben shared the news with her, even though this was not one of his favorite nurses, and the nurse sighed.

"Yes, I know. There's a reporter here to see you, though you have one visitor too many already."

"A reporter?"

"Yes, apparently this record breaking is a big deal. So if you're feeling up to it, and two of you wouldn't mind leaving..."

Dawn smiled. "Ben?"

He nodded. "I'm up to it. "Go on, all of you. Go on."

Dawn gave him a hug and kissed him good-bye. "Don't mention my name," she whispered. Randy and Tom each shook his hand. They left then and the reporter was shown in, a nervous young man in his late twenties.

"Thank you for seeing me, Mr. Miller. My name is Frankie Farrow, and we're uh, going to be doing a feature on your horse All Together. I just have a few questions, if you don't mind?"

Mind? Ben shook his head. "Have a seat. What would you like to know?"

"Well, for one..." The young man scanned his list. "Did you know the track record was set over fourteen years ago?"

Ben nodded. "That was before they resurfaced the track and slowed it down. I believe it was Queen's Court in a minute, thirty-six and one."

The young man smiled. Obviously he'd had some reservations about interviewing a man hospitalized due to a stroke, and now realized he could relax.

The Rib was abuzz with talk of All Together's new track record, and a filly yet. Bud Meyers stopped by the table, offering congratulations and saying how she was by far the nicest thing he'd ever seen. He looked at Tom saying this, only daring to glance at Dawn, nodded to his daughter Ginney, who laughed at how formal he was being, and the celebration continued.

Rounds of drinks for the table kept coming from all directions. Twice the waitress put one down in front of Fred, and twice Tom picked it up and handed it back. Fred flipped him off, whining and complaining, and Tom laughed. "Look at Randy," he said. "Do you want to end up like him?"

Randy was well on his way. His and Raffin's offer to buy Jake's practice was all but a done deal as of early this afternoon, and things couldn't be better with Dawn, so he had more than one reason to celebrate.

"Cheers!"

Dawn, for that matter, kept her drinking to a minimum, mainly in support of Tom, but also because she was still reeling from those *iced teas* of last week. "Never again!" But she too was having a good time. Tom appeared to have gotten through whatever was bothering him earlier. And if not, at least for the moment he seemed in control.

Everyone had Caesar salad, strip steak and lasagna, served family style, hot Italian bread, and for dessert, Cassada cake. Tom led them all in his own rendition of "The Run For The Roses." Even people at the far end of the bar joined in. And Mama Leone made her way to their table, where her son, who towered over her tiny frame, poured her a shot glass full of her private stock. Their table fell quiet instantly, and after that, the one next to them, then the next, and soon all were looking on as she raised her glass.

"I am proxy for Ben," she said in broken English. "He phone me now and I make toast for him."

Everyone hoisted their glasses.

"From bottom of my heart! From Ben's heart. Salud!"

"Salud!" everyone echoed, and here came another round, on the house.

Ben could imagine the festivities, and in fact his heart was there. He remembered years ago, that it was Meg who insisted they celebrate a win. Every win. Even when the years weren't so good, when money was tight, and the wins were few and far between. "We deserve it," she'd say. "You deserve it."

It was late, but he'd convinced the nurse to let him keep his television on for the eleven o'clock news. He promised to turn it off right after the sports, and sat in bed, with the volume down until it aired. Baseball first, pre-season football, tennis, and finally the races. He turned it up.

"At Nottingham today, All Together, a three-year-old filly, set a new track record of 135 and 1/5 for the mile. Some are calling this filly the finest distaffer since the likes of Ruffian. Undefeated in her three lifetime starts, this rising star is trained by Ben Miller, who is presently in the hospital recovering from a stroke, but still managing her career. Some of you racing enthusiasts may remember that it was

Ben Miller who trained the impressive Beau Born, retired earlier this year to stud, and also the 1974 Ohio Derby hopeful, Dandy Ladd."

Ben stared at the small screen.

"That wraps up the sports for tonight," the announcer said. "Join us again tomorrow at six and noon. Ben Miller...this is for you. Godspeed."

Tears filled Ben's eyes as they played the tape of All Together's stretch run, every stride, and through the tears he smiled at the finish. This was more than he'd hoped for. More than he could imagine. Meg would have been so proud. "You bet I would," he could hear her saying. "You bet I would."

"Good night, Meg." He turned off the television and then turned out the light.

"Good night, Mr. Miller. Sleep tight."

Randy's early morning hangover was mild compared to Dawn's the other day. "I know when to stop," he said, and Dawn had to laugh. "Get up or I'm leaving you." She picked up a pillow and threw it at him from the bedroom doorway. "And your truck's at the track, so..."

Randy covered his head with the sheet.

"And I won't be back till noon."

Randy sighed, moaned, uncovered his head and looked at her. "You people have to stop winning races."

"Why? And miss out on your repeat-repeat performances."

"What?"

When Dawn turned and started down the hall, Randy sat up, wrapped the sheet around him, tripped and almost fell getting out of bed, to follow her. "What do you mean, repeat performance?"

Dawn smiled. "Five minutes, and I'm out of here, Randy. I mean it."

Tom was in a good mood when she arrived at the track, which was reassuring, but then Dave showed up with donuts, and all of a sudden his attitude changed. "I've got to go enter," he said, leaving in a hurry.

"Ooh, custard," Fred said, and Dawn swung around and looked at him.

"Don't you dare."

Dave laughed, said he'd brought plenty, and motioned to Tom's back as he turned the far corner of the barn. "What's the matter with him?"

"Nothing," Dawn said. "He's just a little tired and has a lot to do this morning."

This morning was also exceptionally busy for a certain nurse. Nothing was going right. She was exhausted as she fluffed the patients' pillows, brought them their breakfast trays, and sighed when she had to go back to the desk and retrieve the morning paper that should have been on one particular tray.

The patient turned to the sports section, read the headline, and put down his coffee. He turned the page and read the article slowly, closed his eyes, then read it again when he had the strength, and rang for the nurse.

"Yes?" she said, sticking her head in the door.

"I need to make a phone call."

Again the nurse sighed. "I'm sorry. It's not allowed."

"Make an exception."

The nurse studied the old man's distinguished face, nodded, said she'd see what she could do, and disappeared. When the phone rang and Ben picked it up, a thready, feeble-sounding voice responded. "Mr. Miller? Is this Mr. Miller?"

"Yes," Ben said hesitantly. "Who's this?"

"Winston Vandervoort."

Ben frowned. Who? The name was vaguely familiar, he couldn't place it, then it came to him.

"I've been meaning to contact you for some time, but getting a phone here is almost impossible. They suspect I'm senile, and don't want me bothering anyone."

Ben didn't know what to say, how to respond. Part of him thought this had to be a joke.

"I want to congratulate you," Mr. Vandervoort said, pausing to replenish his oxygen with a mask. "On your horse, All Together."

"Thank you," Ben said.

"You see, I bred and raised her."

Ben nodded to himself, as again, Mr. Vandervoort drew on his oxygen.

"It has delighted me so, her career. She was such a strong, robust filly. So beautiful, much like my daughter."

Ben recalled the story the groom told them, and again didn't know what to say. "Um...there's a young woman, All Together's groom. She's curious about her name." Ben hesitated, realizing the man probably wouldn't know what he meant.

But he did, laughed, and then coughed. "I'm sorry. Excuse me, it's my lungs." He relied on his oxygen mask again. "It was a game my daughter made up. She had so few friends. There was a kidnap attempt when she was young."

Ben waited as obviously a nurse assisted the man, told him to relax, breathe deeply. "I'm fine, I'm fine," he could hear Mr. Vandervoort say before getting back on the line. "We sheltered her after that, but she had imaginary friends, that she would lead in games and songs." He pulled the phone away to cough. "I can see her now, playing with them, always starting their games by saying 'All Together.'"

Ben smiled.

"I have to go now. The nurse tells me I am done," he said, breathing hard. "I can't put into words what I want to say, why I called. Take care of her sums it up. Good day, Mr. Miller. And again, thank you."

Ben said, "You're welcome," slowly hung up the phone, and told Tom and Dawn about the conversation later. "It really threw me. I've been laying here thinking about everything I could have said since, but..."

Dawn smiled and squeezed his hand. Tears welled up in Ben's eyes then, and Tom said he had to leave. "You coming?" he asked Dawn.

"No, go ahead. I'll see you in a little while."

Ben wiped his eyes when Tom left and apologized to Dawn for being so emotional. Dawn sat there, feeling rather emotional herself, but managed a smile for Ben's sake as she thought about Vandervoort's daughter, to have led such a lonely life, and to die so young.

"Ben...?"

He looked at her.

"I need to talk to you about Tom."

"What about him?"

Dawn hesitated. "I'm not sure if I should be bothering you with this, but..."

"Dawn...?" Ben motioned for her to just say it.

"All right." Again she hesitated. "He's fighting drinking."

Ben looked at her. "What? Are you sure?"

"Yes. He told me himself and he'd die if he knew I was talking to you about it."

Ben sat back.

"He's edgy. He shakes. And he's become so paranoid. You know how he used to be happy when Dave came by. Well, he dreads it now."

"I was afraid of this," Ben said.

"You were?"

He nodded. "There's something in him that snaps. He has so much talent, why, he can train better than anyone I know. But he doesn't like dealing with the owners, making the decisions. They seem to pressure him without saying a word."

Dawn had to agree, having watched him lately. "I suggested he talk to someone, a counselor..." she said, careful not to use the words psychiatrist or psychologist, first with Tom and now Ben, knowing...

"A shrink? Not on your life. And I don't blame him," Ben said, frowning at her for even mentioning such a thing as he sat thinking. "I'll tell you what, do you have Gloria's number?"

Dawn shook her head. What could Gloria do?

"Get her number and call her for me. Tell her I need to see her."

"All right. But..."

"Don't worry. I'll handle it," he said. "Does anyone else know about this?"

"No." She hadn't even told Randy.

"Good. Don't worry about a thing. I'll take care of it."

Dawn left the hospital feeling hopeful, stopped for a burger at Wendy's, and ate it on the way to meet Randy at Saks, at one as planned.

"I've only got about a half hour," Randy said, "so let's get to it."

Dawn shook her head. A half hour to pick out a dress and a dinner jacket. Oh sure. "Dream on," she told him, and never had such fun shopping.

"No."

"No."

"No." He didn't like one dress Miss Diane brought out, even the ones Dawn insisted she should try on, because you can never tell with them on a hanger. And time was running out.

"One more," Miss Diane said, and vanished. She liked Dawn's young man, and by now was getting a feel for the kind of dress he might be looking for.

"Yes!" Randy said, as soon as he saw it.

It was pale blue, mid-knee in length, relatively low-cut in front, had a bare back, and was silky. "Try it on," he told Dawn when she shook her head. "You can't ever tell when it's on a hanger."

Dawn laughed and followed Miss Diane back into the dressing room. "Randy, this isn't me. It's too..."

"Try it on."

It took about a minute.

"Wow!" he whispered, when she emerged.

Dawn rolled her eyes, barefoot, and pulled at the front to bring it up higher. "Maybe if..."

"It's perfect the way it is, Dawn," Randy said. "Right?" He looked at Miss Diane, who nodded. "See?" And that was that. He kissed her and said he had to go.

"But what about your jacket?"

"We'll do it tomorrow."

"When?" Son of Royalty was running tomorrow and so was Lady. "When tomorrow?"

Too late. He was gone.

Dr. Martin had a fit. What Ben was proposing was ludicrous, not to mention dangerous. "I can't let you do this."

"Why not?" Ben said. "I'll have a nurse with me at all times."

Gloria nodded, standing efficiently at his side.

"I can get in and out of the wheelchair on my own," Ben insisted. "So I know I can get in and out of a car. And it'll only be an hour or so a day."

Dr. Martin shook his head. "It's too dangerous."

Ben sighed. "What's dangerous is staring at these walls. The racetrack is where I belong. It's my life."

Dr. Martin looked at him.

"It's my occ-u-pation."

James smiled in spite of himself, thinking they really should change the title of that form of therapy. He and Ben had been having this stand-off for well over ten minutes.

"What if I just sign myself out? Discharge myself?"

James shook his head. "I don't want you doing that, Ben. Please. Your rehab is going so well."

"I agree. And that's why I think it's time to move on."

James sighed. If this were him, admittedly, he'd probably feel the same way. "All right, listen. Maybe. Depending on how much red tape this is going to involve..."

"Well?" It was the first thing Randy wanted to know when he got to Dawn's apartment that evening. "Did you get the dress?"

"Yes."

And second, "What's the special downstairs? I'm starved."

Dawn picked up the phone, asked, and relayed the information. "Butterfly shrimp, egg role and fried rice."

Randy nodded. It sounded good enough for him. "Get me a couple of extra hot mustards." He gave Dawn the money, said he was going to take a quick shower, and was drying off when the phone rang. He picked it up in the bedroom when he realized after at least six rings, that Dawn was probably still downstairs.

"Hello?"

"Hello?" It was a terrible connection. "Dawnetta?"

"No, this is Randy," he said, and had to shout it again.

"Oh, Randy! How nice!" the woman shouted back. "This is Dawnetta's Aunt Maeve, dear."

"Well, hi!" The infamous Aunt Maeve. "Dawn'll be right back."

"Where is she?" Aunt Maeve shouted, the connection even worse now.

"She went for food!"

"Not that dreadful Chinese?"

Randy laughed. "Yes!"

"What?"

"I said yes!"

Dawn came in then and Randy handed her the phone. "It's your Aunt Maeve."

"Aunt Maeve! How are you?"

"What, dear? I can't hear you?"

"I said how are you?"

"Oh, wonderful! Fine, fine! And you?"

Randy went back into the bathroom, closed the door, finished drying off, and laughed at Dawn's end of the conversation.

"When?!"

"Of course!"

"Yes! Yes! I'll tell him!"

"Love you too!"

She hung up and had to clear her throat from shouting, tapped on the door, and when Randy answered, entered.

"That was Aunt Maeve."

Randy smiled, glancing at her as he finished shaving around his beard. "Where was she calling from?"

"Some ship. They're in a storm."

Randy lowered his razor and stared at her in the mirror.

"A rather lovely one, she said. She was calling from the bow."

Randy laughed, rinsed his razor, made one last pass down his neck, and reached for the towel.

Dawn handed it to him. "She's going to stay with me for the weekend. She says under the circumstances, she doesn't want to be at Uncle Matt and Aunt Rebecca's."

Randy nodded, wondering where that left him. "You were able to understand all that?"

Dawn shrugged. "Most of it. She's says she's looking forward to meeting you." She ran her eyes over the deeply defined muscles across his shoulders and arms as he hung up the towel and reached for his shirt. "Are you on call this weekend?"

"No, tonight and tomorrow."

Dawn smiled, watching him as he slipped on his shirt and then combed his hair.

"Who's side of the family is your Aunt Maeve on?"

"My father's," Dawn·said, and though she probably didn't realize it, she'd said it defensively. "Why? Why do you ask?"

"I don't know, just curious," Randy said. "Does that mean she's a Bask-Fioritto then?"

Dawn stared. "Yes," she said, and turned to leave.

Randy stopped her. "Which means...?"

Dawn raised her eyes and hesitated. He was doing this on purpose to see if she'd answer, to see if she'd hold anything back. "Which means she's my father's full sister."

"And that's all?"

"That's all."

Chapter Thirty-One

"Well I'll be go to hell." Tom's mouth dropped. "Dawn! Dawn, come see!"

Dawn stuck her head out of one of the stalls, warily, not knowing what to expect, took one look, and smiled. It was Ben, in his wheelchair, with Gloria behind him and James Martin at his side.

"How in the...?" Tom fought back the urge to run down the shedrow and hug the old man, walking instead. "How'd you get here?"

Dawn hurried down and asked the same thing.

"I came with Gloria," he said, matter-of-factly. "We're doing occupational therapy. Where's this Fred at?"

Tom and Dawn glanced around. He was always underfoot. "Here," Fred said, from the first stall, where he'd been brushing off the filly. "Hi!"

Ben said hi, sized the kid up, and motioned to the tack room doorway. "Can you build me a ramp here?"

"Sure," Fred said, as if he did that type of thing all the time. "How wide?"

Ben looked at him. "How about as wide as the doorway?"

"Great! Where do I get the wood?"

Ben glanced at Dawn and Tom; an acknowledgment of what they'd been talking about in reference to this kid, and smiled. "Help me," he told Tom, nodding toward the tack room. Dave appeared with donuts at this point and a lot of laughing and joking followed, just like old times.

Ben was in heaven at his desk, and Gloria, thrilled to be able to help. It was lonely without Charlie around the house during the day. At least this would give her something to do with her mornings. Dawn realized now why Ben wanted to contact her, and was enormously grateful, even more so when Gloria tasted the coffee and promptly shuddered.

"Oh my. Who made this?"

Everyone turned to Fred. He shrugged. "Why? What's wrong with it? I don't drink it."

Tom stared and told him to quit making it then, "Please!" And everyone laughed, James Martin included, who said the coffee tasted fine to him, and gulped the rest of his cup.

"Where's Ginney's barn, by the way?" he asked.

"I'll take you there." Tom walked with him as far as the restrooms. "Two barns down and to your left. They're in the annex."

James looked at him.

"The far end," Tom said, and went into the men's room, where he leaned over the sink and splashed cold water on his face. He stared at his reflection in the mirror, a dirty mirror with streaks all over it, and remembered a time years ago, and how whenever he looked in a mirror, he hated what he saw so much, he wanted to shatter it to pieces.

"Take me," he'd said to God, when that boy's life hung in the balance. "Take me. Not him."

He glanced in the trash, took out a discarded coffee cup, filled it with water, and splashed it against the glass, did it again, and wiped the mirror down. "There," he said, and dried his hands and walked back to the barn.

"Where the hell you been?" Fred asked. "I was looking all over for you."

Tom looked at him and laughed. "I was in the friggin' john. What, you want to hold my hand next time?"

Fred blushed. All he'd wanted to know was where the hammer was kept. But Tom started singing, "I want to hold your hand," adding his own version of the words, and Fred laughed. This was a side of Tom he hadn't seen yet, and a lot more fun.

"This must be family week," Randy said, arriving at Dawn's apartment the evening of Aunt Maeve's expected stay. He handed Dawn a letter from his mom, and headed into the kitchen for a beer. When he opened the refrigerator, he was surprised to find it stocked with food, snack food actually on closer inspection, and quite a variety.

"What's this?" he said.

Dawn glanced up from reading the letter and smiled. "They're Aunt Maeve's."

Randy nodded, walked back in, and sat down across from her. The newlyweds, Cindy and Marvin, were doing fine, according to his mother. Back from the honeymoon, they were both working and studying, and settling into a married routine. And Randy's father's burns were almost completely healed. He still needed an additional skin graft between his right thumb and forefinger, a sensitive area which had rejected the last one, but aside from that, all was well. "Aunt Helen sends both of you her love," she wrote, referring to him and Dawn. "And so do your mother and father. Write, or at least call. Love, Mom."

Dawn folded it neatly, smiled, and handed it back to him. There were numerous references to her in the letter, and it felt nice to be included, warm. At the same time though, she felt a longing for her own mother and father.

"Well? When's she coming? Your Aunt Maeve?"

"Soon." The plan was for the three of them to go out to dinner and become acquainted. "I don't know when we're going to find time to go shopping tomorrow."

"For what?" Randy slugged a mouthful of beer. "My dinner jacket? It's done. Can I wear it with a turtleneck?"

Dawn looked surprised. "When did you go?"

"This afternoon."

"Where?"

"Shumann Brothers. It's navy blue, a perfect fit, and if I don't wear it for the whole night, I can return it."

Dawn laughed. He was kidding. "Come on, seriously."

"I am serious, except for the part about returning it."

Aunt Maeve swept in like a whirlwind. "It's so nice to finally meet. I've heard so much about you," she said, shaking Randy's hand, and with a rather firm handshake at that.

"It's nice to meet you too," Randy said, and meant it. The woman reminded him of Katherine Hepburn; billowy clothes, layers and layers it appeared, hair piled on top of her head and no jewelry. "How was your cruise?"

"Wonderful," Aunt Maeve said. "Though I'm still a little wobbly in the knees."

"Here, sit down," Dawn said.

"Thank you, dear. Thank you. Did my goodies arrive?"

"Yes, this afternoon."

Randy sat down across from them and smiled at the similarities in their appearance. Not so much their features, but their mannerisms and the look in their eyes.

Aunt Maeve loved to talk, and loved to eat. "I've had the best and the worst," she said to Randy, and cringed at a recent memory. "Stewed peanut chicken, every day for two weeks. In line behind the men I might add. May I never eat fowl again."

When the valet brought up Aunt Maeve's luggage, Randy carried it down the hall to Linda's bedroom for her. She said she wanted to lie down for a little while and freshen up, and emerged twenty minutes later ready to go.

"Well, where to?"

They decided on a restaurant which was one of her favorites whenever she was in town. "It's a cross between Mexican and Chilean," she said, smiling as she recalled another distant and much more pleasant culinary experience. "Hot tamales to die for."

Randy laughed, and would continue to laugh throughout the night, beginning with the type of car Aunt Maeve drove, a Jeep, complete with canvas top and roll bar. And the way she climbed in behind the wheel, no muss, no fuss, and ground the gears when shifting. In fact, Randy was so taken by her, he didn't notice Dawn becoming quieter and quieter as the evening rolled on.

"Well, you know," Aunt Maeve said to him, in response to his question about the Basks. "It's a long story."

Dawn excused herself to go to the ladies room. "Aunt Maeve...?" she said, hoping she would come with her, which she did.

"Dawnetta, what's the matter?"

Dawn fluffed her hair and shook her head. "Nothing."

"Nothing?" She touched Dawn lightly on the cheek. "I haven't accompanied you to the ladies room since you were about six years old and told me you were, 'plenty old enough, thank you.'"

Dawn smiled. "I just get nervous when Randy asks so much about the family."

"So much?" Aunt Maeve studied her eyes. "One question?"

"No, two. He asked earlier about Nana," which was the way Maeve had referred to her mother. "Remember?"

Aunt Maeve shook her head. "Oh, Dawnetta..." She put her arms around Dawn and hugged her gently. "What are you afraid of?"

"I don't know. He just keeps asking."

Maeve pulled back to look into her eyes again. "There's no harm in that."

Dawn shrugged. There were things even Aunt Maeve didn't understand, didn't know. "You're right." She smiled, and changed the subject, somewhat. "So what do you think of him?"

"Randy? I like him. He's uh, how do you say, drop-dead gorgeous."

Dawn laughed.

"And so nice."

At the apartment, Aunt Maeve said she was tired and going straight to bed, bid them good-night and, vanished. It was past Dawn's bedtime as well, so Randy prepared himself to leave. He kissed Dawn, then kissed her again, and didn't want to go.

"What if we just wait a few minutes," he said, "and just quietly walk down the hall?"

Dawn smiled, but shook her head.

"Come on," he said. "Where does she think Linda is anyway?"

"At home," Dawn replied. "Because that's where she is, for tonight and tomorrow."

Randy smiled and tried again. "How do I love thee," he whispered softly, gazing into her eyes. "Let me show you the ways."

Dawn chuckled, told him to leave, and kissed him at the door. "You are going home, aren't you?" she asked.

He nodded. "Call me. In about a half hour," he said, which she did, curled up in bed, lying on his pillow, and missing him.

Ben couldn't put into words how good it felt being back at the racetrack, even if it was only for an hour or so a day, and couldn't thank Gloria enough. If it weren't for her...

"When are we running Cajun again?" she asked.

Ben smiled, remembering back when, and shook his head. "We'll see." The smell of lilac overwhelmed him, made him think of life, flowers, and the smell of Meg's clean skin. "We'll see." He had another thought then, as he watched All Together and Cajun on the walking machine, listened, and heard the sounds around him. If and when I do die, let me die right here. That's how happy he was. "Happy as a lark," he said out loud. And Gloria nodded, glancing up from her condition book.

"How about this race?" She had one marked.

Ben rolled his eyes and laughed.

Randy stopped by the barn a short time later on his way to farm calls, reminding Dawn he had appointments lined up until seven, and took off in a hurry. "I'll see you later," he said.

"Don't be late, please."

"I'll try."

"Randy...?"

He smiled.

Dawn had plans to meet Aunt Maeve and Linda for lunch at the club. Then she and Aunt Maeve were going to visit Ben at the hospital. Aunt Maeve insisted it was time they meet. And after that they were going to the racetrack so Dawn could show her All Together.

Aunt Maeve and Ben hit it off great. They talked all about Dawn, who blushed and sighed repeatedly. They complained about hospital food. Maeve had undergone two hip replacements in the past ten years, and swore she'd have recovered much faster each time with some decent food, and Ben agreed wholeheartedly. And they talked about the signs of the time.

Soon, they were off to the racetrack, where it was Tom's turn to be charmed and charming. And the filly couldn't have been gentler. Ginney stopped by while they were there, and Aunt Maeve couldn't help overhear part of Dawn and Ginney's conversation. When she asked her about it in the car on the way home, Dawn explained.

"How awful," Maeve said, staring out her window and then looking at Dawn. "But Dawnetta, dear. Are you sure you...?"

"I'm fine, Aunt Maeve. Honest," she added, when Maeve still looked concerned. "I want to be there for her."

Aunt Maeve nodded, squeezed Dawn's hand, and stared out her window again. "Well, at least Matt and Rebecca are going to have good weather."

Dawn feared Randy would be late, told Aunt Maeve to go on without her, and started pacing. Why am I so nervous, she asked herself? Why? She stared out the window. It was getting dark so soon now. Where is he? She glanced at her watch, her mother's watch, as voices from the past mingled in her head. "Merry Christmas! Happy Holidays! Merry Christmas!"

She closed the drapes and walked back across the room. What would make her think of that now? Merry Christmas? The watch. She glanced at it again, turned when she heard a key in the door, and smiled as her eyes met Randy's.

"Wow..." he said, the same thing he'd said at the store, and with the same look on his face. "When your Aunt Maeve leaves, you're going to have to put this dress on just for me, okay?"

"Okay."

He motioned for her to twirl around, whistled under his breath, and drew her into his arms. "And the high heels too. Better yet, why don't we just stay here for a while."

Dawn laughed, told him how nice he looked, so handsome, and motioned to the door. "We're already late. Let's go."

The Fioritto estate was everything Randy suspected it would be. A virtual mansion, all lit up like the White House, with valets, security, landscaping galore, and fountains everywhere. The double-wide circular drive was crowded with limousines, Porsches, BMWs, Devilles, Sevilles, Towne Cars, and an occasional sports car, one of which was totally unfamiliar to Randy. He stopped to look at it, said something to one of the valets, who smiled, and he and Dawn walked up the steps. If he was nervous, he wasn't showing it. But neither was Dawn for that matter, and she, for a fact, was nervous.

Uncle Matt greeted them just inside the door. "It's a pleasure to meet you," he said, shaking Randy's hand. "A real pleasure. And you, Dawnetta..." he said, turning to his niece and kissing her on both cheeks, "have been too much of a stranger lately."

"Sorry, Uncle Matt, but I've been busy," she said, smiling warmly, and then smiling again as Aunt Rebecca appeared at his side.

"Dawn," she said, hugging her. "Thank you for coming."

Dawn held her hand, squeezed it gently to show her support, and looked at Randy to introduce him. "Aunt Rebecca, this is Randy Iredell."

"How nice to finally meet you," Rebecca said, standing on her tiptoes to kiss him on the cheek. "Linda's told me all about you," she added, and glanced at her husband. "Matt, you're needed out on the terrace."

"Well then, that's where I'll be." Matt excused himself, told Randy he was looking forward to talking to him later, and walked away. Randy took a good look at Dawn's Aunt Rebecca, a very attractive woman, and tried to picture her elsewhere with her cab driver.

"If I can just get through this evening," Rebecca said to Dawn, and smiled again at Randy. "Linda and Harland are at the bar."

Dawn took Randy's hand as more guests arrived for Aunt Rebecca to greet, and they weaved their way through the crowded rooms to find Linda. Harland was not what Randy expected. He'd imagined somebody stuffy, especially with the name Harland, but found him to be a genuinely nice guy. Dawn's Uncle Matt wasn't what he'd expected either. He didn't have a Mafia look about him at all. He looked like an everyday business man, out on the town, in his own house. Presidential style.

Linda and Dawn were right at home, telling stories about one another from when they were kids, and laughing. More than once Randy and Harland found themselves saying, "Guess you had to be there," when they didn't get what was so funny. But everyone was definitely enjoying themselves.

Champagne was popped all over, and flowing, hors d'oeuvres were being served throughout. A mime, a clown, and a belly-dancer, mimicked, entertained and performed. And music from the quartet in the great room competed with the rise of voices in conversation. Randy estimated there had to be at least a hundred people there...as he and Harland followed Dawn and Linda from room to room, putting on a big show for her parents' sake, Linda said, "Of everything being hunky-dory."

"Hi, how are you? So nice of you to come."

"Haven't seen you in so long."

"When's the wedding?"

"We haven't set a date."

"Hi, how are you doing?"

Randy half expected to see Dawn's old fiancé around, Dave what's-his-face. And sure enough, another room, and there he was, all smiles and headed their way.

"Dawn! And uh...Randy is it?"

Randy managed a smile as they shook hands.

"So how are you two?"

Dawn sighed. "Fine. How are you?"

"Okay." He glanced from one to the other, shook his head as if amazed to find them still together, and turned to greet Linda and Harland and offer his formal congratulations on their engagement. But it was Randy he really wanted to talk to.

"So tell me, how's business? I understand you've bought into a little practice on the east side?"

No reply. Randy just looked at him, wondering where he'd gotten this information, and sipped his drink. It was an awkward moment for everyone; everyone except Randy, that is, and Uncle Matt, who from across the room, heard, watched, and couldn't help but take notice and smile. Impressed.

"Come on," Linda said, to the rescue. "The last thing we want to be discussing tonight is business. This is a party. Let's party." She swept the group into the great room, motioned for the band to pick up the tempo, and coerced Harland into dancing the tango with her. Dave disappeared as Dawn and Randy sat down next to Aunt Maeve. A testament to how large the house was, this was the first they'd come across her.

"Well now," she said, glancing at them as she bounced a toddler on her knee. "Are you two having fun?"

Dawn nodded, no longer nervous. Randy smiled. He wouldn't necessarily call this fun, but it definitely was interesting. The majority of people were standing, a drink in one hand, a cigarette or occasional cigar in the other. Waiters and waitresses milled about in tuxedos and black and white aproned dresses, carrying trays.

"Say hello to Josh here," Aunt Maeve said. Josh was Rebecca's nephew, the progeny of her brother's third marriage. "Say hello, Josh."

Josh giggled and drooled. He was one of five or six little ones about. "Children are always included in the Fioritto gatherings," Dawn remarked as she and Randy walked out into the garden. Of course, there were nannies to step in when they got out of hand. But most were running around, happy as can be.

"How do you feel about kids?" Randy asked.

Dawn looked at him, studied his eyes reflecting the garden lights. "I don't know. Why?"

Randy shrugged. "Just wondering." He knew she took birth control pills, and for some time now, she'd told him.

"Don't worry," she said. And the way she said it irritated him.

"That's not what I meant, Dawn. And you know it."

"I know." Dawn nodded, having realized that, and smiled apologetically. "Come on, I want to show you something." She took him to the dining room, closed off for the evening, and inside, gazed around with nostalgia in her eyes. "This furniture was in my parents' house." The table and chairs that sat twelve, the china cabinet, dry sink, and serving tables, all imported Italian Provincial made of mahogany, the wet bar. "It's all that's left," she said. "I sold everything else."

Randy studied the sadness of her expression, and for once didn't ask. Anything at this point, he could see, would be hard for her to talk about. She then took him into the foyer, which was empty now, everyone having arrived and no one leaving, and showed him the gallery of family portraits that adorned the spiral staircase wall.

"Here, see..." she said, pointing to her great-grandfather, grandfather, and father. "We all have the same eyes."

Randy smiled, saw for himself, and kissed her lightly on the mouth. "I love you," he said, and Dawn smiled.

"Come on, one more thing." They walked outside, through the side garden, under an oak tree, and along a short path, no longer worn but still very familiar. "There..." she said, pointing. "That's where I grew up."

They heard Linda's voice behind them, and turned. "I thought this was where you were headed," Linda said, dragging Harland along with her. "What are you doing?"

Dawn laughed. "Showing Randy the house."

"Dawn and I used to sneak back and forth this way," Linda said, amazed at how long ago that seemed now. "Come on," she told Dawn. "Mom says it's time to eat, and I want you guys sitting next to us."

Randy glanced over his shoulder at the estate next door before following them back inside. "Who lives there now?" he asked, when Dawn and he were seated.

"I don't know," she said. "I had Uncle Matt sell it after my parents died."

"Were you living at home then?"

"No."

Randy looked at her thoughtfully, smoothed her hair. And here came the food. Platters and platters of it; antipasto first, then lobster, crab, scampies, prime rib, chicken breast. Randy and Dawn laughed when they saw Aunt Maeve wave that one by. And then there were the vegetable dishes. Asparagus, roasted red peppers, artichokes, snow peas, red potatoes, and stuffed onions. And dessert. "Every delicacy and pastry known to Italy," Randy heard someone say. And lots of espresso.

Randy wondered how Linda's parents were going to top this for the real engagement party, let alone the wedding, and couldn't remember eating so much at one time in his whole life.

The party was just beginning. It was already past eleven, but there were wish dances. "Actually, it's more like giving advice," Dawn explained. "All the married men dance with the bride to be, and tell her what they think makes a good marriage. And the married women do the same with the groom."

Randy smiled, passed on the brandy being served, and sat and watched. Some of the wishes were outrageous, and had everyone laughing. Some were sentimental and touching. Some incoherent, due to the particular person's having had a bit too much to drink.

Linda's mother's was short and to the point. "Honesty."

Matt wished his daughter, "Love. Undying love."

Rebecca managed a smile having heard this, and watched stoically until she could no longer hold back the tears. The guests clapped and cheered, believing they were witnessing a tender moment as Matt walked over and put his arm around her. Aunt Maeve said it was her turn then, married or not, which diverted everyone's attention and had them laughing.

About this time, Dave appeared at Randy's side again, full of the evening's festivities himself. "Well now," he said, tipping his drink in some kind of toast. "If I could pull you away from Dawn here, we'd like you to settle something for us."

We? Randy looked at the bar, where three men stood staring in their direction, and placed his hand on Dawn's arm. She was about to object. "I'll be right back," he said. And he and Dave walked over to join the other three.

"Here's the problem," Dave said. "We were having a discussion on politics and decided what we really needed was a democrat's opinion. No offense."

Randy smiled a nondescript smile. "None taken." He glanced at each of the other three men, noticed a hint of reluctance in two, and turned back to Dave. "You know what I think, Dave. I think you have a little dick."

"What?"

One of the men laughed.

"No offense," Randy said.

"None taken," the man laughing sputtered, and with that, Randy turned and walked away.

"What did they want?" Dawn asked, when he sat down next to her.

"Nothing." Randy put his arm around her. "What other traditions are there?"

"I don't think there are any more," Dawn replied, yawning.

Aunt Rebecca sat down to talk with them for a few minutes, then Uncle Matt. Linda and Harland were toasted one last time, and Randy drove Dawn home.

"How long do we have before Aunt Maeve gets here?" he asked.

Dawn smiled. He was so relentless. "She said she'd be right behind us."

Randy kissed her, and then kissed her again. "You're so beautiful," he said, mesmerized with the sleepy look in her eyes. "And so very, very tall."

Dawn chuckled. "Well? What did you think?"

"About your family?"

She nodded.

"They're nice. Your friend Dave is an asshole, but everyone else seemed okay."

Dawn laughed.

"What did you see in him anyway?"

She shook her head. "I don't know."

Randy gazed at her. "Are you sure I can't stay?"

"Positive. Tomorrow."

He nodded, and smiled at her from the door. "We're all clear now. Right?" he said. "Families? Old friends?"

Dawn laughed.

"I just don't want anything to come between us. All right?"

Dawn hesitated, but not so much that it concerned him. After all, she was tired, and he was tired. And they'd had such a nice time. "All right."

Chapter Thirty-Two

Randy and his new partner, Dr. Raffin, signed on the dotted line, shook hands, and were in business. The way they figured it, if all went well, in about ten or twelve or fifteen years, they'd be in the clear.

"But who's counting?" Raffin said.

Randy laughed. All kidding aside, they were both a little nervous. Their biggest commitment was the addition to the existing building, on the gamble they'd get enough large animal surgery over the years to justify the investment. It was practically unheard of for two lone veterinarians to take on such a venture. But they were both young, dedicated, and ambitious. Also to their credit, the loan officer pointed out to his superiors, they were going to keep costs to a minimum by doing a lot of the actual construction themselves. There were only five weeks remaining in this year's racing season at Nottingham. Business would slack off then, which would allow them the time. And if they were lucky, at least they'd get the outer shell of the building up before the first snow.

Presently, however, even with the season winding down, Sunday was promising to be the biggest day of the year for the Miller barn. All Together was running in her first stakes race, and against the boys. There was no doubt in Ben or Tom's mind that she was ready. She'd been kicking and squealing since the day after her last race, and could barely be kept from running off in the morning when galloped.

"I'm leaving!" Dawn yelled to Ben and Tom.

Ben waved with his good hand from the tack room.

She had to leave now in order to go home, shower and get dressed and meet Ginney at the courthouse at ten. A jury had been seated, media coverage approved, and opening statements were today.

"I can't do this," Ginney kept insisting, over and over. "I just can't. Look at all these people."

Dawn did her best to calm her, reassure her, gripped her hand, but felt like a hypocrite. Who did she think she was telling Ginney she could do it, to be brave? "I'll be here the whole time, right here behind you."

The defendant entered the courtroom, glared at Ginney, and was nudged toward his seat by his attorney.

"All rise."

Ginney stood erect and stared straight ahead.

"The Honorable Judge John McMurphy presiding."

Voices blended in Dawn's head, back and forth. "Prove without a reasonable doubt."

"All we're asking ladies and gentlemen, is that you ask yourselves, is there a reasonable doubt?"

"An act of violence."

"A lover's quarrel."

"An innocent man."

"A woman, brutally beaten and raped."

"The evidence will support..."

"Members of the jury, all that the ensuing evidence will prove, is that sexual relations took place. The defendant is not denying that."

"The medical examiner's report will support..."

"A reasonable doubt."

"No is no."

"A disagreement. Nothing more. Nothing less."

"Rape, by all accounts, is rape."

"All rise!"

Ginney's knees trembled as she stood.

"How did it go today?" Randy asked, as he and Dawn ate Chinese for dinner again, and just barely before closing time.

"All right, I guess."

He looked at her. "How's Ginney?"

"Okay," she said. "Her dad was there today. It meant a lot to her."

Bud Meyers was there the following day too, but left the courtroom in a fit of anger, when, as predicted, Ginney's reputation was brought up.

"Objection, your honor!" her attorney said.

"Sustained."

But the damage was done. Stricken from the record meant nothing. The jurors had heard, the media had heard. Ginney glanced over her shoulder as her father stormed out, and then looked helplessly at Dawn.

"It's okay," Dawn whispered. "It's okay."

Her attorney told her the same thing. "We'll have our say. Relax. What's good for the goose is good for the gander."

Ginney stared at the man.

"No interviews, please," he told the media afterwards when they wanted Ginney's opinion of the day's proceedings. He repeated the saying then, "What's good for the goose is good for the gander," and demonstrated it the following day.

"Remember you are under oath."

"Objection! Counsel is badgering the witness."

"Overruled."

Ginney's attorney nodded to the judge, scanned his notes, appeared to be counting, and asked the question again. "What are we talking here, five, ten, fifteen, twenty?"

The man was a character witness for the defense, a friend of the accused, and fellow exercise boy.

"How many?"

The man shrugged. The question had been, according to reputation, how many women did he think the defendant had sexual relations with over the past five years?

"A ball-park figure?" Ginney's attorney said, which had several people in the back snickering and laughing.

Again the man shrugged. "I don't know. I have no way of knowing. Not for sure anyway."

"I see," Ginney's attorney said. "Because anything would be speculation on your part. Unless we did a survey, of course, and compared notes, did interviews, proved who was lying and who wasn't, and..."

The defendant's attorney struggled visibly with whether or not to object. "Your honor!"

"No further questions."

Dawn drove out to Ben's farm to visit Beau Born on Thursday evening, and found him lazy, happy, and getting fat. "He still recognizes me," she told Ben.

Cajun had run yesterday and finished second again. Lady ran fourth the day before. Ben talked Dave into turning Branden out, and as a result, got two ship-ins from his Chicago trainer, which were both running today.

Constantly coming and going, Dawn and Randy had actually cooked last night, and at eleven o'clock yet. "What's that?" she'd asked Randy, when he came in with a grocery bag.

"Macaroni and cheese," he said. "I have a taste for it. And," he added, kissing her, "I think we can handle it."

Dawn laughed, and handed him a postcard off the counter.

"Who's this from?"

"Aunt Maeve." Dawn took out the box of macaroni and cheese and read the directions on the back as Randy read the card. She glanced in the bag to see if he'd bought butter and milk. He had.

"What's this about a trip abroad?" Randy asked, looking at her.

"Oh, nothing. Aunt Maeve mentioned it when she was here, and asked if I wanted to join her."

"When?"

Dawn shrugged. "I don't know, sometime in November."

"Wait a minute. For how long?"

Dawn smiled. "I never said I was going, Randy. I'm not sure I want to, particularly now with you cooking and everything."

Randy laughed. "I even bought salt and pepper."

Dawn cringed as the photographs showing Ginney's injuries were displayed. James Martin, sitting next to her, leaned forward, took them all in with a single glance, and sat back shaking his head.

"I hope they nail this guy to the wall," he whispered. And Dawn nodded.

"He must pay, Dawnetta," a voice in her head said. "He must pay."

"Please, for the jury," Ginney's attorney instructed the doctor on the witness stand. "Describe in detail the extent of the injuries."

"Objection."

"Overruled."

Dawn lowered her eyes, stared at the floor.

"Multiple contusions."

"Dawnetta. Dawnetta, listen to me."

"Labia minora, majora."

"Dawnetta."

"Dawn..." She felt a hand on hers, not a gentle hand, a firm hand. "Dawn." It was James. She stared at him, wondered why he was looking at her this way. "Come with me," he said, but she shook her head.

"I can't," she whispered, and turned back in support of Ginney. James took out his handkerchief and wiped the blood from her palm.

"Laceration of the lip. Right eyebrow."

James pressed the handkerchief into place, motioning for her to hold it tight, kept his hand on top of hers, and watched her out of the corner of his eye.

"All rise!"

"Please," Dawn said to James, as she shook her head. This was nothing for him to be concerned about. She felt bad for Ginney having to sit through this, and couldn't do anything to help. That's all. This isn't about me. "Please..."

Randy was as concerned that evening as well. "How'd you do this?"

She shrugged. "My fingernails."

"Are you all right?"

"I'm fine. Why does everyone keep asking me that? Come on, it's embarrassing. This isn't about me. It's about Ginney."

"How is Ginney?" Randy asked, day after day. His schedule had been so hectic, he'd only been at the trial once, and even then just for a few minutes.

"She's doing good. You'd have been proud of her. She never even blinked and looked right at the jurors."

Randy smiled sadly. If someone had asked him six months ago what he thought of Ginney, he'd have had to honestly say he pretty much thought of her as a good time. Now she was a good friend. One he was rooting for.

Tom sat in the tack room and read the article on the filly again. It was worth reading twice. And out loud.

"All Together, said to be one of the finest hopefuls in racing's distaff history, will challenge the boys tomorrow in the Harvard Stake. This filly, undefeated, who recently broke the long-held track record for the mile, has black-letter worked from the day she arrived at the racetrack. Bred and raised by Vandervoort Farms, in her stake debut, All Together will school the boys and no doubt show them the way home. She is favored to win."

He folded the racing form, laid it aside, and got up and poured another cup of coffee. Brownie was scheduled to shoe Son of Royalty and was due any minute. In the meantime, Tom was basically just killing time, and in a good mood. Randy stopped by later, talked to him and Brownie a second, and took off, saying he was supposed to meet Dawn at some swim club.

"Does she have to feed?"

Tom nodded. He'd offered to feed for her, since he was going to be here anyway. But she insisted it was her turn, and that she wanted to stay busy for fear she'd start hiccuping or something. He wondered that afternoon as he pulled feed tubs, how she was going to make it until tomorrow.

As much as Ben would have liked, staying to watch the race or even postponing his visit until later in the afternoon was out of the question, his doctor had said, no ifs, ands, or buts.

"Need I remind you that you suffer from hypertension?"

Dawn walked with him and Gloria to the car, promised to call him just as soon as the phones came back on, and headed back to the barn. They were in the ninth race, and would be able to phone him right after the tenth had run.

"Do you want to play some cards?" Fred asked, when she and Tom kept walking back and forth, practically running into each other trying to find things to do.

"Cards?" Dawn frowned. "Like what?"

"I don't know. Rummy."

"Deal," Tom said.

Randy showed up as they were playing their third hand, said he had to go out for two farm calls, but would be back in plenty of time for the race, and left. Barn Kitty meandered into the tack room. She'd already visited them once today, when they were eating Kentucky Fried Chicken, and had them laughing when she scarfed up the leftover coleslaw. This time she was dangling a dead mouse.

Dawn chased her out. "Go!"

"Rummy!"

Tom shook his head. "I think you cheat," he told Fred.

"Sore loser."

Tom sat where he could keep a watchful eye on the shedrow, and chewed on a toothpick as he dealt the next hand.

"I wish I could take a nap," Dawn said.

"Go ahead." Tom nodded toward the cot.

"I can't, I'm not even tired. I just said I wish I could. That way time would go faster."

"What time is it anyway?" Tom nudged Barn Kitty with his boot when she relentlessly started back in, told her to, "Git!" and named kings and aces wild.

"It's five after three," Fred said, glancing at his watch.

Dawn had two pair right off the bat, and for the first time in her life, "Honest, my whole life," she ended up winning a game. They quit playing then, ran the stalls, and pulled the feed tubs. After that, Dawn raked the shedrow again, just for something to do, being careful to stay away from the vicinity of the filly's stall. And Tom tacked Red.

Finally, the ten-minute call for the ninth race came.

Tom brushed off the filly and did her back legs up in Vet Wrap while Dawn held her. They put her bridle on, and rinsed her mouth out. Waited. Waited. And waited.

"They've run!" Fred yelled from the road.

"All right, let's go!" Tom said. Dawn went down to get Red, Tom got on and tightened his girth, Fred led the filly out, handed her over, and off they went.

Onlookers clamored three-deep against the paddock railing to get a close-up of the dappled-gray wonder, in all her glory, tossing her head, cow-kicking, dancing, and now something new, rearing.

"Keep her moving." Tom gritted his teeth.

"There now... There now..." Fred kept saying.

"Hold her! Hold her!" was the valet's constant plea, as ardent as Tom's. "Hold her!" And all the while, Dawn watched with her stomach in knots from the number-six paddock stall, the filly's post position.

A fan with a camera waited until the filly was practically right under the railing to snap a picture, and she shied when the flash went off, dragging Fred back twenty yards, and scattering people everywhere. Tom was sweating, "Like a stuck pig," by the time they finished saddling her, and walked out to where the ponies were assembled, mopping his brow with his shirt sleeve. "Jesus!"

Fred waited until the last minute to lead the filly into the stall, turned her around quick, Dawn gave Johnny a leg up, and Fred led her right back out, jogging, dancing, sidestepping, and tossing her head.

"Don't do that!" Fred yelled to the person about to take another snapshot. "Don't!" He held up his hand, blocking the lens, and guided the filly out onto the racetrack and to Tom.

The race was a mile and a sixteenth, the track listed as fast. Dawn climbed up on the fence support at two minutes to post. She looked and saw that Randy's truck was by the kitchen as Fred climbed up next to her.

"She's even money," he said.

Dawn nodded. What was there to say?

The horses were loaded one by one.

"No boss! No boss!"

"Not yet boss!"

The seven horse was the last to go in. They all stood. The latch was sprung.

"And they're off!"

All Together broke on top, ears pinned, and went head to head with Crimson Treasury down the stretch and through the first turn. They ran the first quarter in a blistering .22 flat, a length and a half in front of the rest of the field, went shoulder to shoulder starting down the backside, the half in 45 and 1/5. And then All Together started drawing away.

Dawn held her breath, waiting until they came into view from behind the tote board. "Come on, All Together. Come on."

The announcer called her name again and again, in front by a length, then two, two and a half. Fred started banging on the fence. "Come on, filly. Come on."

"At the three eighths pole, it's All Together by four lengths! Crimson Treasury is running second. And third... Oh no! Ladies and gentlemen, All Together has gone down."

"What?!" Dawn gasped, straining to see. Fred strained to see. A split second later, further down the rail, Randy strained to see. All in disbelief.

"Oh my God!" Dawn jumped off the fence and started running in the filly's direction, with Fred right behind her. She dodged horsemen, race fans, benches, chairs, ran the length of the grandstand to just before the parking lot, climbed the chain link fence, and dropped onto the track on the other side.

"Dawn, wait!" Fred yelled.

She never even heard him.

The announcer called Crimson Treasury as the unofficial winner of the race as the rest of the field trickled under the wire in front of a stunned crowd.

"Shit!" Randy's decision to take the back way to the quarter pole, thinking it would be quickest, turned out to be a huge mistake. "Shit!" Two-thirds of the way there, he found it blocked by a hay truck. He threw his truck into reverse, backed up past three barns, slid to a stop, and weaved his way up through the north end.

Dawn gripped her side as she ran down the surface of the track, tripped and rolled, and rose only to see All Together struggling to her feet and going right back down again.

"Oh God, no!"

Johnny stood next to her, his one hand on the rein, the other on her shoulder. He was hobbling on one foot, trying to touch the other, to grab it, while still holding onto the filly. Tom got to her from the other end, flew off Red to take hold of the filly's rein, and gripped Johnny's shoulder to steady him.

"What happened? What happened?" he asked Johnny frantically. "What happened?" And swore under his breath when the filly tried to stand, and couldn't. "Oh Jesus...fuck!"

All Together rocked her body back and forth, struggled again to get up, and laid back down, her sides heaving and lathered from all the exertion.

When Dawn reached them, Tom wasn't letting the filly even attempt to stand anymore and kept her down by pressing his weight on her neck.

"Tom...?"

He shook his head, glanced past her to the meat wagon, already on its way, the track veterinarian riding up front. Dawn darted her eyes over her shoulder, shook her head no. No! We have to get her up! We have to get her up! Don't let her be laying there when they come. Oh God, Tom... She opened her mouth, but nothing came out. Fred was kneeling next to Tom. The filly's chest was quivering, her side heaving, her legs twitching. Oh, God...

"Let's see what we got here," the track vet said. He bent down to look at the filly's right front leg, touched her, and she started freaking out, picking up her head, kicking, throwing her weight about and knocking Tom aside. And then with a great moan from deep inside her chest, she sat with her front legs sprawled in front of her, dug her chin into the dirt, and pulled herself to her feet.

"Son of a bitch!" Tom said, at the sight of her right ankle, dangling from the joint to the ground. "Son of a bitch!"

Dawn gasped and covered her mouth with her hands as she stared at the filly's injured leg. "Let's get her off the track," she heard a voice say. "Pull the trailer around. We'll probably have to put her down."

"No!" Dawn stood paralyzed, her head registering the voices and sounds, but sounding miles away. No... If she stood in front of the trailer, refused to move, maybe she could stop this from happening.

Randy slammed his truck into park, hurried out and jumped over the fence.

"Dawn..." Tom looked at her. The ramp was dropped and the filly was urged toward it, only to go down on her knees. Randy got to them, pushed Dawn out of the way, took a quick look at the filly's leg, and gripping it tightly, kept it bent at the knee underneath her as she was urged back up.

They unsaddled her then and coaxed her into the trailer with Randy still holding her knee bent to spare her the pain of putting weight on her ankle and to prevent any further injury. The ramp was raised and the trailer turned slowly, heading for the quarter pole. Randy rode inside with her, still grasping her leg and fighting her to keep it bent, and pushing with all his own weight to help keep her standing.

Johnny was being put into an ambulance, clutching his saddle as the filly was hauled away. "She tripped," he was telling Tom. "In the turn. It was something shiny."

Dawn could hear them talking behind her as she followed the trailer, and turned. The ambulance looked like an amusement ride to her. And Johnny, a child, who grew smaller and smaller in the distance.

Once the trailer was off the track and the gates closed, the track veterinarian climbed onto the wheel well, both he and Randy angling to get a better look at the filly's leg.

"What do you think, Randy, sesamoid?"

Randy nodded, the strain of holding her leg bulging all the veins in his neck and arm. He motioned for Tom to come take his place. Tom climbed up and over slowly so as not to spook the filly, talked to her, and Randy climbed out, went to his truck, and came back with a sedative, which he quickly administered.

"You want to switch?" he asked Tom.

Tom shook his head. "No, I got her. Let's go."

Randy nodded to the man driving the tractor. "Barn fourteen," he told him, and turned to Dawn. "We're going to ride over with her. Drive my truck and meet us there." Dawn stared past him at the filly's quivering hindquarters. "Dawn, do you hear me?" he urged, taking hold of her arm, pointing her to his truck. "Drive my truck to the barn, we need to X-ray her."

"Is...is she going to be all right?"

"I don't know. Just go to the barn, okay?"

The tractor and trailer jerked forward. Randy had just climbed back in and was able to balance the filly on the off side. As they made the long trip around the back of the racetrack and out the far gap, Fred followed behind them on Red.

Dawn had the X-ray equipment in the shedrow when the trailer pulled up. Raffin drove in right behind them. When the ramp was dropped, he took one look and shook his head. Randy edged around to relieve Tom, and had him and Raffin link their arms behind her in the event she tried to unload too fast, which would no doubt cause him to lose his grip.

"All right," he said, making sure they were all in place. The driver took hold of her reins, stayed up front, and slowly, one lumbering step back and stopping, then another, and another, they got her unloaded. "Keep her going," Randy said, as they coaxed and braced her weight until she was in her stall. Randy gave the task of holding her leg back to Tom as he and Raffin put on lead-lined aprons and took several shots of her ankle.

When Dr. Raffin left with the X-ray plates, saying he'd develop them and be right back, Dawn sat down on the ramp to the tack room and buried her face in her hands. Randy glanced at her as he came out of the stall and walked to his truck.

"Should I bed her stall down?" Fred asked, devastated and in need of something to do.

Randy nodded. "In a minute. I'm going to put a cast on her first."

Dawn watched him walk back and forth, could hear him telling Tom how they were lucky the skin hadn't torn, and that this was only a temporary cast, but would give her some support. "Bend the leg a little more, yeah, that's good. Now a little more."

He had Tom put her leg down then, finished wrapping it, and wound another cast over that. When he stood up and stepped back, he noticed Dawn standing in the doorway. She reached up and touched the filly's face, rubbing it when the filly leaned into her.

"Is she in a lot of pain, Randy?" she asked, her voice so strained it didn't sound like her.

"No, not really," he said. "I have her pretty well sedated. Between that and the shock, she's not feeling much."

"Do you think...? she started to say.

Randy shook his head. "Dawn, don't ask. Just hang on, okay? We've got to see the results of the X-rays."

Dawn nodded, pressed her face against the filly's, and stroked her neck. She had to be all right, she just had to be. "You're going to be just fine," she said softly, her voice cracking. "Just fine."

Dr. Raffin returned a few minutes later. Randy walked out to the truck, and Tom followed him. Fred kept busy bedding down her stall, while Dawn held onto her halter, talking to her and keeping her calm.

"Fuck!" she heard Randy say, and froze.

"No..." She shook her head, told herself, "Don't listen to them."

"Shattered sesamoid."

"Shit!"

"Like somebody set off a bomb."

"Don't listen to them."

"Dawn..."

She heard Raffin's truck drive away.

"Dawn..."

She shook her head. "No." She stared into the filly's eyes. "No, you're mistaken. Take more X-rays. You're mistaken."

Tom turned away, Fred left the stall, and Randy stepped closer. "Dawn, I'm sorry. There's nothing we can do for her."

Dawn looked at him with tears in her eyes. "Randy, you have to. Take more X-rays. You just need to take more X-rays. It's a mistake."

Randy shook his head, swallowing hard.

"Please help her," Dawn pleaded. "Randy, look at her. She's standing, see. Look at her...."

Randy hesitated. "It's the cast, Dawn. If we take it off..."

"No," Dawn said. "This is all a mistake."

Randy shook his head and looked at Tom.

"You'd better go talk to Ben," he said, and Randy nodded.

"Dawn...?" He reached for her arm, but she pulled away, and he walked out.

Ben was sitting in his wheelchair by the window, and felt the blood drain from his face in response to Randy's pained expression when he entered the room. He didn't beat around the bush either.

"Ben, the filly broke down."

"How?" Ben asked, his voice trembling.

Randy shrugged. "Tom said Johnny saw something shiny on the track. It could have been a shoe, who knows? She was on the lead when it happened."

"And Johnny?"

"He's okay. I saw him walk to the ambulance."

Ben nodded, stared at the floor, and then looked up. "How bad is she?"

"She shattered her right sesamoid."

"Oh my God," Ben said slowly. He turned and stared out the window. "Did you...?"

Randy shook his head. "We got her back to the barn to X-ray her. She's still there now, but..."

"I know." Ben nodded, wiping at a tear trickling down his face. "I know." He cleared his throat and drew a deep breath, and had to clear his throat again. "Is there anything you can...?"

Randy sat down on the bed and sighed. "Not much. The chances of infection..." All the risks ran through his mind. "We can cast it. I have a temporary one on her now, but..."

Ben searched his eyes. He knew the risks, one of the biggest being the most basic, the lack of activity and what it does to a horse's digestive tract.

"I honestly can't even see her keeping a cast on, not with her temperament," Randy said. "And there's no guarantee even if she does, that when we go to take it off..."

Ben wanted odds. "Give me odds, Randy."

"That she'll survive? Slim. That she'll be able to walk some day on her own, I don't know. We'd have to keep her tranquilized and somehow eating, otherwise she colics. That joint needs rest to heal, and yet we'd have to keep her moving around. If it isn't one thing, it'd be another." He raised his hands in exasperation. "And even then..."

Ben looked at him. "You don't leave me much choice."

Randy hesitated, wondering what Jake would do at this moment. "Ben, there's a part of me that would like to defy the odds. But I don't think that part is too objective right now. Maybe you ought to get a second opinion."

"That won't be necessary," Ben said, his voice quivering, but firm. "Put her down."

Randy nodded, swallowed hard, and got up and walked to the door, where he turned to say good-bye, to say how sorry he was, and saw the way Ben looked up and met his eyes. He walked back in then and sat down.

Dawn rushed over to the truck as soon as he returned. "Well?" she asked, holding onto the door.

"Ben wants to see you," Randy said.

"What did you tell him?" she asked, her voice rising.

Randy got out of the truck and glanced at Tom. "I advised she be put down."

"What?!" she gasped. "You're not even going to try?"

"There's nothing to try, Dawn!" he said, not meaning to sound so harsh, but wanting her to accept it. "There's nothing we can do."

Dawn backed up, shaking her head and glaring at him. "I'll get another vet. Don't you touch her. You understand? Don't you touch her."

"Dawn.... It's Ben's decision."

Dawn stared at him, a long grievous stare. "I will never forgive you for this, Randy. Do you hear me? Ever! You won't even try. How can you not try?"

"Dawn, listen to me. It's no use." He took a step toward her, but she held up her hands, turned, and grabbed her purse from the tack room and left.

Ginney entered The Rib, looked around, and walked over to the corner booth where Dawn was seated, and sat down across from her. "I'm sorry, Dawn," she said. "I'm so sorry."

Dawn nodded. "Me too." She took a swallow of beer.

"I was just by the barn. She's gone."

Dawn stared at her glass. "Was Tom still there?"

"No. Fred said he went to the hospital."

Dawn nodded again. "That's where I'm supposed to be. This is as far as I got."

"Do you want me to go with you?"

Dawn shrugged. "I'm not ready yet. I'm kind of hating Ben at the moment, I'm sorry to say."

"Why? I'm sure he's hurting too, Dawn."

Dawn looked at her, studied the concern in her eyes, and smiled sadly. "You're right. It's not his fault we have a spineless vet."

Ginney shook her head. "Dawn, this isn't Randy's fault. These things happen."

Dawn sighed.

"Come on. Ben's probably worried sick about you."

Ginney drove and waited for her outside Ben's room.

Tom was still there, sitting next to Ben's bed. Ben's face was red and his eyes bloodshot. Tom stood when Dawn appeared, his expression upon seeing her a tremendous sign of relief. Ben motioned for her to come sit on the side of the bed, and there she embraced him, holding on tightly as he caressed her hair.

"It's the best thing," he whispered to her. "It's easier to let go now. I had to do it this way." He was shaking, his body trembling as he spoke, but solid. And it was comforting holding on to him, his strength reminiscent of her father's in the past. When she sat up and faced him, behind her, Tom turned away to wipe his eyes.

"Now what?" she asked, her voice quiet and flat.

Ben shrugged. "We go on," he said. "It's simple."

"Just like that?"

"Yes," he said, patting her hand. "We still have Beau Born."

"You have Beau Born," Dawn said. "I don't want any more horses."

Ben shook his head. "Beau Born is yours, and has been since the day we came back from the sale. It's in my will. You and Tom are my only beneficiaries."

"Ben, I don't think..." Dawn started to say.

"Bullshit," Ben said. "And damned if I die, you had better take good care of him, or I'll come back and haunt you."

Dawn forced a smile, a feeble one, but a smile nonetheless. As quickly as it came though, it left. She sighed deeply, shaking her head, and swallowed hard. "Why couldn't Randy do something?"

"Randy's not God, Dawn," Tom said, and she turned. "You have to be realistic. You can't blame him for what happened."

Dawn looked at him, seeing how hurt he was in all this. He was crushed. Still... "I blame him for not trying. For doing nothing. I'll never forgive him for that."

"Dawn..." Ben said.

She shook her head. "I'm sorry, Ben. But that's just the way I feel."

"You're wrong, Dawn." Ben searched her eyes. "You're hurt, and you're angry, but you're wrong."

Dawn shrugged helplessly. "I don't want to talk about it anymore. Nothing's going to change." She hesitated. "I dread going back to the barn. I can't even imagine..." Her voice cracked, tears filling her eyes. "Oh, God, Ben."

He wrapped his arms around her and let her cry. "It's all right," he said. "It's all right. But you'll go back. You'll go back, because that's what horsemen do."

Ginney talked Dawn into coming in for a drink when they got back to The Rib, which turned into another source of anguish for Dawn. "If one more person stops and tells me how sorry they are, I'm going to scream."

Ginney looked at her. "Why? They are sorry, Dawn. She was a great racehorse. Christ, my dad even took it hard."

"Really?" Dawn stared. "What'd he say?"

Ginney smiled. "He said it was a fucking shame."

Dawn shook her head, but smiled as well. "You're quite a friend, you know."

The two of them just sat there a moment, then Dawn stood up to leave. "I'm going to go over to the barn."

"What for?" Ginney asked.

Dawn hesitated, her bottom lip unsteady as she spoke. "To get her bridle. I'm sure it needs cleaned. I'll see you tomorrow."

"Do you want me to come with you?"

Dawn shook her head and left.

The guard watched her as she walked to the barn. She walked so tall, so proud, her instinctive posture hiding any indication of grief. Any struggle. She unlocked the tack room door, turned on the light, and stood staring at everything familiar to her. She'd only meant to go in, get the bridle and leave, not wanting to see it hanging there in the morning. But she found herself going in and sitting down...looking around, and recalling all the important things in her life centered around this room. The times she sat with Ben and Tom. All her endless questions. The explanations. Tom's joking and singing. The planning. The hope.

She looked at the bridle, hanging there, and remembered her surprise birthday and Ben's anticipation as she unwrapped it. "Come on, open it." She took it down off its hook, wiped the dirt and mud from the bit, and traced her finger over All Together's nameplate.

Voices and scenes flashed in her mind. She could see Ben sitting at his desk, smiling, and Tom leaning over his shoulder.

"I'm going to buy this filly," she remembered telling them. "I am."

"Dawn...?"

She could see Randy the morning he was furious with her, ages ago, when he slammed the desk and demanded to know where she'd been. And she could see Ben as he sat contemplating, second-guessing his decision to retire Beau. And ultimately, the morning he lay slumped in his chair.

"Gloria! Gloria, come quick!"

She closed her eyes and sighed, heard Tom saying, "I need a drink. I need it bad." Felt his pain. And heard Ginney crying.

"Dawn?"

"Dawnetta...?"

She stood up, shivering, looked around one more time, and turned out the light and locked the door behind her. Cajun nickered to her then, and she walked down to talk to him, to pet him, smiled when he twitched, and started back down the shedrow to leave.

As she neared the first stall she stopped and stared into the emptiness. No more hopes, no more dreams. She leaned against the doorway, and hugged the filly's bridle to her chest, remembering...and could almost feel the softness of the filly's nose against her face.

"Good-bye," she said. "I'll never forget you. Good-bye."

Chapter Thirty-Three

Randy stopped and bought two sub sandwiches and a soft drink, and drove to his apartment, exhausted. It was after ten. He took a couple of aspirins, sat down on the couch to eat, and turned on the television. What timing. The news was replaying the stretch run from Nottingham showing where All Together broke down. He hoped Dawn wasn't watching, turned it off, and glanced at his watch.

He thought about showering and going over to see her, to be with her, but didn't really want another confrontation. He was too tired, and she was too hurt. And chances are he'd have to leave to take a call, so why bother? He didn't like to think of her being alone at the moment, but then again, considering her response to him earlier today, maybe that's the way she wanted it. Maybe that's the way she always wanted it, everyone at arm's length. He sat back, yawning, and shook his head. Everything was always life and death with them.

"I will never forgive you," she'd said. "Ever."

He closed his eyes, remembering, and after a moment or two caught himself dozing off. He checked to see if his pager was on, looked at the phone, and picked it up and dialed.

"Hello."

"Dawn, it's Randy. Are you okay?"

"Yes, I'm fine," she replied, giving no clue as to her real state of mind.

"I just got home. If you want, I can come over," Randy said, so unsure of himself, of them.

"You don't have to." Dawn sighed. "I'm just going to go to bed and put this day behind me."

"I'll see you tomorrow."

"Good night."

Randy hung up the phone and stared. Every instinct told him he should go over there, hold her, try to comfort her, make some sense of what happened and accept what followed. But instead, glancing at his pager again, he decided to shower, not wait for a call, and headed back out.

Dawn slept restlessly and was haunted with nightmares. From a distance, from the clouds, she heard her father's voice as she lay in a field, half-clothed and beaten. Her ankle was broken, twisted and deformed, and she was surrounded by hundreds of stuffed animals. "Okay, all together now," she kept saying to them. "Help me stand."

"Dawnetta."

"Father..."

"Dawnetta."

"Father, Randy has her leg, and he won't fix it. Make him fix it."

"Dawnetta."

"Help me, I can't walk," she cried. "Help me!"

"I can't, Dawnetta. I'm dead."

"No!" She woke in a sweat, her heart pounding and with her hair clinging to her face. She got out of bed, went in and turned the shower on as cold as she could stand it, stood under the spray until she was shivering, numb, then dressed and left.

She was determined that every detail, down to the exact time she would arrive at the racetrack, be the same. Her schedule, her entire focus that morning as she pulled into the racetrack, five minutes early. Five minutes? How did I get here so early? She ran back through the traffic lights, searched her memory. One, two. She'd stopped at three. Four, was it green? She couldn't remember. Did she stop? Yes. Five... She glanced at her watch again. Two minutes. Two more minutes. She gulped her coffee, spilled some in her lap; she was trembling so, and forced herself to finish the rest. Did I stop at the light on Mapes Road? Was it red? No, it was green. How many more? How did I get here this early?

Charlie stood to greet her when she finally got out of her car. "Good morning, Dawn."

"Hi, Charlie," she said, and smiled, darting her eyes at the barn and back at her car. "How are you?"

"Oh, I'm all right I guess. What about you?"

Dawn looked at him. "I'm fine. These things happen."

Charlie nodded, hesitated, and took something out of his pocket. "This is from Gloria," he said, and got choked up saying it, tears welling in his eyes.

Dawn lowered her gaze, looked at the tiny medal in his hand, and bit hard on her bottom lip to try and keep it from trembling.

"She said to tell you..." Charlie swallowed hard. "She said to tell you to be strong."

It was St. Christopher. Dawn took it from him, and clutched it tightly in her hand as she smiled. "Leave it to Gloria."

Charlie chuckled, wiping at his eyes. "Ben's being transferred today, you know."

Dawn stared a long time. "No, I didn't know that."

When Charlie nodded, she thanked him for the information, and the medal, turned, and walked to the barn. Tom too, tried to ease her pain. "I promoted Red," he said, and motioned to the first stall. "He ain't never been this close to the feed room in his life. He'll probably have an orgasm come dinner time."

Dawn laughed bravely, was grateful to not have to face the emptiness, and morning chores began. Ben arrived at his usual time and barked orders left and right, Dave came with donuts, and Fred got in the way. Dawn grabbed her purse at ten to leave. Since it was Monday and no racing, she wouldn't be back later. It was Fred's turn to feed.

"I'll see you tomorrow," she told Ben.

The attorneys in Ginney's rape trial were giving their closing statements today.

"Come here," Ben said. "I want to show you something."

Dawn walked back into the tack room, glanced at the newspaper he handed her, and shook her head. She didn't want to read about...

She looked again. It was the obituary. Winston Vandervoort had passed away Saturday. The day before... She looked at Ben and smiled. Winston Vandervoort had been spared.

The courtroom was packed, the crowd quiet as first the prosecution, then the defense presented their closing arguments.

Both were positive, they said, that they had proved their case. Both were confident, ladies and gentlemen of the jury, "That you will do the right thing." Both appreciated their time.

Judge McMurphy gave them a lecture of sorts then. He too said he appreciated their time, but encouraged them not to be in a hurry. To weigh the evidence. And to remember, guilty means guilty, beyond a reasonable doubt.

"All rise!"

"Well?" Bud Meyers asked Ginney's attorney, when they assembled in the hall.

The man shrugged and glanced at the barrage of reporters awaiting them. "Well, now we wait."

"For how long you think?"

"It's hard to say. A day, two. The longer it takes, the better for us."

"How will we know? Will they uh...?"

"You'll be contacted. Nothing will be done without you." He looked at Ginney and smiled. "We've done our part. It's up to them now."

Randy felt strange entering the lobby of Dawn's apartment building, and even stranger as he stood outside her door, the key in his hand, and knocked instead.

It took Dawn a long time to answer, and then she just looked at him for a moment. "Did you lose your key?"

He shook his head, walked in, and shut the door behind him. "No, I just..." When she sat down on the couch, he sat down next to her, studying her face, hoping to see some sign of warmth to encourage him. To let him know they were still together, no matter what. "Do you want to talk about it?"

Dawn shook her head. "Not really. Nobody listened to me before, why listen now?" When she started to stand, he reached for her hand.

"Do you want me to leave?"

She looked at him. "No. I just don't want to talk about it any more."

"All right," he said, and did his best to change the subject. "How'd the trial go today?"

Dawn sat back and sighed. "It's over. The jury's deliberating."

Randy nodded. "How's Ginney doing?"

Dawn hesitated. "She's fine, I think."

Randy gazed into her eyes. She looked so sad. "I understand Ben's transferring to a nursing home to finish out his rehab."

Dawn nodded. "Tomorrow. He was supposed to go today, but..."

Randy touched her hair, ached for her, wished he could say something to bring her out of this mood. "Dawn, I'm sorry."

"I know." She looked at him. "It's just that everywhere I look, people are crying. It seems like..." She drew a breath, paused, and looked at him again. "When this is all over, I'm going to go away for a while."

"When what's all over?"

"Ginney's trial, Ben and..."

Randy stared. He was losing her. It was evident in her eyes, in her every word. "Are you going to go with your Aunt Maeve?"

"No, I don't feel much like vacationing. The family has a cabin in Pennsylvania. I think I'll go there. Maybe I can finish my novel, and get some perspective on all of this."

"Where does that leave us, Dawn?"

"Us?" Dawn said sadly. "I don't know. I love you, Randy. I've never loved anyone more. But I'm losing touch. I'm hearing voices. And all this crying... I think I just need to get away."

Randy put his arms around her and held her close. Don't leave, Dawn, he wanted to say. Don't leave. But instead, he just held her. Twice in the night, Dawn woke frightened by her dreams. Both times he cradled her next to him, whispered he loved her. And both times, she said the same thing. "I love you too."

When she woke in the morning he was gone, having left a note in his place. "Had an emergency, but will see you at the track." She dressed and drove to work.

Ginney got paged to the stable gate around nine; the message was to phone her attorney right away, and she ran to the Miller barn. "They've done it," she told Dawn, panting and out of breath. "They've reached a verdict. We have to be there at ten-thirty."

They were prepared, both had an extra set of clothes. Ginney hurried down to tell her dad, grabbed her things, and ran to the ladies room to change.

"Calm down," Dawn told her, rather nervous herself.

"Why so soon? That's not good, is it?" Her attorney had said the longer the better. "Oh Jesus Christ!"

Dawn gripped her by her arms, told her again to calm down. And in came Ginney's friend, Julie, frantic and in a hurry to change as well.

"Oh my God," she said. "It's like déjà vu."

The three young women looked at one another, thought about that morning, the morning Ginney was raped, paused only a second, then finished getting ready.

"Let's go."

"Oh no!" Ginney said. "I forgot my purse!"

Dawn told them she'd wait for them at the barn, that she wanted to tell Ben something, and entered the tack room with trepidation.

"Ben?"

He looked up from his condition book and peered at her over his glasses.

"Um..."

"I thought you left."

"We're going right now. I wanted to talk to you a minute."

"All right." Ben took off his glasses and laid them on his desk, then turned his wheelchair to face her. "What's on your mind?"

"I'm thinking about going away for a while. Fred's here to help Tom and..."

"I see." Ben nodded. "You aren't running away, are you?"

Dawn shook her head, forcing a smile. "No. I just thought that since things were slowing down, that maybe..." She trailed off. Ben could see right through her. "I thought maybe I'd go to the family's cabin in Pennsylvania and work on my novel."

Ginney and Julie came around the corner, said they were ready, and Dawn turned to leave. "I'll talk to you later," she told Ben.

Ben nodded. He looked at Ginney, told her good luck, and Ginney crossed her fingers in response.

"I'm proud of you," Ben said. "What you're doing."

Ginney swallowed hard and rushed over and hugged him. All choked up, she managed a thank you, and they left in a hurry.

"Call me and let me know," Ben yelled to them, and Dawn said she would.

On the way to the stable gate, they came across Randy, getting something out of the back of his truck. "The verdict's in," Ginney told him. "It's at ten-thirty."

Randy glanced at his watch. "I'll see you there," he said, and reached for Dawn's hand when they turned to leave. He looked at her, just looked at her, and she smiled.

"Hurry," she said.

He nodded.

The courtroom was standing room only, friends, family, reporters, photographers, onlookers. "A circus," Randy heard someone say as he edged his way through.

"All rise!"

Randy stepped in next to Dawn, slipped his hand in hers, and nodded to Bud, who was standing on the other side of Julie.

"The Honorable Judge John McMurphy presiding."

Everyone sat back down amidst an echo of shuffled feet, collective murmuring. Someone sneezed in the back, a cough over on the side. Someone laughed. Someone cleared their throat. Then silence.

The bailiff recorded the date and exact time the defendant was asked to stand and face the jury for the foreman to read the verdict.

Ginney held her breath.

"We find the defendant guilty as charged."

Ginney gasped, covered her mouth, turned to look at her dad, Julie, Dawn...Randy, and way in the back of the room, having just arrived, James, as cheers and cries of shock drowned out the judge's gavel.

"Order! I'll have order!" The judge pounded again and again, demanding the courtroom settle down, whereupon he informed the defendant, who was still standing next to his attorney, stunned, that his sentence would be delayed pending a pre-sentence investigation. And court was adjourned.

Bud Meyers cried, unable to utter a word as Ginney hugged him. Ginney was in tears as well as she hugged Julie and Dawn, then Randy, and finally James, who had to work his way through the crowd.

"I can't believe it."

"Believe it," Dawn said.

"What's a pre-sentence investigation?" Ginney asked, and everyone turned to her attorney.

"Just a technicality," he said, and smiled as he guided her toward the swarm of reporters awaiting them.

"I'll see you later," Dawn whispered, and she and Randy left. "I have to call Ben," she told him, and phoned him when they stopped to eat. "Yes, yes," she repeated. "Guilty. Tell Tom when he comes in, okay?"

Ben said he would, and for the moment, to Randy at least, Dawn seemed to have come out of her depression. He talked her into riding with him on farm calls, and they dropped her car off at her apartment and spent the whole afternoon together.

"I've missed you," he said, glancing at her as they rode down the highway.

Dawn smiled, thought about the first time she went on calls with him, and saddened. So much had happened since then.

Randy got paged as they were driving home and pulled into a service station to phone his answering service. Dawn watched him as he walked back to the truck and climbed in behind the wheel.

"Well?"

He shook his head, put the truck in gear, and didn't reply until he'd pulled out onto the highway. "Oh, it's just another emergency out at the Durans'. That little black shit. It's probably nothing."

Dawn looked at him.

"I'll drop you off; you don't need to go."

"Are you sure?"

He nodded. At her apartment, he kissed her good-bye, motioned when she started in, to come back, and kissed her again. "We'll do Chinese tonight, okay? We don't need to go anywhere."

"All right. When do you want me to order it?"

"I don't know. I'm not sure how long this is going to take. You'd better wait till I get back."

Dawn didn't wait. She didn't hurry, but didn't waste any time either. She made a phone call, gathered her things, grabbed a set of keys out of the bottom of her desk, wrote Randy a note, and when the garage attendant buzzed, she left.

When Randy returned a little after eight, the attendant was covering the Jaguar with a tarp. He'd tried to phone her several times to give her an idea of when he'd be home, but hadn't gotten an answer and assumed she'd gone to the club. He parked, got out, and walked around to talk to the attendant. "What? Is it going to snow?"

The attendant smiled. "I hope not."

Randy waved and went upstairs, to find an empty apartment. "Dawn?" He checked her bedroom and bathroom, library, the kitchen, Linda's bedroom and bath, and then the library again, getting more and more apprehensive with each passing second. "Dawn?"

He stared at her desk. The typewriter was gone. The manuscript was gone. He turned, and with his heart pounding hard, checked her bedroom closet, then the bathroom again. Her toothbrush was gone. Her shampoo. Her robe. He walked back and sat down on the bed, and that's when he saw the note under the phone.

> *Randy,*
> *I'm sorry, but I have to get away.*
> *Dawn*

He stared at it, picked it up, read it again, crumpled it in his fist and threw it on the floor, and hurried back down to the garage. "When did she leave?" he asked the attendant.

The man hesitated. "I don't know. A couple of hours ago."

"How?"

Again the man hesitated. Randy looked mad enough to hit him. "In a jeep."

"What?"

"A jeep. I think it was a rental. Someone delivered it."

Randy turned, stared at the covered Jaguar, and raked his fingers through his hair.

"I'm sorry," the man said, for whatever reason. Randy nodded, glanced at him, and got in his truck and left. Ben, he thought. Ben would know where she was. She might leave without telling him, but not Ben. He drove to the hospital, forgot Ben had been transferred that afternoon, and had to drive back across town, even more frantic now. "What the hell? Where is she?"

Ben didn't know, and became concerned as well, but not as much as Randy, at least not that it showed. "She did say something about taking some time off. I didn't think it was this soon though."

Randy sat down next to his bed, stared at the floor, and heaved a frustrated sigh. "Ben, did we do the right thing? Tell me we did the right thing."

"We did," Ben said. "Come on, you know that. There were too many ifs."

Randy looked at him and shook his head.

"Give her some time. She's got a good head on her shoulders; she'll be back. She just needs some time."

Chapter Thirty-Four

Twenty-one days after Dawn had left, Ben shipped his last horse from the racetrack. He stood at the side of the barn, his right leg supported by a brace and a cane, his hand trembling from the strain. He watched as Son of Royalty was led up the van ramp and backed into a stall. Randy pulled up next to him and rolled down his window.

As usual, his first question was, "Have you heard from her?"

To which Ben always replied, "No, but we'll hear something soon. Any day now, I suspect."

One more week and the racing season would be ending, but already a lot of the trainers had shipped elsewhere. A different track, a brighter day. Tom was preparing to go to Florida for the winter, and had already turned Red out at Ben's farm. Fred had gotten a job at a breeding farm in northern Kentucky. And there was a chill in the air blowing out of the north.

Randy glanced at his hands, sore and callused from all the construction he and Raffin had been doing, and checked his clipboard to see where he was headed next.

Ben had resolved himself to one more month of rehab, and was looking forward to going home after that. He'd never felt the cold like he did this year, and chalked it up to the nursing home being too damned hot. He liked it warm, but certainly didn't need to be sweating in his sheets.

"So, is that it?" Randy asked, motioning to the van.

Ben nodded.

"Well, I guess I'll see you out at the home then. I'm out that way most every day."

Ben smiled. "Now listen, I don't want you fussing and coming up there all the time. Don't feel obligated to do that."

"It's not an obligation, Ben," Randy said, smiling but with a serious look in his eyes. "Besides, like I said, I'm out that way most every day. That and all the trips to your farm."

Ben nodded, and leaned to the side to adjust his weight and relieve the pressure on his hip.

"I'll see you later." Randy stopped next at Ginney's barn, also routine by now, but Ginney hadn't heard a word from Dawn either.

Somewhere in the mountains of western Pennsylvania, Dawn stood on the back porch of her cabin, overlooking the river, her jacket pulled tight as she watched a chipmunk skip over the rocks and climb a tree.

"Dawnetta."

She turned and smiled at her Aunt Maeve.

"Are you sure you don't want to reconsider and come with me? I hate leaving you alone."

"Why? I love it here," Dawn said, sounding almost cheerful. "I can write. I can go for walks. I need the time, Aunt Maeve."

"All right," she said. "If you're sure?" She took hold of Dawn's hands.

"I am."

Aunt Maeve searched her eyes. "And what about Randy?"

"I don't know. Maybe he'll find someone else. Who knows, maybe he already has."

"Dawnetta, you don't believe that for a minute," Maeve said, and paused. "Well," she sighed, resigned. "I've said it all before."

"Bye, Aunt Maeve. Write to me, okay?"

Aunt Maeve hugged her tight. "You know I will. You take care of yourself, and watch out for the bears."

Dawn laughed. "I will."

Aunt Maeve got choked up then, touched the side of Dawn's face, and turned and walked to her car. She waved from the end of the drive and honked from the highway. She always honked from the highway, and was gone.

Dawn went back into the cabin, put two more logs on the fire, poked at them for a moment, and then sat down in front of her typewriter.

Randy received a message from Ben later that day, and phoned him on the road between calls. Good news. He'd heard from Dawn. "I got a card. She says she's fine, not to worry about her. And that she's working on her book."

"That's it? That's all she said?"

"No, she asked about Beau, and told me to give him a big hug."

Randy stared at the traffic whizzing past him. "Where is she? Did she tell you?"

"No."

"What's it say on the card?"

Ben looked, tried to read it, but couldn't. "It's smeared. One of the nurse's aides spilled coffee on it when she brought in my tray."

"Wonderful." Randy shook his head in disbelief. "Can you make out anything?"

"Yeah. PA. Somewhere in PA."

Randy sighed. That, they already knew. A thought occurred to him then. "Maybe she sent me one too. I'll see you later." He drove across town, checked his mail, and walked inside his apartment, hurt and angry. "Fuck her!"

No letter. No card. Nothing.

He sat down on the couch, leaned his head back, and stared at the ceiling. He'd had enough. She obviously didn't want to have anything to do with him anymore. They were through. Finished. Done. History.

He thought of what Ben said about her working on her book, that stinking book. And figured he'd have to wait until it got published to find out what went wrong between them. Or for that matter, if they ever had anything to begin with.

He glanced at his watch. No more waiting. No more wondering. Get on with your life, he told himself. Go find somebody else. At least for the night. He washed up and left, stopped at the first bar he came to, and ordered a beer. The place was hopping. "Ducks on a pond," he could hear his voice of old saying, as he looked around at all the pretty faces.

And why not?

Because he didn't want to, and realizing that, he paid for his beer, downed the rest, and headed for more familiar territory, The Rib.

It was quiet tonight, an indication of all the horsemen having shipped south already, though there were a few trainers there he knew, clients of his. He had a drink with them, then excused himself to make a phone call.

"Is Ginney home?" he asked Bud.

"No." He told him she and James were on their way to The Rib to eat.

"Thanks," Randy said, and watched for them.

"Did you get a card from Dawn today?" he asked, practically as soon as they came through the door.

"Yes, why?" Ginney said.

"I need to know the postmark. Do you have it with you?"

Ginney laughed and made a face. "No. I take it you didn't get one?"

Randy looked at her. Wasn't that obvious? "What'd she say?" He motioned to the bartender as the three of them sat down at a table. "What do you want?"

"Vodka on the rocks," Ginney said, and James nodded.

"Two vodkas on the rocks." Randy grabbed his wallet, took out a ten-dollar bill, and asked again. "So, what'd she say?"

"Oh," Ginney paused, thinking. "Well, she asked how I was doing, and then asked about James." She smiled as she and James looked at one another. "And that's about it."

"Call your dad."

"What?"

"Call him and ask him what the postmark is?"

"Randy...?"

"Please."

Ginney shook her head, sighed, walked to the pay phone by the ladies room, and returned moments later.

"Cooksburg."

Randy stared. "Cooksburg?"

"Probably Cook Forest," James said.

Randy looked at him. "What?"

"I was there hunting once."

"What, so it's a lodge?"

"No, it's a forest, literally. There's cabins and lodges all over the place. Hundreds of them."

Randy sat back.

"Sorry."

Randy nodded, thought of something else, then dug into his jeans for a quarter, came up with a roofing nail and two screws, and checked his other pocket. Two dimes and a nickel. "I'll be right back." He phoned information, got the listing for Matthew Fioritto, and walked back dejected, another dead end.

"Who'd you call?"

"Her Uncle Matt. They're out of the country." He propped his elbow on the table and stared into the wood grain. Another idea crossed his mind then. Harland. If he could just remember his last name? Harland what? He looked up. "The club. They'll know. I'll see you later. Thanks."

He drove back across town, approached the desk, and pled his case. "Jeremy, please. I just want Harland's last name. It that too much to ask?"

"Yes, Dr. Iredell, it is. The club has strict rules about this sort of thing. I could be fired," he said, sounding genuinely sorry. "I wish I could help, but..."

Randy nodded, dejected yet again, and turned to leave, when who approached him but Dave. He shook his head, in no mood for the guy. And good ole Dave should have been able to see that.

"Well, well. If it isn't Randy."

Randy held up his hand and started past him, but Dave grabbed hold of his arm. "What's your hurry?" he said. "Seems we have more in common now than ever."

"Oh yeah?" Randy hauled off and flattened him, just like that. Jeremy screamed. Randy warned Dave, "Get up and you're going to regret it."

Dave wisely stayed down. Jeremy rushed over, urged Randy to, "Go. Please, Dr. Iredell, go..." And Randy walked out.

Furious, Randy started his truck and headed home. Halfway there, though, he turned around and drove to Dawn's apartment instead. He still had the keys. There had to be a clue there to where she'd gone, an envelope, an address book.

"Oh my God..." As he pulled into the parking garage, his heart stopped. There was a jeep sitting next to the Jaguar. Was she home...? No. He should've known better. When he got out and looked, it was obvious that it wasn't a new jeep, the kind one would lease. It was Aunt Maeve's. He recognized it from the dent in the right fender. He pulled around to the front and parked on the street. As he entered the lobby, Aunt Maeve was walking toward the elevator, her hands full of Chinese food containers.

"Maeve."

She turned, saw who it was, and smiled. "Oh, Randy. How nice. Have you eaten yet? I was just about to go up and try some of this concoction." She handed over several of the containers. "I don't plan to eat it all, I just didn't know what I would like. If it weren't for prowling alone, believe me, I would have gone out for some real food."

Randy smiled.

"So why are you here?" she asked, once off the elevator, unlocking the apartment door, and standing back for him to enter.

"I came over to ransack the place for a clue as to where Dawn might be."

"She's at the cabin in Cook Forest, dear."

Randy smiled. "Any chance of you being more specific than that?"

Maeve shook her head, which came as no surprise.

Randy put her food down on the table, motioned into the kitchen, and went in and got himself a beer. "What can I get you?" he asked, and felt a little odd. After all, she was the one staying here.

Aunt Maeve looked up. "Oh, beer's fine."

He got her a glass, and walked back into the living room where she was positioning all her food on the coffee table in some sort of order. He sat down in the chair across from her, and waited a moment. "Would it be treason on your part to allow me to look for an address book?"

Maeve smiled sadly. "I would only have to call her and warn her that you're coming."

Randy figured as much, deciding she wouldn't be there then, and glanced around the apartment as Maeve sampled the different containers.

"It's not that this stuff tastes so bad, it's just that it looks so dreadful." She gazed thoughtfully at him. "Aren't you hungry, dear?"

Randy shook his head, and stared at the terrace, remembering the night he and Dawn slept there through a lightning storm, and how she'd held onto him. "I have to find her, Maeve," he said. "You have to understand, I love her. And at times I could swear she loved me."

"She does love you, Randy." Maeve said, putting her fork down and sitting back. "That's why all this is resurfacing."

"What? What's resurfacing?" Randy stood up, his hands held out in frustration. "Her horse broke down. I'm sorry. But what does that have to do with us?" He turned his back to her, the anger mounting.

"Randy, it's not just that. It started long before this. You're a threat to her," Maeve said quietly.

Randy swung around. "What? I would never hurt her. What are you talking about? You're as mysterious as she is."

Maeve hesitated, sympathizing with him. "I wish I could tell you, Randy, but I can't betray her. I would go to my grave never forgiving myself if I caused her one moment of pain. She has been hurt enough."

Randy swallowed hard. "Maeve, I promise you, I will never hurt her. I want to help her. Tell me where she is. Please."

Maeve lowered her eyes to her lap and stared, agonizing over what to do, what to say, and drew a deep breath in resignation. She folded her hands together. "Dawnetta was raped."

Randy stared. "What? When?"

"Sit down, dear."

Randy shook his head, asking again. "When?"

"When she was seventeen."

"Oh my God..." Randy said, his thoughts quickly going to Ginney and Dawn's compassion, her insistence she prosecute.

"Please. There's more," Maeve said with regret.

Randy looked at her and sat down. "Don't tell me she got pregnant." He recalled her article on abortion, his hands trembling as he gripped the arms of the chair.

"No, dear. It was. She was...she was raped by two men." Tears filled Maeve's eyes, and she couldn't continue for several minutes.

"Where?" Randy asked, after giving her some time and unable to stand it anymore.

"In the garage, at their summer home."

"What? With servants everywhere?"

Maeve's voice quivered. "It was somebody the family knew. An employee, and... Charles had no way of knowing," she said, tears streaming down her cheeks. "Till the day he died, he blamed himself."

Randy shook his head, trying to take all this in. "And?"

"And they..." Maeve wiped her eyes, trying to compose herself. "You see, they... This is so hard to talk about. They hurt her then," she said, and had to give herself another moment before going on. "She had to have surgery."

Randy looked at her.

"They hurt her on purpose."

Randy felt the blood drain from his face.

"It was... Oh God," Maeve said, her voice a sob. "An instrument or something." She cradled her face in her hands, prayed for the strength to continue, to make Randy understand, even when he shook his head and didn't want to hear anymore. "They threatened her if she told. But they hurt her so badly, they knew she'd have to tell. She could hardly stand, Randy. She could hardly stand. And then they dressed her. They dressed her and left her at the door."

Randy stood up, strangling on his own anger, and walked to the terrace. Put his back to her for a long, long time, thinking, agonizing, remembering fragments of his and Dawn's conversations. "She can't have children, can she?"

Maeve shook her head. "The doctors don't know. She suffered cervical damage." She wiped her eyes, raised her chin, and cleared her throat. "Something prompted her last month to see her doctor, to ask if they could tell now that she was older. But they still don't know. The only way she will ever find out is if and when she becomes pregnant."

Randy nodded, remembering Dawn's reaction when they talked about children. "Did they get the men who did this?"

Maeve stared at the floor.

"Maeve?"

She looked up at him. "One of them was found murdered a week later."

"How?"

"He was shot."

"And the other one?"

Maeve paused. "He turned himself in. He's serving a life sentence."

Randy nodded and walked back and sat down. "Do you know who murdered the man?"

Maeve looked at him.

"Was it Dawn's father? Is that why the other man turned himself in? Was he next?"

Maeve swallowed hard. "I don't know."

Randy studied her eyes. "Does Dawn know?"

Maeve hesitated, then decided not to answer.

"Wasn't there an investigation?"

Maeve held up her hands in a protective gesture. "Charles was a proud man; he wanted no publicity. There was no connection to Dawnetta."

"I don't understand. When they found this man murdered, didn't they connect it to the rape?"

Maeve shook her head. "Randy, you have to understand, the rape was never reported. Charles wouldn't have it. She was too young. An innocent child. No." She bit her bottom lip, pressed her fist against it, and willed herself not to cry. "Don't you see? It was because of who he was that this happened."

Randy's eyes hardened.

"The media would have destroyed what was left of her. Charles couldn't allow that. He handled it the way he thought best."

Randy shook his head, trying to make sense of all this. "But she was in the hospital. What charge was brought against the other man?"

"I don't know. I only know the sentence. Life."

Randy lowered his eyes, stared, and sat back. "How did her parents die? She told me it was a plane crash."

"It was," Maeve said. "Charles had his own plane and flew it himself." She paused to reach for a tissue. "Their death has hurt her so much. She blames herself."

"Why?"

"She and Charles had an argument that morning. Dawnetta was to fly with them. It was a horrible argument. Charles was so upset." She looked away. "The cause of the crash couldn't be determined. It could have been pilot error or turbulence." She raised her shoulders. "We'll never know."

"Does Dawn think the argument caused the crash?"

"Yes. She's convinced it did."

Randy sat there a moment. "Is there more?" he asked.

"No, I've told you all I know. If there is, it's burièd deep inside Dawnetta, and with her parents."

Randy thanked her for telling him, and apologized for the pain it put her through, having to relive the details for his sake, but had one more question. "Maeve, please tell me where she is?"

"I can't, dear. If she wants to see you, she'll contact you. My prayers are with you...I hope to God I've done the right thing by telling you this. But the rest is up to her."

Randy nodded, and stood up and walked to the door. "Is she okay?"

"I think she will be. What she's struggling with is seeing herself through your eyes. And she hasn't been able to do that just yet."

Randy lay awake for hours that night. For the first time since he'd met Dawn, everything made sense. Her rape, the murder, blaming herself for her parent's death, almost losing Ben, first because of the stroke and then the argument, Ginney's rape and the trial, and then losing the filly. No wonder she chose to run.

"No wonder," he said out loud to himself. "And you pushed her." Always nagging at her, asking her questions, wanting to know who she was and where she'd been. Tell me everything. Everything. When all she wanted to do was forget.

Chapter Thirty-Five

Several days passed from the time Randy had talked to Aunt Maeve, long and hectic days between farm calls, surgery, the continued construction on the hospital, and his visits to Ben and out to the farm.

"You're going to kill yourself," Raffin told him, who was putting in some pretty long hours himself.

"So bury me," Randy said. "Right over there between those two boards. Standing up."

Raffin laughed. He'd pointed to the final section in need of drywall. "Let's do it." The two were eager to put this phase behind them, and as a result, Randy arrived later than usual that evening to see Ben.

"Where have you been?" Ben glanced impatiently at his watch. "Dawn was here."

"What?" Randy's mouth dropped. "When?"

"An hour ago you would have run into her."

Randy stared, too tired to even sit down. "Wait. You mean she's back in town?"

"No, just for today."

"Maybe she's still at her apartment," Randy said, already headed for the door.

"No, not hardly." Ben called him back. "She said she was going straight to the cabin, because she wanted to get there before dark."

Randy looked at him. "Did she say where it's at?"

"Yes, in Cook Forest."

"Where in Cook Forest?"

"I don't know. I asked, but she wouldn't say."

Randy sighed, walked back in, and sat down. She wouldn't say. "Did she say anything?"

"She asked how you were."

"What did you tell her?"

"I told her you were fine."

Randy shook his head. "That's a lie, Ben. I'm not fine."

Ben smiled sadly as Randy stood up and walked over to the window. "Why won't she contact me, Ben? Am I kidding myself thinking she will?"

"Well, she did ask about you."

"Big fucking deal," Randy said, arms stretched to the ceiling. "She asked about me."

Ben couldn't think of an appropriate response and remained quiet as Randy turned to leave. "I'm going to go find her. I'm tired of her wishes. Dawn this and Dawn that. What about me?"

Ben shrugged.

"And don't try talking me out of it. Enough is enough."

"I wasn't going to say a word," Ben said, smiling. "I don't want you decking me like you did Dawn's old boyfriend."

Randy looked at him from the door. "How'd you find out about that?"

"Dawn told me."

"Dawwnnn told you?" Randy said, dragging out her name. "How in the hell did she find out?"

"Oh, I guess a Jeremy somebody told her when she went swimming today. I hear you laid him right out."

"Listen, he had it coming. But wait a second. She went swimming? She *went swimming*?"

Ben nodded, smiling throughout.

"That does it. I'm going to find her. I don't care where she is." He waved over his shoulder, drove home, showered and dressed, called Raffin, and left, wasting no time.

He stopped for a map inside the Pennsylvania line, took Route 80 to Clarion, through town, continued north on a winding two-lane highway, turned right at the sign, which he almost missed, and drove directly into Cook Forest.

"Now what?" He pulled into the first restaurant he came to, which turned out to be more of a bar, that specialized in beer-batter-dipped and deep-fried everything and anything.

"The fried veggies," Randy said, handing the menu back to the waitress. "And a beer, draft." When the woman walked away, he stretched his legs under the table, heard a roar like a freight train, and watched a loaded logging truck barrel down the hill on the highway not a car length away. He glanced at the clock on the wall. It was eight-fifteen. "Excuse me," he said, to the waitress as she passed by on her way to the next table. "Do you know a Dawn Fioritto?"

"Nope. Sorry, never heard of her."

"Thanks." Randy ate, asked where the next closest restaurant or bar was, which drew a funny look from the waitress, and drove another mile and a half and stopped again. Same question. "Do you know a Dawn Fioritto?"

"No," the bartender said. And the next, and the next, and the next. He was on a wild goose chase, a little old lady serving him beer in a frosted mug said as she wiped the counter again and again. "You'd have more luck finding a needle in a haystack."

Randy smiled a weary smile.

"Course if it's a private cabin..."

Randy perked up.

"You might try asking at the River Inn. They're back up the road a piece where things are spread out a little more. Maybe they'll know her."

Randy followed her directions, made a sharp right just over the bridge, and drove along the river for at least four miles.

"Dawn Fioritto? No, can't say that I do," a server in the lounge said.

Randy's heart dropped. This was his last hope, and he was just about to describe her, the way he had with all the others, she's real tall and pretty, red hair down to here, when the man added, "Not personally at least."

Randy looked at him.

"The Fioritto family have a cabin nearby here though."

"How nearby?"

"Well, are you familiar with the area?"

"Very," Randy said.

And familiar he was, even in the dark. He drove back to Route 36, turned right, up the hill to the left, left again at the stop sign, another left, and onto a private road. "There's only three or four cabins there, I'm not sure which one. You'll have to check the mailboxes."

It was the third. He turned into the drive, drove at least six hundred yards before there was any clearing in the woods, and thought of the Ponderosa at first sight of this log cabin; rambling, two-story, and all lit up. If there was any doubt he was in the right place, it vanished at the sight of a new jeep with Ohio plates, parked to the side. When he pulled in next to it and turned off his truck, only then did it occur to him that he might frighten Dawn showing up this late, which was the last thing he wanted to do, and decided he probably should've waited until the morning. But he was here now, and after coming this far...

He got out and knocked on the front door, glanced over his shoulder as all the flood lights came on, and waited. Dawn looked out the side window, saw his truck first, and looking out the next window, him, and walked over to turn off the security system. When she finally opened the door, for a brief moment, the two of them just looked at one another. Dawn stepped back then, and he came in and closed the door behind him.

Dawn walked to the fireplace, where she drew a deep breath and turned, and again, just looked at him for a moment. "How did you know where I was?"

"I didn't," Randy said, watching her. "I knew it was in this area, so I stopped at all the bars till I found someone who knew where you might be."

Dawn nodded, more to herself than him, and sat down on the hearth, the crackling fire the only sound in the massive room.

"Why didn't you stop to see me today?" Randy asked, taking a step forward.

"I don't know." She stared down at her hands, turning the ring on her finger.

"I would've liked to have known if you were all right."

Dawn glanced at him as he sat down next to her. "I'm not all right, Randy," she said, as if he couldn't see that. She was thinner, paler, trembling. "If only I could fall asleep and wake up new. You know, to be able to forget everything and start over."

Randy smoothed her hair, tucked it behind her ear, and when she looked at him, swallowed hard. "I saw Maeve," he said. "Dawn, she told me. She told me everything."

Dawn searched his eyes, and shook her head. "Randy, what am I going to do?" Tears welled up and spilled onto her cheeks. "What am I going to do?"

"I don't know," Randy said, pulling her close. "I just know whatever it is, we're going to do it together. You and me." He turned her face to his. "Understand? Together."

October mornings in Cook Forest are always cool with a heavy fog blanketing the river. The one they woke to was no different. Randy gazed out from the back porch of the cabin, taking in the rainbow of autumn colors interspersed with the lush pines. "This is beautiful," he said, his arms around Dawn as she stood in front of him. "Absolutely beautiful."

"I was here the day my parents died," Dawn said softly, leaning against him for warmth.

"Come on," Randy said, tugging her toward the door. They'd put it off long enough. It was time to talk.

Dawn sat down by the fireplace and watched him as he added more wood to the fire, stoking it before he walked over and sat down across from her.

"Has this cabin been in the family long?" he asked, not knowing where to begin, or quite how.

"Yes, as long as I can remember."

"Dawn, I'm sorry, but we have to talk about it," he said, seeing the all-too-familiar defenses surfacing. "I know I pushed you here with all my questions, but the only way we can deal with this, is to face it, and put it all behind us."

Dawn shook her head. "Aunt Maeve told you everything. Let's let it go at that," she said, her bottom lip starting to quiver.

Randy lowered his eyes and stared, a part of him not wanting to discuss it either. The part that ached at the thought of her being raped, and that would never come to grips with it. He stared a long time. "You know," he said, his voice cracking. "I've got everything Maeve told me gagging me right here." He pressed a clenched fist to his chest. "But I think there's more, Dawn. And that's what we have to talk about."

Dawn shook her head and turned away, unable to bear the tears in his eyes.

"Dawn..." he insisted. "Tell me about your father."

"Father?" She looked at him. "He was the best."

Randy hesitated. "The day he died, what did you fight about?"

Dawn shrugged, and stared into the fire.

"I've given it a lot of thought," Randy said, when it was obvious she wasn't going to answer. "So you tell me if I'm right. I think that even though years had passed, the argument was about the rape."

Dawn looked at him.

"Am I right?"

She nodded, tears flooding her eyes again and with the same request. "Randy, please. Let's just let it go at that."

"I'm sorry, Dawn. But we can't."

Dawn looked at him, wiped her face and got up and walked to the other side of the room. "Oh God."

Randy moved to get up, to go to her, but she turned, held up her hands, and he sat back down. She drew a deep breath then, prayed for strength to get through this, and started. "To understand, you have to understand my father. For days after the rape, he would come to see me and cry by my bed. I'd never seen him cry before, Randy, ever." She hesitated, wiping her eyes again, and had to clear her throat. "Over and over he would say, they're going to pay for this. They're going to pay." She turned then, stared at the wall, her body trembling.

"Go on..." Randy said.

Dawn heaved her shoulders, turning back to face him, and hesitated again. "Father's men caught up with one of them."

Randy nodded.

"And..." Again Dawn paused, unable to continue, and bit at her bottom lip. "And..."

Randy waited, and waited, and finally, because it was breaking his heart to see her struggling like this, asked, "Did your father kill him, Dawn?"

She looked at him, searching his eyes. "I wish you could've known him. That way maybe..." She brought her hands to her mouth, a sob sounding from deep inside her throat. "Father had arranged to have this man brought back."

"Back to where, Dawn?"

"I don't know. He called me at the hospital." Her voice got thick, her eyes distant. "And he said... He said, I have one of the men that hurt you. I asked where. He was crying again, Randy, and he said here. I have him with me now. What do you want me to do with him. What do you want me to do...? I said kill him. And then I heard the shot."

Randy swallowed hard.

"I know he deserved to die. They both did. They hurt me so bad. I begged them to stop. I begged them, Randy. I knew them." She choked on her tears, wiped her eyes and her nose, and once more, held up her hands when Randy started toward her. "No..." she said. "And I almost got away too, but they'd locked the door. They just made me think I could escape. And then they laughed."

Randy had heard enough, walked over and wrapped his arms around her, held her tight, and said only one thing. "He deserved to die; they both did." He rocked her gently, kissed her forehead, and looked into her eyes. Dawn stepped back then, shivering, determined to tell him everything, and wiped her face again and again.

"We did fight about the rape," she said.

"What was there to fight about?"

"I don't know." Dawn shook her head. "Guilt. I couldn't get over it. Father refused to talk about it, like it never happened. But it did. We killed a man."

"Dawn, your father killed him. Not you."

"Randy, that's the toughest part. Because I know in my heart had I not said kill him, Father wouldn't have. Why else did he have the other man jailed?"

Randy shook his head, and for a second, a split second, could almost see Charles Fioritto in Dawn's eyes. And knew.

Dawn turned and stared into the fire. "The day my parents died was the first and only time Father and I..." She hugged her arms to her sides, stared and stared and stared, and started rocking back and forth.

"Dawn...?"

She drew a breath and pushed her hair off her face. "I wanted to go to the authorities. I'd been researching similar cases, where the parties were found innocent on grounds of temporary insanity. I had this thing, this feeling, that somehow the pain, the anguish, and the guilt we never talked about, could be relieved if, if..." She paused and looked at him. "Do you know what I'm trying to say?"

Randy nodded.

"So, we fought. I can still see him. He was so angry. He kept holding his hands up to his ears, and screaming. And my mother was crying. Oh God..." Dawn covered her mouth, started rocking again. "And I left. I left and came up here. I was supposed to go with them."

"Dawn, it was an accident. It happens. You were raped; that wasn't your fault. Neither one of them was your fault."

Dawn looked at him. "When Aunt Maeve called me..."

Randy shook his head. She needn't tell him anymore.

"No," she said. "No more secrets."

Randy stared at her, a feeling of dread washing over him, a feeling that what she about to reveal...

"I went home and in my room was a letter." She walked over and took it out of her wallet and handed it to him. "I kept it."

Randy looked up at her, watched as she walked back across the room, then unfolded it and read it.

Dawnetta,

I understand what you are going through, but I can not let you experience that pain again. It would destroy you, as it has done to me. I don't fear the legal system, I fear only the increased pain. Please forgive me. I would have given my life freely so that you would never be hurt. I have failed. On my memory, let it go.

Love, Father

Randy read the last line again, and then again, folded the letter and raised his eyes to Dawn's. He didn't know what to say. Dawn took the letter from him, and sat down on the hearth.

"I don't know what to do, Randy," she said. "I've never shown that to anyone, not even Aunt Meave."

Randy shook his head. "There's nothing to do."

"There has to be."

"No," Randy said. "There's nothing to be accomplished by it. A man is dead, and the man who killed him is dead. What would going to the authorities and confessing your part change? Nothing. Listen to your father, Dawn."

She looked at him.

"Let it go."

"I don't know how," Dawn said. "I thought maybe with time." She shrugged. "But then lately..."

"I didn't help there, I'm sorry."

"It wasn't just you. When Ben..." Tears welled up in her eyes again. "When he had his stroke and I thought he was going to die, and then with Ginney's trial. I wanted to be there for her, for her, not me, but then it started feeling wrong somehow. Like..." She shook her head. "It felt like everything I did was a lie. The fight with Ben, and when he was so angry with me, and..." She stared down at the letter in her hands, started to unfold it again, to read it again, and that's when Randy walked over and asked her to give it to him.

"Here," he said, and glanced at the fire. Dawn watched him toss it into the flames, watched as it caught fire, and watched as it disintegrated into ashes. She just watched.

"I'm going to get us some coffee," Randy told her, and left her alone a while. When he returned, Dawn reached for the cup, took a sip, and smiled at him.

"How do you feel?" he asked.

"I don't know," she said, the ashes from the letter no longer distinguishable from the rest. "I'm not sure." But she said it with another smile.

"Just promise you won't run away from me again, okay? No matter what?"

She nodded. "No matter what."

Randy leaned over and kissed her, sat down, and after a moment, had to ask. "So how's the book coming?"

Dawn sighed and glanced at her typewriter. "Not very well. But while we're on the subject. Why does it bother you so much that I'm writing it?"

Randy shrugged.

"The truth," she said, and he laughed.

"Well, I thought you were using me for research. And that when you finished it, we'd be through."

"What?"

"Hey, you asked. I thought Ben and Tom, and then Ginney, and even James..."

"Randy..."

"Sorry."

Dawn smiled and took another sip of her coffee.

"When are you coming back?" Randy asked.

"I don't know. How long can you stay?"

Randy smiled. "Just a day or so." His smile faded then. If they were clearing the air, there was one more thing they needed to discuss. "Dawn, about the filly..."

She paused. "I'm still having trouble with that. Randy, you never even tried. I wanted you to fix it so badly, and you never even tried."

Randy looked at her, just looked at her, and nodded. "I hope you come back soon."

"I will. But..."

"But what?"

"I'm not going back to the racetrack. I don't think I'll ever go back."

"If that's what you decide, fine. Just come back to me, okay?"

"Okay. But I'm not going to finish my book either. I can't."

Chapter Thirty-Six

"Are you sure she's okay?" Ben asked, looking earnestly at Randy.

"She's fine; she's just trying to sort some things out. She's had some really tough kicks in her life, a lot of things she's kept bottled up inside that she has to deal with."

Ben nodded. He'd seen that in her the first time he met her. "When is she coming back?"

"Soon, I hope. I just left there this morning and I miss her already. I'll tell you, Ben, it's beautiful up there."

"Did she finish her novel?"

"No, I brought it back with me. She told me she wasn't going to finish it. She also said she's not going back to the track."

"She'll go back," Ben said, smiling.

"You sound sure of it."

"Positive."

Later that night at his apartment, Randy propped his feet on the coffee table, opened the folder, and started reading the manuscript. It was morning before he put it down. He re-read the last page, laid it on the cushion next to him, and leaned his head back. She'd captured it all, the excitement, the heartbreak, the passion, the competition. At times when he'd been reading it, he could almost feel the rain hitting his face, taste the mud in his mouth, smell the shedrow in the air...

He rubbed his eyes and yawned. She'd taken the sport of kings all the way from Kentucky to the bush tracks in the small towns; telling, relating, forcing you to see and feel what it's like to lead a horse to the paddock, and what it took to get to that point. It was all there. All but the ending.

A week from Thanksgiving, Randy still hadn't heard from Dawn, and though he'd promised to give her time, he was starting to worry again. Ben had hoped to be discharged by now, but was still having difficulty building up the strength in his right leg. Tom called regularly from Florida, and Charlie and Gloria visited at least once a week. Even Ginney and James visited him occasionally.

"Don't you be billing me," Ben would tease each time, and James would always laugh.

Randy walked down the corridor, nodded to the nurse, one of the ones Ben liked, started into his room, and stopped. Just like the day she'd gone...without warning, Dawn had returned. He smiled and wrapped her in his arms and swung her around.

"Are you back for good?"

"Yes."

"See," Ben said. "Didn't I tell you he'd be here any minute. I tell you I can't get any rest. No wonder I'm still in this place."

Dawn and Randy laughed, gazed at one another, and instinctively grasped one another's hand.

"When did you get back?"

"Just now." She turned to Ben. "Ben was just telling me about Beau. We're going to go see him tomorrow."

Randy nodded, glanced at Ben, and looked at her again. Then, Ben told them to leave, insisting he wanted to take a nap before the Browns game. "Go on," he said. "And don't forget, tomorrow at one. Come to the side door, Randy'll show you where."

When Dawn gave Ben a hug, he held her tight. He'd missed her these past few months. "I hear you might not be going back to the track for a while."

"I think I just need a little more time," Dawn said, not wanting to disappoint him.

"We'll see," he said, he and Randy exchanging looks of concern. "Now go on."

Randy kissed her in the hall and took her by the hand. "I read your book. It's really good, Dawn. I couldn't put it down till I was done. You have to finish it."

Dawn smiled. "I think I will."

Randy nodded, walking along, and then all of a sudden stopped. "Wait a minute. I just realized...I'm not in it."

"I told you," Dawn said, laughing. "But you never believed me."

It was exactly three in the morning when Randy woke up, rolled over, and nudged Dawn.

She moved closer to him.

"Will you marry me?" he asked.

"Randy..." She looked at him sleepily. "What if I can't have children?"

"Then we'll adopt," he said.

Dawn smiled, shook her head, and kissed him.

"Is that a yes?"

"Yes."

The next time Dawn woke, it was to the ringing phone. Randy'll get it, she told herself, it's on his side. But it kept ringing. She turned over, discovered he was gone, and squinted at the clock. She couldn't remember the last time she'd slept past six, let alone eleven.

"Good morning," Randy said, in response to the groggy sound of her voice. "Rise and shine."

She laughed. "When did you leave?"

"A little after seven. You'd better get a move on it if you're going to pick up Ben on time. I'll try to swing by and meet you there."

Ben was waiting, pacing back and forth when she pulled up, climbed into the jeep without much of a problem, and told her the best way to get to the farm.

"It's going to be good to go home once and for all," he said. "There's nothing like going home."

"I know," Dawn said, smiling and feeling the same.

Ben stared out the side window. "I don't know what I would've done without Gloria and Charlie these past few months. Not to mention Randy. He's a fine man, Dawn."

Dawn glanced at him. "Ben, I hope you don't think I let you down by leaving."

"No, not a bit. Though I have to admit I did miss you. It's not going to be the same at the track without you."

Dawn turned into the drive at the farm, parked close to the barn, but instead of getting out right away, just sat there. And so did Ben. "On the way to the home to get you today, I was thinking about it. The racetrack." She paused, looking straight ahead, her hands firmly gripping the steering wheel. "I was remembering something you told me a long time ago. It was when I was doing that story for the paper. You told me that it gets in your blood. You turned my hand and you pointed to the veins in my arm, and you said, it gets right in there. Do you remember that, Ben?" She looked at him and smiled when he nodded. "Well, you were right."

Ben nodded again. "Some things you just know," he said. "Now come on, we ain't got all day. If I don't show up when I'm supposed to, they'll come looking for me."

Dawn laughed, got out, and walked around to help him if he needed it. "I'm fine," he said, bracing himself and pivoting on his good leg to gaze into the pasture. The wind was cold in their faces. "It feels like snow."

George, Ben's farmhand, walked out to greet them. He too said it looked like snow, and the three of them went inside the barn. Beau Born nickered at the sound of Dawn's voice, came to the front of the stall, and pushed against her as she rubbed his shoulder.

"Did you miss me?" she said, over and over. "Did you miss me?"

Ben laughed. "They're standing in line to breed to him. I'll tell you, it even surprised me how many."

"Well, that's because he's the best," Dawn said, in that talking-to-the-animals voice of hers. "Aren't you? Aren't you?" she said again. And just like that, she got choked up. She pressed her face against Beau's neck and tried to fight back the tears rushing to her eyes. Oh God, she said to herself, you're supposed to have gotten over this. She turned away, stared at the stall across the aisle, and in an effort to focus her attention elsewhere, walked over to look at the horse.

It had its backside to her, a large gray horse with an already ample winter coat. She stared at its hip, tried to look at it the way Tom might, judging for conformation, and ran her eyes down over its legs, pausing as she looked at the right front, which was large and disfigured. She stopped, stared harder, and then looked quickly at the horse's face. "All Together...?" She glanced at Ben, then back. "Ben, is it her? Is it All Together?"

He nodded, all choked up himself at this point, because right about then the filly turned around. And Dawn opened the stall door and went in and hugged her. "Oh my God. It is you... Oh my God," she said, stroking her neck, her face, and hugging her again, and again.

Randy walked up next to Ben, patted the old man on the shoulder, and Ben shrugged, wiping his eyes. Dawn saw him standing there, and couldn't believe... "I don't understand. Why didn't you tell me?"

Randy hesitated. "Because odds were, she wouldn't make it. As it was, we came close to losing her twice."

Ben nodded, and took out his handkerchief and blew his nose.

"But what about at the cabin? Why didn't you tell me then?"

Randy didn't answer right away. "Partly because she wasn't out of the woods yet at the time. But mostly because I wanted you to face things, this...us, you and me, as it was."

Dawn shook her head, smiled, and hugged the filly again. "Do you think she remembers me?"

Ben laughed. "I don't know, but I'll bet she remembers Randy."

Randy nodded. "She's only now getting around to forgiving me. Aren't you, girl?"

When the filly pinned her ears, they all laughed. "That's all right," Randy said. "Come spring, she'll thank me."

Dawn looked at him and knew that he was referring to breeding her to Beau and glanced at the filly's ankle. "Will she be all right?"

Randy nodded. "I think so. She'll never have any flexibility in that joint, but she'll get around well enough."

"And won't they be something when they get to the track," Ben said, referring to their offspring. "They'll be some class there."

Randy agreed and looked at Dawn. "It's a shame you won't be there to see them."

"Oh, she'll be there," Ben said. "We covered that earlier. She'll be back."

Randy's expression was anything but surprised. As he examined the filly's ankle, Dawn wanted to know the details and how all this came about.

"Well," Randy said. "Ben had made up his mind and then..." It was when he'd walked back in and sat down and they'd talked more.

"We decided if we were going to do it," Ben explained, "with all the risks we were facing, it would have to be without you knowing about it. It was the only way."

"But where did you take her?"

"Out to the Durans'," Randy said, "for a week or so. Then here. Which reminds me, I just came from there. They've had it with that black colt and want to sell him. You might want to take a look at him," he told Ben.

"Why? How's he bred?"

"Common."

Ben laughed. "Then why would I want to look at him?"

"Because he owes me," Randy said.

"He's the one that broke Randy's arm," Dawn added. "He's put together really nice. He's just mean."

"You say he's still a colt?" Ben asked.

Randy nodded. "Yeah, and that's half his problem."

Ben sat in the jeep as Randy jogged the horse back and forth twice. "You're right, you really can't fault him. Though I do wish he were a little taller."

"He is pretty, from a distance." Dawn said, somewhat apprehensively.

"Jog him again," Ben said, and pointed something else out.

"What?"

"Look at his hoof prints. I like that in a horse. He's as wide in front as he is in back."

Dawn smiled, asked Mr. Duran the colt's name, and Ben rolled his eyes.

"Shadow Pine?" She loved it.

"Yep, Shadow Pine." Mr. Duran chuckled, said he liked it too, and it was time to talk business. He looked at Ben. "Well?"

"How much are you asking for him?"

"Ten thousand, exactly what I paid for him, even though I have a whole year in him, and half a barn's reconstruction."

Ben laughed, and just about then, the colt cow-kicked and just missed clipping the jeep. "All right, we'll take him."

"You and me?" Dawn asked.

Ben nodded. "Equal partners. All right?"

"All right. Why not?"

Ben told Mr. Duran he'd have a check sent over tomorrow. Mr. Duran went to break the news to his wife, whom he suspected deep down would be greatly relieved. And Ben looked at Randy.

"First chance you get, Doc," he said. "Cut him."

Randy grinned. "My pleasure."

Under the tree Christmas morning, Dawn found several boxes wrapped in the Sunday comics. A very small box was the first she opened. It was an engagement ring, a diamond solitaire set in white gold.

"Do you like it?" Randy asked.

She slipped it on her finger. "I love it."

He smiled.

"I love you."

"Open the rest," he said, and told her he picked everything out himself. Two sweaters, one kelly green, and the other white, both a perfect fit. "All right, so Miss Diane helped me a little with the size," he confessed. And cologne, Chantilly, and pearl earrings. Then it was his turn.

"Come on, open them," Dawn said, when he kept picking up the boxes, shaking them, and turning them upside down. "That one first."

He, also, got a sweater and tried it on, and socks, a pen set, and a digital watch, which he set five minutes fast right off the bat, and that left just one more gift. Dawn handed him a tiny box and a card.

"What's this?" he said. "Do I get an engagement ring too?"

Dawn shook her head and smiled. "Open the present first."

Randy unwrapped it carefully, looked to see what it was, and gazed at her. "Keys?"

"Read the card," she said.

He opened the envelope, took out the card, and inside found the title to the Jaguar, in his name. He smiled. "I guess it's official then. We're getting married."

At the ten-minute call for the fifth race, Dawn returned from the ladies room, having lost count of how many trips she'd already made that day. It was the third week of racing, the barn was full, and Shadow Pine, the black gelding she and Ben owned together was going to make his maiden debut. He wasn't the favorite, but he had a shot, Ben said, and just might run off and hide.

"No, *I'm* going to run off and hide," Dawn said, and Tom laughed.

"Let's go get them." He climbed up on Red, took Shadow Pine's reins, and Dawn followed them to the paddock. This would be the first horse Ben saddled since his recovery, and according to him, some things you just don't forget.

Shadow Pine was still a little feisty, but knew how to behave by now, thanks to being schooled by Tom on more than one occasion, and aside from breaking out in a sweat, stood like an old pro in the paddock. Johnny came out of the jocks' room and huddled close to Ben.

"Well?"

Ben looked at him. "Go to the front and take the horse with you."

Johnny laughed. "Got it."

"Riders up!"

Dawn led Shadow Pine out to where Tom was waiting, climbed up onto the fence, looked to see if Randy's truck was by the kitchen, and smiled. Ben walked down to join her at two minutes to post and glanced at the tote board as the seconds ticked away. The horses were loaded, the jocks adjusted their goggles, and Dawn held her breath.

Shadow Pine's odds flashed seven to two.

"And they're off!"

An equestrian, horse trainer, and environmentalist,
MaryAnn Myers lives with her family in northeast Ohio,
and is currently working on her seventh novel, *Ellie's Crows*.